THE PREHIST~~ORIC~~ ~~~~
SOUGHT A NEW FUTURE
BEYOND THE SEA OF ICE

TORKA—Bold, intelligent, passionate, a hunter of great skill and cunning. Heartbroken over the loss of his family, he summons the courage to lead a band of survivors toward the unknown eastern steppes, where he believes a new life awaits him and his clan.

LONIT—A strange round-eyed girl who has loved Torka all her life. She is but a girl when the momentous journey with Torka begins, but on the trek she blossoms into womanhood. She hopes Torka's grief will soon turn to desire, and desire to the love she yearns for desperately.

UMAK—Torka's grandfather and a "spirit master." His life regains purpose on the odyssey of survival, as he grows to understand that the old ways of his people are no longer possible in 'he brave new world.

KARANA—A boy child who has been abandoned by his own people. He lives like an animal on the mountain to which Torka and his tribe come. He, too, must adapt to new ways when Torka adopts him as a son.

GALEENA—The wily leader of a band decimated by the same great mammoth that killed Torka's family. Galeena competes fiercely with Torka for leadership when their two bands unite—in a vicious battle that can end only in blood.

BOOK 1 * THE FIRST AMERICANS

THE
FIRST
AMERICANS

BEYOND
THE SEA
OF ICE

WILLIAM
SARABANDE

™

Created by the producers of
**Wagons West, White Indian,
Wolves of the Dawn,** and
Children of the Lion.

Book Creations Inc., Canaan, NY · Lyle Kenyon Engel, Founder

BANTAM BOOKS
NEW YORK · TORONTO · LONDON · SYDNEY · AUCKLAND

THE FIRST AMERICANS: BEYOND THE SEA OF ICE
A Bantam Book / December 1987

ISBN 0-553-26889-0

Published simultaneously in the United States and Canada

Bantam Books are published by Bantam Books, Inc. Its trademark, consisting of the words "Bantam Books" and the portrayal of a rooster, is Registered in U.S. Patent and Trademark Office and in other countries. Marca Registrada. Bantam Books, Inc., 666 Fifth Avenue, New York, New York 10103.

PRINTED IN THE UNITED STATES OF AMERICA

O   0 9 8 7 6 5 4

To Lyle

CAST OF
CHARACTERS

Torka's band

Torka — Twenty-year-old Ice Age Paleo-Indian hunter from northeast Asia

*****Umak** — Torka's grandfather, an ancient man at forty-five

Egatsop — Torka's wife, eighteen years old

Kipu — Torka's son, five years old

*****Lonit** — Torka's female, twelve years old and on the brink of womanhood

Galeena's band

Galeena — Hunter from farther east than Torka's people

Ai — Galeena's favorite woman

*****Manaak** — Hunter Torka's age

*****Iana** — Manaak's woman

Ninip — Young boy

*****Naknaktup** — Matron

Oklahnoo — Matron

Supnah's band

Supnah — Mammoth-spurning hunter

*****Karana** — Supnah's son

Navahk — Magic man

*Left the cavelike ledge with Torka

ANIMAL
GLOSSARY

Woolly mammoth — Gigantic elephantlike mammal with huge curling tusks and flat teeth perfect for grinding leaves and twigs. The skull was double domed, and the body was covered with thick red hair. Stood sixteen feet at the shoulder.

Dire wolf — A wolf that was taller and heavier than today's wolves.

Saber-toothed lion — Almost as large as today's African lion, the saber-toothed cat had strong front legs and shorter hind legs. Its upper canine teeth were enlarged into two great sabers with serrated edges, with which it would stab its victims.

Ptarmigan — Small bird, slightly larger than today's quail.

Short-faced bear — One-third larger than today's bears, this beast was primarily a carnivore.

Teratorni — A condor with a wingspan of more than twelve feet.

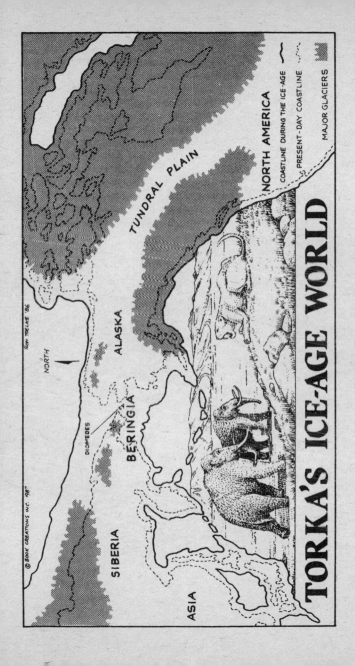

PART I

THE
CROOKED
SPIRIT

1

Something walked within the night—something huge. Something silent. Something terrible.

The hunter stopped dead in his tracks, listening, attuned to some inner thrum of warning that caused adrenalin to run hot within his veins as all his senses screamed: *Danger!*

He was a young man, winter lean, graceful even though he stood tense within his multilayered garments of skins and furs. Braced upon strong, heavily clad limbs like a running beast, he was poised and ready to hurl himself from danger.

He had felt it stalking him for hours, as relentlessly as death. Twice he had doubled back to check for tracks, but blowing ground snow had mocked his efforts, and he had seen nothing—only the vast, wind-driven distances of snow-covered, perpetually frozen tundra and the endless darkness of the Arctic winter night. As the wind wicked away whorls of dry snow and sent them rivering beneath the shimmering blue patterns of the northern lights, he had seen a ridge that rose out of the broad, flat, tundral face like the broken nose of a long-dead giant.

He had made for that veiled, distant refuge at a trot, not looking back, knowing that Alinak and Nap would follow. During the last few days they had tacitly allowed him to lead them. He had not been surprised—for he was Torka, and the blood of many generations of spirit masters flowed within him. It was well known that his hunting instincts never failed him. Alinak and Nap would know that he had sought safety on the high ground of the ridge, which would allow them at least some advantage over whatever it was that was stalking them.

Now he looked back, out across the vistas fogged by thick

clouds of blowing ground snow. Through these he could see his companions, two figures emerging out of the freezing mists, ascending the spine of the ridge toward him. Hunching against the wind, leaning on their spears for balance, they wore the skins of beasts. Antlers branched outward from their hooded heads. Half-human, half-animal, Alinak and Nap had the look of horned apparitions ripped from the nightmare fabric of a dream.

But this was no dream. This was the Age of Ice. At least forty thousand years would pass before hunters of another epoch would call this land Siberia. There would be forests here then, and new races of men and beasts. Now there was only a dark and savage landscape across which the wind wailed and the cries of dire wolves ululated like women keening their dead.

Far to the east, above the towering, ice-girdled mountain ranges that encircled the treeless tundra plain, the first glow of dawn was leaching the sky to gold. It was the faintest banding of light, but it would stay long enough to be called morning, to set shadows of mauve and gray upon a land that had not seen sunlight for months. The time of the long dark was ending. The time of light was returning after the longest, cruelest winter that Torka had ever known.

His two antlered companions came to stand beside him. Like Torka, they were shielded against the weather in many layers of clothing. Their undergarments were of the supplest skins of caribou fawns. Trousers of dog pelts protected their legs from the subzero bite of the Arctic wind. Within these were stockings of buckskin, chewed by their women to the consistency of velvet, and over the trousers were hairy leggings of bison hide, cross-laced over knee-high boots lined in fur and triple-soled to form a barrier against the cold. Each man wore a tunic of caribou hide and, over this, with the hair facing inward, a coat cut from the skins of the same reindeerlike animal.

No skins were warmer than those of winter-killed caribou. Although the caribou was relatively short-haired when compared to the pelage of the shaggy musk ox or the woolly shouldered giant bison, each shaft of caribou hair was an air-filled, insulating cylinder, which kept the warmth of a man in and the death-dealing cold of the Arctic out. In garments sewn of such fur, a hunter could stay out upon the wind-ravaged tundra indefinitely without feeling the cold.

But, although these men were warm, they had been away from their people's winter encampment for three days. The warmth of their clothing could not protect them from fatigue or hunger. Or from bad judgment.

They stood together with the light of dawn upon them, and Torka went dry-mouthed with apprehension as he eyed his companions' horned cloaks. It was sacrilege to don the stalking cloak before the game was sighted. His own cloak was still strapped to his pack frame, rolled tightly, with the antlers upright like skeletal wings projecting outward from his back.

A deep roaring suddenly rent the wind-scoured morning. Torka stood immobile, his face impassive, although once again his senses screamed: *Danger!* He turned, as did the two men beside him. They listened, squinting into the distance and trying to ascertain from which direction the sound had come. Within the faraway, glacier-ridden mountains, the dire wolves fell silent. Torka wondered if they, too, sensed that what they had heard had been more than the commonplace thundering of an avalanche from the towering frontal flanks of the many glaciers on the tundral plain.

This had been the sound of something *alive*—something passing below and well beyond the ridge upon which the three hunters stood. It was made invisible by blowing ground snow and distance but was so large that its footfall set up vibrations in the permafrost and caused the earth to tremble. Its scent reached them, and they drew it in, seeking definition of it as only those refined to the kill could recognize the smell of life within the lung-searing cold of the Arctic wind. It was the merest inference of the warmth of living flesh and breath. The wind brought it to them, tainted them with it, then took it away before they could put name to it.

The moments passed. Long. Breathless. The hunters waited, but the sound did not recur. Nap and Alinak salivated with want. Their bellies were tight and aching with hunger. Unlike Torka, they sensed no threat in the wind, no danger in the dawn. Fatigue had dulled their instincts. Their minds were filled with visions of what they so desperately wanted to see: *caribou*. They yearned to see vast herds of migrating cows and young, with the bulls following in separate traveling units, pouring out across the tundra from the distant mountains en route to their calving grounds far to the east.

The herds were long overdue. The starving moon had

risen and set over the winter encampment that their people
had erected against the brutal storms of the time of the long
dark. Theirs was a small band. Composed of fewer than forty
souls, the group had worked together to dig pit huts into the
frozen tundra, to raise domed roofs of bison skins over frames
of mammoth ribs. With provisions cached against the long,
dark months to come, they had settled in to await the return
of the time of light.

As always, they had encamped along a known route of
caribou migration, certain that, before starvation set in, the
herds would return to nourish them. But the caribou had *not*
returned. The winter had been more severe than any winter
that even the eldest members of the band could remember.
There had been a brief thaw. Then the cold had returned,
and storms had raged down upon them from out of the north
like ravening wolves. Despite the weather, the hunters had
gone out each day in search of game, only to return empty-
handed. Soon their provisions had been exhausted. Women
stared blank-eyed at empty snares as their breast milk dried
and their babies wailed unceasingly. Ptarmigan fences of the
leg bones of freshly killed steppe antelope, raised by the
children earlier in the season, failed to confuse and entrap
any more of the low-flying, winter-white birds. As a sacrifice
to the spirits to bring the caribou back, Teenak, the headman's youngest woman, had exposed her newborn infant. In
sympathy, the sky spirits had taken the suffering baby's body
along with its soul. The baby would feed upon the clouds
until Teenak could give birth to it again in better times. Two
other women had followed Teenak's example with their own
offspring. But still the caribou had not returned.

So it was that the hunters of the band had been sent out
to find the herds. For three days now, they had been fanning
out from the encampment, desperately searching for any sort
of game, each hoping to be the first to sight the long-awaited
herds upon which the band had come to depend for all those
things that were the very blood of life to them: No meat was
sweeter, no hides were warmer or more versatile, no antlers
or bones were more malleable. No sinew was stronger or
more resilient, no fat burned longer in the concave ovals of
the burning stones that served as lamps. The caribou was the
staff of life to the nomads of the Arctic tundra. Without the
caribou, they could not survive.

Alinak and Nap stared into the growing light of the snow-driven morning, each man trying to see what had brought Torka to such an abrupt stop. Surely, there *was* something moving out there in the mists. It *had* to be caribou! When Torka had suddenly made for the ridge at a run, optimism had caused both men to assume that the herds had at last been sighted. They had followed, donning their stalking cloaks without breaking stride, certain that Torka was leading them to high ground so that they might gain an overview of their prey.

Nap's gloved hand curled tightly about the bone shaft of his spear. Above his high, round cheekbones, his black eyes slitted with anticipatory pleasure. He could see himself now, trotting home, bent forward under a load of fresh-killed meat, his belly full for the first time in months, his blood singing.

Alinak shared his brother's vision. He could almost smell the sour, steamy stink of caribou dung and feel it grainy-slick between his gloves as he imagined himself smearing it over his garments so that he might take on the scent of his prey, insinuate himself into the fringes of the herd, and with Torka and Nap hunting close by, easily make his kills.

The brothers nodded, one to the other, acknowledging their unspoken thoughts. An Arctic hunter's ability to communicate without sound was a sixth sense, as it was with all predators whose survival depended upon their ability to hunt in packs. To speak was to alert prey to their presence, and to break the concentration of others when game was being stalked was unthinkable.

It was hunger, coupled with exhaustion, that put the word on Nap's tongue. He did not know that he spoke until the wind blew his voice back into his face and slapped him with it.

"Caribou . . ."

The enormity of his transgression hit him at once. He sucked in a half-strangled gasp of alarm, as though he might draw back his utterance, but it was too late. The word was out, running free upon the wind.

Torka and Alinak stood stunned to silence. Nap had just broken one of the most ancient taboos of the Arctic. They all knew that to name a thing was to give it the spirit of life. And life spirits had wills of their own. If called forth without the proper ceremony or chants of respect, they were dishonored and would seek to punish those who had shamed them. In the case of game, they might not come forth at all, thus punishing the transgressors through starvation. Or they might transform themselves into crooked spirits, half-flesh, half-phantom . . . clawed, fanged, invisible, and malevolent . . . big enough to make prey of men and eat them . . . slowly.

Nap felt sick. He could see Alinak's wide face scowling at him out of the shadowed recesses of his antlered headdress. Torka's hood was fashioned from the pelt of a dire wolf, with the tail of the beast stitched end to end to form an encircling ruff, within which his face was but a pool of darkness in the meager light of the morning; but Nap did not have to see the strong, even features to know that Torka's dark brows had merged into one black sprawl above his all too expressive eyes. He could visualize the well-formed mouth snarling back from the white teeth as Torka hissed an exhalation that was more damning than any rebuke.

Torka did not have to tell Nap that what he had done was unforgivable. His lapse might well cost all three of them their lives. And if, by some chance, they *did* manage to get safely back to the winter encampment of their band, Nap's reputation as a hunter would be sullied forever. Yet, as the initial flaring of his anger cooled, Torka could not condemn Nap for his blunder. They were *all* exhausted, *all* hungry and dangerously near to starvation. It was said that starvation fed the light of vision. It was also said that hunger made men careless. Any one of them might have blurted the word of longing and thus, inadvertently, broken the ancient taboo. But if Nap *had* loosed a crooked spirit, it would be a separate entity from the one that Torka sensed stalking them. *That* phantom had been following them for hours. And whatever it was, Torka was now more certain than ever that it was no herd of caribou.

The three hunters stood immobile. They all saw specters, listened for the voice of danger, and imagined that they saw death stalking them in the wind-driven mists.

Torka stood with his fleshing dagger in one hand and his stabbing spear balanced and at the ready in the other. He could taste bile at the back of his throat as he recalled the words of old Umak, the grandfather who had raised him and taught him to hunt after his parents had been killed: *There is a light that burns at the back of a man's eyes when death is near, stalking, waiting for the hunter to make the final error. The hunter must face into this light. Only by facing death may his spirit overcome it.*

The light that burns. Torka could feel it now. It seared the back of his eyes and transformed his vision. The world was ignited by it, bright, as white and bold as the great white bear of the north, and he thought: *Whatever is out there, the wind is in its favor now. It will have our scent. And if it is a bear, it will be mad with hunger after months of living off its own fat. It will come for us, even here upon high ground. It will come.*

Restlessness ran in his blood, heating it. Despite the cold, he could smell the acrid scent brought on by his tension. He wished that his grandfather were with him now. Alinak and Nap were both in their prime and experienced hunters, but when old Umak was at his side, Torka always felt that he had the courage and the wisdom of two men. But Umak had injured his leg while chasing down a steppe antelope earlier in the season. Now he sheltered within Torka's pit hut back at the winter camp with Egatsop, who was Torka's woman, their newborn infant, and Kipu, their little son.

Kipu! The boy grew paler and weaker every day. And here was Torka, the brave hunter, dry-mouthed and in fear of an unseen prey whose flesh would feed his son and save his people from starvation. Self-revulsion caused him to scowl. What sort of a man was he? Why was he standing here in silence when he should be making the chants that would summon the unknown prey to him?

But what if the prey was a crooked spirit? Or worse, what if it was a bear? He had seen what the great white bear could do. When Torka was a child he had seen his father slashed and torn by those great paws. He had seen his father die as many others were mauled, until at last the huge, short-faced, lumbering marauder had been driven off. Later it had been found dead from wounds it had suffered in the encampment. The surviving members of the band had eaten it, but the bear had ruined ten spears and taken the lives of three hunters and one woman, Torka's mother, to the spirit world with it.

The memory roused anger and a fully formed resolve that drove away his fear. Umak had stood against that bear. Umak's courage had enabled him to place the killing spear. Not even the great white bear had been bolder than Umak. *And I am Torka. I am the son of Umak's son. I can be bold. I, too, am mad with hunger after months of living off my own fat.*

The wind was gusting now, its power ebbing as morning claimed the tundra and banished the terrors of the dark.

Torka's black eyes stared into the settling ground snow, searching for a bear that was not there. Nap and Alinak frowned into the distance, expecting crooked spirits to take shape and come at them to take their lives. But, to their infinite relief, there was only the familiar, empty tundra spreading out before them, with the mountains circling the far horizon and, on that horizon, the frozen jewel of a shallow little lake glinting in the cold colors of the morning. The lake was at the base of the shouldering rise of a terminal moraine, no doubt the result of the recent thaw and ensuing freeze. A huge embankment of loose stones and rocky debris rose at the foot of a glacier. And mired at the edge of the lake, its shape a dark scab upon the ice, was a corpse whose color was unmistakable. Red. Deep red, the color of blood rising from a wound.

The hunters exhaled in disbelieving unison. The terrors of the night and caution were forgotten. Hunger took complete control of their senses as they realized that at last they had found enough food to gorge upon until they were sated and still have more than enough to bring back to their starving people.

Torka laughed with relief. So his instincts had failed him at last! What a fool he had been! The only thing that had stalked him in the night had been the beast of his own fear! The light that had burned behind his eyes had only been the color of that fear!

"Do you see it?" questioned Alinak softly, as though he dared not trust his own eyes and feared a negative answer.

"I see it!" Torka affirmed, and put a name to that which lay before them, obviously dead, fresh-frozen in the ice, waiting to be taken. "Mammoth!"

Nap winced, but Torka reached out and gave him a friendly shoulder jab that told the other man that everything was going to be all right. Nap *had* broken a taboo, but it seemed as though the spirits were going to overlook it.

They put the ridge behind them and went on toward the lake at a jog, grateful for the light of morning, forgetful of the terrors of the dark. They blessed whatever spirit had misled the mammoth and sent it plodding into the quagmire of the lakeshore during the last thaw; they knew that its weight must have entrapped it, and death must have come either by starvation or in the storms that had followed the thaw to freeze the lake solid.

They chanted as they ran, verses of gratitude to the spirits. Although the flesh of the woolly mammoth was not their favorite meat—it was bitter with the taste of the scrub spruce that was its favorite fodder—starving men were not discriminating, nor were they curious as to what had drawn the mammoth far from its preferred habitat in the hill country close to the base of the mountains. They knew only that whatever had set it on its course out onto the tundra had set it directly in their path. They made incantations that would appease the soul of the huge beast, whose flesh would now save their lives and the lives of their people.

They were breathless when they reached the lake and paused before the corpse of the mammoth. It lay on its side, two legs totally submerged, and most of its great head imbedded in the ice. It was an enormous cow. And, strangely, it was untouched by predators. They should have noted this, but they did not. Hunger had consumed their caution.

The cold had lessened somewhat with the drop of the wind, although, in the shadow of the towering moraine and the massive wall of the glacier behind it, the air temperature was well below freezing. The long hair of the mammoth was frozen into twisted pillars of ice above its equally rigid hide. It would take all the hunters' energy to hack through the hair and hide to the frozen flesh beneath; but they did not care, nor did they hesitate.

They leaped onto the body of the behemoth and set to work with their spears, chipping and wedging away at the hair, then bending to work with their fleshing daggers to open the hide. Weariness soon dulled their excitement as they took up bits of frozen flesh and sucked the blood from them, silently acknowledging that unless there was another thaw, the meat of the mammoth would remain rock hard. It would take better tools than they had to cut enough steaks from it to transport back to their people. They would have to go back to the winter encampment and bring others to help them, leaving one of their number to keep predators from the corpse.

As they crouched upon the body of the mammoth, trying to decide who should stay and who should go, a shadow fell upon them. They paid it no heed at first. They were already in the shadow of the moraine and what fell upon them seemed to be only a deepening of that shadow.

It was Torka who was first distracted by the sensation of being watched. He looked up into the eyes of death.

A full eighteen feet tall at the shoulder, the bull mammoth stood on stanchion limbs, with over half a ton of ivory curling forward in its tusks. Nearly as long as the beast was tall, the tusks were discolored at their tips, where, in its endless foraging, the bull had ripped and torn into the fragile flesh of the tundra as deeply as it had also ripped into the flesh of its own kind during many a battle for mating supremacy.

Torka rose. *This* was what he had sensed walked within the night. His instincts had not betrayed him. Never had he imagined that any living creature could be so huge or so menacing. It was a haunting, risen from the tales that the old men told in the winter dark, close to the warming fire within the Man House—stories of monsters to frighten adolescent hunters, to emphasize the meaning of danger, to stress the full consequences of breaking a taboo. The beast that stood staring down at Torka from the top of the moraine made the great white bear of his memories seem as puny as a half-starved Arctic hare. It made the most malevolent of crooked spirits seem less threatening than a winter-weakened ptarmigan flapping its wings in a snare.

Instinctively, Torka knew that the bull must be the mate of the mired cow whose body he and the others were carving, whose flesh they had eaten to nourish their own. It was the bull who had kept predators from the body until, at last, it had wandered off, only to be drawn back to its mate again, following the hunters.

The mammoth's great head lowered and swung back and forth. Alinak and Nap saw it now. They crouched, gaping, incredulous as the low, measured exhalations of its breath reached them. Then, impossibly, it reared back and pawed at the air. Its huge trunk rose, and its long, sloppy-lipped jaw opened as it trumpeted its rage at them.

Torka would never be certain of the exact moment in which it charged. He only knew that it was suddenly coming at him, and he and Alinak and Nap were grabbing for the spears that they had set aside. They leaped from the cow, slipping and scrambling madly along the ice-rimed embankment of the lake as they ran for safety. But there was nowhere to run.

Torka heard Alinak scream. The choking retching gurgle that followed put the hideous manner of his death into his companions' minds, but neither Torka nor Nap looked back. They could not help Alinak now.

They ran close together. Nap was sobbing as he rasped in terror, "Run wide of me, Torka. It is *my* crooked spirit. It comes for *me*. Make for high ground! Run for the ridge! I will lead it away!"

"We run together!" was Torka's reply, even though he knew that there was wisdom in Nap's advice. If they ran wide of one another, the beast could not take them both at once. But if they both made for the ridge, running in an erratic pattern, perhaps they could confuse it, and then they could both make it to safety. The beast was the largest mammoth that Torka had ever seen, but somehow he knew that it *was* a mammoth and not a crooked spirit. And mammoths could not climb.

It was this certainty that gave him the power to quicken his pace, to lengthen his stride into long, earth-eating steps that would surely have brought him to the ridge in time had Nap not veered away, turning back toward the lake, directly into the path of the mammoth.

"No!" Torka cried. "Run with me! We're almost there!"

But Nap had paused. He stood dead still, facing back across the open tundra to where the mammoth trotted toward them, its gait slow now, but gaining. It had stopped after knocking Alinak down. It had wheeled around and ground his body into a bloody mash within the heavy casing of his clothes. His blood was on its trunk and tusks and huge, toed feet. Its head was down, and its hairy ears twitched forward like wings below the high, twin domes of its skull. It eyed Nap, then nodded, huffing as it increased its speed from a trot to a gallop as it moved directly toward him.

Torka stood frozen. "Run, Nap. Now! Run!"

Incredibly, Nap did not run. He stood his ground before the charging mammoth, not raising his spear until the very end. Perhaps, in that last moment, when he smelled the stench of the beast's breath and the acrid stink of its body, superstition fell away and he knew that what rushed down upon him was no crooked spirit but a creature of flesh and blood, as fully mortal as he. He screamed then and turned to flee. It was too late. The mammoth had him in its trunk. His weapon fell away, snarling uselessly in the beast's thick, tangled red hair. He was thrown down and trampled, his organs exploding out through his mouth as every bone in his body was broken and every fiber of his being was reduced to jellied rubble.

Immobilized by the horror of what he had just witnessed, Torka stood in shock, shaken by the mind-splitting reverberations of the mammoth's trumpetings of victory over those who had profaned the body of its mate. It was as though the sound of its roarings permeated the skin of the world. The earth shook. Within Torka, the sound reached down into a never-before-tapped core of molten rage that rose slowly to burn white-hot behind his eyes.

The mammoth was staring at him. Its eyes were round and dilated with its hatred of Man. Its great trunk swung upward. Its enormous body swayed. One massive forelimb lifted, then came down to strike the earth again and again until it seemed that all the world trembled.

But Torka did not tremble. Terror had taken him beyond fear. Rage steadied his nerves. He waited, knowing that there was no escape for him now. The ridge was too far. Death was too near. The light that burns was bright behind his eyes. He thought of Umak and remembered the old man's words: *The hunter must face into the light. Only by facing death may his spirit overcome it.*

Torka faced death. With his body poised and his weapons balanced, he waited for it. And when, at last, the mammoth charged, Torka did not turn away. He ran to meet it, screaming.

2

The hunter's cry cracked the stillness of the Arctic noon.
It was a shout loosed like a well-flung spear, hurled upward
toward the sun so that it flew across the snow whitened
tundra as though it were a ptarmigan flushed from winter
cover.

But here, in this place, there was no sun. Morning had
come and gone, and that was all there would be of day. There
was no hunter. There was no spear. There was no winter-
white bird flying in terror of death. There was only an old
man crying out of his dreams within the domed shelter of a
pit hut beneath the appalling cold and returning dark of the
Asian winter sky.

"Behold! They come! The people shall not starve!"

Joy propelled the old man bolt upright upon his narrow
mattress. It was a jumbled piling of time-worn hides stretched
over the much-mended patchwork of oiled caribou intestines
that, together with an underlayering of leather tarpaulin,
formed the flooring of the little hut. The cold dampness of
the permafrost, into which the floor had been cut, had melted
to congeal into a soggy ooze beneath the waterproof covering;
but it did not soak through to permeate the old man's bed-
ding, nor did the frigid darkness bite at his bony brown body
as his bed furs tumbled down around him into his lap. Since
the death of his woman, he had taken to sleeping fully clothed.
Now he was sweating with excitement within his sleeved
tunic of caribou hide and his meticulously stitched vest of
vertically aligned foxtails.

"Yes . . ." he exhaled with a reverence born of pure
longing. The caribou *were* coming. They poured out of his
dream and into the darkness of the little hut in a tide so vast

that he could see neither its beginning nor its end. Caribou! The annual spring migration to their calving grounds had begun at last! Soon the hunters would be returning with food for all!

The old man's prominently lidded black eyes squinted as his tongue emerged to lick the imagined sweetness of caribou fat from his desiccated lips. He rested his strong, lean hands upon his mattressing. He pressed down hard. Yes! He could feel the hoofbeats of the approaching herd roaring deep within the earth. It was a rising, thundering reverberation of life pounding toward the little valley in which his people had made their winter encampment. The caribou were coming at last from out of a thousand secret sheltering canyons deep within the encircling mountains, where they had sought refuge from the seemingly endless storms of the time of the long dark.

Yes, the caribou were coming at last! Or were they?

Suddenly disoriented, the old man cocked his head, listening, straining to hold onto his dream as it dissolved into wakefulness, taking the vision of caribou with it. The roaring sound of the animals' hooves melded into something else, something deeper—something dangerous somehow, although very far away. Then that, too, was gone, and the old man heard only the growling voice of his own hunger. His intestines lurched and contracted, hurting him with the gnawing, pitiless ache of starvation. He had not eaten a full meal in weeks, and for the last three days he had not eaten at all.

"Umak's belly speaks through his mouth." The woman's voice was a whispered monotone reeking of contempt.

His face burned with shame as, through the long, unbraided strands of his black, as yet ungrayed hair, he allowed his gaze to meet the woman's. So he had awakened her once again with his blasphemous cries of caribou sightings, which were nothing more than the pathetic outpourings of an old man's wishful thinking.

"Would that we could eat of Umak's dreams, we would all grow fat," she said, watching him out of her wide black eyes, eyes as cold and compassionless as the Arctic night.

Her words shriveled his pride. Had he lost his dignity as well as his youth? How could he shame Egatsop, as well as himself, by allowing her to know that he suffered from the pangs of hunger while, by right, she ate his portion of the family's remaining food?

He could barely see her in the darkness. Sitting cross-legged upon the piled sleeping skins that she shared with her man and children, she had pulled the bed furs up over the back of her head, so that they fell around her small, compact form like a tent. Her man was not there. She sat with her infant at her breast while her little son, Kipu, slept close by.

In front of her, within the pebble-lined central fire pit, a small stone settled beneath the thick layering of banked embers. The stone, superheated, cracked and fell into two halves. Its movement caused the banked ashes of burned bones and dung to sag and separate, allowing a little fissure of heat and light to rise. Umak stared across the resulting light and saw the woman's face shimmering red and gold. For all of its undisguised hatred of him, it was the face of a young and undeniably beautiful woman: Egatsop, Torka's woman.

Within the fire pit, another stone cracked. It made a sharp, explosive sound, which roused the nursing infant. The baby uttered a sleepy, plaintive cry, then took suck again, making small gasps of satisfaction.

Egatsop continued to stare at the old man, her mouth downturned between her small nose and pointed chin. Her black eyes flayed him. "All the hunters have returned without meat. All but Torka, Alinak, and Nap. If they do not soon come with game, my breasts will begin to dry. Then this little one will be like the others . . . abandoned to the wolves or wild dogs or—"

"The hunters *will* return. They *will* bring game. Your breasts will *not* dry."

"Have you seen this in your dreams, Spirit Master?"

"I have seen this." He resented her sarcastic reminder of his title. Once it was said that he, Umak, was the greatest hunter of them all, that he could communicate with the spirits of his prey and command the herds of game to appear or disappear at his command. These days, it was growing painfully clear to him, as well as to the rest of the band, that he could command nothing. Especially the tongue of his grandson's cold-eyed woman.

"Old men see many things," she said with a rude snort of derision. "But never do they see with the clarity of youth, or they would be out with the hunters, scouting for game, not consuming the food of others when they are unable to provide for themselves."

"I will hunt again. My leg is nearly healed."

"Nearly is not good enough. Torka hunts for you. Torka shall always hunt for you. And give to an old man what should be for his woman and children."

Her words struck at his sense of justice. At forty-five, Umak was the eldest member of the band. He knew that many considered him to be ancient; but he did not *feel* old. Surely, even a youth could have slipped and sprained a knee while running down and tackling a steppe antelope, as he had done earlier in the winter. Recently widowed, without a woman of his own to care for him, he had agreed to spend the remainder of the time of the long dark with Torka. From the very first, sensing Egatsop's sullen resentment of his presence within her pit hut, he had made certain that half of everything that Torka apportioned to him went to her and the children. Food, drink, furs. When Torka had objected, Umak simply claimed that his needs were less than they truly were. And for the past three days, since Torka had been gone from the encampment, every morsel of his food had gone to Egatsop so that she would continue to have milk for the baby. He reminded her of that now.

She snarled at him. She told him that it was his duty to give up his food. She held no gratitude toward him, only disgust. "You should have fed your spirit to the storms long ago, old man. Torka has been too kind to you. It is a weakness in him. But now the headman has said that if Torka and the others do not soon return, we will be forced to break camp and move on without them in search of game. It will be better than staying here to starve. But without Torka to walk at your side, how will you keep up, old man? This woman will not help you."

Once again his belly lurched. He thought of his game-filled dream. Had it been the vision of a spirit master? Or had it been only the wishful thinking of a hungry old man who could not hunt for himself? The winter had been so long, so cold—perhaps snow still blocked the passes through which the caribou made their migrations. Perhaps the herds would not appear at all this year. And what of Torka? Why had he not returned? He, Alinak, and Nap had been the first group of hunters to go out from the encampment. They should have been back by now . . . if they were going to return at all.

For the first time in his life, Umak felt the weight of his years. All of his children were dead, and the last of his women. Torka was all he had left to remind him that they had ever lived at all. Torka and little Kipu and the infant. How the old man loved the children! Almost as much as he loved Torka. He knew that he had allowed himself to feel too much affection for his grandson. Their years together had formed a bond that choked him now as he thought of what his days would be like if Torka did not return. Egatsop would take another man. She would send Umak from her pit hut, and he would be alone, without shelter. And who, in these starving times, would see to it that one old man, who could not hunt for himself, was fed? Little Kipu would, but the boy was only five. Egatsop would forbid him to show compassion for one who was useless. She was a wise woman who would make him understand that survival was for the strong. The old, the weak, the children who showed no potential for becoming contributing members of the band had no right to a place within it.

Despair was a cold and alien wind that stirred within the old man's soul. He was *not* old! He was *not* weak! His leg was taking a long time to heal, but it *would* heal! The knee was only sprained. He could already hobble about on it. Soon it would be as strong as it had ever been. Soon.

"Soon we will go from this place." Egatsop's voice was low; she did not want to wake Kipu or disturb the infant who now slept, still sucking fitfully, at her breast. "If Torka returns, he will care for you, Spirit Master. He will walk at your side across the long miles and deprive himself of strength for your sake. He will see to it that Umak has food that should be for the mouths of his woman and children. One who is not worthy to live *will* live. Torka will see to it. Then we will all starve, because soon he will be too weak to hunt."

Shame filled him. He could not speak. He knew that she spoke the truth and that the other members of the band would view Torka's kindness as weakness.

Her voice continued on, barely audible, a croon, not to the old man, but to the sleeping infant. "You sap me of my strength, little one. There is not much milk for you now. If the hunters do not soon return with game, the band will move on. But do not be afraid. Sleep. Dream. In this place where you shall stay alone, the spirits will ease your hunger. Dream of that. And know that, in better times, this woman will give birth to you again."

Beyond the pit hut, far away across the cold darkness of the Arctic winter noon, a wild dog barked, and Egatsop tensed, listening. "So it is still there. Yesterday it came close, close enough to trip the snares that we women have set for it. But it is wise and wary. It will take better bait than we have to make it abandon caution in the hope of satisfying its hunger."

Umak drew his bed furs up about his bony shoulders. He shivered. He knew what she was going to say.

She rocked the sleeping infant. It made small, fretful mewings. "It would come for you. Yes. Now, while you are still strong enough to cry. It would come for you. A good-sized dog, if properly portioned and prepared, could nourish your people for many days. They would sing praises to you. Your death would serve the band. This woman would be proud."

"Woman, you will *not* feed this man's offspring to wild dogs!"

"The child is Torka's, not yours, old man!"

"Torka will not allow it!"

"Torka is not here. And even if he were, he would know what this woman knows: He left the encampment before this newborn was old enough to be named. Without a name, it has no life spirit. It only looks alive. If the band moves on in search of new hunting grounds, this woman will need all her strength to carry her share of the traveling burden. Egatsop will not be the only woman to abandon her baby to the spirits. Do not look at me like that, old man. You know I speak wisdom. Egatsop can make more babies only if she is strong. Be glad that I am not so unfeeling as the headman's woman. Although she said that the spirits took both the soul *and* the body of that little one, they did not. Teenak herself took the corpse of her newborn. Her family have been eating off it for many days."

Umak hung his head. He, who had faced down and slain a great white bear in his youth, who had raced down and killed a steppe antelope with his bare hands in his old age, could not bear to listen to Egatsop's words. What was wrong with him? Why did he feel such loathing and anger toward the woman? She was such a practical creature. Torka was the envy of the men of the band for having won her. She was right in everything that she had just said—right and honest and practical. And strong. Yes. Strong of mind and body. While he was old and weak and not as fit to live as the spiritless suckling whom she held to her breast.

She saw his anguish and smiled. Her teeth were small and sharp and even, but it was her words that bit deep. "Go now, old man. Feed your spirit to the winter dark before Torka returns to stop you. Go. Go, and this woman vows that she will suckle this little one as long as there is milk within her breasts. Stay, and this woman vows that what she holds within her arms will be offered as bait for wild dogs. Go. End your shame. And mine. And Torka's."

He took no weapons. He took no food. He went out wearing only the clothes upon his back and the boots that he had neglected to remove before lying down to rest. Around himself he draped the heavy bison hide that had served him as a traveling cloak for many years. He did not wear it as protection against the cold. It was something in which to hide his shame.

Beyond the pit hut, in the pale blue light of the aurora borealis, he looked out upon a landscape that was as savage and uncompromising and beautiful as Torka's woman.

Torka. He could only hope that he was still alive, out there somewhere with Alinak and Nap, even now en route back to the winter camp with game for all.

But not for Umak. No. He would not eat again.

He made his way through the encampment, past the other little pit huts within which his people sheltered against the rising bite of the wind. No one was outside. He could hear their voices. The sounds of life. But he had put that behind him. The future lay here, with these little families, with Egatsop and her children, and with Torka, if he still lived. He, Umak, was the past.

He accepted the finality of that truth, wondering why it did not come easily. He had always imagined that it would. He had assumed that, if not killed on a hunt, one day he would awake and *know* that he was old, and after that his spirit would seek release and he would walk out upon that final trek, at peace, as had so many others before him.

But there was no sense of peace within him as he walked on, fighting against the knowledge that he did not want to die. Is this what the others had felt? Rage? Frustration? A terrible sense of betrayal? A young man's soul trapped within an old man's body, scratching at his gut, digging in, trying to take control of his tongue and scream: *I have lived and loved and hunted and grieved with you for all of my life. I have*

*been your spirit master. I have brought down the great
white bear and taught your young men to hunt as only I,
Umak, know how to hunt. In starving times, I have shared
my food with you, and now can it truly be that there is none
for me? Am I to be thrown away like an old bone? Can you
not know that, from the marrow of my spirit, my soul cries
out for life?*

Ahead of him, the figure of a female emerged from the
last pit hut of the encampment. It was Lonit. He knew her at
once, despite her heavy garments; for although she was not
much more than a child, she was already taller than any
woman of the band and as strong and gangly as a colt born to
the wild horses that ranged the summer tundra.

She had come out of her family's shelter to secure one of
the lashing thongs that laced the hide roof cover tautly over
the arching mammoth rib bones of the roof frame. When she
saw Umak, she paused, instinctively knowing his intent.

With the wind rising around them, the old man felt her
eyes upon him, those unusual eyes that were as softly brown
and deeply lidded as an antelope's, almost totally devoid of
the elongated fold of eyelid tissue that was considered to be a
mark of beauty among the women and girls of the band. He
knew that the skin around one of those strange eyes was black
and blue from her father's latest beating. It was a wonder
how the girl had lived to grow up. Since the death of her
mother, she had become the focus of her family's abuse. No
doubt it had something to do with her odd appearance. Many
said that her father, Kiuk, should never have allowed such an
ugly girl to live in the first place; but Kiuk was a fine hunter,
an asset to the band, and what he did with his women was his
concern. Still, Umak had always felt pity toward the girl. She
was a strong, stalwart, uncomplaining child who, for reasons
he could never understand, went out of her way to be kind to
the very young and the very old. For a moment he was
certain that she was going to speak his name, to call him away
from his purpose. If she did, she would shatter his resolve
and ruin this last act of dignity, thus shaming him forever.
But the girl stood motionless in the wind, and the moment
passed, and Umak walked past her in silence, committing
himself to the final trek. Death awaited him. He would seek
it now. For the good of all.

*   *   *

"Where is Umak?"

Little Kipu awoke, looking for his great-grandfather. The old man had promised to help him perfect his skill at bone toss; it was a game that grown men played with sticks whittled out of leftover bone fragments for which the women had no use. In all of the band, no man was better at bone toss than Umak.

The little boy frowned. He missed his father. Torka had been gone so long on the hunt. Kipu sat up and rubbed his eyes. His mother had an odd look on her face. Expressionless. As flat as a much-used cooking rock. And as smooth, with all detail worn away after years of marrow bones being rubbed and splintered on their surface. Cooking rocks were pretty things. Glossy. They looked strong, as though they could last forever, but stress them too much or put them too close to the fire, and they would crack. Kipu thought about that as he looked at his mother.

"When will Torka return?"

"Soon," she replied with absolute certainty.

Kipu's frown deepened. She sounded certain only because she was not. He had come to know that it was her way when she was afraid. His dark eyes took in the equally dark interior of the pit hut; there was not even enough fat left to burn in the hollow stones that served as lamps. How he wished that winter would end! How he longed for summer!

"Umak has promised to teach me to chase down a steppe antelope," he confided. "When the time of the long dark is over, Umak has said that Kipu will be old enough to begin to learn to hunt like a man."

"Umak has gone to set his spirit free upon the wind."

Kipu cocked his head. "When will he come back?"

"He will *not* come back."

The child stared. He was five, but he had been born and raised among the nomads of the tundra. Far beyond the pit hut, a wild dog howled, and Kipu listened, understanding what his great-grandfather had gone to do, and why. Tears stung the back of his eyes. He adored his great-grandfather. He would miss him more than he had words to say. But he would not cry for him. He was Torka's son and of Umak's line. He would have thrust his hand into the fire pit before he would allow himself to cry.

Egatsop watched him, waiting to see tears, a display of weakness; she was relieved when the child sat dry-eyed, stoically staring straight ahead, saying nothing. She knew what the moment was costing him. Against her breast, the infant stirred, and although Umak would have found it impossible to believe, she fought down a wave of tenderness for it that came close to overwhelming her. If she were to be forced to expose this baby, she dared not let herself care for it, lest grief weaken her and make her unable to give her full attention to Kipu and Torka.

Torka! She almost called his name aloud with longing. Where was her man? Why had he not returned to her?

3

Blood. And pain. Torka awoke to these two realities and lay dazed, in agony and confusion.

Where was he? Why was he alone? He remembered watching the sunrise, and now it was dark. And cold. The wind was a constant slur of sound coming to him from across the tundra. He listened. For a long while, that was all that he could do. It hurt to move, to think; even breathing was painful. He sucked in shallow little takes of air, as carefully as he would have sipped at liquid if anyone had brought him something to drink.

Thirsty. In a black, aching limbo, his thirst was suddenly more intense than his pain. He lay with his face down, his cheek half-frozen into the earth. His mouth was open. He could taste the tundra. It was salty, and sweet, as though the skin of the permafrost were the flesh of a living being that had been flayed alive and now bled into his mouth.

Blood. Somehow reality was linked to that. And to his pain. And to the fact that he was alone. Through blood-caked lashes, he looked out across the miles, and suddenly it all came back to him.

The mammoth.

The deaths of Alinak and Nap.

And his own death. He remembered his raging charge. With his spear raised, he had run to meet the mammoth head-on. As it had lowered its head, he had leaped forward onto one of its tusks. As it had thrown up its head to dislodge him, he had hurled himself against the beast's vast shoulder. With one hand curled into its hair, he had held on and stabbed and stabbed until, at last, the monster had pitched him off. He had been hurled up and away as though he were a stone being loosed from a mighty sling. And when he had hit the ground, he had known that he was dead.

But, incredibly, he was *alive*. He was in too much pain *not* to be alive. His instincts told him that the mammoth was gone. Why? Why had it not finished him as it had finished Alinak and Nap?

The answer came as he tried to rise, and levering upward with his hands, gasping against the pain of several broken ribs, he looked down at the ground beneath him. What he had tasted *had* been the flesh of a living being that had been flayed alive. It was the bloodied mass of what was left of Nap. The slowly ebbing warmth of his flattened, mangled corpse had kept the unconscious Torka from freezing to death; the smell of Nap's blood on Torka's body had caused the mammoth to assume that Torka, whose body it had inadvertently thrown atop Nap's, was also dead. Its rage sated, its thick, hairy hide barely pierced by Torka's stabbings, it had gone on its way.

With the bloodied gore of Nap's exposed entrails upon his gloved hands, Torka rose and turned away, retching, nearly fainting from pain. Twice in one day, Nap had saved his life—once when Nap was alive, and once when he was dead. When Torka returned to the winter camp, he would make chants of honor to his name. Nap's woman would be proud in her grief; Torka would see to that.

If he returned to the winter camp. The wind was rising. A thin veil of high clouds obscured the light of the aurora borealis. It was a dark, cold world across which Torka began to make his way toward home.

Hours passed. The miles slipped away. He was weak, in pain, and several times he had to stop to rest. A thin, dry snow began to fall at about the same time that he first crossed the mammoth's tracks. Tramping on, he knew that it was moving ahead of him, following the route that he and Alinak and Nap had taken outward days ago from the winter camp.

Half sobbing, fighting against the pain and weakness that threatened to overwhelm him, Torka hurried on. He knew what was in the mammoth's mind. Poor, foolish Nap had been right. It *was* a crooked spirit, and its rage was *not* spent. It was on the scent of Man. It would stay on that scent until it reached the encampment of Torka's people. Once there, it would kill them all.

*   *   *

Umak walked alone within the night. He tried not to wonder about how long he had been walking or how far from the encampment he had come; these things should no longer concern him. Yet he knew exactly and could have found his way back to the camp blindfolded and in a snowstorm. His knee ached, but not nearly so badly as he had expected it would; perhaps it *was* nearly healed after all?

No matter. It is the time of death, not of life and healing. For Umak these things will be no more.

Still, he walked on and wondered at his own stamina, for although he was ancient and starving, he was not tired. He walked in the slow, measured, steady manner of one who moves as easily as he breathes—in the gait of a nomad whose feet have taken him across the world beneath the broad and savage Arctic sky.

He looked up. The sky was filled with clouds. Hard pellets of snow no larger than dust particles stung against his face. He found himself gauging the weather. There would be no storm, but the wind was rising. In a few hours the snow would stop, the sky would be swept clear, and a deep cold would settle upon the tundra. It would be dangerous to anyone not sheltered against it.

Umak harrumphed to himself. Ahead lay the gentle rise of a tundral hillock. It was a scabby, wind-scoured mound, but it would offer a pleasant view across the tundra to a man who sat upon its summit, exposing himself to the wind, waiting to die.

This Umak did. And the wind came, speaking to him of many things: of past hunts and of wives who had shared his pride, of long-dead children, of . . . everything but how to die. He was not even cold. It occurred to him that he could strip naked. That would certainly hurry the process, but he could find nothing dignified in the thought of shivering himself into death with his old bones showing under his skin, and all of the spirits seeing that, beneath his clothes, Umak was not the man he once was.

Again he harrumphed. He gathered up his composure and began to chant, to make his life song. The wind would take it to the spirit world. Death would hear it and know that it was time to come. Umak might no longer be able to call down the spirits of the game. But what sort of spirit master would he be if he could not call down the spirit of his own death?

He sang and sang. It was an atonal rhythm, a chanting meld of word and vibrations of his throat. He tried to match its resonance to the wind, but could not quite get it right. The chant went on. He ran out of words. Now the song was only sound. It bored him. Perhaps it was boring Death as well? The thought piqued him. He was Umak! What hunter could boast of more daring deeds than he? Death should be impressed. But even the Arctic's greatest spirit master could only fill a life song with so many stories. How many great bears could a man challenge in one lifetime, or saber-toothed cats, or stampeding herds of giant bison? He was, after all, only a man, despite his extraordinary prowess. What did Death want of him? He could not very well make up stories to extend his life song; that was a taboo that no man would break lest his life spirit be thrown away upon the winds. He thought about it for a while and decided that perhaps Death liked his tales so much that Umak was being urged to repeat them.

Umak did this, several times. But his stories did not summon Death. They summoned a wild dog instead. It was the same animal that had been lurking around the peripheries of the winter encampment for the last few days. Umak was not surprised to see it now. The dog had been wise enough to avoid the snares that Egatsop and the other women had set for it; no doubt, seeing a lone hunter wandering out of the encampment, the dog had decided to trail him as potential prey.

It was very close to the old man now, a large, wolfish animal with a mask of dark pelage surrounding its light blue eyes. It moved into the wind so that its prey would not pick up its scent. But Umak knew that it was there. Although he did not move but sat cross-legged, hands resting open upon his knees, head upturned to the great, cloud-filled vault of the sky, he knew. And smiled.

You will not sneak up on this old man, Brother Dog. Before you make prey of Umak, he shall break your bones and suck the marrow from them to keep the fire of his own life alive.

He did not speak aloud. Yet somehow the dog understood that it had been threatened. It paused, head down, tail tucked, watching, waiting for the unmoving figure to show the first sign of vulnerability.

Umak was not about to oblige it. He remained as he was.

From the corners of his eyes, he saw the dog fold its rear limbs into a seated position. Despite its size, the animal's disproportionately long limbs and gangling carriage betrayed its youth. It was an adolescent, a young male on its own, perhaps driven out of its pack after unwisely and unsuccessfully challenging the dominant male of the group. Umak did not know very much about dogs. He assumed them to be much like the more commonly seen wolves: social animals, pack hunters, dependent upon the group for survival. A disturbing feeling of empathy with the dog made Umak painfully aware of his own situation. Young or old, man or beast, neither could long hope to survive alone.

Not that Umak intended to survive. No. He was resolved to die. Now, for the first time, he moved, just enough so that he could eye the wild dog over one shoulder. Perhaps this was the way the spirits intended to answer his life song? He had called for death. Perhaps this masked, blue-eyed wild dog was his deliverer?

"Hmmph!" The exhalation was so loud and vehement that both man and dog were startled by it.

The dog was on its feet, growling. The two castaways stared at one another, and taking in the bone-thin animal, noting its flesh-colored, scarred nose and wound-scabbed ears, Umak suddenly became angry.

"This old man has not lived this long to be eaten by dogs! Umak deserves a better death than this!" With these words, he snapped to his feet, raised his arms, and charged, howling, straight at the dog.

Terrified, the animal wheeled and, without taking the time to bark or yip, ran into the night, across the snowy tundra, vanishing as completely as though it had never been there at all.

For a long while the old man stood looking after it. He wondered if it had been a creature of flesh or spirit. Its tracks gave him his answer. It had been real enough. And in all likelihood, all too soon, it would be back. In the meantime, it was possibly headed back for the winter camp. Umak thought of Egatsop and her promise not to abandon her newborn to the storms. He thought of the other women who had. He wondered if the wild dog had been surviving off the flesh of those infants whose mothers had not been as practical as the headman's woman, who had fed her family from the corpse of her newborn.

His hands flexed. He wished that he had killed the dog. He wished that he had brought his spears with him, or at least one of his daggers. His long mouth twisted down into a scowl. If the dog came back, he would kill it with his bare hands. It would be his last brave deed. Perhaps then Death would not be bored by his stories and would decide to come to him in a more honorable manner than through the jaws of an emaciated cur.

But the dog did not return. Strangely, Umak found himself missing it. What would come for him now? He shrugged. Whatever it was, he would face it, even if it came as he suspected it must—in stealth, sneaking up on him while he slept.

He went back to the summit of the little hill and seated himself. The wind was dying. Snow had ceased to fall. He could see stars where, only moments ago, clouds had covered the darkness. It was very cold as, once again, he began his life song. He would slowly freeze, and his spirit would ease away from the casing of bones and skin that had held it captive since his birth. It would not be such a bad death. He could feel sleepiness growing within him as he sang. But he was warm and comfortable within his heavy garments and the encircling windbreak of his bison-skin robe. It occurred to him that, in these same clothes and robe, he had weathered many a winter gale upon the open tundra. He was not likely to freeze to death in them now.

So, without ceremony, he cast them away. The wind cut through his undergarments. It bit at his skin as deeply as any wild dog could have done. When he breathed, the cold seared his lungs, and he thought: *This old man shall die now. In his sleep, Death shall come.*

He sat down. He waited for Death. Time passed slowly. It was too cold to chant. Too cold to sleep. He thought that he might make the time pass more quickly if he did a spirit dance. Movement would promote circulation; he would feel warmer until, at last, Death came for him and he collapsed. He tried it for a while, but his knee ached, and he felt foolish dancing when there was no one to watch. He hunkered down upon the little hill, beneath the savage sweep of the Arctic sky, and stoically waited for the end to come.

It did not. He shivered. His extremities went numb. His penis shriveled, and his testes retreated upward against that warm hollow from which they had descended when he was a boy. He thought of his boyhood. It did not seem so long ago. Memories came. Yesterday was closer than tomorrow.

Time continued to pass. Umak did not die. He sat and at length conceded that it was not possible for one who had spent his entire life fighting the cold to succumb passively to it—especially when the warm garments were close at hand. He stared at them and rationalized: *This old man is too cold to sleep. In sleep, death will come. Umak will put on the robe. He will freeze . . . but slowly.*

He made a tent of the robe. Without his caribou-skin tunic and vest of foxtails, without his outer trousers and leggings, he was still cold; but he had put on his boots and gloves. Within the windbreak of the old robe, the cold's bite was lessened, and he slept, albeit fitfully. Now and again he awoke, expecting to be dead, but he was still alive. He grumbled, vexed, and slept again.

Sometime before dawn, he felt Death come close. It called his name, and only the growling of a dog roused him before he answered and allowed his spirit to follow.

The wild dog was back, standing very close. It must have been watching him for hours, waiting for Death to come before it made its move. Umak cursed it. He spoke to it aloud.

"Stupid beast! This old man was about to enter the spirit world! Could you not wait! Umak has been *trying* to die! Were it not for you, my spirit would be free and you would be feasting off my useless bones! But those bones are *not* useless now! And you will not eat this old man while he is still alive!"

The dog listened. Its head was down, its ears and lips back. Its growl was deep and full of threat.

Umak growled back at it. "*Aar* . . . go away! If you come too close, this old man shall eat *you!*"

The dog did not move. Its growl continued. A single thrum of threat, as cold and full of menace as a rising wind out of the north.

Umak was not intimidated. The dog was large, but it was also young and thin and probably as weak as the starving man whom it had singled out to be its next meal. Experience told Umak that he could brazen out the dog's threat. He rose, then pulled the bison-skin robe about him so that he looked twice his size. He growled at the dog again and, in doing so, gave the creature a name.

"*Aar* . . ." snarled the old man.

And the dog answered, but did not back away. "*Aarrr* . . ."

"Hmmph!" said Umak, annoyed with the situation. As long as the dog stayed, his body would not allow his spirit to leave it. He bent and reached for a stone to hurl at the animal. His aim was good; the dog yipped and ran. But the action made the old man pant. He *was* weak. He *was* dying. And suddenly he was frightened because he knew that he did not want to die.

He retrieved his clothes, put them on, and began to walk. He did not know where he was going. He only knew that he would walk until he dropped. And then the dog, which Umak knew was following, would attack. The dog, being young, would outlast an old man. It *would* be the death that he had called for. The death that Umak no longer wanted.

The old man and the dog saw the abandoned wolf-kill at the same time. They made for it, and Umak's hunger renewed his strength as fully as it made him bold. He moved like a youth, shouting and waving and forcing the dog to back away in confusion. The animal stood cowed as the old man fell upon the mutilated steppe antelope, snarling and sobbing with relief as he tasted the sweet blood of life and knew just how much he did not want to die.

He ate and ate and did not know when the dog joined him. Somewhere halfway through a haunch, he looked up to see the dog eating across the carcass from him. Their eyes met. The dog paused; its manner was submissive. Umak went on eating. Strangely, the old man felt no desire to drive the dog away. The raw, near-frozen meat was restoring his energy, and he knew that were it not for the dog, he would be dead, back upon the hillock, and the dog would be feasting off his flesh rather than the flesh of the prey they now shared. As he continued eating, he wondered if, perhaps, the spirits had not sent this half-grown, half-starved dog to tell him that they did not want Umak's death. But why?

He pulled back from the carcass, his appetite, if not his questions, sated. He watched the dog. It occurred to him that he was strong enough now to stone the beast successfully. And now was the time to kill it, while its guard was down. He could live off its carcass for many days. He could even take it back to the band. There he could flaunt his prowess with it. He could show Egatsop how thoroughly she had misjudged him. Egatsop. He remembered her readiness to use her own child as bait with which to snare the dog. Loathing of the woman made him frown. *No*, he thought, watching the dog, *you will not go into that one's belly. The band has cast away this old man. But you have given back to Umak the spirit to live. Now that we have eaten of the same prey, we are of one flesh, Brother Dog. And Umak, he will not eat of the flesh of his brother.*

He rose, then stood looking down at the dog. Sensing his stare, the dog looked up, studied him out of its blue, black-masked eyes. The animal sensed a change in the man. There was renewed strength and purpose in his stance and a strange, undeniable power shining in his black, slitted eyes. The threat had gone out of him. The man had allowed the dog to share in "his" kill. In the unspoken, instinctive language of all animals that run in packs, this sharing was a statement of acceptance into the pack. Those that ate of the same kill were forever bonded by the mutually ingested life-giving blood of that kill. Predator and prey might never eat together. The dog understood this. He sensed that the man understood it, too. Visibly, the dog relaxed. He turned his eyes away from the man and set to eating his fill. The man would not harm him. He would not harm the man. A covenant had been made between them. They were of one pack now.

Umak and the dog stayed beside the carcass of the steppe antelope until they had eaten it all. It had been a fresh kill, only partially consumed by the wolves who had taken it, and it was not until Umak sat cracking the last of the bones and sucking the marrow from them that he began to wonder why wolves would abandon so much meat.

To Umak the question was sobering, for wolves were as frugal as men, carrying away and caching what they could not eat on the spot; and these were starving times for hunters, be they men or beasts.

The tenuous morning of the Arctic spring passed into dusk. It was night again. The old man huddled in his tentlike robe of bison hide and slept, with the wild dog close, but not too near. They were no longer adversaries, these two, but they were not yet friends. The night passed. Then it was dawn again. Umak awoke and smiled because he was alive, and he was glad, although he was not quite sure why.

He walked on. The dog followed. When he stopped, the

dog stopped. When he went on again, the dog was still with
him. In the fragile light of the Arctic morning, they picked up
the trail that Nap and Alinak and Torka had taken out of the
winter encampment many days ago. Umak paused, wondering if they had yet returned to the band. With Torka as a part
of their team, Umak had little doubt that they had. His
grandson was a hunter of extraordinary skill, a man of profound instincts. Torka would be a spirit master someday,
when Umak had taught him all that there was to know.

The old man ground his teeth. He remembered that he
had been cast out, and that he would teach Torka no more.
Whatever his grandson had learned, that would be all of it.
They would never meet again.

There was such pain in that thought that the old man
wished that he *had* died, for surely to be alone upon the
tundra, cast out of the band, never to see his loved ones
again, that *was* death.

The dog's sudden excitement put an end to Umak's black
reverie. Up ahead, another set of tracks crossed those of
Umak's kinsmen. The dog circled and sniffed, and the old
man went to investigate.

Mammoth.

He knew better than to speak the word aloud lest he call
down the spirit of the game without the proper ceremony;
but it was mammoth, all right. A single mammoth, and from
the size of its footprints, it was the biggest mammoth that
Umak had ever seen.

He checked the tracks. Touched them. Smelled them.
They crossed and recrossed the hunters' trail in several places—
often enough to suggest to Umak that the mammoth was
following the route that the men had taken when they had
come out from the encampment.

Strange behavior, thought the old man. Mammoths usually traveled in small, close-knit family groups near to the
scrub forests by the base of the distant mountains, with the
cows and calves clustering together, while their bulls ranged
alone or in pairs, shadowing the herd only in mating season.
They avoided Man.

The tracks of the solitary giant informed Umak that they
belonged to a big male. He knelt, one hand splayed across
the width of the enormous footprint. Memories stirred of
tales heard in times long gone by, of a legend whispered by
the old men when he was a little boy. Of Thunder Speaker.

Of World Shaker. Of One Who Parts the Clouds. Of a mammoth that men called the Destroyer, for where it walked no man might follow, and all who fell beneath its shadow died.

He shrugged off the memories. He smiled at his own foolishness. The beast of his boyhood recollection was only a fable. Mammoths were shy, evasive creatures. If this old male was heading in the direction of the encampment of the band, then his people's days of starvation were at an end at last. The hunters who went out from the camp each day would see it; they would feel the shock of its footfall quivering in the permafrost. Although they were near starvation, their need would make them strong. They would gather their weapons and their wits, and with their combined strength, they would kill the beast.

He rose, happy for his people and sorry that he had listened to Egatsop and chosen to die. It had been years since he had hunted mammoth. His experience would be valuable to the band. But he could not go back; once the decision to walk with Death was made, it was irrevocable. To return after having called to Death might cause Death to follow and eat of the life spirits of the entire band.

He drew in a little breath. Too bad. He would like to help, to tell them that a mammoth the size of a walking mountain was coming toward them.

"Hmmph," he said aloud, not realizing that he was talking to the dog. "They will not need this old man. A mammoth as big as a mountain will also be as old as a mountain. Perhaps, like Umak, it wanders alone, waiting to die. It will be weak. It will be easy to kill."

The dog looked at him. And clearly, as though the animal spoke the words, Umak understood its thoughts and was rebuked. Had he not come to know from personal experience that not everything that is old is necessarily weak . . . or easy to kill?

Night came down, and its wind was bitterly cold. The old man sat in his contrived tent of bison hide and conjured past hunts and glorious battles waged against big game. He chanted. The wind took his words and blew them away across the tundra.

The dog listened. He lay nearby but not too close, curled against the wind, nose tucked beneath his tail, dreaming his own dreams, twitching against memories of his own past battles.

Not far away, Umak's chanting rode upon the wind, and Torka heard it, disbelieving. He tried to rise and cried out as he fell again, half-conscious, where he had collapsed hours ago.

The wild dog heard his cry. Its head went up as every hair along its back bristled. Umak heard it, too, but it had come and gone so quickly that he could not identify it.

He stopped his chanting. Had he heard the cry of prey or predator? Unable to answer that question, all recollections of his youth vanished, leaving him an old man again, alone and unarmed and waiting to die upon the dark and savage tundra. Perhaps he had heard the voice of Death?

He rose. His head went up. His chin jerked outward defiantly. He was Umak! He would not be afraid. Yet, despite his best efforts, his hands flexed as he longed to hold his weapons. There was an acidic dryness at the back of his throat that tasted too much like fear. He *was* afraid. He was old and weak and alone, but he did *not* want to die. Death should have come when he had first summoned it; he had wanted it then. But no more. The drive to live was strong in him now. His eyes squinted resolutely into the wind. His chin went down. *If Umak is still the spirit master that he once was, then what he has called he can also send away.*

He began to chant again. A new song. A loud song. Noise always sent the spirits of fear scattering out of a man's belly. Perhaps it would send Death fleeing as well. But Umak's song scattered out upon the tundral wind and reached Torka instead, into his ebbing consciousness. It roused the dying embers of the young hunter's life spirit and brought it up through pain and desolation into a new hope.

"Umak?" *Yes!* He would know that beloved voice in the darkest night, in the whitest storm, in the fiercest gale. "Umak!" He hurled the name against the wind.

Umak heard it.

With the dog trotting on ahead of him, the old man soon found his grandson and knelt to cradle Torka in his arms, listening to his tale of bloody terror.

"Umak . . . father of my father . . . you must warn the people . . . you must . . . get back to them in time. . . ." Torka's words bled out of him as he fought to hold on to consciousness and lost.

The old man held him close. There, beneath the winter dark, Umak knew at last why Death had not come to take the spirit of one old man—it had been feeding off younger, weaker life spirits. And now, with Torka severely wounded, Umak understood that in the guise of Thunder Speaker, of World Shaker, of a giant woolly mammoth whom men called the Destroyer, Death, the ultimate predator, was moving toward the winter encampment of his people.

Only one old man was left to stop it.

"And this old man will try!"

4

Across the long miles, across what was left of the long night, Umak jogged toward home with an unconscious Torka upon his back and the wild dog loping at his side. Dawn had not yet bloomed upon the horizon when he paused, gagging on fatigue, forcing himself to suck in deep breaths of the darkness as though it were a food that might nourish him.

It did not. He stood bent forward, with Torka deadweight across his shoulders as wolves howled in the distance and, deep inside him, the voice of exhaustion counseled: *Old man, it is not far now. Only a few miles. But your knee aches, and your body fails you. You will never make it—not with Torka on your back.*

Truth, or temptation to expediency? He could not tell which. He only knew that he would not abandon his grandson, not as long as there was a breath of life left in either of them.

He felt the eyes of the wild dog watching him, measuring him, and he thought of the censure of Egatsop, Torka's woman. *Weakness.* Yes. She would have called it that. He knew that he *must* get back to the encampment of his people as quickly as he could. He knew that he should leave Torka behind. If Torka were able, he would insist upon it.

"Hmmph," said the old man, listening to the wolves. "What Thunder Speaker could not kill, Umak will not abandon to be meat for beasts."

It took all of his energy and concentration to force himself to go on, but this he did, hefting his grandson, speaking aloud to the dog and the wolves and the savage distances of open tundra that still lay ahead of him. "This man is Umak. He is spirit master. He will run with the wind, and it will speed him on his way. Soon Umak will be home. He will warn his people. Together they will stand against the great mammoth. They will feast upon its flesh and send its spirit away."

And because he *was* a spirit master, it seemed to him that the wind *did* rise to speed him on his way, giving power to his limbs to keep them moving, bending, lifting, falling; in his mind he flew across the night, with Torka weightless upon his back and the wild dog leaping across the sky beside him.

It came upon them out of the night, as all true terrors must ultimately come—in silence, from out of that black pit in which fear is cradled, and from which crawl all of the horrors that evade the light of day. It came in stealth, walking into the wind so that its scent at first blew back and away. Only the pressure of its footfall onto the shallow skin of the permafrost betrayed its approach.

Within Torka's pit hut, little Kipu stirred in his sleep. It was the deep sleep that comes toward night's end, when the heartbeats slow, and the blood runs deep, and the mind lies inert and dreamless.

Across the warm, black substance of that dreamlessness, a vague and undefined awareness of danger ran like wind currents across the black surface of a pitch pool on a moonless night: invisible but sending subtle tremors deep. There was nothing tangible to fear—only the darkness, only the silence, only the familiar rank and musty life smells of the pit hut and the soft, arrhythmic rubbings and creakings of hide chafing against bone as gusts of wind intermittently sucked and slapped at the exterior walls of the hut.

The boy sighed and changed position beneath his bed furs. He moaned softly, still deeply asleep but no longer peaceful in his slumber.

Egatsop heard him. With the sleeping infant curled against her breasts, she lay half-awake, listening. Her nostrils picked up the faintest essence of crushed spruce bark and clotted blood as an inference of enormous height and weight slurred across her senses. The hide walls of the conical little pit hut strained softly against the thong-lashed bone framework that held the structure upright.

It is only the wind, she decided. *It blows from the distant mountains where the spruce forests grow. But why the smell of blood?*

She opened her eyes, staring into darkness, scenting the air like a small animal huddled in its burrow, fearing that something huge and hungry stalks it from above. But she could hear no one moving about outside. If there were a predator lurking within the encampment, the hunters would have sensed its presence, been up and in pursuit with spears and blades and bold shouts to warn the women and children to stay inside until all was safe. But the hunters evidently slept undisturbed, each within his own shelter.

Egatsop lay with her infant daughter and little son, feeling vulnerable and alone as she longed for the warmth and reassurance of her man. *Torka!* She had never missed him more. Why had he not returned? If he did not come back to the encampment soon, Egatsop would have to accept another man. The headman would insist upon it. A woman could not live alone.

A small, hard knot tightened hurtfully at the back of her throat. There were other men who wanted her, but she would not think of that yet. Not as long as there was a chance that Torka might still be alive.

She lay very still. Something *was* outside. But what? She resolved not to be afraid. She told herself that it was only her fear that walked within the night.

A pang of regret caused her briefly to lament her earlier goading of Umak. Had he been here, he would have ventured out to check. But he was gone, and she was not really sorry. For reasons that had always eluded her, the old man had made her feel less than worthy to be Torka's woman and the mother of Umak's great-grandchildren. She wondered if he was dead yet. She hoped that he was, then remembered that the spirits of the dead always lingered around an encampment until a newborn infant was named for them, thus allowing them to reenter the world of the living. Perhaps what had awakened her was only old Umak's ghost plucking at the walls of the little hut, trying to get in out of the cold.

Egatsop drew her baby close, for the first time glad that it was not a male child. Now that the old man had released his life spirit, custom would have decreed that a male child be named for Umak so that the old man could live again within the baby's body. Egatsop frowned with revulsion as she thought of that possibility; of old Umak sucking new life from the breasts of the very one who had sent him out to die.

As though sensing her thoughts, the sleeping infant rooted

at her breasts, found a nipple, and closed in hard, pulling
fretfully with hot, hard gums.

Egatsop winced. Had the old man already occupied the
infant's body? Umak had been a spirit master in his day, and
a good one. Perhaps he would maneuver his way back into
the world through trickery. Egatsop recalled how tenaciously
he had clung to life, how he had refused to acknowledge his
age or the extent of his injury, and how she had been forced
to shame him into abandoning his spirit to the winds. But
would any male be so hungry for life that he would willingly
degrade his masculine spirit by consigning it to live as a
female? No. Not even Umak would do that.

The baby made sleepy little bleats of dissatisfaction as it
nursed. Egatsop had not lied to the old man when she had
told him she feared her breasts were beginning to dry. It was
already happening. If Torka and the others did not return
with game by tomorrow's dark, she would expose this infant
before it began to sap her of the strength she would need to
keep herself and her son alive.

She lay quietly, thinking about how she would do it.
*Without ceremony. Since it has no name, it has no spirit. It is
not alive. Its fate is of no consequence. This woman will carry
it well out from the camp. This woman will pack its mouth
and nostrils with snow so that none of the living will be
disturbed by the cries of the dead as it is abandoned naked to
the cold.* That was how she would prefer to do it; but for the
sake of her son and the starving members of her band, she
knew that she could not be so wasteful. This baby would be
bait for wild dogs while it still had strength enough to cry and
lure them to the traps.

The smell of spruce and blood was suddenly very strong
in the air as the shallow skin of the permafrost twitched and
rolled, like the flesh of a gnat-stung giant. Egatsop sat up,
startled and frightened. The movement stopped, then began
again in hard, sharp jolts. Footfalls.

Kipu was awake. He sat up, knuckling sleep from his
eyes. "W-what is it?" His voice was tremulous, but he tried
to put a masculine edge to it, flat, uncaring, as though he
asked not out of fear and curiosity but out of indolent after-
thought, like a hunter asking politely about what sort of prey
his friend has sighted when he himself has already taken all
the game he can hope to eat in an entire winter.

Egatsop's eyes were round with dread. The little boy saw

his mother's fear and reacted to it. He was on his feet, five years old and protector of his father's woman.

The scent of crushed spruce bark was overpowering. Kipu's head went up. His nostrils dilated. He drew in the scent and tried to define it, as Umak had taught him to do: *Take the scent deep into memory, into that place where a man's images are collected.* But Kipu was not a man. He was a little boy. The place within him where images were collected was still a reservoir far from brimming. He had never been to the faraway mountains. He had never seen a forest or a tree of any kind.

But Egatsop had and knew now that her fear had been well-founded. The stench that filled her nostrils was less the stink of spruce than of the animal that ate it—an animal whose diet was composed almost entirely of spruce, so that its flesh and hide and hair and breath all stank of that sap-rich tree even when it strayed far from the forests onto the tundral plain.

"MAMMOTH!"

It was the cry of the headman. A shout of warning was given just as the beast itself cracked the sky with its trumpeting.

Beyond the walls of the little pit hut, the encampment was suddenly rent with screaming. The confused shouts of men, the startled cries of women, and the screams of frightened children told Egatsop all that she needed to know.

Thunder Speaker . . . World Shaker . . . He Who Parts the Clouds and Destroys the Lives of Men . . , the litany of dreaded names rolled through her mind as she remembered the old tales of terror. She drew in the stink of the mammoth's breath and bloodied hair and hide and knew, with a sick, sinking certainty that the blood she smelled was Torka's. The Destroyer had killed her man.

The beast was on a rampage now, cutting back and forth across the encampment. She could feel its movements in the earth. Scenes conjured from the nightmare stories of her childhood were afire within her brain as Egatsop leaped to her feet, clutching her daughter to her breast, forgetting that the infant was a spiritless suckling. She was a real child to her now.

It was *all* too real to her now.

Kipu was gathering up the spears that old Umak had left behind, spears that would be useless in the hands of a child.

Egatsop kicked out at him. He fell flat on his belly as she bent and scooped him up by an armpit with one hand.

"We must run. If we stay within the hut, it will smash us flat."

It.

"I will kill this mammoth!" brazened the child, daring to name his intended prey, fighting against his mother as she shoved him out into the fading night through the piece of hide that served as a door. He was furious with her as he turned back from several paces ahead to tell her that he was her only protector now, that he must retrieve his weapons. She had stopped, still bending low, with one hand holding the hide door open as she looked up and beyond Kipu. She had the strangest expression on her face, and he could not comprehend why she screamed his name the way she did— high-pitched and half-strangling, with her pretty features twisted into ugliness.

She was the last thing that he saw, and he did not even see her very well through the blue darkness of the Arctic dawn. But for one split second everything went very bright as something hit him from behind and above. Kipu did not even have time to wonder what it was that killed him.

But Egatsop knew. It paused as it crushed her little son beneath one vast foot and then came at her. She could have run—she was a small, lithe woman. She could have ducked away like a dancer at a hunting feast, throwing the spiritless suckling at the monster to distract it from its charge. But she did not, could not. In that last moment, when Torka's woman looked up into the eyes of Death, she tried her best to throw herself out of its path, curling her body protectively around her baby in a vain attempt to save its life at the cost of her own.

The world was blue. Above, below, snow, sky, even the air and the distant sounds of death and terror—all seemed blue. And Torka fell through the blueness, through miles of it, like a man tumbling into a glacial crevasse, hurtling downward through a bottomless chasm of blue ice, plummeting while a companion called helplessly from above, his voice dwindling . . . dwindling . . . until there was no sound but that of his own frightened breaths and gasps and sobs of terror as he fell . . . and fell . . . his body bouncing off ragged, ever-narrowing walls of ice until—

"Torka!"

Umak's voice. Far away, at the top of the crevasse, above the blue, parting it somehow. The old man called down, as if by magic arresting Torka's fall into oblivion, drawing him back up into the pain and reality.

He lay on his side in the snow, hurting; it did not seem possible that he could hurt so much. The fall to death within the blue abyss seemed preferable to so much pain. He sank back into it for a moment, but Umak, beside him in the snow, pulled him up, gripping him with gloved, unrelenting hands, and shook him hard.

"Torka! We must go on. But this old man, his knee will no longer bend to his power as spirit master. It has tripped him. He has fallen. Umak can carry you no farther."

"Carry?" The word was less question than protest. He was Torka. No man carried Torka. Not even Umak. *Unless*— With this half-formed supposition, he fell into the abyss again, only this time it was not blue and filled with ice; it was bright and filled with memories, which stabbed at him and erased any vestiges of torpor.

With Umak's help, he sat up, half-fainting with pain; then, drawing strength *from* the pain, he told himself that it was not there and almost believed it. He leaned against Umak, against that old, hard body with a heart inside it as deep and full of power as the unchanging, rock-hard under-pinnings of the tundral plain. There had always been comfort and renewed strength for him in the mere closeness of that old man, and he drew upon it now, as the dying dawn tangled itself in the shimmering sweep of the aurora borealis, stole its color, and bathed the world with the full golden light of morning.

"Listen!" commanded Umak, and there was something in the old man's voice that sharpened Torka's battered senses and brought him up out of pain-dulled lethargy.

He listened to the silence of the Arctic morning, the unnatural absence of wind, the erratic beat of his heart, the even suck of the old man's breath, and the uneven, shallow wheeze of his own. It was quiet . . . too quiet . . . as though, within the entire world and sky, only he and Umak were left alive.

"We have come too late," said the old man, his flat voice revealing none of his anguish. He had come so far. Driving himself beyond exhaustion, he had reached the final boundary that any other man would have recognized and accepted as the ultimate limit of human endurance. But he, Umak, had willed himself to leap over it. With Torka on his back, he had gone on and on—young again, powerful again, invincible—until even the panting wild dog had looked at him with disbelief as it had strained to continue running beside him.

Now the dog lay in the snow, not far off, on a gentle slope of tundral rise, which lay above the little valley where Umak's band had made its winter camp. It was upon that slope that the old man's knee now made a mockery of his power. A spirit master he might be, but kneecaps were spiritless things, and his buckled without warning. He had fallen down hard, trying to hold onto Torka but failing, lying stunned and breathless and winded in the snow.

The trumpeting of the mammoth cleared his head. But no startled shouts and cries of his people reached him, and he knew that it was too late for him to warn them. He limped to the top of the rise, and what he saw caused him to drop to his knees. Gone was Umak, spirit master and slayer of beasts. He became an old man again—old and unarmed, no longer invincible but impotent. He bowed his head, and as the silence of his people's catastrophe washed over him, he willed his own spirit to wash away with those among them who had died. But Umak had already learned that Death wanted no part of one stringy old man or of the injured hunter who lay in the snow moaning in delirium.

He went to Torka, knelt, then lifted his grandson, attempting to soothe him, drawing strength from the young man's need of him. He had been too late to warn his people of danger, but they would still have need of their spirit master's skills as a healer in its aftermath. The thought restored a little of his sense of self-worth. He spoke to Torka, telling him that they must go on.

The silence continued, and Umak listened, knowing that the mammoth had gone its way. Soon, when the shock of its passing had ridden over the people like a great and terrible wave, the survivors of its devastation would begin to weep and wail. For Torka's sake, Umak would try not to take too much noticeable pleasure in proving to Egatsop just how sorely she had underrated his worth as a healer.

But the moments passed. The silence did not abate. It thickened; it became palpable. And suddenly, Umak knew the truth, as Torka also knew it.

The Destroyer had come and gone. And within all of the world, and beneath all of the broad, compassionless sky, only Torka and Umak were left alive to hear the renewed song of the wind and to listen to the desolate lament of a lone wolf as it cried out to them from the edges of the valley far below.

5

They sat in silence, listening as a wolf sang a song that deepened their anguish.

Neither Torka nor Umak knew which of them first realized that it was *not* the song of a wolf. But the wild dog knew and was on its feet, head held out and low, ears back, recognizing the sound of potential prey.

Umak rose slowly, as did Torka. He leaned on the old man for support, fighting and winning against pain and dizziness. He stood into the wind. It had turned and was from the east now, blowing out of the valley, across the devastated encampment, redefining the song of the wolf, transforming it into what, in fact, it was: the grief-maddened howls and wails of a woman.

They went down into the valley together, with the dog trailing at a wary distance. They paid no heed to it; Umak had forgotten that it existed.

The wailing of the woman had stopped, yet Torka willed himself to hear it anyway. The sound of that voice gave him back his strength and set his pulse pounding and his heart racing with hope: It was his woman's voice! He was certain of it! Even though he was exhausted from pain and loss of blood, a new day was dawning. There was no way of knowing how many more of their people had been killed or injured, but Torka was alive, with Umak at his side. Egatsop called to him. Kipu would need him. The other survivors would also need him.

Somewhere deep inside the innermost core of what was left of his reason, Torka knew that his thoughts were irrational ramblings. But he could not face the truth. His thoughts

were scabs, which covered a dangerous wound. They soothed
him and lessened the pain that every step and breath cost
him. Without them, he would succumb to insanity.

When at last he came to the edge of the encampment and
saw what his mind would not allow him to grasp, he paused,
stared, and told himself that somehow, amid the total carnage
and ominous silence, survivors waited . . . his woman and
children waited . . . but the scabs cracked a little, and the
wound beneath them began to bleed. His next step was less
certain than the one before.

It was Umak who first saw the form of the woman. She
knelt at the opposite end of the ruined encampment, across a
bloodied lake of collapsed huts and scattered corpses. He
focused past the bodies, not wanting to see them, for most
were crushed beyond recognition, their garments dark with
blood and fouled with gore. The mammoth had not been
content merely to kill; it had ground and crushed and mutilated until most of what had once been men and women and
children was now a part of the tundral earth, joined to it in a
final hideous melding so that, in places, Umak could not tell
where flesh ended and earth began.

The woman had knelt with her back to the carnage. She
had covered herself with a swathe of hide and looked like a
little tent sitting alone amid the devastation until she moved,
rocking back and forth—as Umak had all too often seen
mothers do when their infant sons have died, clutching the
babes to the breast, tragically attempting to nurse and croon
them back to life.

It was understandable that Torka assumed that it was
Egatsop who sat there with his baby in her arms; he wanted
it so badly. He crossed the encampment to her. He lifted her
by the shoulders, turning her toward him as he spoke her
name. The hide fell away, taking his illusions with it. It was
not Egatsop. It was the girl Lonit.

Huge-eyed, dirty-faced, pale with shock, she held no
child but had crossed her arms protectively over her chest,
cradling herself as she had sat and rocked and tried to prevent her terror from taking control of her mind. It had
already done that once, when she had been awakened by the
screams of her people, to her world collapsing all around her.
Her father's pit hut had fallen down, smothering her, it had
seemed, as her father's women had clambered over her,
stumbling and fighting their way out of the tangled mass of

hides and bones, and left her to suffocate. She had heard her father shouting, and the other men, too; all screaming about gathering up spears and blades and making torches to drive "it" away. His voice had been lost, then; there had been too many voices, blending into one mass of sound. And above it all, she had heard "it" and had lain wrapped in her bed skins, trapped beneath the collapsed frame of her father's hut, unable to move, nearly unable to breathe, screaming in strangled terror as the world shook and shook and then went silent.

She had fought her way free of the hut to see what had brought madness to her: Her people were dead, all of them, and she was glad. *Glad!* Her mind had filled with memories of hurt and humiliation, of cruelty and lack of compassion. Of late, Kiuk had come to pound her in the dark, and although she was not yet a woman, he had pierced her as was his right as her father. Until another man spoke for her, she was Kiuk's to do with as he pleased. Since his two women were both big with child, he used her to ease himself. He rode her hard, stabbing deep. Sometimes she thought he was trying to ram straight through into her heart so that he might kill her. He pumped and pumped until her thighs were bruised and the place that he entered was raw and sore and bleeding from his brutal handling. She had not cried out. Not once. Not even when he blacked her eye because he was slow to come to his release. When he finished and rolled away, she had cried herself to sleep; a silent, inward sob that she had learned to make so that he, or his women, would not hear her and beat her for disturbing them. It was the females' place to be silent. It was the females' place to be strong. It was the females' place to oblige the men in all things. She lamented her inability to satisfy her father when he rode her in the night. It was her duty to satisfy him, but nothing that she did ever pleased him. And now nothing would please him ever again. He was dead. They were *all* dead. And she was glad! Who among them had ever shown kindness to her? Only old Umak. Only Torka. But they were both gone, perhaps as dead as all the others.

The enormity of that possibility had nearly struck her down. In an instant, her gladness had become guilt. What a wretched creature she was! Her father had been right to despise her. They had *all* been right to despise her. And now they were dead, and only she, a half-grown, miserable excuse for a girl, was left alive, to run about the encampment, howling her grief like a frenzied animal until she had collapsed, unable to cry or howl anymore. Without her people she would die. Without the protection of the band, the huge wolves, and bears, and lions would come to feed upon her flesh. They, at least, would find her satisfying. For them, perhaps, she had been born.

Now she stared at Torka as though she dared not believe that he was real. The blank look of madness was in her eyes. She could feel it. She blinked, willing herself back from the brink of insanity, back from that mindless world in which she had taken refuge since the mammoth had gone its way, leaving bloodied, tangled ruins all around her, leaving her alone with no hope of survival. Until now.

"Torka?" She spoke his name. Her knees nearly buckled, but she kept them locked lest she faint and shame herself before him. He was *real*. The hard, hurtful grip of his hands told her that. She was glad for the pain. She was alive, and Torka was with her. He was *not* dead. He *had* come home. The spirits *had* heard the supplications that she had made over and over since he had failed to return to the encampment with the others. He *had* come back, as she had known that he would, even though everyone believed that he would not. No one had spoken the words, but Lonit had sensed them seeping through the encampment like smoke from an ill-made fire. Bad smoke. Dark and foul with unburned things, such as envy and covetousness and resentment. Torka had been a friend to all. All would mourn his loss. Many would lament the starvation that had rendered them too weak to go in search of him. But others would remember that he was potentially better at so many things than they, and if he did not return, how much braver and stronger and more clever they themselves would seem to their women and children . . . and to themselves.

It was the way of the People. Lonit had learned it long ago. One did not set oneself apart. One strove to be like all others, to unify the band, to exist within it for the sole purpose of the survival of the whole. The band was a living, functioning organism that was only as strong as the whole of its parts. So it was that its weak members were cast away. So it was that its superior members hid their strength in order to inspire the lesser members to reach toward a level of excellence that all might achieve. Experience had taught that twenty good, steady hunters would always bring home more meat than a single stalker, no matter how superlative his skills or extraordinary his bravery. Torka had understood this. Lonit had watched him from afar, marveling at the way he had paced himself. He was like a runner holding back at the end of a race, knowing that he has won too often and too well; for the sake of others, he held himself back, allowing others their pride, not realizing that his very deference to them shattered it. Torka was the best. They all knew it. Lonit knew it. She could not remember a time when she had not adored him.

Now shame filled her as she looked up at him. She was aware of the wind blowing across the devastated encampment. It surrounded her, whispered to remind her that she alone was left alive to speak the traditional, obligatory greeting of a female to a returning hunter.

Her mind went blank. It did not occur to her that, in such a scene, words of welcome would be obscenities—she only knew that she could not remember them. Her shame intensified. She was not worthy to be alive when all of her people lay dead around her. How Torka must hate the sight of ugly, awkward Lonit when his own woman was dead, when *all* of the women were dead . . . all the pretty ones with their small, compact bodies and uniformly beautiful faces, which were as round and flat and fair as moons. Torka would want no greeting from one who would have been exposed at birth had she not been born to Kiuk's favorite woman during a season of plentiful game. She had been so ugly that she would not have been allowed to suckle had not her father, in a moment of weakness, seen fit to indulge a poor female who had never before been able to bring an infant to full term.

Her mother had thought her beautiful. Lonit had never understood why. From the first, it must have been obvious that she was different. Her face was oval rather than wide and circular. The bridge of her nose was not flat. She was big for a female, and most unforgivable of all, she had been born without the taut span of skin that covered each eyelid and stretched from the inner edge of the tear duct to the temple. A shield against wind and snow glare, this fold was more than a requirement for female beauty; without it, no girl-child was allowed to live. But Lonit had lived, despite her deformity. Her mother had begged for her to be named and thus allowed a life spirit. Kiuk had conceded. No doubt he had hoped that she would outgrow her ugliness. She had not; she had grown strong instead. After the death of her mother, her father's other women had not turned her out. Kiuk would have done so; her ugliness embarrassed him. But the women always had work for her to do. Hers were the heaviest loads, the most tedious chores. She was grateful. She was worthy of no better life. Someday, when she came to her time of blood, a man might take her to be his woman; an older man, perhaps, widowed or scarred or in some other way undesirable. In the meantime, Kiuk found his own uses for her. But, although eleven times of the long dark had come and gone since her birth, she had not yet bled as a woman. Others of her age had sucklings at their breasts, but it did not matter. Her desire to live was fierce. Sometimes she found this puzzling, but always she remembered her mother's dying words:

"You are not like the others, my little one. They call you ugly. They say that there is no place in the band for an ugly girl. So you must be useful. You must be brave. And above all, you must be strong. If you are not, you will be cast out and your spirit will walk upon the wind while foxes follow wolves to feast upon your bones."

She had listened. She had learned. She had made herself useful. She forced herself to be brave. Lonit knew that as long as she was strong she would have a place within the band.

But now the band was gone. Her father was dead, and his women, and all the young girls, and all the sucklings. All dead. And here she was, the most unworthy member of the band, alive and unhurt and as strong as ever. She was confused. How could she stand before Torka, the most worthy of them all, and presume to speak to him?

"Where is Torka's woman . . . his son . . . his infant?"

She flushed at the sound of his voice. Now, for the first time, she noticed that he was badly injured. She could see it in his stance and in his fevered eyes. His voice sounded strange to her—distant and hollow, as dry and brittle as old bones. Lonit knew that when she spoke the truth, something inside him would break.

And something did. He felt it bleeding deep within his chest. Instinctively, he knew he would not accept Lonit's words as truth until he saw Egatsop and Kipu with his own eyes. And perhaps even then . . . somehow . . . it would not be so.

Umak watched Torka and the girl from the edge of the ruined encampment. He too felt the wind blowing around him. His eyes squinted against it as they scanned the sky and the far, encircling horizon. Birds of prey had already found the encampment. It was still early morning, but Umak knew that, at this time of the year, the dark would soon come. With it, drawn by the smell of so much blood, foxes, lynx, wild dogs, and dire wolves would follow.

The thought of wolves was sobering. Their broad, crushing jaws could easily snap a man's thigh. The wolves' strong, sharp teeth were perfectly designed for cracking bone and ripping through skin and muscle. He tried not to think of that, but the wolves walked within his mind and fed upon his courage, and visions of the huge, voracious, meat-eaters joined them: towering, fleet-footed, short-faced bears; shaggy-coated, maned lions; saber-toothed, springing cats. With stabbing fangs nearly as long as the forearm of a man and nostrils set far back and high upon their muzzles, these lionlike felines could breathe while they rooted their faces into their prey and sucked their victims' blood before it ran, wasted, out of the wounds.

Umak stood facing into the wind. Against such predators, he knew that one old man, a young girl, and a severely injured hunter would be virtually defenseless. They dared not linger here. The wind had steadied and grown colder. Umak could sense the threat of a storm in it. He, Torka, and Lonit must salvage what they could from the ravaged pit huts and be far from here by tomorrow, protected against predators and the storm within some rough shelter, with the makings of a new life gleaned from the remnants of the old.

Umak frowned. It would be no easy task to convince Torka and Lonit of this. Indeed, the premise was upsetting to him. The living were not allowed to claim the belongings of the dead—to do so would deprive the departed spirits of their weapons, tools, and shelter in the spirit world. They would wander the wind forever, unable to hunt or rest, haunting those who had robbed them until they, too, became spirits. But what life would the three of them have if they did *not* take up these things? Perhaps if the correct chants were made, the spirits would understand. . . . It would be Umak's task, as spirit master, to *make* them understand.

Umak watched Torka moving through the remains of the winter camp. He walked stiffly, obviously forcing himself to ignore the pain of his injuries, and was unaware that the girl, Lonit, followed at his heels like a stunned colt terrified of abandonment. His step was slow, cautious, as though he walked upon spring ice across the surface of a deep and dangerous lake. And in a way, thought Umak, he did. When Torka found what he was seeking, the ice would break and he would fall through it to drown in his grief. Then he would die a little. . . . A portion of his heart would always walk the spirit world with his dead woman and children; but the man who would be reborn through the searing agony of the truth that Torka must face would be a harder, stronger man. Like the killing point of a well-made spear, Torka must now be shaped and redefined in the fire of his anguish.

Umak wished that he could help his grandson endure the pain; but he knew that Torka, for the sake of pride, must suffer it alone. Umak could not share or lessen the pain. Yet, despite his resolve to remain a stoic observer inured to suffering by age and wisdom, the old man's chin quivered when he saw Torka kneel amid the rubble of what had been his pit hut. Umak knew what Torka was seeing now and longed to go to him. He wished that he had the power to command the pit huts to rise again and to order life back into the bodies of his people. A *true* spirit master would be able to do these things. A *true* spirit master would not have stumbled in the snow. A *true* spirit master would have arrived in time to send an invisible spear into the mammoth's heart.

But Egatsop had been right about him: Umak was no longer a spirit master. He was a useless old man who could only stand and watch as Torka bent and lifted something into his arms . . . something small and mangled and as limp as the dolls of caribou skin that the women made for their little girls—dolls stuffed with ptarmigan down and bits of lichen and soft scrapings of fur from old hides gone stiff and dark with rot. Shapeless, its seams torn, its bloodied stuffing spilling out, its little arms and legs hanging at grotesque angles out of a flattened torso held together by the blood-sodden casing of its clothes, this doll was not a doll. It was all that remained of a child.

"Kipu!" Umak cried the name aloud. He answered Torka's

terrible wail of anguish with a wail of his own. Until this moment, he had forgotten the little boy. He had been so full of himself, so full of misery over his failure to prove that he was still Umak, master of spirits, hurdler of all obstacles. Now, the sight of Torka holding the crushed and lifeless body of his beloved little Kipu broke his pride.

Umak closed his eyes. Tears seared his lids. His long, unbound hair flew forward in the wind, whipping his face as he thought: *This old man is old. This old man is master of nothing. This old man has lived too long.*

But not long enough.

The sharp, staccato bark of a wild dog brought Umak up out of the drowning pool of despair. The dog stood nearby but not too close, watching the old man out of its familiar sky-blue eyes.

Umak stared back thoughtfully. So, once again, Brother Dog had followed. Once again, the intrusion of the animal into his thoughts caused him to know that it was not yet time for him to die. Old he might be, and unworthy to call himself spirit master, but he was still alive. He was still Umak, a man. And if Torka and Lonit were to survive, there was much for him to do before he set his spirit free to walk upon the wind.

6

They worked together to arrange the corpses in the traditional manner: men, women, and children in family groups, on their backs in the position that was called looking at the sky. It was an ugly task, and when at last the grisly assemblage was complete, the three survivors stood together, contemplating the terrible finality of the scene before them.

As Torka dropped to his knees beside the bodies of his family, Lonit shivered uncontrollably and Umak raised his arms, offering up the death song. It was a brief incantation broken now and again by cracks of desolation in the old man's voice, but he continued until the end, and when the chant was concluded, he had a further plea.

"Go now, Life Spirits. Leave this place of death. Be now riders of the wind and the guardians of Umak and Torka and Lonit. Be born again through this female and live on in the words of these men who shall sing of you always in their songs of life."

His arms came down. He looked at the girl. "Come. We must prepare now to leave this place before the darkness comes."

Lonit stood mute, her face pinched and tight with cold, her eyes wide with apprehension. What was Umak suggesting? Had he forgotten that they must remain with their dead for five days? This was the time of the obligatory death watch, when the spirits of the deceased lingered around their fallen bodies and sometimes chose to return to life. Family and friends alike would need assistance if they chose to awake from their death sleep. They would need food and care, shelter and protection from predators. To abandon their people during this critical time was unthinkable.

She waited for Torka to question the old man's order, but the young hunter was in no condition to question anyone. She saw that he had taken little Kipu's body into his arms again, and her heart bled for him. He had placed his sleeping robe over the bodies of Egatsop and his infant. The fur rippled like spring grass in the cold winter wind. Torka stared across it, his dark eyes glassy with fever. Chanting softly, imploring the life spirit of his son to return to Kipu's poor, mangled body, he seemed to be in another world, entranced, beyond this place of death.

"No spirit shall ever again come to live within the body of that little one," said Umak softly, thus making his peace with a truth that Torka would accept in time. "Now Torka must rest." He looked at the girl again. "Come. Lonit and Umak have much to do."

Her strange eyes were round with confusion, enormous in her unusually shaped face. With smooth, highly defined cheekbones set forward in a way that differed markedly from the flat, moon-faced standard of beauty for females of the band, she looked like a startled antelope as she stared at Umak and then quickly looked away. To hold the glance of another for any length of time was forbidden; life spirits could be sucked from the eyes of one person right into the eyes of another. And in that short span of time in which she had held Umak's gaze, she had felt the power of his life spirit boring right into her. It sapped her own spirit. It made her feel small and frightened and faint.

Umak understood Lonit's reaction to his words; it was what he had expected, and now he must deal with it. He put a hand upon each of the girl's shoulders and shook her a little. "Listen to me, Lonit, daughter of the People. The People are no more. We cannot stay in this place. If we are to have life, we must go. Now. Before the eaters of the dead come to feast. Before we find ourselves defenseless against them and without shelter from the storm that shall soon come. But first we must take the things of life from the dead. We are all that is left of them. If we die, the People die forever. Do you understand?"

She did not, but it was not a female's place to challenge the authority of a male. Especially *this* male. She was terrified of him. Not because he was a spirit master—not because he was old and wise and strong, despite his years. She was terrified because she was certain that he was more than a man. She had seen him limping out of the encampment to give his life spirit to the wind. He had been a bent and ancient hunter, taking a journey from which no one had ever returned.

But Umak *had* returned. When she had first seen him standing at the edge of the ruined encampment, with a ghost-eyed dog staring at her out of his shadow, she had known that he was a ghost man. And the dog was a ghost dog; otherwise it would have followed Umak into the encampment to feed upon the dead. Instead, it had kept its distance, sitting now where she had first seen it, at the edge of the encampment. Its thick coat ruffled in the wind like the fur that covered the bodies of Torka's dead.

Lonit trembled violently. Umak's hands tightened around her shoulders, and she could feel the hardness of his bones within his sinewy palms and long, strong fingers as he pressed them into the thick layering of her tattered tunic of caribou skin. Did ghost men have bones? Could they grip the living with such sure, consoling strength of purpose? She dared a quick look at the ghost man's face. He did not look dead. He looked like Umak. He looked like the spirit master. He looked like the old hunter who had saved Torka's life and returned to his people's winter encampment in time to help an ugly girl lay out the dead.

Hot, stinging tears came unbidden into Lonit's eyes. The old man drew her close and held her in his arms. In the cold wind, his was the smell of life. She drew it in. She knew that he was no ghost. He was alive. She clung to him and wept. And when there were no more tears, she whispered, "I am afraid."

He held her for a while longer, as comforted by her closeness as she was by his. Then he said gently, "Come, Lonit. There is no more time to be afraid."

Yet she was afraid as she helped him to rummage through the ruined camp, gathering tools and weapons, clothes and skins and scraps of food. What they were doing was forbidden and would surely anger the spirits of the dead. Umak made incantations of apology, which Lonit fearfully echoed, as he picked through the rubble and brought his gleanings to be added to hers.

Torka's own chanting grew fainter until, at last, he slumped protectively over the body of his son. Lonit would have gone to him, but Umak assured her that they could do nothing for the young hunter now. "Sleep is good medicine," he said, and kept her at the task at hand.

They placed their gatherings on a bison skin: the few unbroken spears that Umak found, daggers, strips of leather, rolls of sinew, knapping tools, and stakes of bone. Lonit had found a net woven from the coarse guard hairs of a musk ox, fleshing knives and wedges, three good sewing awls, a fine adz of greenstone, and a chisel made from one of the stabbing teeth of a great, short-faced bear.

It seemed to her that there were a thousand items on the hide, but Umak grumbled and shook his head and told her to go in search of this or that while he also sought out other necessities. Within her family's downed pit hut, she found her collection of bone needles inside the strip of badger skin where she kept them. The skin had been half-mired in the muddied ooze of the permafrost. Incredibly, only a few needles were broken. She drew out the good ones, washed them in her own spittle, and rubbed them clean upon her sleeve before inserting them through the carrying hole that all women of the band had at the base of the nose—pierced for this purpose in infancy. When not transporting fragile sewing needles from camp to camp, the nose hole was used for ornamentation like stone beads or freshwater shells. Pretty things. Lonit had never considered herself worthy to wear them, but they had looked lovely on the other girls and women. The memory saddened her. She was glad when Umak called and told her to get back to her gathering.

Satisfied at last, he began to assemble a large sledge, which would carry the bulk of their supplies, and also hold the weight and length of a reclining man. It was clear that Torka, now delirious, would be unable to travel on his own.

The sledge was a simple enough contrivance of bison hides secured by sinew thongs over a frame of caribou antlers, with runners of mammoth ribs that would later double as support posts for the shelter that they would raise against the coming storm. With Lonit's assistance, the sledge was soon assembled. Umak grunted his approval.

As Lonit watched, he began the all-important glazing of the runners—coating the mammoth ribs with a sludge of mud, moss, and snow, which she mixed for him in a stone mortar. It was difficult to keep the mess from congealing in the cold, but soon Umak had managed to smear it on the runners. He sat back, allowing it to freeze solid in the rising wind before scraping it smooth with his dagger.

Lonit volunteered to build a fire over which she would melt snow into water in a skin bag, this for the final ice-glazing of the runners. Umak shook his head and cast a worried look at the sky. Day was rapidly fading into dark.

"No time to waste," he grumbled, and walked around, scouting out a scrap of bear fur. "This will be faster and will work just as well."

As the girl watched, impressed by the old man's resourcefulness, he urinated onto the swatch of bear fur. The hot, steaming liquid penetrated the thick pelage. He nodded and told her to observe as he gently ran the liquid-soaked fur over the frozen sludge. After several meticulous rubbings, he had produced a hard, slick veneer of thin ice that would allow the runners to glide smoothly over the snowy tundra.

"Now we go! Like the wind," he said.

They worked to divide their collection of tools and supplies into three piles. Two were wrapped and secured to pack frames; the third was rolled into a bison hide and loaded onto the sledge. The old man gently persuaded his grandson to release Kipu's body; Torka stared vacant-eyed at his grandfather.

"Torka will not leave Kipu," he muttered in his delirium.

"Kipu is not here. His spirit waits. In a far place."

Torka's face was a blank mask. "We will go there?"

"We will go," said the old man, fighting against the bitter upwelling of a terrible sadness as Torka slumped forward, unconscious, into his arms.

PART II

WALKERS OF THE WIND

1

"The tracks of the great mammoth lead off toward the south. So we shall go east, along the path that the caribou take when they migrate out of the face of the rising sun. Soon we will intercept the herds. Soon we will eat."

With these words of optimism from Umak, they moved out across the frozen land, beneath a lowering storm sky, heading eastward into unknown country, the wild dog following not far behind.

Lonit looked back, wishing that the dog would go away. Perhaps it was a ghost dog after all. Why else would the spirit master have made no attempt to kill it? It would make a feast for them. It would give them strength to go on until larger, more palatable game was sighted, but the old man showed no interest in either killing it or driving it away, and Lonit, as a female, knew she had no right to question him.

They went on and on, bent double under the weight of their packs, sharing the weight of the sledge and of Torka, who lay unconscious upon it. After a while, the girl forgot about the dog. It was all that she could do to concentrate on her next step. The dragging of the sledge was nearly unbearable; it seemed to be growing heavier and more cumbersome with each passing mile. Lonit told herself that it did not matter. Torka's weight would never be a burden to her. *Never.* She had loved him since the first days of her memory. Torka was the handsome one, the best of all the hunters, the one who would be spirit master someday, and who would lead the band when the headman grew too old. Torka was the one man who had never mocked her for her odd appearance. And once, when she was a very little girl and had blundered into her father's way to win a kicking from Kiuk, Torka had watched her punishment, stern-eyed and frowning. When her father had stalked away, Torka had come to her and put her on her feet again. He had smiled at her . . . a smile of encouragement . . . a smile that had erased her hurt. She would never forget the moment. It was the first time since the death of her mother that anyone had shown kindness to her.

"Be brave, little Antelope Eyes," he had said, and on his tongue, the usually caustic reference to her large, uncommonly round eyes had seemed almost an endearment.

She had loved him ever since. It did not matter that he would never love her in return. She was not worthy of his concern, much less of his affection. It was enough to live within his shadow, to see him, to hear his voice. If Torka's spirit left his body to walk away upon the wind, Lonit knew that her spirit would follow as surely as her body now followed Umak's lead, eastward beneath the gathering storm, across the snow-whitened tundra, putting all that she had ever known behind her.

But how long could she go on? She was hungry and tired, not only from the day's ordeal, but from weeks of near-starvation. She and Umak had eaten only a few small wedges of rancid fat that the old man had discovered in the ruins of the headman's pit hut. He had consumed his share with distaste, eating with a revulsion that had puzzled her. Food was food, no matter how foul. She would have gulped it all down had he not insisted that half of it be saved, sliced thin, and placed within a storage sack of oiled bird intestine. This he had pressed flat and placed inside Lonit's traveling coat, between its soft inner lining and her tunic, with the weight of her pack frame to hold it in place against her back. In this manner, the strips of fat rode safely secured, out of the wind, warmed by whatever body heat escaped outward through her tunic, and rubbed soft by her movement as she plodded forward through the snow. When she and Umak finally made camp and sat down to consume this treasure, sharing it with Torka, it would be soft and broken into greasy globs that would grant precious energy to them as they slept and drew strength from its meager sustenance. The girl salivated as she thought of it, and as her stomach began to ache with hunger, so did her body also ache with need of rest.

The wind was rising. Daylight was only a vague, cold aura glimmering beyond the clouded horizon. Night was spilling across the tundra. Lonit wondered how long she could keep up with Umak. She cast a sideward glance at him through the long guard hairs of her foxskin ruff.

Umak walked resolutely beside her, bent forward, head out. She could see his profile jutting out from the fall of his heavy bearskin robe. Long wisps of hair whipped in the wind above his wide, furrowed brow. A heavy-lidded, wiry-lashed eye stared straight ahead above the high, humping crag of his nose. His mouth was pursed and seemed shut above his rounded chin. It was a strong face. It was the face of a true spirit master. But it was also the face of a very old man.

Lonit felt suddenly sick with fear. If anything were to happen to Umak, how would she care for herself and Torka? And what if Torka were to die? No! She would not allow herself to think such thoughts. They were more burdensome than the weight of her pack.

With grim determination, the girl leaned into the wind. It whispered all around her, rousing memories of the many dead who now lay far behind, reminding her that she and Umak had stolen the belongings of those who now lay looking at the sky.

You will not get away.

We will follow.

We will take back from you all that you have stolen.

We will eat of your life spirit and throw it away upon the wind.

You will die. Forever.

Had the wind spoken? Or had she only heard the voice of her own fear? She could not be certain. She lowered her head. She would not listen to the wind. She would not think of the past or the future—both were too frightening to consider. She would think only of the moment. Of the next step. And the next. For Torka's sake, she must go on.

Umak sensed a change in the way the girl was carrying her side of the sledge. It surprised him, for rather than lagging, her step seemed suddenly revitalized. The girl was strong; that had been apparent from the first. She had yet to utter a complaint or to falter beneath the weight of her pack. But she was still only a female, and despite her height, she was only a half-grown girl. Soon she would tire. Soon she would stumble. And in the days ahead, until Torka recovered— *if* he recovered—Umak would have to hunt for her and see to it that she was sheltered against the weather and protected against any predators that might come against her.

The old man thought about this as he walked. Since the death of his last woman so many moons ago, he had had no one to care for but himself; and since he had injured his leg, he had been cared for by others. Now he was needed again. Torka and Lonit depended upon him for their survival. If he failed them, they would die. And if they died, it would be as though the People had never lived at all.

It was nearly dark now. The wind was very strong. Yet the old man was not chilled, nor did he slow his step. His awareness of his responsibility to Torka and Lonit did not intimidate him. For them he would be young again. For them he would be strong—as strong as the girl who matched her stride to his. He eyed her thoughtfully out of the corner of his eye, thinking: *This one has courage. This one will someday be a woman who will make brave sons.*

Her face was hidden deep within her ruff. This was just as well, for Umak knew that she was no beauty. It did not matter. In the vast, hostile, unknown land that lay ahead, a woman's beauty would be measured by her stamina and strength of will, not by the shape of her features.

But now, as darkness claimed the last of day, the woman was just a girl, and the "young" spirit master's leg ached within the confines of the old man's skin. When Torka stirred upon the sledge, both of those who carried him were thrown off balance. They went to their knees in the snow.

"Hmmph," snorted Umak, rising, extending a hand to the girl. "I think now it is time to rest." His hand was steady. He was glad for the darkness. It would keep her from seeing his weariness upon his face.

But Lonit was not looking at Umak. She was looking beyond him, back along the way they had come, with an expression of terror frozen upon her face.

Eyes.

Hundreds of staring eyes. They seemed to hang suspended within the night. Floating, disembodied, blinking now and then, like sparks hovering above an unseen fire.

Lonit was certain that they were the eyes of the dead . . . watching . . . following across the miles . . . waiting for the dark . . . preparing to steal the life spirits of those who had stolen the belongings that should have been theirs in the spirit world.

But Umak knew better. He could just make out the form of the wild dog. It stood between him and the watching eyes. The dog's tail was tucked. Its ears were laid back. Its head was out, and its teeth were bared as it growled deep in its throat. It was the warning growl of one animal to another.

Now Umak growled—at his failure to sense the threat. The wind had blown the scent away, but that was no excuse. The dog had picked it up. In other days, a younger and less tired spirit master would have known that it was there. He grimaced with self-disgust, then squinted into the darkness, willing himself to see the sleek forms that crouched there, as white as snow in their winter coats.

Foxes.

How long had they been following? Emboldened by starvation, gathered into a great and ravenous pack, they would be as dangerous as wolves when they moved to the attack.

And Umak knew that they would attack. They had seen their prey stumble and fall. They had smelled the weakness of an old man and a young girl and the blood of Torka's injuries upon the wind.

Slowly, purposefully, Umak slung off his pack and told the girl to do the same. She obeyed, hesitating only when he told her to hand him two of his spears and to take up two of them herself. She blanched; it was forbidden for a female to touch the weapons of a male lest the contaminating influences of her weaker gender sap their killing powers. She had scrupulously avoided doing so when they had gathered the belongings of the dead. Now she stared at the old man, hoping that she had not heard him correctly; but when he scolded her sharply and repeated the command, she did as she was told.

It took her only a moment to loosen his pack and draw the weapons from it. There were seven spears in all. Long, slender lengths of bone sliced from the leg bones of mammoths killed long ago by hunters of the band, each was tipped with a flaked or chipped point of stone or ivory that was secured to its killing end by sinew binding. The old man had inserted the spears horizontally through the center of his rolled stalking cloak. Normally he would have carried two or three of them in one hand, their weight resting across one shoulder; but with the sledge to drag, and the added burden of a pack frame loaded with supplies that, under usual traveling conditions, would have been distributed among several members of the band, the spears were an unnecessary hindrance. He had not intended to hunt. For protection, he had his stone dagger and a club made from the fire-hardened thigh joint of a long-horned bison tucked into his belt beneath his traveling cloak. In an emergency, the spears could be taken up quickly enough to be used against large predators— as he chose to use them now against the foxes.

He stood tall. He puffed out his chest so that he would look big and bold to the watching predators. He growled again, as the dog growled. He snarled, as the dog snarled. With a brash gesturing of his spears and a telling grunt or two, he showed Lonit what she must do.

The spears seemed awkward in her hands, but they did not melt or sag as her female fists tensed around their shafts. Perhaps, now that the band was no more, the usual prohibitions concerning the use of weaponry were no longer in effect? The girl had no way of knowing. She only knew that she must follow Umak's instructions. If she did not, it would be his right to beat her or abandon her.

He strutted forward toward the foxes, and Lonit strutted beside him, silently invoking the spirits that lived within the spears.

Forgive this unworthy girl for holding you. Give strength to her hands and courage to her spirit. For Torka and for Umak, be strong and swift. Strike true.

The spears responded to her plea as, with Umak beside her, her arms seemed suddenly strong. The old man took huge, stomping, swaggering steps forward. He shouted at the foxes to retreat. Lonit copied him, surprised at the sound of her own voice. It did not sound afraid.

Ahead of them, some of the eyes blinked and vanished; but others glared and glowed as the remaining foxes stood their ground. As Lonit and Umak stalked forward, the wild dog looked back at them. The leaders of the fox pack took advantage of the dog's movement. They sprang at it from out of the darkness. Lonit saw them clearly now for the first time. She gasped. They were like lemmings, surging toward the dog in droves. Never had she seen so many foxes in one place, nor had she imagined that there could be so many of them in all the world. For a moment the strength went out of her arms, and her throat constricted with fear. She could not move.

The wild dog could easily have run. It could have turned tail and vanished into the night. Instead, it stood its ground, circling, snapping and snarling, savaging its adversaries as they swarmed around it and leaped against it with ripping teeth and slashing jaws.

Instinct told Lonit to turn and flee. The foxes would consume the dog. If she and Umak went quickly from this place, the foxes would not follow; they would be content to stay and feed. But why was the dog staying to fight them? It was as though the animal were deliberately putting itself at risk for them; as though, somehow, it considered them its pack and found itself bound to protect them.

"Aar!"

Umak's scream caused the girl to jump with fright as the old man ran howling to the dog's side. He was knee-deep in foxes as he stomped and stabbed downward with his spears. She heard yips and barks of pain. And then, like a wedge of birds suddenly banking away across the sky, the main body of the fox pack was gone. Umak and the dog stood together, panting, surrounded by the torn and bloodied bodies of foxes that would never rise to follow their kindred. Umak raised one of his spears. He shook it, along with the spitted body of the fox that was impaled upon it.

"Now we feast!" he proclaimed in triumph.

Lonit blinked, staring as the old man looked down at the dog. Except for a torn ear and a bloody snout, the animal seemed unhurt; its thick coat had evidently prevented the foxes from doing much damage. It stood so close to Umak that, had the old hunter wished to touch it or to drive his spear downward through its back into its heart, he could have done so. The dog looked up at the old man and, obviously unafraid, made no move to back away as Umak slid the body of the fox from his spear and dropped it at the feet of the animal. The dog sniffed it, then calmly lay down and began to feed upon it, as though it were the most natural thing in the world for a dog to keep company with a man.

But it was not natural. Lonit continued to stare at Umak. Truly, he *was* a spirit master, a hunter so skilled and powerful that, by magic, he could enter the mind of an animal and coerce it to work his will. Not only had he frightened the foxes away and killed others to make a meal for them, he had also put his spirit into the dog. He had made it stand and fight beside him as though it were his brother.

2

With the wind rising steadily around them, they hunkered down in the snow and devoured two of the foxes raw, skinning the carcasses with their stone daggers as they ate, sucking sweet, hot, life-giving blood from the fibrous flesh.

Energy returned slowly to their starved, exhausted bodies. They worked together to assemble a pit hut to shelter them against the coming storm. Umak used a stone ax and wedge to break the surface of the permafrost. He whisked the snow away with the side of his ax and hacked the broken surface into small, uneven sods. These Lonit carried away to stack into a pile for later use. With the pronged stalk of a caribou antler, the old man and girl took turns scraping out a hollow circle, approximately six feet around and one foot deep. When the hut was complete, Umak, Torka, and Lonit would be able to recline fully within, with room to spare for their supplies; and the below-ground floor would prove an effective protection against the wind and cold once the warm air from their bodies and their cooking fire filled the interior.

When the circle was dug and smoothed, they dismantled the sledge and laid the still-unconscious Torka down upon the snow-covered earth, on a bison skin that they then wrapped around him. With the runners of mammoth ribs and with the large antlers that had formed the body of the sledge, they quickly erected the domed framework of their shelter. It was cross-braced with thong wrappings at all critical joinings, and the bottom ends of the ribs were stabbed as deep into the frozen ground as it would allow. Next they brought in the floor skin of oiled hide, the only one that they had been able to salvage from the ruined camp. It was ripped in several places, but Lonit would mend it later.

The walls of fur and hide were staked and raised, draped in layers over the frame and cross-lashed with thongs all around the bottom and across the top. The last touch was the piling of sods at the base, not only to weight the bottom of the walls but to serve as additional insulation.

When this was done, they brought Torka in and laid him down gently, close to where they would build their fire. He lay inert. Umak touched his pulse, high at his temple. He was still feverish, but the beat of his heart was strong and even. The old man smiled. Torka would live, Umak was certain. He dared not speak this certainty to the girl lest the utterance rouse crooked spirits that would work against his belief, but he told her that Torka seemed improved and heard her exhale with relief and joy.

Now they dragged in their supplies, including one of the foxes, which had frozen stiff. They would skin and butcher it later when the growing warmth of the hut softened it a little. The rest of the dead animals, six in all, they stacked in a small, hastily dug pit close to the hut. Covered with a staked-down skin, the pit would serve as a deep freeze; even in summer camps, meat could be kept cold indefinitely in such storage holes because, beneath the thin top layer of the tundral soil, the earth was perpetually frozen.

Umak seated himself as Lonit laced the hide door skin closed from the inside. It was dark within the hut. Outside, the wind lessened a little, then changed direction. Almost instantly, the air grew noticeably colder. Experience told the old man that the storm that would now descend upon them would be so viciously cold that only the hardiest creatures would survive against it.

We will survive, thought the old man. He was beginning to relax now and thought of the dog, wishing that he had been able to lure it into the shelter of the hut. It had accepted food from him, but it had backed away when he had beckoned to it, inviting it into the hut. Now it lay outside, close against the skin walls, using them as a windbreak as it curled protectively about the remains of its fox. With a belly full of meat and marrow to generate body heat, the dog's thick winter coat would provide adequate protection against the cold.

It too will survive, thought the old man.

As if affirming the old man's thought, the wild dog lifted its head and howled in defiance of the rising storm.

Lonit sat very still, listening, trembling against a sudden desolate sense of loneliness. She and Umak and Torka were all that was left of the People. The full impact of this settled upon her now. Within her heart there was no gladness, no guilt; there was only the terrible, crushing weight of despair. Outside in the darkness, the wind and storm and wild beasts ruled a world that stretched on forever. They were alone in that world—a girl, an old man, and a wounded hunter. Beneath the vast and savage Arctic sky, the wild dog sang a lament to the endless night.

"What does your brother dog cry to the wind, Spirit Master?" she asked the old man, trying hard not to sound frightened, hoping that he would not strike her for daring to put a question to him.

He listened to the dog. He heard tremulousness in the girl's voice and knew it for what it was. He too felt the desolation of loneliness and the nagging beginnings of fear, but unlike the girl, he was Umak, spirit master, and would have none of it. "That we are *alive*," he replied with the grim ferocity of absolute resolve. "And that we shall *stay* alive."

The wind slapped at the little shelter, but it held fast even though snow blew into its interior through the seams that Lonit had been too exhausted to mend. In the darkness, with the wind drowning the howling of the dog, Umak felt the temperature falling dangerously low. Alarmed, he rose, hunching forward, for although the pit hut would accommodate the full length of his reclining body, he could not stand erect within it.

"Up!" he half shouted at the startled girl. He commanded her to undress, so they might bundle together beneath the combined weight of their furs. The combined heat of their naked bodies would serve to warm them against the worst of any storm.

Shivering, Lonit complied as Umak stripped himself, then bent over Torka and, not without effort, peeled off the bulk of his grandson's torn and bloodstained garments.

"Come!" he then demanded of the girl, and told her to lie down against Torka's right side, while he stretched out against his left.

With the bison hide beneath them all, skin side down so that its thick, rough hair cushioned their bodies, they shivered themselves warm beneath their piled sleeping skins. For a long while they lay awake, listening to the storm while

Torka slept, oblivious to it, between them. After a while, only the hut shivered in the wind, and in the darkness, Lonit heard the old man speak with quiet, absolute determination.

"You see? We *are* alive. We *shall* survive."

But for how long? wondered the girl, not certain if Umak had spoken to her or to the storm. It did not matter. She sensed his drifting off to sleep and knew that she was following. Within the soft, warm limbo of total exhaustion, with her slender body naked against Torka's side, she closed her eyes and shivered once again, but not with cold as she thought: *In all the world, there is no woman for Torka now. There is only Lonit. I am his woman. He shall be my man. In time. Yes. It shall be so. He shall forget that I am ugly. I shall make myself so worthy that he shall have to forget!* A sweet sense of euphoria nearly overwhelmed her. She pressed closer to him. She felt the heat of his fevered flesh melding into the heat of her own skin, into the rising pulse rate of what was more than a child's infatuation. She was *not* a child—not after today, not ever again. One small hand strayed upward to rest open upon Torka's shoulder.

"Lonit is Torka's woman," she whispered barely audibly, sleepily, feeling herself slipping into dreams.

But suddenly she was wide awake. Staring. Every muscle in her body rigid. Umak slept on. Torka breathed evenly. But outside, the storm had reached a demonic intensity. There was something unnatural about it, something threatening. Lonit sat upright. Wind-driven snow was streaming into the interior through the gaps in the seams. As she stared, the streams of snow ribboned out, whirled in the air, took on the forms of ghosts and demons as they swirled around her, plucking at her bare skin.

She gasped. She knew the faces of these ghosts. They were the members of her band, yet they were changed. They had no form, no substance. They were the stuff of storms and snow, as gray and as dank as mists as they solidified into a single diaphanous column. The column took on the form of a woman, but unlike that of any woman who had ever lived. Its flesh was ice rimed, broken, and torn. It bled mist from a thousand wounds. Out of a frozen, ruined face that had once been beautiful, eyes as cold and unforgiving as the Arctic night fastened upon Lonit and, from out of a skeleton's mouth came a single moaning word.

"Torka . . ."

Lonit stared, knowing that the ghost woman was Egatsop, Torka's woman, come to claim the life spirit of her man. "No!" Lonit cried, throwing herself across Torka, feeling the snow-driven hands of death raking downward across her back. "He is alive! You cannot have him! He is my man now!"

The wind intensified; it roared inside Lonit's ears. The cold was so bitter that it burned her nostrils and filled her lungs until she could not breathe. She could feel bone-sharp spears of ice, Egatsop's fingers, piercing through her body to get at the man who lay beneath her. She felt Torka move as he suddenly cried out the names of his dead woman and children.

A terrible wave of anguish ran through her. What a fool she had been to imagine that Torka would want her, even if she was the last woman in the world. Here was the woman he loved, come back from the dead, to claim him. But she could not let him die—not Torka, not the one whom she loved more than her own life.

She rose, turning to face the spirit. "Take me! Come! Live again in my body if you would be with him!"

It seemed then that the specter laughed at her, and never in her worst nightmares had Lonit seen anything more ugly than the sight of Egatsop's ghost. Half-fainting with terror, Lonit flung herself back across Torka's body and sobbed in terror as the wind rose and the pit hut shook. Suddenly, above the storm of death, she heard the snarling of the dog, and as quickly as they had appeared, the apparitions vanished.

She turned to see that Umak had risen. He was doing what he could to close the seams and asked her to help him. He had seen no ghosts. He had heard no voices. It had all been a dream, he assured her.

In the darkness, fumbling amid her belongings, she found her sinew thread and with trembling hands managed to thread her needles and sew the seams as best she could. By the time she finished, the wind had dropped. She helped Umak to remove the snow from the hut and crawled back under the sleeping skins to shiver herself back to sleep.

But she did not sleep. Beyond the walls of the pit hut, the wild dog growled, and all night long, although Umak swore that it was not so, crooked spirits walked the night while Lonit kept watch against them.

3

Dawn rose out of the east. The wind rushed toward it across the crumpled, glacier-laden peaks and frigid polar steppes of Siberia. It blew past the barren, storm-blasted expanse of tundra upon which Umak and Lonit had labored to raise their little shelter of bones and fur. If crooked spirits had ridden the wind, they were silent now, for the wind was gentler. The storm had spent itself, leaving a dusting of dry snow on the arching roof of the pit hut and on the coat of the sleeping wild dog.

Lonit slept at last; the deep, dreamless sleep of total exhaustion. Beside her, Torka awoke, his fever broken. For a long while he lay still, staring into darkness, feeling the warmth of the two who slept on either side of him.

Their presence gave no comfort, for the memories that washed through him were more painful than the dull ache of his injuries. The ghosts of the past lived within his eyes—his woman, his infant, the faces of friends lost to him forever. He saw the bloodied snow of his people's devastated winter camp. He saw little Kipu and heard his cries as a terrible shadow fell upon him. He saw the mammoth . . . Thunder Speaker . . . World Shaker . . . He Who Parts the Clouds. With eyes round and dilated with its hatred of Man, the Destroyer thundered within Torka's head as its impossibly huge body raged over little Kipu and nearly everything that Torka had ever known and loved.

Anguish choked him. The confines of the pit hut were suddenly suffocating. Torka could not bear his memories. He rose, wincing against his pain. He stepped over his sleeping grandfather, took up one of the sleeping skins of caribou hide, and wrapped it around himself as he unlaced the door skin and went out.

The world was white and unfamiliar. It stretched eastward for miles in broad, rolling waves that shimmered with a lustrous patina of ice in the Arctic dawn's light. To his left, a snow-covered mound of fur suddenly rose, shook itself, and backed away, growling.

Startled, Torka hunched forward into a defensive posture, ready to strangle the beast if it came at him; but he had awakened Umak when he had left the pit hut, and now the old man appeared at his side.

"It is only Brother Dog," explained Umak. "He too is alone, without a band. He has followed this old man and prevented his spirit from walking away upon the wind. He has fought beside Umak. He has won his place within this encampment."

Torka frowned, feeling suddenly weak and disoriented. He had no recollection of the hours that had passed since he had succumbed to delirium in the winter camp. Umak's words made no sense to him. The moment seemed unreal, a part of his dreams. He reached out and put his hand upon his grandfather's forearm to make certain that he was real.

Umak nodded, understanding. "It is so," he said. "Umak lives because Brother Dog would not let him die. So it was that this old man found you. Together with the girl, I have brought you out of the place of death to a new life. We are all that is left of our people. But we will survive."

Within Torka, weariness and pain merged to become something else, something harder and darker and sharp with the bitter edge of total desolation. "For what purpose?"

Now it was the old man's turn to frown. "For what purpose do men ever survive? To make new life! To hear the laughter of their children! To hunt boldly for their women! And to sing the songs of life in the winter dark."

Torka closed his eyes. "This man will sing no song of life until he has dipped his spear in the blood of the Destroyer. This man's life spirit will be as dead as the spirits of his people until he eats of the flesh of World Shaker and leaves the bones to bleach beneath the eye of the midnight sun."

Umak stared at his grandson, aghast. "The Destroyer is a crooked spirit. It cannot be killed!"

Torka's eyes met the eyes of the old man unflinchingly. "For my woman. For my unnamed infant. For Kipu, my son.

For all of those who now lie looking at the sky. Torka will kill Thunder Speaker. Or he will join it in the spirit world, to hunt it forever as it walks upon the wind."

The days passed. In the clear, brutal cold that followed the storm, ice crusted the land, covering the tracks of man and beast alike. Even if Torka had been well, he could not have backtracked to pick up the trail of the mammoth. Umak and Lonit had brought him farther than the band of hunters had ever ranged. Not a single familiar landmark pointed the way back to the winter camp, and yet he remained obsessed with the need to return, to pick up the trail of the beast that had killed his people, to stalk it, face it, and kill it. He knew that he had virtually no chance of surviving the confrontation. He did not care. As far as he was concerned, his life was over. It had ended days ago, miles away, in the bloodied snow where his woman and children now lay looking at the sky forever.

It was warm and dark within the pit hut. Umak sat cross-legged, scowling at Torka through the gloom. "The mammoth you seek, you will never find. Forget him. Before he kills you."

Torka scowled back at him. "Thanks to you, the Destroyer walks one part of the world while I walk another. If I cannot find the mammoth, how can it kill me?"

Umak harrumphed. "The beast that walks within you is feeding on your life spirit. Let it go, Torka, before it is too late."

"It is already too late."

Lonit listened in silence. The two hunters sat opposite her, close to the little lake of fire that danced within the concave stone that served as both lamp and a source of cooking heat. It was not a large stone; she had easily carried it rolled in her traveling pack, along with her fire-making tools: the notched, well-worn fire stick of bone; the drill stick, also of bone, with its mouthpiece of polished stone and its double-handed drill cord. These had lain close to Lonit when the mammoth had charged the hut. Like the girl, they had not been damaged.

The making of fire with the stick and drill was art. Today, sensing the depths of Torka's black mood, she had prolonged the ritual. Through the light and warmth of her fire, she hoped to drive back the darkness in which Torka's sadness grew. With the capstone held in her mouth and the end of the drill inserted into one of the notches of the fire stick, Lonit had held the ends of the cord in each hand, the tension of the sinew strung around the drill. With expert manipulation, she was able to keep the drill spinning in the stick until friction sparked a flame; this she nourished with bits of dried moss pinched out of her tinder box of hollowed antler.

Fire starting was woman's work. Lonit's mother had taught her well. The girl was proud of her skill; in this, at least, she did excel, and she had wanted Torka to be cheered by her fine fire. She had made a thick oil by pounding the last of the fat that she had packed out of the winter camp on a scrap of leather with the heel of her hand. This she had placed into the hollow of the stone, and into this she had dipped one of her few remaining wicks of moss. Saturated with precious oil, it was the wick that took the flame and held it, burning smokelessly under Lonit's constant vigil. The stone bowl now glowed softly, held in place by a circle of sods. Cut from the skin of the tundra, the sods were composed of moss and lichen. They absorbed the heat of the little fire and then radiated warmth outward to cut the chill of the interior of the pit hut.

But neither Torka nor Umak paid much attention to her fire. They were too absorbed in their conversation and simply took it for granted that, as a female, Lonit would possess the skills of hearth making.

Torka stared into the flame. "I *will* return to the winter camp to pick up the trail of the Destroyer. The days are growing longer and are bound to become warmer. I will be stronger soon. With the weight of your packs and sledge, your marks will be deep in the land. The tundra holds its scars forever. When the ice melts, I will follow the trail that you have left beneath it."

"There will be no footprints," replied Umak. "The tundra was frozen hard. We walked in snow all the way."

"Hmmph!" Torka muttered, and Lonit looked up from her fire tending, startled to note how similar the speech patterns of Torka and Umak were. "Then I will look for circling birds," said Torka. "The carrion eaters of both land and sky will come to feast upon the dead."

"They have already come. Before the storm, Umak sensed their threat. It was for this reason that this old man chose to walk ahead of the storm."

Lonit shuddered against her memories.

Torka's face was set, shadowed by weariness and sadness in the fire glow. "You have taught me well, father of my father. I will walk west until the land is familiar. I will find the camp. *I* will keep death watch. Then I will hunt the Destroyer."

"This old man will not go with you!" snapped Umak, angry and impatient all at once. "This old man will continue east and seek the caribou. Umak has been given back his life; he will not throw it away. Umak has Lonit to care for. She is a girl now, but she *will* be a woman. The People may yet be reborn through her, to make a new band, to begin a new life for us all. But life feeds on life, Torka. When you find the Destroyer, *if* you kill it, how will it feed you? It is a crooked spirit. When it dies, it will disappear, into the mists of the ghost wind."

"Its flesh will feed me." A muscle pulsed high at Torka's temple. He recalled the smell of the mammoth's blood. He remembered stabbing it again and again before, at last, it had hurled him to what had seemed certain death. "It bleeds. . . ."

"Hmmph!" Umak was so upset that he cracked the edge of the spearhead that he had been reknapping. "So do you!"

Torka would never know exactly when he began to accept Umak's opinion about the mammoth. Time was passing quickly. His bruises faded. His gashes and abrasions were becoming scars. Spring was beginning to drive back the winter dark. Each day, during the brief hours of light, he went out. He searched for the way back to the winter camp but could not find it. He searched for game and mammoth sign but found his strength instead. Slowly, his body healed. His spirit did not.

He was obsessed by his memories. Whether he was awake or asleep, Thunder Speaker dominated his thoughts. Then, one night, he slept and did not dream. For the first time since the mammoth had walked into his life to destroy it, he awoke refreshed, glad to be alive. He could not forgive himself for this. His people, his woman, his infant, and his beloved son were dead. He could not allow himself to forget them. He *would* not. As Umak had warned, the beast that walked within him fed upon his spirit. He let it browse. In some dark, perverted way that he did not wish to analyze, it soothed him even as it sapped the joy from his life.

They ate the remaining fox, and even before they scraped the marrow from the last of the bones, Lonit was busy setting snares. Soon there were lemming and pika to roast. Umak speared a motley-feathered ptarmigan. The first of the season's returning migratory birds were skeining across the sky. Shyly, Lonit came to Torka to present him with a new tunic that she had made for him out of the skins and tails of the foxes. It was a beautiful garment. The girl's workmanship far excelled his dead woman's skills with the needle. He resented her for causing him to make such a comparison and was loath to wear it. With his own tunic in tatters, he had no choice, but he lamented the loss of Egatsop. She should have been there to mend and make for him, not this coltish girl with her round eyes and her long, boyish gait. He had admired the child once. The tenacity with which she clung to life despite adversity was admirable in one so young. But he hated her now. His feelings toward her were irrational and he knew it, but he did not care. She was alive when his woman was dead. She was alive when his son and infant daughter were dead. She was alive, and because of Umak's concern for her, the old man would not seek out the Destroyer.

For this Torka hated her. She was the only female left alive in all the world, and Umak was right when he said that, if the People were not to die forever, they must someday be reborn through her. The thought was so repugnant that Torka would not dwell upon it. But then the day came when he awoke and ate a meal of roasted lemming, and as he went out of the pit hut to stand in the warmth of the rising sun, he reluctantly admitted that it was good to be alive. The beast of memory stirred, but unlike the last time when he thought of the Destroyer, he knew that, in truth, he never wished to see it again—unless it was on his own terms and he had a chance of coming away from the encounter alive. He could never do that alone. Nor would he put Umak and the girl at risk by allowing them to follow him into the shadow of the Destroyer. Umak was an old man. Lonit was a half-grown child. In this savage, hostile world, they were all that was left of his people. Torka would not abandon them.

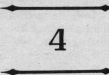

4

They broke camp and moved eastward into the light of the rising sun, seeking the caribou. With the return of light and rising temperatures, the texture of the tundra was changing. Land that had lain hard and brittle beneath winter's thin layering of snow and ice now began to emerge resilient and yielding beneath the feet of the travelers.

They walked out across a landscape that differed from any other on earth. As in other lands and times, moisture and sunlight were the determining factors of life, but here the cold, bitter wind was ever dominant. Except during the longest days of summer, when the sun never set, the chill breath of the polar wind kept the air temperature low enough to prevent snow from melting on the north-facing slopes. Even on the warmest days, when the tundra swarmed with insects and flamed with the colors of hundreds of species of flora, snow lay in hard-packed drifts on windward hills and in the shaded fissures of boulders. Although rivers and ponds were free of ice, less than a yard beneath the tundral earth the ground was perpetually frozen. The mountains that reached to the western edge of the known world were never bare— snows that fell upon them in winter remained to greet the snows of the following autumn, growing thicker and thicker until the combined weight formed great, smothering blankets of white that lay upon the ranges, burying all but the highest peaks.

Far to the west, much of Eurasia was entombed in ice. Eastward, beyond the distant horizon toward which Torka, Umak, and Lonit plodded, bent beneath their pack frames while the wild dog trotted after them, an unknown land also lay entombed. Beyond savage, soaring, ice-mantled peaks, this land mass had almost vanished beneath the crushing weight of an ice sheet two miles thick and over four thousand miles wide.

The little traveling band, however, saw only the greening tundra as they walked ever eastward in their search for the returning herds of caribou. The going was slow. The tundra had split into oddly uniform wedges, the result of the ground's contracting during periods of intense cold, then cracking open. Now that the days were growing warmer, melting snow seeped into the fissures. When temperatures dropped, the meltwater froze and expanded, forming ice wedges that filled shallow gullies ten to one hundred feet in length.

But neither Umak nor Torka nor Lonit complained. Skirting the gullies, they gave thanks to the spirits that the long, rolling valley within which they walked had only a thin coating of snow and was alive with the sound of meltwater running off into icy streams and rivulets.

They paused, breathing hard. Umak nodded, content with what he saw. "Soon many birds will come to nest. To raise young and be food for us."

Lonit was heartened by his words. Within her pack, she carried more than enough sinew thong with which to fashion a stone hurler. If she could find four small stones of equal weight, she could put together an admirable weapon with which to capture waterfowl in the time-honored way of the women of the band—by hurling the bolalike device so that its stone-tipped thongs wrapped around the feet of its victim, grounded it, and prevented it from flying. Lonit was as adept with a stone hurler as she was with the setting of snares and the weaving of nets for either birding or fishing. She thought of this and was glad for her skills and of the many hours that she had worked to perfect them, knowing that an ugly girl must be good for something if she was to be of value and worthy of survival.

Torka stared ahead into the narrowing neck of the valley. How far had they come? How many miles now lay between him and the desolation of the winter camp? He thought of Egatsop and the infant; it had been such a pretty girl, with its mother's long, sloping eyes and lashes. How he longed for her! And for little Kipu. He closed his eyes. He felt suddenly weary beyond bearing.

"Look!" Umak shouted, suddenly rigid, pointing a bony finger skyward.

Torka and Lonit looked. High above and perhaps as far as a mile ahead of them, an enormous broad-winged bird was riding the thermals.

"Sun eater!" exclaimed the old man, naming the bird for its ability to block out the light of the sun when it flew before it. Weighing at least fifty pounds, with a wingspan of some fifteen feet, the giant condor made Umak's heart leap with joy, and the wild dog, standing close but not too near, looked up at him as though he had suddenly become addled. Umak hopped on one foot, and then upon the other, feeling so strong and happy that he could not remember which was his good leg and which was his lame. "Sun eater! We will follow your shadow!" he proclaimed, knowing that the giant condor was a scavenger of big game and that where sun eater flew, in the shadow of its great wings, there walked the caribou!

Hope walked with them now. They proceeded onward, across the shallows of an oxbowed river. They had been traveling for hours. Weariness brought them to a halt. They set up a temporary camp in which they would pass the night, raising a lean-to instead of a pit hut, for they had no intention of lingering, certain that, only a few miles ahead, they would encounter the herds of caribou.

As Umak and Torka took up their spears and went to scout for any small game that might be in the vicinity, Lonit drew a scoop net of sinew meshing from her back. While the wild dog sniffed at marmot sign and chased the molting male ptarmigans that issued raucous mating challenges to one another from every knoll and snowbank, Lonit knelt by the river. Careful to cast no shadow across the water, she leaned out and dipped her net into the flowing current. She held it with its open end facing upstream. In no time at all, a sleek, fat grayling was splashing in the pale light of day's end; then another was entrapped beside it, and another, until the girl's net was filled to bursting.

She laid the fish in a neat line upon the bank, kneeling back to admire them until the wild dog caught her attention. She was afraid of the dog. She knew that Torka also distrusted it. The animal's size was such that, if it chose to attack, it could do damage to a man, and a girl would be no match for it at all. But the dog was Umak's spirit brother, and if it was a ghost dog, there was nothing very frightening about it now. It chased the elusive ptarmigan, dashing from one knoll to another, snapping at flying feathers as the pugnacious birds squawked and cheeped and succeeded in frustrating the dog's best efforts.

"Did your mother dog not teach you to hunt? You will catch no meat like that!"

Shaking water from her scooping net, Lonit bent to break two stalks from a clump of dwarf willow that grew, fuzzy with catkins, at the edge of the embankment, close to the water and out of the wind. With these, and the net in one hand, she walked slowly to a nearby knoll, one of the few that were not occupied by courting ptarmigan. Snow lay banked on the northern slope of the little rise. It was hard packed in the main, but she was able to dig out enough soft snow to form two small balls. The larger of these, about the size of a ptarmigan's body, she placed atop the knoll. The smaller, a tiny, slightly elongated ball the size of a bird's head, she placed firmly atop the larger. At the joining of the two, she placed a few pickings of brown moss that grew at the edge of the snowpack; this approximated the first tufts of summer plumage that were appearing at the necks of each bird amid the molting fluff of its white winter feathers.

She observed her creation, remembering others that she had made in happier times. She forced herself not to think of the past. It was gone. But she was alive, satisfied with her work. From a distance, her snowbird would look real enough to fool any featherbrained, eager-to-mate ptarmigan. She smiled a little as she packed snow in front of her decoy, placing her net over it, staking it down with the twigs of willow.

Now she scooted out of sight. She lay flat, concealed behind the knoll, listening to the calls of the ptarmigan as, having paid not the slightest attention to her efforts, they continued to sound their territorial challenges to one another. With well-practiced skill, the girl echoed them. Within moments a nearby bird was flying to attack the decoy. It swooped low, feet forward, squawking a warning; but when its talons raked into the snow that lay before its opponent, they tangled in the net. Off-balance, the ptarmigan fell, flapping its wings, into the decoy, as Lonit, alerted by its cries, raced to the top of the knoll, pounced upon it, and promptly broke its neck. Holding her trophy high, she gave a little whoop of triumph. When Umak and Torka returned to camp, they would feast upon bird and fish. They would be pleased and would find her worthy.

She could see them now, trotting toward her out of the distance. Both had their spears raised. They were gesturing, no doubt in pleasure, as they saw the ptarmigan held high in her hand. She shook it so that they could not fail to see it. Umak shouted her name. He and Torka began to run. Lonit was elated.

But not for long. The cries of another species of bird caused her to wheel around. Facing back toward the river, she cried out in dismay. The wild dog stood at the edge of the embankment, wolfing down the last of her fish. Above him, a shadow turned the last of day into dusk, as the giant condor tucked back its enormous wings and dove straight down at her.

Lonit froze. It was a huge blur of black and white feathers streaking downward through the sky; its vulturine neck extended, its skull resembling both eagle and condor with its flattened cranium and long, aquiline, dangerously massive beak. That hornlike hook, so perfectly designed for its rapacious, carnivorous feeding, gaped open as it dove. The girl stared upward in horror, seeing its round, red eyes, its equally red stab of tongue, and the huge, concave openings of its nasal passages. It shrieked as it reached to rip the ptarmigan from her hand, just as the wild dog leaped out of nowhere to knock her from her feet.

The force of the dog's impact caused Lonit to release the ptarmigan just in time; had she not done so, the condor would have ripped off her hand. She fell in a stunned heap, half expecting the dog to eat her; but it was gone in an instant, after the huge bird that was banking downward, screaming as it fell from the sky with one of Torka's spears in its breast.

Lonit heard the hunters shouting now.

Her mouth had gone dry. She felt small and foolish and ashamed as she watched the great condor come down on its side, squawking, wheezing, and hacking blood. It was still dangerous, with its beak snapping and its enormous legs kicking out. Torka and Umak ran to kill it, bravely stepping close to plunge their spears deep as the wild dog kept close to Umak's side, snarling and snapping and spitting feathers as, sneezing, the animal helped its brother man to make the kill.

Lonit watched. Her own foolishness had caused her to lose her fish and her ptarmigan. Tonight Torka and Umak and

Brother Dog would gorge themselves upon the meat of the condor. Lonit would not eat. An ugly, unworthy girl had no right to partake of a feast to which she had contributed nothing.

5

Umak teased her when she said that she had no right to share in the meat of the condor. He looked at her with a droll, but not unkindly, smile. "Little girl, without you and your ptarmigan, what would we have used as bait to bring the sun eater down from the sky?"

"I am not a little girl. I am almost a woman."

Torka eyed her sternly. "Then, Almost A Woman, you will butcher the carcass of the condor. You will make a fire. You will roast the meat for Umak and Torka. This is a woman's work. Complete it, and you shall be worthy of your share."

She flushed to her hairline. Grateful for any word from him, she set to work gladly.

Umak at least was easy to please. While out from the camp, he and Torka had walked as far as the neck of the valley and climbed a low hill to look beyond, across a vast plain where, upon the horizon, they had seen what they had so long yearned to see.

"Tonight we eat the flesh of the condor," said Umak, "and grow strong upon the blood and marrow of the sun eater, for we must not dishonor its life spirit by wasting that which we have killed. But tomorrow we go from this place. Tomorrow we walk far. Tomorrow we make a hunting camp in which we will stay many days. Tomorrow we prepare to hunt the caribou!"

His eyes glistened with excitement. "The herd walks toward us from out of the east, as this old man has promised. The herd walks from horizon to horizon, across a plain that stretches from forever to forever. Never has this old man seen so wide a land. Never has this spirit master seen so many caribou!"

Umak's enthusiasm was contagious. Lonit listened as she worked, saddened at first as she recalled the long days of the starving moon, remembering the suffering of her people, wishing that the caribou instead of the mammoth had come to them, wishing that they had met life instead of death. But the band was no more. All that were left of the People were here, sheltering in this little encampment. Torka, Umak, and Lonit composed a new band. And when the hunters brought caribou to their camp, Lonit would make certain that her woman wisdom was put to good purpose. She would provide well for her men. Her sadness drifted away. She smiled a little, and dimples formed hollows beneath her high cheekbones as she thought of all of the fine things that she would make out of the caribou.

Torka was troubled as he listened to his grandfather—not by the old man's words, but by his thoughts as he watched Lonit working at her butchering. As always, the sight of the girl distressed him. She was a strong, hardy, uncomplaining child, but he longed for his own woman now. And for his children. Again the longing ignited his hatred for the girl. Why had she survived when all of the others had died? *Why?*

He stood beside the lean-to that they had raised, staring out across the world. It seemed so empty. It *was* so empty. Would he ever hear the laughter of children again? Or the sound of women talking low in the lonely dark and of men arguing over a friendly game of bone toss?

As he stooped to enter the lean-to, wishing to seat himself out of the wind beside Umak, the wild dog growled at him. The animal lay on the other side of the old man's extended limbs—close but at a wary distance, just out of Umak's reach. Always, the dog kept itself within the fall of the old man's shadow. Always, when Torka came anywhere near it, it warned him away.

"Be at ease, Brother Dog," Umak assured the animal. "Torka is a member of our band and flesh of this old man's flesh. You must get used to him. He is also your brother."

The dog lowered its head, visibly relaxing a little; but it did not take its eyes from Torka. "Aarrr . . ." It continued growling, albeit more softly.

"Aar!" repeated Torka in annoyance, seating himself beside his grandfather. Truly, Umak *was* a spirit master to have won the following of a beast. As for Torka, if it were up to him, he would brain the creature. A young dog would make good eating. Its pelt would make good fur. But it would never make a brother to a man. *Never*. No matter what Umak might say to the contrary, Torka did not trust the dog. Someday it would revert to kind. Someday, instead of leaping to the assistance of the girl, it would attack her. Someday, instead of assisting Umak with a kill, the old man's powers over it would wane, and the dog would turn to try to kill one who no longer was master over its spirit. Torka would wait for that day; then he would kill "Brother" Dog.

"Look," said Lonit, holding up one of the long wing bones of the condor. She had cut the meat and tendons from it with her fleshing dagger and now openly marveled at its light-weight structure. "How can such a fragile bone support the weight of such a great wing?"

Umak grunted. It was not a question that a man, even a spirit master, could answer. But Torka rose, intrigued. What the girl had noted was, in fact, worth considering, if for no other reason than to satisfy his innately curious nature.

He knelt across the carcass from her, balancing his weight on the balls of his feet within his multilayered boots. He took up not the bone, but the entire other wing of the condor. The girl had cut it cleanly away from the shoulder socket. It was intact, its intricate layering of feathers sleek beneath his ungloved hand. Never had he seen flight feathers of such size. He plucked one out and swept the air with it, remarking that the lay of the feathering along the flexible, hollow shaft created a powerful pull against the air.

Lonit eyed the feather. Her feminine eyes took note of more practical attributes. Sewn together along a belting of sinew cord, the feathers were long enough to make a skirt for summer wear, or a magnificent ornamental collar for a spirit master to wear when he called upon his powers, or an effective fan to keep away the biting flies that swarmed across the land on windless days of endless sun. She ventured shyly to share her thoughts with Torka, but he did not seem to hear her, or else showed no interest as he worked the wing, fascinated by its anatomical structure, intrigued by the strength and elasticity of the powerful tendons that gave a springlike movement to the muscles and bones.

"This is how it flies. . . ." he said thoughtfully.

Not to be outdone by his grandson, Umak got to his feet. He went to Torka and took the wing from him.

"Hmmph!" He scrutinized the severed member, nodded, and hefted it upon his back, extending it outward along one arm as he began to move about, slowly at first, pretending that he was a condor. He made a dance of it, mimicking the flight and vulturine sounds of the deceased creature.

Torka could not help but laugh aloud. Lonit covered her own laughter with her hands lest, coming from such an unworthy girl, it offend the spirit master. The wild dog whined and backed away, not knowing what to make of such behavior.

Umak danced on, improvising as he went, moving the wing as though it were an extension of his arm, chanting a song of praise of the great bird whose flesh they would soon consume.

This is how it flies, Umak thought, and for a while he did not feel the weight of his years in his old body. He danced. He turned. He soared. And then, at last, he was a man again, and tired. He stopped, burdened by his years and by the long miles across which he had come since leaving the ruined winter camp of his people behind. He thought of the broad plain that he and Torka had sighted, of the caribou, and of the miles that still separated him from the long-sought-for herds. He dropped the wing of the condor and stood, hands on his hips, breathing hard, all too aware of the ache in his bad leg and of the pain in his feet.

"Hmmph! If only this old man could sprout wings like a sun eater! If only we could *all* fly with the wings of the condor! Think of the distance we could cover! Think of the things we would see! And think of the wear and tear it would save our feet!"

Lonit made a fire of dried fox bones and sods, which she had carried in her pack for this purpose. They roasted the sun eater and ate all that they could, sharing the meat with the wild dog, then bundling beneath their sleeping skins to seek much-needed rest.

With bellies full of meat, warmed by the heat of the fire, they slept huddled close beneath the lean-to. Torka dreamed strange dreams in which he saw himself as a man with the wings of a condor—wings that carried him high above the world, that made him weightless and allowed him to experience the awesome thrust and power of flight. He was like a spear hurtling across the sky, a spear that could control its own passage, that could see with the eyes of a man.

He looked down upon the earth, the soaring peaks and ice-choked canyons, the tundral valleys and the vast plains where the caribou walked in an unending, continuous river of life across the land. And there, upon the easternmost horizon, he saw a mammoth grazing . . . a mammoth like no other . . . a beast with shoulders as high as mountains, tusks as hard and cold and relentless as glaciers, and eyes dilated with hatred of man. It looked up and saw his flight and trumpeted with a voice that shook the sky.

Torka answered that voice. He cried aloud in his dream as his wings folded flat and he hurled himself from the sky, downward, transformed into a spear that struck the mammoth with the killing power of a lightning bolt. The Destroyer fell where it stood, and Torka awoke, shaking, with the taste of blood and death and absolute frustration in his mouth.

For a long while he lay awake, thinking about the dream. Where did the mammoth graze now? he wondered. And was there ever a spear made—or a man born—capable of killing it?

6

The looped end of the leather thong hissed as it left
Torka's hand. The sleeping dog heard it, but too late. The
loop encircled its head, and when the startled animal leaped
to its feet, the noose tightened about its neck. The weight
and stricture of the unknown thing set panic loose within the
dog. He turned to run, only to be brought up short and
half-strangled as Torka fastened the other end of the thong to
a bone stake that he had driven deep into the tundra the
night before.

Stunned, the dog stood still, head lowered, its body straining forward against the pull of the thong. The animal stared at
Torka. Slowly, understanding dawned in the blue eyes as
they traced the slim run of leather to the man's hand. A growl
formed deep in the dog's throat. Without further warning, it
lunged forward, teeth bared, and would have bitten right
through the thick layering of Torka's sleeve had the hunter
not jumped away in time. The dog yipped in pain as it fell
hard on its side, jerked off its feet by the fully extended
length of its tether.

Lonit looked up, startled. They had come far since taking
down the lean-to and heading eastward toward the distant
hills. They had raised a pit hut in the lee of those hills and
had spent another night resting and readying themselves to
hunt the caribou that grazed by the hundreds of thousands
upon the plain that stretched before them. The girl would not
participate in the killing, of course, but she would do the
bulk of the butchering. With this in mind, she had awakened
before her men, eager to assemble her scrapers and fleshers,
the sharp tools of stone and bone that would render caribou
carcasses into meat and hides. She had crept from the pit hut

and had seated herself before it, facing into the sunrise, placing her tool bag of lynx skin upon her lap. The wild dog had looked up to eye her once, then had dropped its head and gone back to sleep. The short, silken hair of the lynx had felt sleek and cold beneath her ungloved fingers. She had admired the meticulous stitching of its seams. It was her bag now, but it had belonged to another woman, as had the tools within it. Her own bag, which had been lost somewhere within the tumbled ruins of her family's pit hut, was made of the skin of a marmot, peeled whole from the body with legs attached and head serving as a flap closure. She had searched for it to no avail. Stroking the lynx skin, she had remembered Enilik, maker of this bag, the bright-eyed woman of Nap. She closed her eyes, hoping that Enilik's life spirit would understand why Lonit had taken her bag and tools and would forgive an unworthy girl for having survived.

Lost in thought, she had not heard Torka come out of the pit hut, nor did she see him cast the loop-ended thong toward the dog. He had given no advance notice of his intent to tether the animal, nor did she understand why he would wish to do so.

Umak burst from the hut, still naked. "What have you done?" he cried, taking in the scene, distraught as he watched the dog roll and strain, half-dislocating its neck as it arched back in a frenzied attempt to get its teeth into the thong to pull it loose.

Lonit gasped. She bowed her head. She lowered her eyes. Not against the sight of the old man's nudity, for, among the People, families often slept naked together, although Lonit, Umak, and Torka had not slept so since the night of the great storm. It was the tone of the old man's voice that had shocked the girl. He had shouted at Torka. It was to avoid seeing Torka's shame that Lonit had lowered her eyes. One man did not speak so to another. Ever. Only females might be so abraded.

Torka paled, not understanding what he had done to so anger his grandfather. "One whiff of dog, and the caribou will scatter like willow leaves driven before an autumn gale," he explained, then added that he had thought Umak would want the dog to be restrained before they readied themselves for the hunt.

"A man does not bind his brother!" Umak shivered violently against the morning cold. One weathered, high-veined hand went to his throat. He could feel the stricture of the dog's tether closing about his own neck. He was sorry that he had shouted. Torka's words were not without substance, and he had obviously meant well. But when he had tethered the dog, he had dishonored it, and Umak as well. "Between brothers, there must be trust. That is the only bond that may exist between them. Without it . . ." He let the words trail off and took a step toward the dog, knowing that his fear had not been misplaced.

Seeing his approach, the dog got to its feet. Its black-masked head went down as every hair along the crest of its spine stood on end. A deep, reverberating growl came from its throat as its quivering lips rolled up to reveal the threat of its bared teeth. Umak paused. A terrible sense of remorse filled him. He knew that he had lost a friend.

The dog took several backward steps, then ran forward, throwing all of its weight against the thong. Stressed beyond its limits, the loop around the dog's neck snapped, and the stake that held the thong broke in two. For an instant, it seemed as though the dog was hurling itself at Umak's throat. Lonit cried out, spilling the tools and bag from her lap as she jumped to her feet. Torka whirled to grab one of his spears from where he had placed them, upright, against the pit hut. But the dog leaped past the old man, hit the ground with its two forepaws, and kept on going.

Torka readied to throw a spear after it, but Umak stopped him with an imperative shout.

Respect for his grandfather stayed Torka's hand, but that hand trembled with frustration as he said, "The dog will drive away the caribou."

Umak's eyes narrowed. Torka was looking at him with an expression that was more chilling than the air. There was pity in the young man's eyes, pity for one who was old and no longer capable of making decisions that could stand unchallenged. A defensive anger sparked within Umak, warming him with the heat of pride. Dignity kept him from reminding his grandson that he would be lying dead upon the tundra, looking at the sky forever, had it not been for Umak's strength and ability to make lifesaving decisions. He scowled with the regal disdain that only the very old could feel for the ignorance and impatience and arrogance of youth.

"Torka has acted for the good of the band. Torka believes that Brother Dog cannot be trusted. But Torka has driven off one who has saved Umak's life, and Lonit's, and, yes, Torka's too. Umak and Brother Dog have walked many miles together. We have eaten of the same kills and have slept in the same camps. Aar *is* this spirit master's brother. And if he comes back to claim his rightful place as a member of this band, Torka will raise no hand against him."

Umak had spoken quietly, but clearly the words had been as much a rebuke as a command. "The dog will not come back," replied Torka, frowning. Had he heard correctly? Had Umak actually called the beast a name, as though it were a man? Although he had already pressed his grandfather beyond the bounds that propriety and tradition allowed, he could not resist pressing for an answer. "Aar?"

Umak's chin jabbed imperiously at the sky. "My grandson has a name. So, too, has my brother."

"Your brother is a *dog*, Grandfather," reminded Torka. He was deeply troubled. The old man looked so frail standing stark naked in the cold, with his lean, sinewy arms locked together across the bony expanse of his chest. Torka recalled the many times that Egatsop had pointed out Umak's failings to him. Her voice seemed to be whispering contemptuously upon the rising wind of morning. *Umak is old. Umak has lost his powers. Umak is no longer the man that he once was. Umak is no longer a spirit master. Umak is no longer even master of his own mind. Umak is a liability to the People.*

But now the People were no more. Torka was alone in the world with Umak and Lonit. Both had worked to save his life; but now that he was well and strong again, he knew the truth, which Umak might well deny. Their lives depended upon Torka. The girl was so young, and until this moment, Torka had not realized just how old Umak really was. Perhaps Egatsop had been right about him. Perhaps his wisdom, like the resiliency of his body, was a thing of the past. His strange attachment to the dog seemed to confirm this.

Gently Torka said to him: "Grandfather. It is time to forget the dog. Torka did not intend to drive it away, but now that it is gone, Torka says that this is a good thing. Never before have dogs and men walked together. Never before have they shared their kills or their encampments. If the dog comes back, it will follow us on the hunt. It will drive away the game."

Umak harrumphed, irked by the unmistakable condescension in his grandson's voice. "As it drove the sun eater away from Lonit to send it banking downward onto Torka's spear?"

Lonit felt her face flush. The tension between the two hunters seemed to stress the very air she breathed. She knelt and began to pick up her spilled tools. If only Torka had seen the way the dog had stood with Umak against the foxes! If only he had seen the animal lie down at the feet of the hunter! If only he had seen the beast take food from the hand of a man! If only she were not a female, unfit to speak her thoughts to anyone not of her own gender, she would tell Torka of these things; then he would know that Umak was a great and powerful spirit master and that the wild dog had been under the spell of his magic.

"Torka needs no dog to assist him with his kills!" Torka responded hotly to Umak's cool sarcasm.

"Hmmph!" replied Umak. "We will see. Come. Let us prepare for the hunt. Let us don our stalking cloaks. This old man is cold. This old man would kill caribou. This old man would see how much Torka has remembered of all that Umak has taught him."

They killed. And killed again. When the second cow went down, twitching and slobbering with two spears in her belly, the herd broke and ran before them—a teeming river of bawling calves and snorting, antlered cows, which spread outward before them from horizon to horizon, as far as their eyes could see.

"No dog could drive away so much game!" said Umak.

Torka made no comment. He did not want to admit that the old man was right. Still, he felt better now that his blood was up from the killing, and he was actually glad that Umak had outperformed him. Despite his stiff leg, the old man had been directing their hunt as though he, and not Torka, was a man in his prime. Torka had not allowed Umak his kills. The old man had taken them, and he knew it. Of the five spears that had been thrown, each had found its target; only one of the weapons belonged to Torka.

There was a cagey squint to Umak's eyes and a wry grin of smugly suppressed superiority upon his face as he retrieved his weapons and stood by while Torka withdrew his own.

Their eyes met and held. As often happened between them, their life spirits seemed to meld. Each knew the thoughts of the other.

This old man is not so old that he cannot still out-hunt his grandson.

Torka nodded, chastised. *This man has misjudged one who could still bring down a great white bear if he chose to do so.*

Umak's grin widened to show strong, time-worn teeth. He knelt, peeled off one of his gloves, and thrust a bare hand into the wound that Torka's spear had inflicted upon the now-dead cow. "This was a death wounding," he conceded.

Torka smiled, knowing that his grandfather's words had been meant to soothe feelings from their earlier conflict. He knelt beside the old man, took off one of his gloves, and thrust his hand into the wound that Umak's spear had made.

"Torka and Umak are a good team," he said. "Working together, we have killed this cow twice!"

They killed no more that day. They made the song that generations of hunters of the band had made in gratitude to the spirits of slain game. They tried not to think of those who would not hunt with them again, but they were there, whispering in the wind, watching from the sky.

But the dead could not eat, and Umak and Torka were both ravenous. They gouged out the eyes of the caribou and sucked the bittersweet black juices from them. They pierced the upper bellies of their kills, pulled out the hearts, and ate them, making a ceremony of the eating as they felt the life spirits of the caribou fill them with warmth, strength, and renewed purpose. They smiled at one another. It had been too long since they had eaten of the blood and flesh of the caribou; this was the best meat of all.

The cows that they had taken were relatively small, tender-haunched yearlings with no calves that would starve for want of their milk. The hunters hefted them with ease and plodded back to their encampment, where Lonit awaited them.

She offered the traditional female greeting, which they, as males, pretended to ignore. They dropped their offerings before her, then removed their antlered stalking cloaks and hunkered down by the fire that she had made within a wind-protective nest of stones and sods. Now she began the obligatory litany of praise. Custom decreed that the man speak no acknowledgment, but although they kept their silence, their faces showed their surprise. The cadence of Lonit's praise song was perfect. Her voice was so pleasant and soft, it seemed to gentle the cold, flat breath of the ever-present wind. The little side-stepping dance, performed slowly, with ritual simplicity, took the girl in a graceful circuit of the game. When she paused before them, Umak made a loud exhalation of approval, and although Torka made no comment, Lonit beamed with delight—not only because she was pleased by the game, but because her praise song had been accepted by her men.

Her men. The concept made her giddy with happiness. She set to work, dragging the carcasses downwind and well away from the pit hut, lest predators be drawn by the smell of meat and happen upon man instead. With her sharp fleshing knife, she opened the bellies of the caribou and cut out the blood meats. These she brought to the hunters, carrying the livers and kidneys in her hands. Still warm with life, they steamed in the chill air, and the smell of their rich, dark sweetness was heady. To her amazement, while Torka took his portion and began to eat, Umak magnanimously shared a part of his treasures with her, slicing off dripping ribbons of what were his by right and insisting that the girl consume them on the spot. This she did and was further delighted when she brought the long lengths of intestines to the hunters. These, too, Umak shared with her, portioning off generous sections that were filled with a delicious puddinglike mass of highly nutritious lichens and mosses made soft by the sharp, acidic tang of digestive juices. Not since childhood, when her mother had shared such delicacies with her, had Lonit tasted any of the prized portions of any big game. Her food had been leftovers, cast-off sections of marrowbones with the best parts already chewed by others, scraps of meat too tough to be eaten by any but the most unworthy, and whatever "woman meat" she had been able to catch for herself: birds and rodents and fish, grubs in season—all considered meat unfit for males, except during the time of the long dark when the starving moon rose and the People ate without complaint whatever they could get.

Their hunger sated, Torka and Umak rose and completed the skinning of the caribou while the girl stood by, admiring their skill. The skinning of big game was a man's work; no female would dare even to think of doing it lest she offend the spirit of the deceased animal. Yet Lonit found herself watching curiously, observing the swift, sure movements of the hunters' hands as, with beautifully dressed blades of flint, they lifted the skins and drew them away from the flesh beneath.

This done, the men returned to the fire and seated themselves. They picked at the remaining pieces of liver, kidney, and intestine. Soon they were dozing.

Now Lonit set to the butchering. First she spread out the skins, hair side down, and weighted them with stones. She was careful not to stretch them. Hides stretched when still wet would soon stiffen and become unworkable. The girl eyed the expanse of bloody, cursorily scraped skins. They were already crusting in the dry, freezing wind. Tomorrow, she would scrape more fragments of tissue from them. Several days would pass before they were ready for additional working. When she was satisfied that they were dry enough, she would sleep with the raw skins, flesh side down against her body. The warmth of her skin would permeate them with curative oils that could only be obtained by prolonged contact with human skin. The next day they would be scraped again and stretched tautly in the freezing wind. Eventually, after several more scrapings and stretchings, Lonit would have hides soft enough to be formed into new garments for her men. She would sew them with infinite care and join the seams so that not even the coldest wind could penetrate them. Then, on stormy days, when the hunters went out into the brutal cold of the time of the long dark, they would know that, at least in some small ways, Lonit was not without value. Perhaps then Torka would smile at her. Perhaps then he would begin to see that she was not totally without worth.

She thought these thoughts as she imagined the many caribou that Torka and Umak would bring to her for butchering in the days to come. She would make new clothes for them all! She could see the hides stretched out beneath the sun and smiled as she worked to cut the meat from the bodies of the caribou. Her back ached and her hands were raw, but she did not care. This meat was for Torka and Umak. She was proud to be their woman and to be able to prepare the meat for them. She worked and worked, and soon thin red fillets of muscle tissue were hanging to dry over frames of bone. Ignoring her fatigue, she turned her attention to another task and began to pound the joint bones, cracking them open, preparing to extract the marrow that lay within.

"You will stop now! You will come to the fire!"

Torka's voice startled her. She looked up to see that he

was awake. He scowled at her as he sat cross-legged beside the sleeping mound of a snoring Umak. To her surprise, the world had gone dark. Bold auroral patterns of gold and blue and green pulsed in the night sky. The smell of roasting meat reached her. Her stomach growled. She realized with a start that she was hungry again.

Torka beckoned. His face was immobile as she went to him and took from his hand a bone skewer upon which long strips of caribou tongue had been roasted. In the soft glow of the fire, with the multicolored luminescence of the aurora at his back, Torka's handsomeness was so overwhelming that Lonit could not move. Her hand froze in midair. She trembled visibly.

"Take! Eat! Almost A Woman has done a woman's work . . . the work of a dozen women! Does she not know when it is time to stop? Does she not know when it is time to rest?" He patted the ground beside him irritably. "Here. Sit on the skins beside Torka. Be warm by the fire. Rest. Eat!"

The invitation was so overwhelming that her knees nearly buckled. She sat down. They ate in silence beneath the dancing colors of the night, with the wind whispering all around and sparks rising from the fire like stars trying to climb into the sky. The girl watched them, eating slowly, tasting nothing, thinking only of the closeness of the man who sat beside her. She was so aware of him that every nerve ending in her skin seemed raw, waiting for the slightest word from him, wanting to be touched by him, but he sat in silence, unmoving, staring into the night, lost in his own thoughts. His face was set. Not even the fire glow could warm the sadness that Lonit saw in his eyes. In time, that sadness filled the girl, for she knew that, although he had called her to sit beside him, he was unaware of her. His heart was with his woman, with his children, with all that he had lost and would never be able to hold close again.

As the night deepened, the wind rose and the temperature dropped. They went into the pit hut to take shelter against the cold. Before dawn, Lonit was awakened by the howling of a wild dog. She lay awake in the darkness, wondering if it was Brother Dog, listening to its cries and to the low, even pull and release of Torka's breath. Rolled in his sleeping skins, he slept soundly beside her. It was a while before she realized that she could not hear the familiar snoring of the old man.

She sat up, squinting, trying to see into the dark and succeeding. Umak was gone.

She had been so tired from her labors that she had discarded only her bloodied outer tunic before crawling beneath her bed skins. She did not don it now. She wrapped herself in one of her bed skins and, after pulling on her boots, tiptoed out of the pit hut to stand in the wind and the first blue light of morning.

She saw Umak at once. He stood silhouetted against the dawn. His head was thrown back. His hair whipped in the wind. With arms raised, he cried aloud to the rising sun. But he did not cry with the voice of a man. He howled with the voice of a wild dog.

And as Lonit listened, Brother Dog answered from out of the distant hills, and the voices of man and beast were one.

The next day, when Torka and Umak went out to hunt again, the dog was waiting for them. It stood on a tundral hillock, its thick fur ruffling in the wind. It watched the caribou as they grazed. The wind blew past the dog, taking its scent. The caribou caught no smell of it, nor did they note the smell of man; for as the hunters approached the herd, they rubbed fresh caribou feces onto their stalking cloaks, thus masking their own scent.

The dog watched the hunters as they bent forward, imitating the slow, halting steps of grazing game, disguised as caribou within their antlered stalking cloaks. It was difficult to tell that they were men at all. But the dog knew—it had walked too many miles with Umak not to have been imprinted by him. The old man's howls had drawn it back toward the encampment from across the lonely distances into which it had fled. The pack instinct was strong in the dog. Although its hackles rose when it thought of Torka, Umak *had* become its brother. They were of one pack. And the dog, by nature a social animal, had no wish to hunt or live alone.

Born for the chase, Aar did not have to be instructed in the best way to help the pack make a successful kill. To the amazement of Torka and Umak, the dog trotted down from the hilltop, gaining speed with every step, and raced through the rivering herd, driving caribou in every direction until the entire herd was on the run. Barking aggressively, singling out its intended prey and cutting them from the herd, the dog snapped at flying hooves as it drove several cows and calves straight into the waiting spears of Umak and Torka. Hamstringing the beleaguered game, the dog then backed away and stopped, watching as the men made their kills, and by this behavior conceding to them their dominant role as masters of the pack.

Umak was elated. "Brother Dog drives the game," he said, reminding Torka of his earlier words. "But not *away*. He drives it *to* the hunters!"

Torka stared at the panting, bloody-muzzled dog and tried to make sense of what he had just witnessed. It was not possible for a dog to hunt with the wisdom of a man, but Aar had done just that, and more. The dog had made it possible for Umak and Torka to take twice the game with only half their usual effort. Torka frowned, admitting to himself that Umak must truly have mastered the spirit of the animal. He nodded, wanting to be convinced for the old man's sake; yet he was not entirely satisfied. No matter how he reasoned it out, it was not natural for a dog to keep company with men. Something about it made him uneasy. But the animal *had* earned its portion this day; this much Torka would not debate.

7

Life was good. Even if ghost spirits from the abandoned winter camp followed to whisper on the wind of death and desolation, Torka, Umak, and Lonit were too busy to listen. The girl tended the new camp while the men hunted. The dog always ran ahead of them, driving game toward their waiting spears as though it had been trained to do so. They took much meat, enough to last through the ripening time of light and on into the dreaded return of the time of the long dark. The girl cured many hides, enough to make new garments for them all. Soon there was no need to hunt. Still the caribou continued to move across the land, pouring out of the east in numbers so vast that it seemed as though the herds were not composed of individual animals but were one endless, teeming being.

And then they were gone.

Torka stared across an empty, silent world. He stood upon a tundral hummock. Below, the scars of the caribous' passing lay dark upon the still-frozen land. They had vanished into the far western hills.

"They will return," said Umak. The old man had come to stand beside his grandson. The dog was with him, close, but not too near, and well out of Torka's reach. Umak drew in a deep breath of the morning, then exhaled it with enthusiasm. The last few days of food and rest and good hunting had made him feel young again. "This is a good camp. When the caribou come east, we will be here to greet them. They will be meat for us in the time of the long dark."

"From where do they come? To where do they go?" queried Torka.

Umak harrumphed. "That no man may know. The caribou walk back and forth across the world. They go to secret places where only the caribou may go."

"I wonder. . . ." Torka turned his gaze eastward across the vast, rolling plain over which the caribou had come. On the horizon, a broad, snowcapped mountain shimmered in the haze generated by the distance through which Torka viewed it. Beyond the mountain, the tundral steppe rolled on into infinity. Torka stared at it thoughtfully. "It is from somewhere beyond that mountain that the caribou have come to graze, to calve, to eat of the tundra in the days of sun. But always, when the time of the long dark comes near, the caribou turn back, returning eastward. Where do they go? *Why* do they go? Upon what do they feed when they disappear in the days of the starving moon? If hunters could follow, if men could hunt caribou in the winter dark . . ."

Umak interrupted Torka with another harrumph. "No man may do this! The sun calls to the caribou. They follow, to a secret place in the sky, above the mountains, into the face of the rising sun itself!"

"Is it so?"

"It is so," Umak affirmed, for what the fathers of his father had spoken in days long beyond remembering was sacred. It was not to be questioned.

Beneath a cloud of migrating birds, Lonit searched for stones with which to make a bola. Her head ached, and her breasts were tender as she bent to sort through pebbles that lay about a large, lichen-crusted boulder. On the southern face of the stone, where lichen did not grow, the boulder was so smooth that it seemed to have been scoured. Ordinarily, the girl would have noticed this, for the unusual always caught her eye, but she did not feel well and was absorbed in thoughts of her unworthiness.

Look at this female! she said to herself, her mouth drawn against her teeth. *A few days of butchering, and Lonit is as stiff and sore and grouchy as an old woman! Never has she felt like this before. Lonit dishonors the men who allow her to share their camp. Even the dog is more important than Lonit!*

Her silent self-recriminations went on, intensifying when she could find no pebbles of the right shape or size. How could she make a proper bola without the right stones? She had already prepared the four leather thongs to which the

stones would be tied; each thong was made of three strips of
sinew, meticulously braided into thirty-inch lengths, which
were brought together at one end and secured by yet another
thong. When the loose ends of the four braids were weighted
with stones—with two condor feathers attached to the united
end to stabilize and guide the bola in flight—Lonit would
possess the perfect snare weapon with which to catch the
land birds and waterfowl that filled the sky. Soon they would
be nesting in the thousand pools and lakes that would jewel
the tundra after the spring thaw. Even now the more shallow
lakes were partially free of ice, and tiny, sparrowlike long-
spurs were landing everywhere to pick at the thinly frosted
tundra for bits of new growth and remnants of last year's
grasses. Soon they would be nesting, they and uncounted
other winged nomads of the skies. There would be eggs to
gather and suck.

But now as a dull, deep cramp pulled at Lonit's belly, not
even the thought of such long-anticipated delicacies could
cheer her. Coupled with her aching head and tender breasts,
the cramp was a further sign of her unworthiness. Within her
gloves, her work-worn palms were clammy. She felt so strange.
She wondered if she would die. The speculation was so
engrossing that, when Umak came up behind her, she jumped,
startled.

"Almost A Woman has come far from the camp alone.
This is not a good thing. Always there is danger when one
walks alone. For what does Lonit search?"

She stood before him. His rebuke shamed her. She dared
not look at him. She knew that he was right. She felt so
miserable that she did not doubt for a moment that she was
not fit to look at him. She answered lest her silence offend
him. "Lonit would make a bola. Lonit has come out from the
camp to look for stones."

"There is much meat on the drying frames. There is much
meat in the cache pits. Lonit has no need to make a bola.
Lonit looks tired. Come. Almost A Woman will never *be* a
woman if she does not stop her work and allow herself to rest.
If she walks alone far from camp, flesh eaters will stalk her,
and her men will have to put themselves at risk to save her."

Her shame deepened. She had tried so hard not to allow
either Umak or Torka to see her weakness. She had been so
proud to do a woman's work for them, to have the opportunity to show them that she was skilled at making meat and

hides and garments and a proper encampment. They had been appreciative, in the tacit way that men showed their approval—with grunts, nods, and by taking what she offered without comment; consent was the highest form of flattery a female might hope for. If a man ate her cooking or donned a garment or ornament that she had made for him, her heart sang with pride. And this Lonit's heart had done . . . until the weariness had come upon her. Until her head had begun to ache. Until her breasts had suddenly swelled and begun to hurt. She had remembered then. She had known that Umak and Torka were only tolerating her, accepting her efforts on their behalf because they had no other choice. She was the only female left to do a woman's work.

When Umak looked at her, he must secretly lament the lost lives of all of the fine females who had shared his bed skins during his long life. Now only a homely, unworthy girl was left to flatter him in his old age. If indeed he believed that a new band would someday be born through her, his manhood must shrivel at the thought of coupling with such a weak and insignificant creature. No doubt he would leave this to Torka. And if Torka had his way, new life would simply come out of Lonit as insects emerged from the skin of the tundra—by magic, spawned of themselves as fish spawned of melting ice carried in the currents of a river.

Even then, Lonit was certain that she would not be valuable. When she was old, the children that she had borne would be ashamed to call her mother. She would wander off into the winter dark, leaving them to live their lives, hoping that they would soon forget her.

But in the meantime, she was alive, and when she had gone off in quest of the stones, she had been thinking of her responsibilities to her men. She had been thinking of the future and of the past. She had been remembering the way it had been for the band during those last nights of the starving moon. Yes. The men had brought much meat into this new camp. And Lonit had prepared it and cached it against lean times to come. But could there ever be enough meat in any encampment? If starving times came again, would not even the pink, fatty meat of the great geese and swans that flew ahead of the rising spring sun and disappeared into its dying light at summer's end be welcome? It was "woman meat," but cured by long smoking over fires of dried caribou dung and tundral sod, it would serve to keep her men alive when the last of the caribou "man meat" was gone.

These were Lonit's thoughts as she followed Umak back to the encampment. He had told her to rest, and rest she would; but her belly cramps would not allow her to sleep.

The night would not be fully black again for months. Yet it was dark as Umak and Torka sat before a little fire of bones and dung. They spoke quietly together, savoring the feel of a wind that, for the first time in what seemed too long to remember, bore no sting of winter.

There was no moon. Against a leaden sky, an owl soared, a pale discoloration against the night, for its white winter plumage had still not fully turned to summer brown. Torka looked up. He followed the pale blur of its flight until it disappeared. All around, the night was filled with the awakening sounds of spring, of water running in a thousand streams, dripping beneath melting snowfields into air pockets that insulated the yielding earth beneath. Across the fire from him, Umak chewed on a long strip of caribou meat—holding it in one hand, while he sawed it off, close to his mouth, with a sharp blade of flint that he held in the other. As Torka watched him, Umak's stone dagger cut through the meat as easily as it sliced warm fat. Umak grunted with contentment. Through the mouthful of meat, he said that Lonit had prepared the meat well. Torka nodded begrudgingly. The girl had cut the strips against the grain, and very thin; they had dried quickly in the wind and were as tender as though she had pounded them with stones. She was proving to be a better camp maker than Egatsop had ever been. She was a hard worker and meticulous at every task to which she set her skilled hands. Although she had made no complaint, Torka had seen the strained look of fatigue on her face when Umak had earlier brought her back to camp and had insisted that she rest. He had sensed the weariness growing within her over the last few days. He brooded over it now, thinking that even though he disliked the girl, perhaps he and Umak were going to have to rethink certain traditions of the band. There was man's work and woman's work; but now, in all the world, there were only two men, and only one woman. No. Not even that. Almost A Woman might be nearly as tall as Umak and surprisingly strong for one of her years, but she was still only a girl. She could not be allowed to do too much.

Umak watched Torka as he ate. As so often happened, he knew what his grandson was thinking. The old man spoke thoughtfully. "In a new life, men must seek new ways." He took a mouthful of meat, sliced it off, then vigorously spat it out. It landed unannounced on the nose of the dog that dozed in the firelight. Roused instantly, Aar snapped it up and gulped it down whole.

Umak chuckled. "New times make new kinships. If this old man can become brother to a dog, then Torka may also assist a woman with her work."

"Lonit is no woman. She is a child. She does not need to work so much. We are two. She labors as though she had an entire band to feed. She works too hard. She cooks too much. She shames the memory of the women of the band on purpose, I think. It is not a good thing."

Umak eyed Torka thoughtfully. He had seen himself reborn in his grandson. They were alike in so many ways. Yet, from the first, there was a quality within Torka that even his wise, watchful eyes had been unable to define. When at last Torka had come to his manhood, that quality was still there . . . deep, subtle, a power growing in the spirit of the man . . . unseen, unfathomed, like a current flowing in a great river, hidden by winter ice but there all the same. Someday it would ripple the surface of the water. Someday it would shatter the ice that held it captive. Someday it would break forth to reshape the land. Someday, but not now. Now the scars of a wounded life were too thick upon his spirit. They blinded him to everything but the past. He could not even see the merit of one young girl who tried so hard to please him.

Umak sighed. He mulled over the many miles that he had walked with the girl. His lids came down, and he stared into the fire, allowing memories to spark along with the light that danced into his eyes, through his lashes—multicolored, as though viewed through a crystal.

"Hmmph," said the old man, not feeling old at all but young and warm with his belly full of meat and his body fully rested for the first time in months. "Almost A Woman *is* just that. She is strong. She is brave. She is not a child. She has no wish to shame the memory of the women of the band. She tries hard to please us, because she is ashamed that she is not more like them."

Torka exhaled an Umak-like harrumph and told his grandfather that *he* was not seeing clearly.

The old man measured his grandson across the flames. "Umak has lived long. Umak has seen many things. And Umak will tell you this about Almost A Woman: Even the plainest bud, long dormant beneath the ice of the winter dark, is soon a flower, swelling and open and eager to accept the gift of life beneath the warmth and light of the summer sun."

His meaning was clear. The idea was one that Torka did not even want to consider. "Lonit is *not* a woman!" he insisted.

Umak sighed almost dreamily, flung the last of the meat to the dog, then pulled his bison-skin robe higher about his shoulders. "Now Lonit is a girl," he conceded. His voice was low, thoughtful, weighted by an inner sadness. "Soon she will be a woman . . . the *only* woman. . . ." He laced his arms about his bent knees and rested his head upon them. He was suddenly sleepy. He yawned. He closed his eyes and listened to the wind and the sound of the earth opening itself to spring. "Soon . . ." he said again, drifting into sleep. Dreams came instantly, of far lands, of bounteous hunts, of women who had loved him and walked beside him beneath the savage Arctic skies of his youth. The girl was not a part of the dreams, for they were of the past. Lonit was an unopened flower, awaiting the rising of a future sun as she dreamed her own dreams in the last days of the winter dark.

Torka sat alone by the fire. Wolves howled in the distance. His thoughts turned inward—to his lost woman, his infant, the beloved little son whom he would never see again. He closed his eyes. In the dying light of the fire, only the wild dog saw his tears.

It was the growling of the dog that woke him. From the moment that Torka opened his eyes until the moment of the attack, only seconds passed. It seemed a lifetime.

A fierce alertness coursed in his veins. He was awake instantly. He was aware of being watched, like some captive thing awakening within a trap, with hunters gathered all around, ready to tear him to pieces.

Umak slept on, still sitting wrapped within his bison-skin robe. Not recognizing him as prey, one of the dire wolves leaped right over him, heading straight for Torka. Too late, Torka realized that he was too far from the pit hut to make a grab for his spears. He would have cursed himself for being a careless fool, but there was not even time for that.

The huge wolf was a blur against the night as the dog leaped to intercept its spring. Torka was on his feet, ready to block the beast's attack with his upraised arms, but to his amazement, the wolf was knocked to the ground at his feet. The dog was on top of it. Disbelieving, Torka saw their bodies seem to blend into a shadowed mass of fur and legs as their combined snarls ended with a garbled yap of pain as the dog's ripping teeth and burrowing snout tore out the throat of the dire wolf.

The pack was closing now—heavy jawed, heads down and slavering. There were four of them, with a big male in the lead. Torka dove for his weapons. His spears stood upright with Umak's against the pit hut. Torka grabbed two of them, and the rest collapsed with a clatter as he whirled to face the wolves alone.

"Umak!" He cried the old man's name, but his grandfather slept on, oblivious to danger. There was no time for Torka to rouse him. "Come!" he shouted at the wolves, knowing from experience that a show of bravado was usually sufficient to drive their kind away.

The clouded sky gave off a soft gray light of its own. Torka could see the wolves clearly as they advanced, one halting step at a time. Why did the wolves risk themselves? Had they not also feasted off the passing caribou? They showed no signs of starvation. Their coats were thick, their sides sleek. Their eyes glowed, staring directly into Torka's eyes, and suddenly he understood. They savored the taste of man. They preferred it to less hostile prey. They had eaten their fill of it miles away, westward in the abandoned encampment where Torka's people lay looking at the sky, defenseless against their ravening predations.

The thought filled Torka with rage. He hurled one of his spears. It missed its target by inches. He threw the other, just as the smallest member of the pack leaped for him. Surprised in midair, the wolf impaled itself and fell, twitching and screaming in agony.

The sound filled the night. Umak awoke with a start. He blinked as the scene before him slowly came into focus. One dire wolf was dead upon the ground. Another twitched in its death throes at Torka's feet. And two more were snarling, advancing on Brother Dog. He blinked again. Was he dreaming? It took him several seconds to understand what he was seeing, and several more for his mind to tell his body what it must do. By then, Lonit had come out of the pit hut.

Clad only in her undertunic, with her fleshing dagger in one hand, she did not hesitate. She let out a cry that rivaled that of the dying wolf as she ran boldly toward the interlopers, menacing them as fiercely as they menaced her men. Torka reached for the spear that had fallen short and, lifting it, echoed Lonit's strident cry.

The smaller of the two wolves cringed. It knew that it had lost all hope of any advantage. It wheeled and fled, and its companion followed. But the leader of the pack, the big male, did the unexpected. It, too, wheeled—not to flee, but to lunge for the audacious, knife-wielding girl.

Caught off-balance, Lonit went down with the wolf atop her, its teeth deep in her forearm. The blade flew from her hand.

Now Umak was on his feet, spear in hand as Torka threw his weapon aside and leaped to tackle the wolf. He fell upon the beast, grappling at its neck, feeling its power tense and twist beneath his own. Then the wolf went limp. Umak had thrust his spear downward with all of his weight behind it. It pierced the wolf's skin, passed between its ribs, and drove straight into its heart, killing it instantly.

"Aiyee-eh!" exhaled the old man, withdrawing the spear point with a vengeance. Blood spurted from the wound. It was black in the darkness, almost as black as Umak's mood. His reaction time in the face of danger had been slow, too slow, and he knew it. His youthful spirit had screamed at him to hurry, but his body had betrayed him; it had moved as though made of stone. Because of his failure to leap to the attack, the girl had fallen beneath the wolf. Torka had simply been too far away to do more than he had. Umak felt sick with shame. His cry had not been a shout of victory; it had been an exclamation of self-disgust.

Impatiently, Torka pushed himself off the wolf and rolled its limp body aside. He felt himself go cold with dread as he saw the equally limp, bloodied body of the girl lying beneath it. One arm was folded across her face. The leather of her sleeve was punctured in a dozen places, shredded, saturated with blood. Torka knelt beside her, afraid to touch her, afraid to breathe. Blood was all over her. Hers, or the blood of the wolf? He could not tell. He wondered if she was dead.

Confused emotions swarmed in his head like stinging insects upon the summer tundra. His heart was like ice as he realized how much he would miss her. Not because she was a hard worker, not because she labored unceasingly at the countless skills that were a portion of woman wisdom. Not even because she was the only female in the world. But simply because she was Lonit. The realization was shattering. Yes, she was homely, with her great, round, antelope eyes and her unsightly dimples that formed in the hollows beneath her cheekbones whenever she smiled. Yes, she was too tall for a girl, and too slender, but she was as brave as the proudest hunter and as uncomplaining as any woman of the band had ever hoped to be. Until this moment, Torka had not realized how much he had come to care for her. And he did not want to care. He would not let himself care. His memories of Egatsop would not allow it.

"Lonit?" It was Umak who spoke the girl's name softly, tentatively, half-afraid that her life spirit had left her body. Within his belly, the sickness of shame congealed into nausea. If the wolf had taken Lonit's life, her death would be Umak's fault.

But the girl was not dead. She was merely stunned and hurt—and frightened. Slowly, her injured arm moved. Her eyelids flickered. She looked up at Torka through blood-stained lashes and, without willing herself to do so, flung her arms about his neck and buried her face in the warm hollow of his neck as she sat upright. He was alive! She had been certain that the wolves had eaten him! She clung to him, then remembered that the wolves had also menaced Umak. She peeked over Torka's shoulder to see the old man standing close, with the dog at his side. Relief flooded her. She smiled wanly.

"The wolves are gone? And we are still together . . . all of us . . . Umak and Torka, Brother Dog and Lonit . . . we are still one band?"

"One band," affirmed Umak, wondering if the girl had seen his failure.

She had not. She had eyes only for Torka as, gently, he pried her arms from about his neck. She sat very still as he carefully folded back the tattered layering of her blood-soaked sleeve. She held her arm as steady as she could. She barely winced as he examined her wounds. His brow furrowed as he saw the damage that the wolf had done to the soft skin of her inner forearm.

"This will need sewing," he told her, impressed by her silent endurance of pain. "Almost A Woman is brave." He spoke the acknowledgment aloud, only half-aware of what he was saying. It was not right for a female to be so brave. Egatsop had howled like a gutted wolf during the birth of her children. The sound of a woman wailing made her man feel strong. Was this homely, round-eyed girl trying to unman him?

Unaware of his thoughts, her heart made a little leap of happiness. Coming from his mouth, the observation was a compliment sweeter than life itself had ever been. She spoke her heart to him. "With Torka beside her, Lonit is not afraid . . . of anything!"

She looked so young and vulnerable and trusting that he had to turn away. He did not understand her. He did not *want* to understand her. A terrible sense of desolation filled him. He thought of the wolves, the giant condor, and the mammoth that had destroyed the band. He thought of all of the tundra's hungry, stalking predators, and the vast, lonely miles that stretched out all around. He heard the wind's soft whispering as it moved in the night. It spoke to him about the thousand ways in which a man might die and about how short the lives of a young girl and an old man would be without a hunter in his prime to protect them.

Slowly, weighed by his thoughts, Torka rose. He had not failed to note Umak's inability to respond quickly to the attacking wolves. Had it not been for the warning growls of the dog, the wolves would now be feasting off their bones. With infinite regret and sadness, Torka was forced to admit to himself that Umak *was* old. The days in which he had depended upon his grandfather for all-sustaining strength and wisdom were gone. Umak had allowed him to make a nearly fatal error in judgment when they had set up a butchering camp that two men could not possibly hope to defend. It was an error that might have cost them their lives. They had been lucky so far, but now Torka realized that if they were to survive, they would have to live differently: No longer would they be able to linger in exposed encampments, as their people had always done, while meat and skins were cured and the local game was hunted to depletion by men and boys until, at last, the band was forced to move on, following the herds in search of new hunting grounds.

But how else *could* they live? The question cut deeply into his heart. He was a man of the People. Without them, how long could he hope to hunt alone, with only an old man and a girl at his side?

He was facing eastward, into the glow of dawn. And suddenly, as he saw the shimmering silhouette of the distant mountain, he knew what he must do. Like the herds that turned eastward at the beginning of each time of the long dark, he must lead his little band into the face of the rising sun. They would go to the far mountains, where they would encamp, with high stone walls at their back to protect them from unexpected attacks by meat-eaters. They would hunt the broad sweep of the tundra as the People had always done. But they would rest where the People had never rested before.

He stared straight ahead, letting the high, shouldering image of the mountain fill him with a renewed sense of purpose.

"Lonit is ready."

The girl's voice distracted him. He looked down to see that Umak had brought his medicine bag from the pit hut. The old man knelt beside Lonit, preparing to suture her arm. She sat very still. Very straight. Very bravely.

"Lonit is not afraid," she said.

Torka looked away, back toward the dawn, into the face of the rising sun, hating the girl again, wishing that she were dead and that Egatsop were here in her place. The mountain burned gold, and the tundra rolled on forever, shivering in the cold breath of the ever-blowing wind. Somewhere, far across the miles, thunder growled out of the now-cloudless sky. Torka listened. He knew that it was not thunder. It was the distant trumpeting of a mammoth.

He closed his eyes. Memories of the Destroyer walked within his mind. Around him, the world was silent except for the low, whispering wail of the wind. The mammoth did not roar again, but Torka thought of Nap and Alinak, of Egatsop and of little Kipu, of all whom lay dead, looking at the sky.

He opened his eyes. The wind whirled around him, once again speaking to him of the thousand ways in which a man might die. The wild dog was watching him. Their eyes met. Then Torka looked away, not wanting an animal to see what he would not reveal to Umak or Lonit.

Torka was afraid.

8

"Now we must go from this place."

Torka's announcement stunned both Umak and Lonit. They stared at him. His face was grim. His arms were folded across his chest. He had made a necklace of the paws of the wolves that had been killed, this not to honor the spirits of the beasts but to show mastery of them. They had fed upon the bodies of his people. By taking the paws, he had prevented the beasts' life spirits from walking the spirit world. He had killed the wolves. Forever. And now their claws hung downward over his outer tunic, the paws still bleeding around the thong that pierced their flesh.

He saw the expressions of astonishment upon Umak's and Lonit's faces. He knew that by asking them to abandon this camp, he was also asking them to leave behind most of the meat that they had taken. Hours of work would be wasted. The lives of the caribou that they had killed would be wasted, and this would be a grievous offense to the life spirits of the game. Yet it must be risked.

"In a new life, men must seek new ways." He looked directly at Umak as he quoted the old man's words. "Umak has given new life to Torka and Lonit. Now we must walk from this camp, as Umak walked from the winter camp of the People because he knew that he could not defend the living from the beasts that would come to eat of the dead. The wolves have shown us that this camp cannot be defended." He paused. The next words would be difficult for his listeners to digest. "We must go to the far mountain. Upon its flanks, we will make a new camp and will have the advantage over any predator that would come against us. Upon its flanks, we will have a new life. Here, in this camp, we cannot live, except in the blood of the beasts that will come to eat us."

Lonit flinched. Her face paled. The People had always avoided the mountains. It was well-known that the wind spirits lived there, eternally giving birth to clouds and storms. Lonit had heard their voices many times . . . in terrible, deep roarings and crackings . . . in desolate moanings that echoed in the canyons and wailed out onto the tundra from high, unknown vastnesses where the People had never gone— not even to follow the caribou. To venture into the high realm of the wind spirits was to risk vanishing into the eternal cold and ice of the misted heights where the wind spirits took form in the ephemeral flesh of the clouds. Huge. Churning. Shape changing. Man- and woman-eating.

Lonit shuddered.

Torka did not have to be told what she was thinking. He knew of the tales that were told of the wind spirits. "We will make our camp on the *flank* of the mountain," he emphasized, frowning at her for her unspoken challenge of his decision. "We will not go high."

His words were not comforting. She was still not feeling well. To camp anywhere even near a mountain was unthinkable. She remembered a story that her mother had told:

Long ago, in yesterdays that existed only on the far edges of the People's group memory, a headman whose name was long forgotten led the band to make an encampment close to a high peak. Hunting was good. Many days passed. Then, in the time of the endless sun, the wind spirits grew jealous of the band's good fortune. They caused a great mass of ice to fall from the heights of the mountain. It buried the encampment. Many died. Never again had the People risked offending the wind spirits by venturing too close to their mountains.

Lonit would have liked to remind Torka of this. But surely he knew it! He was Torka. He would suggest nothing that might prove hazardous to them. They *were* at risk upon the open tundra. Her recently stitched and bound arm testified to that. Still, a knot tightened in her stomach when she thought of the far mountain. She told herself that she was being foolish. They could not stay where they were. It was not safe. And they could not go back. There was nothing to go back to—no People, no camp. Only a hostile land where the caribou now grazed the greening tundra and, somewhere, the great, man-killing mammoth walked. Its shadowed, bloody memory was more terrifying than any mountain.

Lonit swallowed down her fear. If Torka's plan was unsound, the spirit master would question it. But Umak remained silent. He did not even harrumph. The girl relaxed. If Torka and the spirit master were in agreement, everything would be all right.

They dismantled the pit hut. Torka observed Umak as they worked. He was concerned. The incident with the wolves had changed the old man. Although the teeth of the beasts had ripped Lonit's arm, they had given Umak a deeper wounding. He moved slowly, lethargically, favoring his bad leg. He showed no interest in the wolf that he had slain; he had killed the beast, but something in him seemed to have died with it.

Torka cut the paws from Umak's wolf. He strung them upon a length of thong. He went to his grandfather and hung them around the old man's neck.

"For Kipu. For Egatsop. For the People who lie looking at the sky. This wolf runs no more, in this world or the next, because Umak has killed him. Forever."

Torka's statement had been meant to bolster the old man's wounded spirit, but it did not succeed. Umak accepted the necklace without so much as a grunt or a nod. He knew that his performance against the wolves had been less than adequate, and he knew that Torka knew it. No words could stanch the inner bleeding that was slowly draining the old man of the last vestiges of his pride.

Now, as Torka watched his grandfather listlessly assembling his traveling pack, Umak seemed to be shrinking before his eyes—aging, growing weaker. Soon he would dry up and disappear altogether. Without a sense of self-esteem, even a young man could lose the will to live, and even the bravest man could become useless on the hunt. For a nomad of the tundra, death must soon follow the ultimate degradation of being proved worthless before one's peers. Torka felt sick with frustration. To live in a world without Umak would be to live in a world eternally deprived of light. He could not bear to think of it; he had lost too much already. Umak had saved his life. And Lonit's. Umak had brought them out of the winter camp, away from certain death, to a new life. Torka would not stand by and watch him slowly waste away. He knew that he must counter his grandfather's will to die, even if it meant trying to shame him back into a sense of pride.

He walked slowly to where the old man crouched beside Lonit. They sorted through their things, readying to roll them into their pack skins. "Hmmph!" said Torka as nastily as he could. "Umak works with the speed of an old woman! Look, even a girl with one arm in a sling works more quickly than Umak!"

Lonit looked up at Torka, her mouth agape.

Umak froze. Never had his grandson spoken to him with such open contempt. He took the words as truth. He let them settle. "Umak *is* old," he said.

"It must be so," agreed Torka disdainfully. "Look at Umak! No doubt he will now ask Torka to carry the bulk of the girl's load plus some of his own because Umak is old and the girl is injured. Hmmph! Or will he put his old man's spirit into Brother Dog so that even a beast will be burdened by the weight of one old man?"

This was too much. Umak reacted as though stung. He was on his feet with the speed and agility of a man half his years. "No man . . . no girl . . . not even Brother Dog will carry Umak's weight! This old man has come this far without assistance! This old man has carried Torka when Torka had not even the strength of a spiritless suckling to lift his own weight off the ground!"

Relief flooded through Torka. It warmed him. It almost made him smile. Insult was a venom with healing power. It had put the fire of life back into Umak's eyes.

Lonit stared from one man to the other, not understanding. She was horrified to think that she might be the cause of enmity between them. "Lonit will carry her own load! Lonit is strong! Lonit needs no help!"

Torka measured her with withering reproof. "Almost A Woman has an arm with many stitches in it. Almost A Woman will *not* carry a full load. She will need Torka *and* Umak to help her. But Umak says that he is old. Perhaps he would prefer to stay in this place. Perhaps he would find it easier to give his life spirit to the wind than to go with Torka and Lonit. Perhaps our life spirits will soon join his because without Umak, our loads will be great and our weariness will slow our steps. Perhaps when next wolves come to feed upon us, they will not go hungry from our camp. They will howl their praises of one old man who was too weak to continue!"

Umak's eyes bulged. His mouth arched downward above the outthrust jab of his chin. "Hrrmph! This old man will show the suckling Torka what he can carry! This old man will see who can walk farthest before growing too weak to continue on!"

Lonit looked at Umak, then at Torka. Suddenly she understood. Umak seemed reborn! She knew what Torka had done. She smiled. She would walk to the mountain with confidence now. She would not be afraid, knowing that she would walk in the company of *two* spirit masters.

They moved on. The hills were behind them now, extending along the western horizon like the mounded forms of sleeping, white-crested animals. Behind those hills, the land of their ancestors lay cold and bleak, icebound save for the east-facing valleys and narrow, tundral plains from which the People had been eking a tenuous existence for countless generations.

Ahead the land rolled eastward toward the distant mountain. To the north and south the tundra stretched for a thousand miles before vanishing into the ice-choked depths of waters that would someday be called the Chukchi and Bering Seas.

Torka led the way. Umak followed behind Lonit. The dog trotted at his side across the broad, taut flexings of the greening land. With the coming of spring, the daytime temperature climbed to just above freezing. The world filled with the sound of the awakening land as snowbanks began to melt and glacial runoff poured out of distant mountains to transform the tundra. In a few hours it would all freeze again, but as the travelers walked across the open, wind-driven miles, streams and rivulets were everywhere. Lakes and ponds, thick with ice-sludge but no longer totally frozen, glistened in the slanting light of the sun.

They were not aware of when the lay of the land began to change. It led them subtly downward over shouldering humps of low hills that were thick with unfamiliar wormwood and sagelike scrub. The inclination was so illusory that they were unaware of it until their shins began to ache from the unrelieved stress.

The dog stopped first, head up, tail curled, nostrils working to sieve the wind. There was something different about it. Torka noticed it, too, as did Umak. They stopped. The girl paused beside them. Her arm ached within the sling made of strips of caribou hide. Her load was lighter by half since Umak and Torka had insisted upon dividing much of it between them. Still, it was a heavy burden; its weight intensified the dull, deep cramps that refused to leave her lower belly. Readjusting her pack frame, she wished that the cramps would go away. She hoped they did not mean her slow but imminent death. She felt miserable as she leaned forward, hefting her pack higher onto her back. As she did so, she looked down, her attention suddenly drawn to a scattering of stones that lay at her feet.

Her first thought was that, at last, she had found the perfect weights for her stone hurler, for they were all of similar size, approximately that of the eyeball of a large caribou. Then, as she bent to pick up one of the stones, she frowned, puzzled. Its sleek, spiraling configurations were so beautiful that she caught her breath. It was like no stone that she had ever seen.

It was not a stone.

It was a shell—or had been, untold millennia ago. Now it was a fossil. It was heavy in the girl's hand. She stared at it, not understanding how a shell could be made of rock, or how a rock could be shaped like a shell. Her frown deepened.

There was no way Lonit could know that the object in her hand had once lain at the bottom of a wide, shallow strait of water. She could not know that the climate of the world had changed, that when glaciers lay upon the earth, they held much of the world's moisture captive, and as they grew, oceans shrank . . . seas atrophied . . . a strait rapidly became a scattering of saltwater lakes and ponds trapped within the low-lying depressions of its exposed sea bed. Gradually such drying bodies of water thickened with the detritus of a dying age, suffocating all living things that had not managed to swim or crawl to deeper, life-sustaining waters. With the passing of years, a strait could completely disappear. And shells such as the one that Lonit held in her hand could be buried in the sediment of centuries, transformed into stone by time and the inexorable processes of fossilization.

Now, brought to the surface by the pawing hooves of migrating caribou, the shell spoke to Lonit of another epoch, of another world; but it spoke in a language that the girl could not understand.

Where once the blue, shining waters of the Bering Strait

had stretched beneath the Arctic sky from the coast of Siberia to the shores of Alaska, now the skin of the continental shelf lay bared beneath Lonit's feet.

It was the fragrance of that skin that had brought Torka, Umak, and the dog to pause. The layering of soil that lay upon the permafrost was thicker, redolent of the vaguely astringent stink of primordial ooze, of the thousand unnamed species of marine flora and fauna that had lived and died and decomposed to form the flesh of this land. It spoke of ancient seas, and of warmer skies in which a more beneficent sun rose and set over a less hostile world. Through their highly developed sense of smell, the hunters knew that the tundral plain that lay ahead of them was different from any land across which they had ever walked, but Torka and Umak could not describe the difference. They were men of the Age of Ice. They had never seen a sea or an ocean, nor could they imagine a gentler world or a wind that blew beneath a benevolent sun.

"Look!" Umak pointed off. Eastward, between them and the still-distant mountain, the shapes of high-humped, shaggy camels could be seen grazing. The old man counted three of them, then squinted and nodded to affirm another. And there were musk ox! "So much game!" he exclaimed.

Torka made no comment; to have spoken would have been to confirm the obvious. The sun was as high as it was going to get this day. Soon it would be dark. The mountain was still far away, and he would not rest content or allow his "band" to hunt until they had made a safe encampment upon its flanks.

"We will go," he said, and after Lonit had scooped up several more fossil shells, he led them on and on, across the wide, rolling land that had once lain at the bottom of the sea.

They trudged toward the broad, snowcapped mountain that, in future millennia, would not be a mountain at all but an island rising out of a shallow sea. It would be called Big Diomede, after a prince of Argos, a hero among a race of men who would not be born for another forty thousand years.

But Torka's thoughts were not of the future as Umak, Lonit, and the wild dog followed him toward that shining mountain. He thought of the past—of the dead, of all that he had left behind him as, unknowing, he lengthened his stride and led his people out of Asia toward a new world.

PART III

MOUNTAIN OF POWER

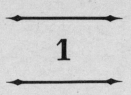

1

They walked until the dark came down, but still the mountain loomed ahead, its huge snowcap glistening in the night.

Exhausted, their bodies aching with fatigue, they stopped and dug a communal burrow into the lee side of a tundral hummock. They spread their sleeping skins, and after eating a meal of dried caribou meat, they bundled together like foxes beneath the windswept indigo sky.

They slept. Umak smiled in his dreams. He was content. He had matched Torka step for step across the miles. It was the young man who had called for rest, not the old.

Lonit also smiled in her dreams, for now she kept a secret from her men. She lay with her back to them, curled up at the very edge of their sleeping burrow. If they knew her secret, they would make her sleep alone, and she was afraid of that—the tundra was too dark, too strange, and too threatening. So she kept her secret, understanding at last that she would not die from the cramps that had been plaguing her. Had she been among the women of the band, she would have understood long before now. She would not have been surprised when she had made her discovery. Never again would Torka have just cause to call her Almost A Woman. The spirits of her gender had found her worthy. Lonit had begun to shed a woman's blood at last. Luckily, she had brought enough scrap cuttings of skin left over from her sewing to conceal her secret from her men.

Torka lay awake for a long while. He would have preferred to go on, but the mountain was farther than he had thought. When at last he succumbed to sleep, his dreams were troubled; they kept him on the edge of wakefulness, and for this he was glad. He wanted to remain alert to danger. He had not forgotten the wolves. He could sense the tension ebb and flow within the dog; he shared it and for the first time was grateful for the presence of Umak's spirit brother, which lay at the crest of the hummock, just out of the wind, a self-appointed sentry. If predators came to sniff out the scent of man, the dog would give warning. Torka conceded that perhaps the animal's loyalty to Umak was not without advantages.

Because of the dog, Torka allowed himself to sleep in fitful spurts. His dreams were troubled, filled with sound—a low, deep roaring that filled the world. He led Umak and Lonit across miles of darkness, spilled across the endless black plain of his dream. A wall of water surged toward him, as black as night, as high as the mountain toward which he led his band. The incomprehensibly huge wave roared as it threatened to sweep across the world and drown everything before it. In his dream, he ran, and Umak and Lonit and the dog ran with him; but the wave came on and on . . . and they were swept away . . . into a black, choking limbo where their life spirits were lost forever.

He awoke with a start and sat bolt upright. He stared eastward, toward the mountain, into the face of the rising sun. The night was gone. A new day had been born. And Torka, who could not know that his dream had been a vision of the past—and of the future—was glad to be alive as he was warmed by the light of the dawn that swept across the tundra and turned the entire world to gold.

They walked on, single file, with the dog in the lead now. Umak strode out ahead of the girl, and Torka walked close behind her. She leaned into the wind and watched the dog trotting on, its tail up, curled high over its back.

Ordinarily, the sight of the animal would have been comforting to Lonit. The dog's manner often amused her, and she was certain that, if danger lay ahead, the dog would alert its human pack. But then Lonit began to sense that they were being watched. She frowned. Aar kept his pace, heading ever eastward toward the mountain. If he sensed eyes watching them, he showed no sign of it.

After a while, although the sensation of being watched remained strong, Lonit told herself that she was being a foolish female. After all, Umak, Torka, and the dog were hunters. Her senses were not nearly as acute as theirs. And it was well-known that when a woman was in her time of blood, her thinking was as erratic as her moods. Had she been traveling with the People, she would have been isolated from all except females in the same condition. They would have trudged along at the very rear of the column lest their condition infect the others with all sorts of bad luck.

Flushed from her guilty feelings, she was glad that neither Torka nor Umak could see her face. Her cheeks blazed with her deception, and if her men saw her, they would know she was keeping something from them and be angry. They might even command her to walk away from them forever. She would deserve no better. But no, she was the only female in the world, and they would not send her away. But they *would* make her walk behind them. Tradition and taboo would demand it. And it was this that she feared, for the one who walked at the end of a traveling column was the one most vulnerable to predators. A group of women might be safe enough, but long ago, when she had been a little girl, she had seen a straggler mauled by a lion. The woman had fallen back to relieve herself, and the huge, shaggy feline had leaped upon her from behind a tundral hummock where it had lain in wait until the entire traveling column had passed. By the time the men of the band had rallied to kill the marauder with their spears, it had been too late for the woman. Lonit had never forgotten what the woman had looked like when the lion had finished with her.

She shivered and kept up with her men. Torka, Umak, and the dog would know if something observed them. In the meantime, she tried not to think of either lions or the wind spirits, which might be observing their approach from the cold, savage heights of their distant mountain. With her eyes turned down, she willed herself to think of nothing but the next step, and the next, and the next, until Umak came to a sudden stop and she bumped right into him.

"Look!" He seemed unaware that she had blundered into him. He pointed off as, wilting, the girl followed his gaze.

There, directly ahead of them, a huge skeleton lay upon the land. Torka's hand curled so tightly around the hafts of his spears that his fingers ached. His teeth clenched. It was all he could do to keep himself from crying out.

The Destroyer . . . Thunder Speaker . . . He Who Parts the Clouds . . . World Shaker . . .

"No!" Torka shouted his disbelief of a truth that was unbearable. If that enormous rubble heap of bones belonged to the great mammoth, then he would never be able to kill it with his own hands. Until this moment, he had not known just how much he still longed to do this, regardless of Umak's sage advice and of all odds and obstacles—even if, in killing the beast, he forfeited his own life. The confrontation was all that mattered, to stare once more into the red, man-hating eyes, to drive his spear home . . . in memory of his slain people, for Egatsop, his woman, and for Kipu, the beloved little son whom he would never hold proudly upon his shoulders while the child's laughter rang out with the joy of life.

Bile was bitter at the back of his throat. Tears stung beneath his lids as he choked back a cry of agonizing frustration. With his spear arm raised, he ran forward, with the dog at his heels and Umak and Lonit racing after him.

They stood together in silence, examining the skeletal remains of a creature unlike any they had ever seen. Torka experienced a soaring sense of relief, even as Umak grunted to express a disappointment that he shared with the girl.

"No mammoth this," said the old man, wondering where the great beast grazed now, hoping that it was far, far from this stretch of tundra.

Lonit stood stiffly against unwelcome memories. She stared at the strange elongated bones. She was sorry that they were not those of the mammoth that had destroyed the lives of the People. Somewhere, that beast still lived. Somewhere, it shook the world with its mighty, hateful trumpetings. Somewhere. But not here. Umak had led them away from it. But what if it had veered eastward? What if it had come out of a tundral valley onto this very plain? What if it walked ahead of them? What if it were the thing that she had sensed watching them across the miles? She shuddered. It was too terrible to consider.

The dog whined softly. It circled the enormous carcass, sniffing ardently before losing interest when its nose told it that these were ancient bones, without promise of a meal. With an exhaled snuff of disdain, it trotted around the massive length of bones, sniffing and snorting, and leg-lifting here and there to mark its places of passage. Seating itself at last, it yawned and stared eastward as though to inform its fellow travelers that there was nothing of interest to keep them here and it would just as soon get on with their journey.

But the carcass had captured Torka's interest. Never had he seen anything even remotely like it. Half-buried in the tundra, from head to toe it was over seventy-five feet long. He paced the distance twice, just to be certain that he was not imagining it. Legless, tuskless, and toothless, it had the look of an enormous fish. But how could a fish have come to its death upon dry land? And of all the streams and pools and rivers he had ever seen, where was there water wide enough or deep enough to contain the swimmings of such a fish?

Umak seemed to know his grandson's mind. Their eyes met. Umak nodded, grunted, and puckered his lips. "In the time of the great rain, when the waters gathered to walk upon the earth, in this time such a fish would have had wide water to swim in and deep water to hide in. It is said that the flesh of the People was food for fish in that time." He paused, and the Creation stories that he had learned from the old men in the long-gone days of his boyhood returned to fill his mind. Again he nodded, comforted now by the sight of the impossibly huge carcass; it confirmed the truth of the tales. Only in great waters could such a fish exist. Still, Umak was a man of his own time, of the tundra. It was difficult for him to imagine an ocean, much less a whale.

Torka recalled his dream, the great black wall of water sweeping across the plain. He reached out and touched a portion of the skeletal remains of the whale. His hand rested upon a portion of fossilized rib. He knew from experience that fish bones dried and blew away in the wind and were not like the hard bones of man and beast. But this . . . beneath his ungloved palm, the bone was rough, as unyielding as rock. The dream washed through his mind again. He saw the wave coming toward him from the south, north, east, and west. It surrounded him, reared up, and showed a mile-high wall of watery death as black as the fluid that filled the eyeball of a caribou. The blackness thickened and shone as sleek as obsidian. It roared. It rose higher and higher, and then it began to fall, to curl into lips that foamed like the mouth of a man filled with mad spirits.

Torka willed himself up and out of his vision before it drowned him. As he did so, he brought his hand up from the whalebone, then down again in a reflex action that had so much power behind it, it cracked the fossilized bone in two. The upper portion fell at his feet.

Umak's eyes went round. Both he and the girl made sounds of wonder, and then the old man's face clouded. Torka took a step back from the broken bone and would have turned away had Umak not cried out to stop him.

"No! The hand of Torka has cleft the bone. The life spirit of the great fish has yielded to Torka's power. It has given a part of itself as a gift to the man. Torka cannot walk away!" He wanted to add: *Or it will follow. It will become a crooked spirit. It will feed off Torka's soul, and Torka will die.* But he dared not speak so, lest he guarantee that his warning come to pass. He said instead: "You take!"

Torka recognized Umak's words as an undeniable command. The old man was right. Although he had not spoken his warning aloud, Torka saw it clearly on his face. He could not disobey. He knelt and stared at that which had fallen at his feet.

Torka sucked in his breath, amazed. The bone was slightly shorter than his forearm, with a natural arch, and it was clear that the force of his blow had done more than merely fracture it from the main portion of the rib. Where the break had been made, the bone was as sharp as a dagger. He could not have flaked it more cleanly if he had tried, nor could his most meticulous knapping have achieved a sharper edge. He ran the inner edge of his thumb lightly along the break to test it, then quickly drew it back again. Although he had applied only the slightest pressure, he had drawn blood.

"Hmmph!" exclaimed Umak. His chin went up, and he nodded his head with approval.

Torka smiled despite his dark mood. He did not like this piece of fish rib that was neither bone nor stone, but it was good to see that Umak was feeling arrogant again, assuming credit for the discovery by having ordered Torka to take the bone. He lifted the blunt end of the broken piece of whalebone into his hand; he hefted this gift from the life spirit of the great fish that he knew was, somehow, not a fish. He raised it high as he got to his feet. He tested it for balance and decided that, like it or not, it would make an extraordinary weapon. "I take," he said, conceding.

Umak harrumphed again.

Once again, they went on toward the mountain. This time, not only Lonit was discomfited by the sensation of being watched. Torka felt it, too, but the eyes of his vision stared from within, and now again he turned to look back, half expecting to see the wave of his nightmare vision rising to follow. There was nothing there—only the empty miles and the skeleton of the whale growing smaller and smaller. Then it was gone.

And still they walked on.

2

The land tilted upward as they neared the mountain. They left behind the broad, open expanse of rolling grassland and entered a realm of high hills. There were grasses here, too, interspersed with wide stretches of tussocked marsh plants and communities of familiar mosses and lichens, but now they passed stands of droop-branched, man-high spruce trees. Umak and Torka instinctively looked for signs of mammoth. They knew that spruce was the favorite fodder of the great beasts; but if mammoth browsed here, they left no sign. Relieved, Umak walked on with Lonit and the dog at his heels.

Torka paused, his eyes inextricably drawn back across the way they had come. The plain lay far below. The miles seemed to tremble in a glaring haze born of distance. And in that haze, upon the far horizon, he could just make out a dark form following . . . its back as high as the distant hills, its tusks glinting in the sun, its color as red as dried blood.

Squinting, he put a hand across his brow to cut the glare and saw . . . nothing.

Still he stared, his eyes burning and his heart pounding. *Mammoth. Thunder Speaker. World Shaker. The Destroyer.* He nearly raged the words aloud. He *wanted* the beast to be there, to be coming toward him across the plain, to be following him into the high hills where, hidden by the scrub spruce, he could lie in ambush. As in the dream that he had dreamt after he and Umak had slain the condor, he could see himself swooping down upon the mammoth from the heights. He could see himself driving home a killing spear. In memory of his lost family, he could see himself—

"Torka!" Umak called, gesturing him on.

He stood still. Memories of the dream ebbed away. He knew that he would need a spear fashioned out of the power of a lightning bolt if he were ever to pierce the hide of that monster and drive a killing point deep enough to rupture its heart. In all the world, there was no such weapon. And except in his dreams, no man could hope to stand against the Destroyer twice and live to tell the tale.

He went on, troubled by his thoughts, satisfied that what he had seen on the horizon had been a trick of the haze induced by his overly active imagination. Still, he thought of the mammoth as he walked. He was so absorbed in his frustrated lust to kill, he took no note of the changing landscape.

The dark stands of fragrant spruce were rare now. The travelers had entered a forest that was unique to the high Arctic: a mixed woodland of tiny conifers and hardwoods, of dwarfed trees that were products of extreme cold and endless wind, of a paucity of light during one half of the year and an excess of it during the other. Composed of willow, spruce, and birch in the main, many of the trees were hundreds of years old, yet not even the most ancient of them reached a height much above the travelers' ankles. They grew with the inexorable slowness of lichens, adapting to their environment so perfectly that, in places, it was difficult to tell that they were trees at all. They grew flat to the ground as though consciously seeking to absorb the maximum warmth of the sun as they sprawled out, not up, extending their branches protectively out of the way of the wind.

The mountain was close now. A huge, black-shouldered, ice-mantled giant, it filled the sky ahead of them. They paused to rest, staring up at it in awed silence. The mountain seemed to exhale its breath upon them from out of the frozen heart of its soaring, glacier-choked canyons. From somewhere within the massive ice cap that sprawled across its summit, there came a grinding, wrenching sound, which caused Lonit to wince against her fear of wind spirits. Umak frowned. Never had he seen a mountain so massive. Torka eyed it with cool speculation. The peak itself was intimidating, but where its tundral flanks rose to merge with hard, unyielding walls of rock, a safe encampment might be made upon any of dozens of wide, high ledges that erosion and time had conspired to carve into a base of the mountain.

"We go," he said at last, impatient to find just such a site before nightfall.

They went on.

Lonit's arm arched within its sling, and a low fever burned within her blood. She felt hot, tired, and irritable, but she made no complaint. She walked resolutely behind Torka, doing her best to keep up with his long stride. Twice she tripped over nothing but kept her balance and did not break her pace. She bit her lip. To do less would prove her unworthiness to Torka. Despite all of her best efforts, she knew he still thought the worst of her. She tried to remember the times when he had been kind to her, so long ago, in another world, when she had been a child. Now she was a woman, the only woman, and he hated her for that. She could not blame him. She drew in a breath and held it, drawing off as much strength from it as she could. In time, perhaps he would see that she was not so bad. In time, she might come to see that, too. But now she was tired, disgusted with herself for being a miserable excuse for a female. Her arm hurt so much. The wolf had done more than rip skin and muscle; it had bruised the bone as well.

Despite herself, she slowed her pace, grateful that Torka did not look back to see her display of weakness. Umak would see to it that she kept up. The old man seemed to be concerned for her. Why? She could not say, other than she was the only female in the world. Still, it was apparent to Lonit that, even with this in her favor, she was not worth much.

Umak watched the girl plodding on ahead of him. It was obvious that she did not feel well. He saw her trip and regain her balance with only the slightest break in stride. Admiration for her sparked. At their last rest stop, he had noted fever shining brightly from her eyes. She had said nothing. He knew that her arm must be hurting; it had taken many sutures to repair the damage that the wolf had done to the tender flesh of her inner forearm. As Umak watched Torka walking steadfastly on, he growled to himself. The dog looked up at him curiously as the old man wondered how Torka could have no concern for the girl. Not once had he turned back to make certain that his pace was not too fast for her. *He* had seen the extent of the wolf's mauling. He had witnessed her bold leap into danger when she had seen the wolves menacing her men. How could he be so calloused toward her? The old man's mouth puckered over his teeth. He worried about Torka. The wounds of grief were not healing.

He had never been a hard man before. *Never*. But he was hard now.

Hmmph, thought Umak, feeling protective and tender toward the girl. *If Torka is too stubborn to see Lonit's merit, Umak is not*. A growing sense of sole responsibility for the girl made him feel almost young again. "Hmmph!" he said aloud, and again the dog looked at him, cocking its black-masked head. Umak directed his conversation toward the dog. "Next time wolves come against this old man, they will see that he is not so old as they would like! Lonit will see this, too."

Umak nodded, satisfied with his boast. He had no doubt that he had spoken truly. He felt strong again, virile again; his bad leg barely ached. He paused beside an ice-flowered freshet that ran through a small grove of finger-high budding willows. Half-buried within a thick embankment of marsh plants, the little stream invited the dog to drink. Umak watched the animal lap at the cold water, then bent and began to break off several twigs from the green-stalked willows. Half of these he stuffed into the all-purpose medicine bag that he carried at his belt; Lonit had made it for him out of the skin of the condor, with the downy breast feathers still attached.

He rose, placing the remainder of the twigs between his teeth as he wiped his hands on his traveling robe. His fingers ached with cold, but he barely noticed as he trotted purposefully after Lonit. He was not the least bit breathless when he caught up with her. He held the twigs in his right hand as, with his left, he cupped her elbow and brought her to a stop, turning her toward him.

"Here. You take. Magic spirits live in the green stalk of the willow. Good spirits, too small for a girl or even a spirit master to see."

She was grateful for the chance to rest but hoped that he did not see this in her stance or expression. She stood still, not understanding what he wanted her to do with his strange gift of twigs.

Seeing her hesitancy, he explained with robust enthusiasm. "You chew stalks! You release willow spirits into your mouth. They will run away into your body. They will do the willow-spirit dance. They will eat your fever. They will steal your pain. Then they will go away, grateful to Lonit for nourishing them."

She bowed her head. He had seen her weariness. He had probably seen her stumble. Umak must think that she was the most unworthy female ever born. But to her surprise and confusion, before she could vilify herself further, the old man's strong, big-knuckled fingers poked at her chin, gently prodding her to look at him. And when she did, she was shocked to see that he was smiling.

"Lonit has walked far with wounds. Lonit is brave. Lonit is strong. To Lonit, Umak gives the willow spirits. They are not for those who are unworthy."

Her face flushed with shame. Did he actually believe what he said? No. He was just being kind. He was trying to make her feel better. Slowly, as she walked beside him, she obliged him by chewing on the willow stalks. They were bitter, but soon she began to marvel at the old man's magic. Not only had he mastered the spirit of a wild dog, but now he commanded the spirits of a tree! As he had promised, her fever lessened. The ache in her arm decreased. She thanked him. He grunted, obviously pleased with himself as he told her to thank the willow spirits instead. This she did and tried to envision them; tiny green feasters dancing within her body. She wondered if they had names, as men and women had names. She wondered if they looked like trees, with branching arms and limbs and leafy hair. She wondered if they ate pain raw or cooked it in the heat of fever.

She walked on, feeling immeasurably better; but as her fever ebbed, her fear grew. The mountain towered ahead, shadowing the world. And from its savage heights, something *was* watching them.

Torka paused. Umak and the girl came to stand beside him. They could all feel it now. The dog stopped near the old man's side, head down.

Wind spirits, thought the girl, and knew that against their fierce and vicious nature, the gentle, healing spirits of the willow would be powerless.

Lions, thought Umak. *Or bears. Or wolves.* Memories pierced through him. His chin went up. He did not want to think of his earlier failure with the wolves, but he did. He wondered how he would perform when they came upon larger and more dangerous prey.

Torka stood tall, his eyes slitted against the wind and glare. *It could be anything*, he thought. A great, stalking mountain cat. A short-faced bear just emerging from its winter sleep. Or only a bird, a falcon or an eagle. Or a lemming, or mouse, or a fat marmot sunning itself on a ridge, its shiny little eyes taking in the progress of human travelers with only the dullest form of interest. Whatever it was, it could not be more threatening than anything that they had already faced on the open tundra. Even if it proved to be a large flesh-eater, its threat was lessened by their knowing that it was there to menace them.

As his eyes scanned the heights, they focused upon a high cornice that jutted out from the up-thrusting, west-facing wall of the mountain. Above that huge, protruding pout of granite, a series of caves pocked the wall. Their size and placement intrigued him. If they could be reached, the largest and deepest would offer excellent shelter from the wind and weather and give them protection from predators as well. *If* the cave were not already occupied by predators. He was certain that Umak would give him an argument. He was not disappointed.

"Hunters of the band do not live like beasts in caves!" the old man protested. "Hunters of the band must live as our fathers have always lived—beneath the open sky!"

The light of day was fading. Rain clouds were gathering. A cold wind was sliding down off the summit ice pack. Far below them on the tundral plain, dire wolves began to howl. Torka saw Lonit cringe against the sound and measured her weariness against his own fatigue and the many miles they had come this day.

"We must make camp," he said. "Soon it will be dark. Wolves or even larger prey hunters may be on our scent. Father of my father, we are all that is left of our band. We are at risk as long as we camp in the open. To camp against the mountain wall would be a good thing. To camp *within* it would be even better. Umak has spoken the words of wisdom himself: In a new life, men must seek new ways."

The old man harrumphed. He looked up at the caves with a hostile squint. He did not like the look of them, but he was a spirit master and could not bring himself openly to oppose his own words of wisdom. "We will see," he pronounced.

And they went on.

They found the way to the caves with little difficulty, although they continued to feel eyes watching them. They had been walking across the tough, spongy skin of the tundra, but now they stepped out across the bare bones of the mountain, traversing the high, sandy shoulder and picking their way across a tumbled outwash of glacial till and scree. They walked around the mountain, and as they looked up from the base of the mountain's eastern wall, the peak seemed to be a part of the gathering night. Although miles around, the mountain was not as high as it had seemed from a distance.

They stood in the lee of a narrow canyon, where an ice-choked stream flowed sluggishly over a stony bed. Here and there were patches of hardy soil, just enough to support a few clumpy mounds of sedge grass and low-growing alpine shrubs. Where the canyon wall absorbed the most sunlight, there was a bedraggled stand of spruce trees. They clustered close together, droop-armed and bent-headed, like costumed hunters frozen in a dream dance. In the rapidly thickening twilight, the trees looked black. The strong, unmistakable stink of a musteline cut the frigid air.

Weasel or wolverine. Not much danger there. While the dog sniffed out the unfamiliar terrain, the travelers searched for signs and scents that would reveal the presence of other, larger animals, but nothing indicated that they were trespassing into the territory of any creature that might prove a threat to them.

They turned their attention to their destination. The caves were some three hundred feet above them, hidden from view by the overhanging lip of the cornice. Torka pointed out a series of horizontal breaks in the narrow fissure that angled steeply upward from the base of the rock wall to the cornice. It looked as though a giant hand had gouged a stairway into the stone. It was the only access route to the caves and would prove a dizzying, difficult climb for any creature that did not possess wings, but its degree of difficulty was proof that no larger cat or bear would have made the climb before them.

Except for the dog, they made the ascension without incident. The precipitous alignment of the route caused the dog to hesitate. It stood at the base of the wall, watching with perplexed apprehension as its pack climbed without it. It barked twice. Umak, the last in line, paused and called down, urging the dog to follow; the way was steep, but with effort, Aar could make it. The dog, not convinced, stood its ground.

"It is nearly dark, and a storm threatens," Torka reminded Umak. "Come, Father of my father. Leave the dog to make its own way."

The old man bristled. "Umak will not leave his brother!"

Torka was distracted by the quick, shallow breathing of the girl. Lonit, right behind him, was obviously exhausted. He reached down and extended a hand, offering to assist her. He would reason with Umak later. The old man had a blind spot when it came to the dog.

"Here," he said, gesturing to the girl to take his hand. "Torka will help you."

She was leaning into the cold, rough face of the rock. The weight of her pack was a frightening burden; not only did its straps cut into her shoulders, but she was desperately afraid that it would throw her off-balance and pull her backward into a fall to her death. Her heart was leaping in her chest, and her mouth was dry. Her wounded arm was hot and aching once again, for using it in the climb had caused it to bleed anew. She was certain that several sutures had pulled free. But she would not let Torka see this further display of weakness. Although she longed to reach up and grip his hand, she demurred.

"Lonit is strong! Lonit needs no help from Torka!"

He hissed his annoyance through his teeth as, disgusted with her, he turned to complete the climb. *What a willful, ungrateful creature she is!* Females! Old men! Dogs! Let them all make their own way!

He reached the lip of the cornice and hauled himself up onto a broad ledge that ran, cavelike, deep into the mountain wall. The girl was close behind him. He could hear her smooth-soled boots slipping on the slag that lay within the footholds. The rasp of her breath came in scrapes of pain. Torka slung off his pack, leaned down, took hold of her pack frame's straps, and pulled her up onto the ledge beside him. She slumped to her knees, head bowed, and visibly trembled as she told him that she had been capable of completing the climb without his assistance. He fought back the impulse to kick her. It never occurred to him that she might not be speaking out of arrogance.

It took Umak a while to convince himself that no amount of persuasion was going to get the dog up onto the ledge without his help. Unfortunately, Aar had not forgotten the unhappy incident with the tether, and although it was Torka who had sought to confine the dog, it did not trust Umak enough to allow the man to touch it. Umak harrumphed. He understood the dog, knew its thoughts as clearly as if the animal had spoken them. Carefully, slowly, he climbed down and tried to assure the dog that if it could not climb as a man climbs, then Umak would carry it. But each time he tried to get close to the dog, Aar backed away from him.

The wolf pack that they had heard earlier was closer now. Its howls sent shivers up and down the old man's back. Torka called down to him, but Umak did not reply. He felt small and vulnerable and very tired beneath the soaring walls of the mountain. It was beginning to rain, and he could not delay his ascent much longer, lest the rocks become too slippery to climb safely. He also felt angry with the dog for not trusting him despite all that they had been through together and frustrated with his powers as spirit master for having failed to coerce the animal into doing his will.

"You! Aar! You will come to Umak!" The command was as bold as the gestures that accompanied it.

The dog cocked its head and looked at Umak as though he were crazy.

"Aar will come to Spirit Master!"

Aar lowered his head. He did not like being shouted at.

"Come! Your brother calls to you! The dog must obey the man!"

The dog began to back away.

Umak leaped at the animal, hoping to grab it and show it that he meant no harm by his touch. But Umak grabbed at air where, scant seconds before, hair and hide and bone had stood. The dog had also leaped. Backward.

Flat on his face, Umak levered up with his gloved hands and glared at the dog. "Stay alone, then! Be meat for wolves! But do not say that Umak did not try to help you!" He rose and wiped clay and pebbles from his trousers and rubbed his bruised knees. "In new times, men must make new ways! So, too, must it be for dogs!"

He turned his back upon the dog. He readjusted the weight of his pack and began to climb. By the time he reached the halfway point, he was feeling guilty. He paused and looked down, then smiled.

Brother Dog was following.

Although the ledge was an alien environment to those born and raised on the open face of the tundra, it had the advantages of being dry, out of the weather, and devoid of threat. A brief exploration revealed that no animal had yet claimed it as a den.

In the darkness, they dropped their packs, spread their sleeping skins, and yielded to exhaustion. They lay at the very back of the enormous, low-ceilinged, roomlike ledge, curled in their furs, close to one another. The dog lay near, but not too close, to Umak. Aar licked his paws, for the way up to the cave had bloodied them, but after a while even the dog slept. The night was filled with the sound of the travelers' deep, even breathing and with the all-pervasive whispering and drumming of the wind and rain. Now and again the rank, musty stink of musteline caused Lonit to stir restlessly in her sleep, as did Torka, but only the dog was roused by it.

Aar raised his head and snuffled. It was pitch black in the cave. Every hair on the dog's back stood upright. Its snuffle became a low, menacing growl. Something was moving in the darkness at the entrance to the cave. It heard the dog and froze.

Suddenly the wind changed. The scent and shadow vanished. The dog, not certain of its own senses, was at the lip of the ledge, where the scent was strongest, sniffing, still growling. Something *had* been there, but the dog could form no picture of it. Its scent was like nothing that the animal had ever smelled before. He lay down. If it came back, he would be ready for it. All night the dog kept vigil for his man pack. Only toward dawn, when the rain turned to snow and the mountain wall became slick with ice, did Aar allow himself to sleep. Nothing could climb the mountain now. Nothing except a wind spirit.

The snow fell in eerie silence—thick, wet snow that smothered the night and filled Lonit's dreams with hauntings. She awoke and saw the dog keeping watch. She let her dreams ebb away. She was glad to release them. Wind spirits had taken form within them, dancing and whirling like snarling, snapping weasels, weasels that stood upright like human hunters as they hacked one another to pieces with bloody, sharpened clubs made of the thighbones of men.

She awoke in a sweat, wishing that she had more of Umak's magic willow stalks to chew on. She knew that she was feverish, but she had no wish to disturb Umak to get more of the stalks from within his medicine bag. She could see it, lying close at his side as he slept, but she would not think of taking anything from it without his permission.

The snowy, clouded light of morning was thin and gray. It gave the stone walls and ceiling of the cave a cold, sinister appearance that seemed to be a remnant from her dreams. But it was real enough, and she did not like it. She longed first for the tundra and the open sky, then for the snug, familiar confines of a pit hut as she rose and began the rituals of morning. Her arm was hot and hurting. She bit her lip. She would tend to it later. Her discomfort was not important. What mattered was to have a fire made and a meal ready by the time her men awoke. She must serve them before she even thought about her own needs.

The snow turned to rain again as she built a small fire of bones and dried sod that she had carried with her in her pack. By the time Torka and Umak were awakened by the scent of its smoke, she had taken strips of dried caribou steaks, wet them with melted snow until they softened a little, then threaded them on thin skewers of bone and set them to cook over the flames.

They sat close together in silence around the little fire. Torka and Umak on one side, Lonit on the other, the dog at a wary distance, watching and salivating until the old man tossed it a portion of his share despite Torka's sullen disapproval. Umak smacked his lips and nodded to show the girl that she had done well. Torka made no effort to display his appreciation. But for Lonit, who had often been severely beaten by her father if he did not like her cooking, his willingness to eat what she had prepared was compliment enough.

The meat was soon gone. The little fire smoked. The sods had been transformed into heat. The burning bones cracked and settled into ashes. Inhibited by their surroundings, the travelers did not speak. Outside, it was still raining hard. Beyond the bleak, barren protection from the elements that their high, rocky aerie afforded, the wind moaned and the rain beat upon the face of the mountain as waterfalls of meltwater cascaded downward from the summit ice pack.

After a while, uncomfortable with their silence, discomfited by the strange sounds of the mountain itself—deep, internal groanings and shiftings that seemed to emanate out of the rock—Umak was inspired to speak. He told the story of how the People came to be created.

"It began on a day like this, long ago. Before the Great Flood, when all living things were male, the first rain fell. It did not turn to snow but stayed as rain for many days and nights, until all living things were drowned except two spirit masters."

Torka and Lonit were enthralled. The old man spoke with the flat, formal cadence of one who has spent over half a lifetime learning to tell a story correctly. He cast an enchantment with his words. Even the dog listened, its head cocked, appearing to understand.

"The two spirit masters took refuge from the rain on a day like this in a cave like this, high on the Mountain of Power. And when at last the waters receded from the world, they were alone. It was not a good thing.

"On a day like this, they sat together. In a cave like this. They grew bored with one another's company. 'Let us put life back into the drowned world,' they said. And this they did. From the Mountain of Power, they made great magic. The sun came back, and day was born again. And the moon came back, spitting out the stars that it had hidden in its mouth, and night was born again. The green plants grew anew, and the animals rose up to live again.

"But when they tried to make new people, they could not do this. They tried and tried again. But the great flood had diluted their powers. They were very tired. They looked out from their cave and were sad. It was not a good thing to be alone in a world with no people."

He paused. His listeners were rapt. It was the most ancient of tales. They had all heard it countless times, but it was comforting to hear it now, on a day like this, in a cave like this, with the rain falling and the mountain holding them high within the clouds as the spirit master's words poured out of the cave and rode upon the back of the wind to tell the spirits of the air and sky of how the People who were no more had been born.

"The two spirit masters slept. The Mountain of Power gave them dreams. On a day like this, in a cave like this, they awoke and knew what they must do if they would make new people. By the magic of the mountain it was done—they copulated, male to male. By the magic of the mountain, one man became pregnant by another. And when the moon had fled from the night nine times, and returned nine times, the first child of the People was delivered out of a man. In blood.

In pain. This was *not* good. So, by the magic of the mountain, First Child became a female. And from that day to this day, woman is created so that males may know the company of other males without ever again being forced to endure the terrible ordeal of childbirth. That is for women. Always and forever."

The story nourished them like a good meal. Umak looked thoughtfully at Torka and Lonit. The cold, high world of the mountain was desolate and strange, but Torka had been right to lead them here. Male and female sat safely together within its sheltering walls of stone. They had survived the destruction of the People, and therefore the People had not been destroyed.

As Lonit sucked the last remnants of flavor from her roasting skewer, the old man found himself appraising her speculatively. Man-need stirred fleetingly in his loins, then disappeared as he chastised himself. *The girl is only a girl. In time she will be a woman. But not now.* He stifled a yawn. The fire was warm. The meat in his belly was as soothing as the juice of the willow. His eyelids felt heavy. He closed them, locked his folded arms around his knees, and allowed himself to nod off to sleep.

For Torka, Umak's Creation tale roused no speculative interest in Lonit's fertility. It roused memories of his lost woman and children. He rose and went to stand at the edge of the cornice, just out of the rain. Looking out across the clouded sky and down to the misted, rainy tundra far below, his thoughts roamed the past.

The sound of falling stone suddenly distracted him, and the rank, glandular stink of musteline intruded into his nostrils. Aar was barking excitedly, standing closer to Torka than he had ever done. Torka walked as close to the edge as he dared and looked over. There was nothing, only the rain, only the clouds, only the precipitous wall of the mountain dropping away into the mists. He cast a glance upward into the rain. When it stopped, he would explore the smaller caves that lay above. Perhaps the musteline lived there and had been drawn down to the larger cave by the smell of roasting meat. Strange that he had not seen it.

Umak was now wide awake and kneeling by Torka's side as he touched the rain-sodden ground, then brought its scent to his nose via his fingertips. Weasel? No. Not quite. The scent was not quite like any animal scent that the old man had ever smelled. It was as though the smells of several species had melded. He sniffed. He did not like it. There was even the vague essence of Man mixed into it. But that was impossible; there were only the three of them alive in all the world. A dark cloud of foreboding rose in him. "If it comes to our cave again, we will kill it," he said, thinking, *before it kills us*.

Torka shrugged. Despite the previous night's rest, he was tired and annoyed with himself for not having seen the intruder before it slipped away. He would have to guard against such carelessness in the future. With Umak at his side and the dog following, he went back to hunker close by the fire where Lonit sat carefully unwrapping her bandages.

She felt so miserably ill that she had barely paid heed to Torka's and Umak's concern over the animal whose essence had permeated the wind. Whatever it had been, it was gone now. She wished that she could say the same for her pain. What she saw beneath the bandages came as no surprise. Her woman's blood had ceased to flow the night before, but her arm was bleeding again and oozing a clear, hot fluid in the few places where Umak's sutures still held fast.

"Aiyee-eh!" exclaimed the old man as he looked at her arm. He dropped to his knees beside the girl and began to examine her wounds with gentle fingers.

Torka was furious with them both. Why had the girl not complained about her arm? Why had she allowed her wounds to fester at the risk of infection? He had seen hunters lose fingers, limbs, and lives because of such carelessness. In her arrogance, did Lonit imagine that she was above the corruption of the flesh? How could Umak coddle her and encourage her irresponsible behavior? What an outrageous, insufferable creature she was! Why, out of all of the women in the band, had she alone survived? Why was his beloved Egatsop not here beside him? The question brought all of the agony back, and the longings.

In a sudden fit of rage, he grabbed Lonit by her good arm, swept her to her feet, and dragged her to the edge of the cornice. She screamed, certain that he was going to throw her off. Instead, he half ripped off her sleeve and held her injured arm out into the rain.

"This female is the only female in the world!" he shouted at Umak. "If the People are to live, they must be born again through her someday! She may think herself above the rest of us, but she is *not*! If she dies, the People die forever. Umak has said this. Umak should remember it. This is *not* the Creation story told again—Torka will not couple with Umak to produce a first child. Of this Umak may be sure! If this female will not care for herself, then Torka will care for her . . . and the care that Torka will give will not be as gentle as that which Umak has given!"

With hard, compassionless fingers he scrubbed her wounds and opened the soft, infected scabs to the cold, clean, healing rain. The girl sobbed and squirmed, but he held her fast until an equally enraged Umak charged him with all the force of a rut-maddened bull caribou.

Taken by surprise by the force of the old man's blow, Torka released his hold on the girl. Lonit collapsed in a heap, and only Umak's strong, broad fist curled tightly into the fabric of Torka's tunic kept him from falling backward off the ledge.

The girl stared in shock, and the dog growled in confusion.

Torka gaped at his grandfather in amazement as rain fell upon them, cooling their tempers.

"Hmmph!" snarled Umak, releasing Torka with disdain. "Torka is brave! Torka is strong! But Torka is blind when it comes to women!"

3

The days passed. Rain continued to fall in intermittent squalls that kept the face of the mountain slippery by day and icy by night. It was not safe to venture out. The travelers were content to remain within the sheltering confines of their aerie. Across the entrance to the ledge they hung the oiled hide that would ordinarily have served as flooring for their pit hut. It proved an effective weather baffle, screening out wind and rain and keeping the floor of their shelter dry. They collected drinking water in bags of oiled skin that Lonit had contrived to hold the rain. They gathered loose stones and placed them in a circle at the back of the cave, making it as good a fire pit as any that they had ever built of sods upon the open tundra. Hungry for warmth after days of wandering in the wind and cold, they piled their skins close to the fire. The stones absorbed the heat of the flames and, unlike sods that burned away to nothing, radiated heat long after the meager fire had died and the meticulously banked coals had cooled.

They slept. They rested. They recouped their strength. Umak filled the hours with tales of the People. Aar lay close to the fire pit, but not so close that any member of the dog's man pack might take it unaware. It watched the entrance to the cave, listening and sniffing for any hint of the foul-smelling intruder, but the mysterious creature did not return. Just in case it did, Torka set a snare across the entrance, hoping to entrap it.

Umak stood by, watching stoically. "Wind spirits will not be caught in the best of Torka's snares. A man cannot hold the mist."

"Perhaps." Torka went to sit by the fire again. He took up

the piece of whalebone that he had taken from the plain and began to wrap a length of sinew binding around its blunt end. "When the rain stops, Torka will hunt it."

"A wise man does not hunt spirits. A wise man makes praise songs to those whose flesh is of air and wind."

"Torka can think of no praise words to sing to a thing that smells like a foul wind blowing out of the hind end of a badger. When the rain stops, this hunter will find out what its flesh is made of. If it is spirit, Torka will praise it. If it is meat, Torka will kill it."

The rain continued. The hunters grew restless. They readied their weapons for future use. Torka began to think of more appetizing prey than mustelines. Like Umak and Lonit, he salivated when he recalled the camels and musk oxen that they had seen on their way to the mountain. When the weather cleared, he would hunt big game before he turned his talents to confrontations with odoriferous mountain dwellers, be they flesh or spirit.

Lonit shared the impatience of her men. She was feeling much better. Her fever was gone, her arm was healing nicely, and her appetite returned just as the supplies of dried caribou meat began to run low. Despite their best conservation efforts, they used most of the sods and bones that she had brought along for fire making. They ate their meals raw and made fires only when it was necessary to cut the chill of the most bitter mornings.

While the men worked to make projectile points out of the odd assortment of stones that they had collected en route to the mountain, Lonit spread out the roughly cured caribou skins that she had packed from their last encampment. It would take hours of meticulous scraping before they were supple enough to be sewn into garments. Undaunted, she applied herself eagerly to the task with her good arm, not only because there was nothing else for her to do, but because she knew that her men would savor the luxury of possessing two sets of clothing again so that they would be able to don clean, dry garments after a day's hunting the muddy tundra. She smiled as she worked. She would make Torka's clothes first: a new pair of trousers to go with the tunic of fox skins that she had stitched for him. *Torka*. She cast him a longing glance, then quickly looked away. She had successfully managed to stay out of his way lest she inadvertently provoke his ire once again. But new clothes would please him, even if they came from a homely, unworthy girl.

The nights were still long and cold. The mountain filled the darkness with strange, otherworldly sounds that made sleeping difficult. The dog would growl now and again. The travelers would awake, but the darkness lay undisturbed, and the snare that Torka had rigged at the entrance to the cave went untripped.

"Whatever walks the dark wind of the mountain night is not of flesh. It is spirit." Umak rose from his sleeping skins, knelt, and raised his arms, rocking back and forth as he chanted a praise song to the invisible spirits of the mountain.

Torka watched him, unconvinced. "We shall see." He burrowed beneath his furs. He went back to sleep and dreamed of mountains made of roaring water and of crooked spirits that walked the earth in the flesh of a mammoth that fed upon the deaths of men. He opened his eyes, suddenly wide awake, listening to the sounds of the summit ice pack shifting in the night. He thought of the Destroyer and knew that if a man dared face it with the right weapon, it *could* be made to bleed.

Lonit curled herself into a little ball within her sleeping skins. She listened to Umak's song of praise to the mountain spirits and was afraid. She did not like the mountain at all.

Two days later, the rain stopped. They drew the weather baffle aside. The clear, brazen light of a cloudless sunrise filled the cave. Far below, scattered across the tundra, game could be seen grazing: a small herd of musk oxen, the family of camels that they had seen before, and a few head of steppe antelope. Without a moment's hesitation, Umak and Torka eagerly took up their weapons and went out to hunt. At Torka's insistence, Lonit stayed behind. He wanted no female at his side to contaminate his luck. Umak reminded him of how helpful the girl had been in the past, but Torka was adamant. Lonit made no complaint. She was certain that he was right. Still, even though Umak assured her that they would stay well within hailing distance, she was apprehensive about remaining alone on the mountain.

With her splaying dagger in her hand to protect herself against any wind spirits who might come to menace her while her men were away, she watched the hunters descend the trail. It was wet and slick, but without the weight of their traveling packs to hinder them and throw them off-balance, they moved easily. The dog followed at its usual wary distance, its tail high and its tongue lolling. Lonit was sorry to see it leave. She would have appreciated its company.

The wind blew softly out of the east. Warmed by the yellow light of the rising sun, it was sweet with the scents of earth and grass, of fragrant spruce and artemisia, of a thousand scents that Lonit knew but could not put name to. Her hand relaxed around the bone haft of her dagger. It was not a morning to sustain thoughts of ghosts.

She forgot all about her fear of wind spirits as she went back into the cave and withdrew the stone shells from the bag in which she had carried them along with her firemaking tools. From her pack, she took the four braided lengths of sinew that would form the arms of her bola. With these in hand, she went back to the lip of the sun-washed cornice and seated herself. It was her intent to begin the assembly of her bola, but the beauty of the morning distracted her.

Never before had she rested in such a high place. Never before had she imagined that such vistas as this could exist. She drew in a satisfying breath of the morning, held it in for a long time—digesting it, savoring it—before she released it and drew in another and another until she felt lightheaded and as radiant as the sun. Perhaps the mountain was not so bad after all.

Far away across the rolling tundra, enormous banks of clouds spanned the horizon. It was a moment before she realized that they were not clouds. They were mountains. Birds flew against them, tiny motes against soaring walls of ice and stone. The birds flew closer. She saw them sweep across the sky, then bank and swoop down to land upon the many ponds, lakes, and swollen rivers that glistened in the morning sun.

She smiled as she turned her attention to the making of her bola. In the days to come, she too would hunt. Not with her men, but in the way of a woman. She would take many birds. She would snare them with her stone hurler, pluck them, and hang them to smoke over smoldering beds of spruce and moss. When the time of the long dark returned, Torka and Umak would have much meat to augment their own stores of game. Smoked waterfowl would serve as a tasty diversion when they were all sated upon the heavier flavors and textures of game meat. They would be pleased with Lonit.

A cascade of small stones fell somewhere high above the ledge. Startled, Lonit ducked and scooted back under the protection of the ceiling of the cave. The rockfall was over in a moment, but it was time enough to turn Lonit cold with fear. The brightness went out of the morning. She was certain that she had heard something slipping and grabbing at the treacherous rock face above the cave. With a gasp, she dropped the unfinished bola and made a dash for her dagger. Clutching it in her hand, she stood ready to defend herself as wild, nightmarish images filled her mind.

But the moment passed. The last of the little avalanche tumbled away onto the scree far below. After a while, there was only the sound of meltwater cascading from the heights as the wind licked gently against the mountain, a wind so warm and sweet with spring that the girl relaxed and told herself that she was a foolish female whose imagination was running away with her common sense. The days' extended rainfall had loosened the stones and caused them to fall. Nothing alive moved on the vertical crags above her. She was alone on the mountain.

She went back to the ledge, where she sat and resumed work on her bola. She basked in the sunlight like a lemming on a rock, but she was not fully at ease. She thought of wind spirits and kept her dagger close, just in case it was needed.

Aar clambered onto the ledge ahead of Umak and Torka. To Lonit's delight, each man had taken an antelope. Their eyes were bright with satisfaction as they slung their kills from their shoulders and dropped the tawny, delicately boned animals at Lonit's feet.

They were impatient to gut and skin their kills. Lonit made her praise dance short and stood aside to watch them as they worked; but there must have been something in her demeanor that alerted them to the fact that she was troubled. She told them that it was nothing. She said that she was a foolish female who had imagined that she heard the sound of footfall on the mountain wall above the ledge when, in fact, all she had heard was the sound of falling stones. She was surprised when they exchanged meaningful looks.

"Perhaps it was not only a trick of the light," said Umak as he put down his knives and rose from the crouch he had taken over the body of his antelope.

Torka was on his feet, wiping his bloody hands on the hairy side of his freshly lifted antelope skin. "Come. Whatever it was, we will find it. Now!"

"It?" Lonit's query came before she could call it back.

"The thing that we thought we saw moving on the mountain wall above the ledge," informed Torka with a surly snap. "Why did Almost A Woman say nothing about it before she was asked? Why did she sit on the ledge like a rock instead of going after it?"

Her face flamed. She bowed her head, choking out an admission that shamed her. "Lonit was afraid of wind spirits."

Umak turned on his grandson angrily. "Almost A Woman cannot climb safely with only one good arm! And if she had tried, Torka would have said that she was wrong to risk herself. Bah! Umak says that Torka is worse than a woman! He cannot make up his mind. One moment he says this, another he says that! *Hrmmph!* Lonit must listen to Umak, who is spirit master! And spirit master says that Only Woman In The World was right not to put herself in danger by trying to chase ghosts!"

"That was no ghost we saw above the cave!" Torka chafed against his grandfather's open censure. Umak had never spoken harshly to him before they had been forced to travel in the company of the girl. He glared at her. "Listen to Umak, then! Torka will climb the mountain wall. Torka will bring back the ghost spirit. Torka will make a sauce of its innards to flavor the flesh of the antelope that he has killed!"

With his dagger gripped between his teeth, he ignored the old man's protests as he set out to fulfill his boast. He had no fear of the shadow thing that he and Umak had seen scooting along the bare face of the mountains. From their distant vantage point, it had seemed to be no more than a shadow, created by light and wind playing on the crenellated, upswept walls of the mountain. Reflecting on it now, he knew that it *had* been more than that; it had been a dark, lithe, hairy thing, larger than a wolverine but a little smaller than a young bear. The girl *had* heard it. They had all *smelled* it on their first night on the ledge. He was certain that it was no wind spirit. For a reason that he could not fathom, he wanted the girl to know that. He wanted to make her see that Umak was not always right. He would bring her the carcass of the old man's ghost spirit, and she would see that it was only an animal. With the razor-edged bludgeon that he had fashioned from the whale rib and now wore scabbarded at his belt, he would smash its skull and open it from throat to crotch. He would drop it at Lonit's feet and say: "Here is the wind spirit! Here is the ghost whom Umak fears. Dance now the dance of praise for Torka, who has killed it. Dance now for the hunter who has driven fear of the mists from our cave!"

The thought gave him immeasurable pleasure. He could not say why. It should not matter to him what the girl thought. It should not, but it did.

As he climbed, his only worry was that he might come upon his quarry when he least expected it. He visualized himself groping upward for a handhold, only to have the shadow creature's claws and fangs rip into his flesh before he could make a grab for his bludgeon. He saw himself thrown off-balance, hurtling to his death while the shadowy thing cowered on a ledge. Umak and Lonit would watch him fall, and the old man would say: It is as Spirit Master has foretold—men do not hunt spirits. To those whose flesh is of air and wind wise men make praise songs.

Hmmph, thought Torka as he climbed. *We will see who is made of air and wind and to whom Lonit will sing her next praise song.*

He carried his dagger in his teeth, using it to slash defensively across each hold before he committed his bare hand to it. The rock was cold, and it crumbled beneath his grasping fingers. Rotten in some places, and hard and slick in others, it made for treacherous climbing. Nevertheless, long, vertical fissures in the stone allowed him good leverage. Soon he found himself upon a broad, shouldering slope. He paused and caught his breath, flexed his hands to relax them, then walked through filmy mists, telling himself that they were only that and not wind spirits.

Above him, clouds were forming over the summit ice pack. He heard occasional groans and cracking sounds emanating from the glacial mass; a less pragmatic man would have imagined that he heard ghost voices, but Torka heard the living power of earth and ice and knew that, as long as he walked wisely and warily, it bore him no threat. Still, he was a hunter of the tundra, of the broad, rolling steppe. He was out of his element and knew it. The mountain made him feel small and vulnerable to forces that he did not understand. Instinctively, he walked quietly, his dagger at the ready.

Now and again he felt the eyes of something observing his progress as he continued up across the slope. *Watch well. Torka is coming. Torka says you die,* he warned in silence.

The surface of the slope granted little traction. He walked as though across hard-packed sand. Composed of a blanket of scree and till that lay hundreds of feet thick over the solid rock underpinnings of the mountain's east wall, the slope stopped abruptly at the base of a soaring precipice that ended where a downward extension of the summit ice pack began. It was a huge lobe of glacial mass. Studded with stones and boulders bigger than mammoths, it overhung the precipice and extruded downward over its sides, showing underlayers that were black and brown with the refuse of the mountain. Meltwater bled from beneath it, sheening the sheer surface of the rock with uncountable raucous, milky waterfalls.

The feeling that he was being watched persisted. Torka picked up the stink of musteline and followed his nose to the series of caves that he had viewed days before from the tundra. They pocked the lower wall of the precipice. Unlike the broad, sheltering expanse of cavelike ledge upon which he and the others had made their encampment, most of these caves were little more than mere depressions in the rock; only one was large and deep enough for a good-sized musteline to live in with room to spare.

Torka did not venture too close. His fingers tightened around the bone haft of his dagger. The entire area reeked of the creature's habitation. Looking for tracks, he drew his bludgeon from its scabbard of caribou hide and advanced, holding the deadly weapon poised in case the animal charged him. But whatever resided within that foul den was not there, nor had it left any telltale paw prints that would have revealed its identity to the experienced tracker. With utmost caution, Torka peered into the cave.

The creature had made a small, filthy nest for itself of grasses and twigs, which it must have carried up from the tundra far below. Lined with an assortment of bird feathers and down, it was littered with bits of chewed bone and fragments of gnawed tendons. There were no feces fouling the nest, but the musklike stench of glandular secretions forced Torka to fight the need to retch.

He backed away and drew in lungfuls of the rapidly

cooling mountain air. What sort of creature could dwell in such a foul nest? It was a cold, hostile place for any kind of animal to chose as a home, although, Torka noted, it did catch the light of the rising sun and afforded a spectacular overview of the tundra while still being out of the direct path of the wind.

He turned, scanning the heights and the slope below. He was still being watched, but from exactly where, he could not say. He wanted to investigate, but the wall was too steep, the glacial lobe too treacherous, to invite further exploration. And, to his surprise, his shadow was growing long. Soon the day would be over. The prospect of descending the mountain in darkness was sobering.

Annoyed, he squelched a rising surge of frustration. Umak's "ghost" would live out this day. But not another if Torka had his way. It did not take him long to position a loop snare around the entrance to the cave. As he worked, he was glad that he had begun his climb with such rash impetuosity—he still had his snare nets and sinews with him. After he and Umak had each brought down an antelope, neither man had seen much sense in taking the time to set snares for smaller, less desirable prey. Torka set them now, placing them at likely places along the slope and at the very lip of the east wall as he began the difficult descent to the cave where Umak and Lonit awaited his return.

His mouth was set as he climbed down. He had set his snares with infinite care. One of them was bound to work. Tomorrow, Umak would look upon his "ghost," and Lonit would see who was more of a spirit master—the man who sang praise songs to the unknown, or the man who dared to seek out his fears and slay them.

4

Torka was in a black mood when he entered the cave. Aar, dozing on the ledge, awoke when it saw him, took one look, growled, and moved well out of his way. If the animal had not moved, Torka would have kicked it. He was tired and hungry and not at all glad to see that, in his absence, Lonit had butchered both of the antelope. His mouth turned down. Egatsop never would have been able to prepare a kill so quickly, nor would she have readied it for eating or laid out the portions to be dried with such neatness. The gathering shadows of the approaching night reflected his mood as he observed the perfection of the small, nearly smokeless cooking fire that the girl had made. Egatsop had never been able to make so fine a fire. *Never*, thought Torka, and once again found cause to despise Lonit for having caused him to think unfavorably of his beautiful beloved.

He paused. The girl had already prepared a meal for Umak. She never failed to show deference to the old man. Again Egatsop compared badly. Again Torka found reason to loathe Lonit. He knew that she worked diligently to discredit Egatsop in his eyes. What a despicable girl she was! How could Umak abide her scheming? Torka's eyes rested upon his grandfather. He sat beside the fire, sound asleep, snoring blissfully with his head on his knees and a half-consumed haunch of antelope still in his hand at his side.

Now the girl was approaching the returning hunter. He glared at her as, with downcast eyes, she offered a roasted haunch from his own kill. Torka snatched it from her hands without a word and walked past her to hunker down by the fire. He ate in sullen silence, not wanting to look at her as she knelt across the fire pit from him, patiently awaiting his command for water or more meat.

He cast her a surreptitious glance. He knew that she must be thinking that he had failed. He had not done what he had set out to do. Defensively, he boasted through a mouthful: "Torka has found a place of the 'spirit's' dwelling. Tomorrow Almost A Woman will see that it is flesh, not mist. Torka has set snares. Tomorrow Almost A Woman will singe its stinking hide in this fire pit. Tomorrow Umak will drink its blood and know that Torka was right!"

She made no reply. None was expected. She could sense the anger in him and wondered what she had done to cause it. She was puzzled as to why he was speaking to her at all. She picked up a water skin and held it out to him. Perhaps he was thirsty? A man should not have to ask for water. His woman should anticipate his need.

Their eyes met. Held. For a moment, Torka was so startled that he stopped chewing. Lighted by the ruddy glow of the little fire, Lonit's face was as smooth and tawny and delicately beautiful as that of the young doe whose flesh he was consuming.

His hunger vanished. A new and long-dormant appetite flared, then was cooled by incredulity. Lonit *beautiful*? Umak was right! There *were* spirits on this mountain! They must have seeped into Torka's head when he had walked upward through the mists. Even now they were feeding off his sanity. To look with desire at a homely, wretched girl like Lonit was to shame the memory of his beloved Egatsop. Suddenly furious, he reached out and backhanded the water skin out of her hands.

"Get away! Tend to your skins and your woman's work! Stay away from me!" He snarled his rage and hatred at her, sorry that he had not hit her. "Torka cannot stand the sight of you!"

She did as she was told. Numbed by his display of wrath and revulsion, she cowered well away from him, huddling in the darkness at the very back of the cave where he could barely see her. Tears stung beneath her lids. She blinked them back, but they fell anyway, and she was grateful for the shadows.

He did not look her way. He did not want to think of her. He turned his full attention to the haunch, eating with a vengeance until he had stripped it of all but the thickest portions of the thigh meat. Slowly, he became aware of the stink of musteline and knew that he had brought the stench of the creature back with him. It permeated his clothes. He gave the back of his hand a tentative sniff, then cursed. It was on his skin, too, and in the long, unbound lengths of his hair. Disgusted, he threw the haunch into the fire pit and got to his feet, peeling off his clothes and tossing them back into the shadows. Lonit would know what to do with them once she caught a whiff of their essence. Meanwhile, he bent and scooped ashes from the edges of the fire pit and scoured his skin with them. He rubbed himself until he was gray from head to foot and the warm, absorbent coating of ashes drew in the stink of the musteline and masked it with its own acrid, smoky scent.

Lonit did not smell or see the reeking garments that lay scattered before her. She saw only the man who stood naked in the firelight. The flames smoked. The haunch that he had thrown into them had disturbed them; they fed on its fat and tissue, giving off a hot, dusky light that cast strange dancing images onto the walls of the cave.

And in this light she saw the maleness of him, and the scars of many hunts. She saw the breadth of his back and shoulders, the leanness of his hips and waist, the power of his thighs and upper arms. Unable to look away, she could barely breathe as she watched him go to the far wall where she had placed the water skins near the entrance of the cave. He took two of the skins and went to the outer edge of the cornice. There, in the cold wind of evening, he emptied them over himself. She heard him gasp, and something deep within her loins caught fire. Dim, dark recollections suddenly flared within her mind. She saw her father, felt him riding her, pounding her, cursing her because she could not "catch fire." She had not understood what he had wanted of her. Now, having looked at Torka in the tremulous light of the flames, she understood, and knew for the first time that a woman could burn as hotly as a man—but not for just any man.

Silhouetted against the dying embers of the day, Torka cleansed his body and shook out his hair. He reentered the cave, took up one of his sleeping skins, and returned to the fire. He seated himself. Within the encircling folds of the dark, hairy bison skin, he began to shiver himself warm. He was tired, unaware of the girl watching him, unaware that she was shivering, too, but not with cold.

The moments passed. Torka dozed, then slept. Lonit could hear the deep, even pull of his breathing. She heard the snores of the old man. In the shadows near the entrance to the cave, Aar gnawed on a bone. She listened to the rasp of the dog's teeth and to the sound of the last of the haunch fat dripping and spitting in the fire pit. The flames were cooler now. The time for "catching fire" had passed.

Now, for the first time, she became aware of the smell of Torka's tainted garments. She understood that he wanted her to cleanse and air them. As quietly as she could, she dragged them—at arm's length—to the fire. She took up ashes and rubbed them into every inch and seam of the clothing. When this was done, she took them out into the rapidly gathering night. She spread them out upon the ledge, and weighted them with stones. The wind and sun would cleanse them. In time the stink of musteline would lessen, but it would never fully disappear. In the near darkness, she ran a palm over the silky fox tails that trimmed the tunic that she had made for Torka. How many hours had gone into its construction? How long would it take her to accumulate so many prime fox skins again?

She sighed. Torka would need a new set of clothes. Although she was tired, the thought inspired her. He had told her to tend to her skins. She would do just that! Perhaps he would stop being so angry with her if she could quickly replace his garments with even better ones. Her injured arm was healing rapidly. She no longer used the sling, and she *could* use her hand again without pain, although the sutured skin often itched.

She sighed again. Torka would never smile at her looks, but he might yet show pleasure at her workmanship. Ignoring her fatigue, she set herself to the task at hand. The real work would begin tomorrow. Now the skins must have their final curing. Tonight she would sleep naked with them wrapped tightly around her. They would absorb oils from her skin and take on a soft resiliency that they had not possessed since the animals that had lived within them had been slain.

As quietly as she could, she went to where the skins were spread and stood above them, undressing. Layer by layer, her garments fell away until she stood naked and shivering in the meager warmth and fading light of the dying fire.

Within the fire pit, the blackened haunch bone settled

and cracked. Marrow swelled out and oozed onto the coals. Steam hissed. The sound roused Torka. He looked up.

At one whom he had never seen before.

She stood at the edge of the darkness. The soft, fading fireglow defined her every curve. Torka stared, entranced, enflamed, and confused. The figure standing naked before him could not be Lonit. Yet the eyes that stared at him could belong to no other. They stared back at him like the eyes of a startled antelope—round, dark pools in which the firelight swam.

But it was not her eyes that held his glance. It was her body.

Almost A Woman *was* a woman. And for the first time since Torka had left the camp of death behind, Egatsop's memory was eclipsed. She was dead. Lonit was alive. And it was life that rose in him now. It banished memory. It banished comparisons. It banished all longings but one. He was hard with need as his eyes moved over the contours of a body that did not belong to any half-grown adolescent. Lonit's skin was as sleek as a young doe's, her form lush and rounded. This was the flower of which Umak had spoken. Long dormant, it was now ripe with life and promise.

Torka stared into the darkness after Lonit had knelt, wrapped herself in the closest skin, lain down, and closed her eyes. Anger stirred within him now. Why had she displayed herself if she had not intended to come to him for gratification? How dare she turn her back upon him now, curling up in her skins like a child after brazenly flaunting the fact that she was anything but that? Among the People, it was a man's right to sate his sexual need with any available female as long as her own man offered no objection. Lonit was the last female in the world whom Torka would have singled out to be a vessel for his pleasure, but since the murderous rampage of the Destroyer, she was the *only* woman in the world. She was his. And Umak's.

Torka looked at his grandfather. As far as he knew, the old man had made no overtures to the girl, but he had made no secret of the fact that he had been considering such possibilities. Now, asleep beside the fire pit, Umak slept heavily. Torka knew that, unless deliberately awakened, he would not stir until dawn.

His eyes strayed back to the girl. She lay on her side,

unmoving in the shadows. He suspected that she was only pretending to be asleep. Now that she had aroused him, she rejected him. A growl formed at the back of his throat. He did not notice that the dog heard him and looked up. It had been too long since he had known a man's release. The flame that Lonit had ignited within him would not be extinguished. She had no right to turn away from him. It was her obligation to yield to his desire.

He went to her and pulled the skins away. He lay down beside her, drawing his own sleeping robe over them both to cut the chill of the deepening night. Her back was to him, as hot and rigid as his need. Roughly, he turned her toward him. Roughly, his hands explored the woman whom he had not known existed until this night.

Lonit yielded to Torka all that he desired, all that she could offer of herself, for his pleasure as much as for her own. Now, at last, she was his woman. Now, at last, he found her useful. Now, at last, he was guiding her in ways that truly pleased him. She followed eagerly, touching him, loving him, opening herself to his questing mouth and hands, arching to accept him when he entered her. Her body was no longer her own. It was one with his. Her movements were his movements, as savage, as intense.

For Torka, her response was shattering. Never, in all of their years together, had Egatsop responded to him as Lonit was responding now. *Never*. Even in *this*, she shamed the memory of his beautiful beloved. But in the darkness, joined to him, moving with him, Lonit was beautiful in ways that he had never imagined. He had intended to use her, to come to a quick and purposefully hurting release, but her unexpected passion had aroused him to heights that he had never thought possible. He forgot everything but the moment, prolonging their union, savoring it, withdrawing and entering in an ecstasy of control that was broken at last when the girl cried out and his release came in a final, probing thrust that brought a sob from her.

In the darkness, Aar turned his back upon them and moved a little closer to the fading warmth of the fire pit. Umak slept on undisturbed. Dazed, Torka and Lonit lay trembling in exhaustion, their bodies joined, still moving, seeking the last ripples of pleasure until, at last, sleep took them. They knew no more until the first of the creature's screams of pain cracked the night in two.

5

The first rays of the sun were just pouring across the eastern plain by the time Torka dressed, took up his weapons, and began the ascent of the wall. Having slept fully clothed, Umak had a head start. The old man had said nothing to either Torka or Lonit when he had noted their unusual sleeping arrangements. The screams of the creature had been too imperative to ignore. He had chosen the lightest of his spears, tightened his belt, and gone out to see for himself just what was howling on the cliff above the cave. He climbed above Torka now, both balancing their spears across their shoulders, using the chin to steady and grip it when necessary. Although it was awkward going, Umak was at his best in the morning. Despite his bad leg, he moved with a natural grace and agility.

The full light of morning bathed the mountain. Above them, screaming like a scalded child, the creature hung upside down over the side of the mountain face; one of its short, hairy legs was caught in the noosed end of the last snare that Torka had set the day before. They could see the animal fairly well now, and smell it. Its head was hidden within the stiff downfalls of hair that were as long and dark as a musk ox's. They could not see its face. As it flailed madly with its thin, furry arms, its small, stinking body spun round and round, propelled by the force of its own frantic movements.

Umak paused, looking down at his grandson as he felt obliged to concede: "No wind spirit that."

But what was it? Neither man had ever seen anything like it. It was much too large for a weasel or wolverine and too small for a mountain cat or bear. As they stared up at it, its screams stopped and became panting moans as it grabbed with handlike paws at its trapped limb, desperately trying to pull itself up and work itself free. If it did the latter, it would fall to its death, but it would die anyway.

Umak took his spear in his right hand. He aimed with the precision of one who seldom missed, leaning back as far as he dared, then hurling the projectile upward with as much weight behind it as his tenuous position on the mountain would allow. It allowed little. The spear fell low. It missed the target's body and lodged itself in one of its thighs.

The scream that came from the animal struck both hunters as sharply as though they, and not the creature, had been pierced.

On the ledge below, Aar cocked his head. Still in a half-dreaming state of bliss induced by the events of the night before, Lonit stopped midway through her dressing. She listened, certain that her ears must be tricking her.

The hunters stood frozen. The little body above them continued to spin. It was no longer screaming. It was sobbing in short, pathetic bursts of sound that only one creature in all the world could make: *words*. This was not an animal. This was not a wind spirit. This was a child.

In one moment, their entire perspective of the world had been changed by a small, sobbing, indescribably filthy child.

They ascended the remainder of the wall and hauled themselves onto the overhang from which the child had fallen. They pulled it up. It fought them all the way, thrashing like a fish on a line. When Torka reached down to grab it, it shrieked and slapped at him. Trying not to breathe in its stink, he grabbed it by the scruff of its neck, hefted it onto the overhang, and attempted to put it on its feet. Its response was to kick out at him with its good leg. The wounded leg offered no support, and the child collapsed, its weight snapping the protruding end of the spear and driving the shaft deeper into the muscles of its thigh. The resulting pain was so excruciating that the child did not cry out; instead it dropped as though it had been brained by a boulder. Unconscious, it lay sprawled at the feet of the hunters, a ragged heap of foul, tattered furs and long, unkempt hair.

Torka and Umak stared at one another in perplexity, wondering if they were both experiencing the same delusion. What lay before them could *not* be a child. In all the world, they were alone. The People were dead. All of the children were dead. The mammoth had slain them. And yet, only a cursory examination revealed the "creature" to be an emaciated, fully human little boy of about nine. When they parted the filthy strands of his hair, both men drew back as though stung. The tear-streaked, dirt-blackened little face was so like that of Torka's beloved son, Kipu, that they gasped, momentarily disoriented.

With tremulous fingers, Torka traced the familiar features. "Father of my father, how can this be?"

For the first time in his life, Umak could not summon a harrumph, much less an answer.

Torka closed his eyes and withdrew his hands. The sight of the child had brought the old agony back—memories of that small, precious boy who was lost to him forever.

Umak was crouching over the boy beside Torka. He examined the wound. Even though still unconscious, the child was murmuring against his pain. The old man was confused. He had thrown the spear and had made the wounding. But how could he have known that this small, foul-smelling thing was not an animal?

As Umak extracted his ruined spear, blood bubbled warm and red and wet out of the boy's wound. Umak dipped his fingers in it and touched what he could not deny.

"Spirits do not bleed," he said, rising, hefting the boy across his shoulders as though he were an antelope taken in a hunt. "Come. Torka and Umak must return to the ledge now. This child's wound must be tended."

Dazed by the implications of their discovery, a befuddled Torka followed. Midway in his descent, he paused. His head was clearer now. Things were suddenly coming into a new and distinctly different focus. The boy had changed everything. He was *real*. Somewhere out there was another band. They were *not* alone! There were people, hunters, men who might be convinced to go in search of the Destroyer. And if they could not be convinced, he would go alone. It would not matter to Umak and Lonit. They would be a part of a band again.

Torka would be free to follow the beast, and find it he would, even if he had to follow it beyond the edge of forever. In memory of all who had died, for Nap and Alinak, for Egatsop and Kipu, for all of those who now lay looking at the sky, this Torka would do!

*   *   *

The boy sat naked at the back of the cave. His leg hurt. He felt hot with fever; but he would not chew upon the sticks that the old man tried to force upon him, nor would he put on the new tunic that the strange-eyed girl had placed before him. The tall, good-looking young hunter knelt before him, asking questions again. The boy pretended not to understand, although the man's words were so similar to those of his band that he knew most of them.

"Why are you here, alone upon the mountain? Where is your band?"

The boy kept his features set, scowling with feigned stoicism, trying hard not to make a face of disgust that might betray his understanding of the hunter's questions. Surely this man had seen children abandoned before? Surely it could not come as a surprise to him that sometimes those who were left to die survived?

The old one was staring at him. He glared up at him, then looked away. The old one's eyes had a way of making him feel invisible.

"This little one has been left alone to set his spirit free to walk upon the wind," the old one said.

Hearing the truth, the boy cast a careful look up at the old man. He stood beside the younger hunter, his arms folded across his chest, his time-runneled face scowling with introspection. The boy knew him for what he was and was afraid of him. He wore the paws of a dire wolf around his neck, as did the younger man, but he carried a medicine bag at his belt, and where he walked, the wild dog was usually close at the heels of his shadow. The boy looked around. The dog lay at the far end of the cave, looking back at him out of a blue-eyed, black-masked face that was as impassive as the old man's. The boy gulped. The dog was in the old one's power. Clearly, the old one was a magic man.

"The boy is strong," the young hunter was saying. "He is beyond the age of name giving. The People would not waste such a boy as this!"

"The People are no more. If there are others in the world, who may say what they would do?"

"Where is your band?" pressed the young hunter.

The boy held his tongue. *My people will come back*, he thought. *They* will *come back for me. Supnah has promised. He has sworn that if they survive the winter, they* will *come back for their children. My father would not lie! If he lives,*

*Supnah will come for Karana. And he will kill these people
and their dog. He will make them pay with their lives for the
way they have treated his only son! So Karana will be silent.
When Supnah comes, these people will howl with surprise.
Then Karana will speak. Then Karana will laugh. Then these
people will die!*

He glared at the young hunter. His thoughts had made
him feel brave. He glared at the old man. Had the strange-
eyed girl not been bent over the cooking fire, he would have
glared at her too. They had all conspired to take him captive.
While he had been in the place of dreams, they had burned
his leg and sewn up the wound that they had made. They had
scrubbed him with water and ashes. They had stripped him
of his garments and of his dignity.

The garments were the last clothes that his mother would
ever make for him. Fringed, and sewn from the furs of all the
kinds of animals that a man might hope to kill, they had been
for his first hunt. She had stitched the many seams and strips
so finely that the stitches were nearly invisible. He had gone
forth with his father boldly, proud of the new clothes, proud
of his new dagger and of the spear that had been made just
for him. It had been a good hunt. But it had been the last of
the good times. The dark times had come and stayed until his
mother was dead, and all of the babies had been exposed,
and all of the old men and old women had walked away into
the endless storms so that the younger men and women
would have enough food to share with each other and their
children.

The band had moved on in search of game. There was no
game. The women grew weak. The surviving children grew
gaunt and ill. The hunters sang the songs that would bring
back the sun. The sun had not returned.

They had moved on again and again. In each camp there
was starvation. In each camp there was death. Then, in the
looming presence of the mountain, Navahk, magic man of the
band, had taken Supnah, the headman, aside. And when at
last their words were done, Supnah had looked old even
though he was young, and Navahk had walked past Karana,
stopping to look at him as though he were of no more worth
than the larva of a blackfly squirming in the beak of a rapacious bird. He had turned and walked on, but not before the
boy had seen him smile.

Supnah had come to him. "Magic Man has seen much

game ahead. It is far across a hard land. We will go there. We will hunt. Karana will wait here with the children who are sick. Karana will guard the little ones until Supnah returns."

Supnah had not returned. Although Karana had done his best to guard the children, they were weak. One by one, they gave their breath to Spirit Sucker until Karana was left alone with his spear, and his dagger, and his fine warm clothes, listening to the remorseless moaning of the wind, remembering the smile of Navahk, knowing that the magic man had wanted this for him and wondering what he had done to make the shaman hate him so.

In the blue shivering light of the aurora borealis, he had seen the eagle flying back and forth from its aerie high upon the mountain wall. Weakened by hunger, he had yet enough reason left in him to know that it was still too early to see the eagle flying above the tundra. But there it was, and Karana had thought that if he could bring down the eagle, he would keep Spirit Sucker at bay, and somehow, across the many miles, Navahk would know that he had survived and would stop smiling.

It was this thought that got him to his feet, but it was the presence of dire wolves arriving to feed upon the dead children of Supnah's band that had put fire to his intent. He had run and run until at last he was on the mountain, hefting his spear, hurling it with his last ounce of energy. Impossibly, it had taken the eagle through its breast. The bird had fallen, and the boy had pounced upon it, devouring it even as it screamed its last; and all the while that he had eaten, he had thought of the smile of Navahk and wished that it was the flesh of the magic man that he was consuming.

For long, uncounted days he slept in the eagle's cave, warm in its nest, safe upon its broad aerie until a huge teratorn sighted him and swept down to pluck him off the cliff. His spear saved him, but in his panic, he stabbed upward once, then drew back, took the weapon in both hands, and whacked at the bird as though the spear were a stave. In a squawking rain of flying feathers and spurting blood, the condor was driven away. He stood shaking, the spear splintered and broken in his hands, and knew that he must seek a smaller, less-conspicuous refuge.

He followed a marmot up to the little caves, then killed the marmot and ate off it for several days. Hunger drove him down off the mountain to hunt; but where there was prey, so too were there predators. A great, fang-toothed cat almost caught him once, and he was nearly mauled by a young, solitary short-faced bear. Soon, inspired by his strong desire to survive, he snared as many weasels as he could, regretfully rubbing their stinking, oily glands into his clothes and hair. It had hurt him to ruin his mother's beautifully made garments, but he smelled so foul that nothing wanted to eat him. Now he was safe. He did not think that his mother would be angry.

Alone on the mountain, he lived by his wits, hunting the lowlands when hunger made it necessary, then retreating to the safe, sheltering heights. Patiently, he awaited his father's return, confident that Supnah would come for him. He longed for that day and dreamed of the moment when he would stand with proud contempt before Navahk. He watched the wide, empty miles for endless hours, but Supnah and his band had not returned. These people and their dog had come instead.

He was disgusted with himself for having been caught. His glare intensified. He had ferreted out each snare except the last one. He knew that he had been right to fear the strangers. They, or at least their magic man, must possess a great and fearful magic to have bent the will of a beast so that it lived with them as though it were a member of their band. Had it not been for the growls of the beast, he would have blundered into their company sooner, drawn irresistibly down from his cave to theirs by the smell of roasting meat.

Now the girl was kneeling before him, offering a sliver of bone upon which she had roasted choice blood meats. The two men had hunted earlier; the smell of the fresh, fire-browned meat was almost too much to refuse.

Nearly. He made a face at the girl. She lowered her unusual eyes, sighed, and went away, leaving the meat beside him. He let it lie, not certain if it was poisoned.

"It is safe! Eat! You are a boy, not game to be taken with bad meat!" snapped the old one.

The boy's eyes widened. The old one *was* a magic man. He had seen into his thoughts. Fear tightened in his gut, obliterating his hunger. Why were these strangers so kind to him? He was not of their band. Perhaps they were going to feed him to the wild dog? But no. If they were going to cut his throat and slice him into fillets for the dog, they would not have stanched and stitched his wound.

A new thought dawned. It made him feel weak and sick with dread. Perhaps they were what all men feared? Members of the Ghost Band. In times of light they came from nowhere and disappeared into nowhere, stealing young women and boys, then vanishing as though they had never been there at all, leaving burning encampments and dead and dying to mark the reality of their raids.

Suddenly shivering and trying hard not to show it lest the strangers know that it was from fear and not cold, he realized that this cave must be the place to which the Ghost Band vanished to dance its ghost dances. Here they must gather after their raids, with their tattooed skin and their huge, flapping labrets of carved bone that so deformed their lower lips, they terrified everyone who had ever seen them and lived to tell the tale.

"Where is your band?" pressed the young hunter again, speaking slowly, with an intensity that made his voice sound as though it was ready to snap. "If your people abandoned you, in which direction did they go? Can you tell this man nothing? Can you understand not even a word of what this man says?"

The boy slapped his arms across his chest and locked his hands beneath his elbows in an effort to keep himself from shivering. The young man bore no tattoos, nor was his lower lip pierced to hold a labret of any kind. And why did he care so much about one small boy who had been left behind by others? Maybe he was of the Ghost Band, waiting here for his fellow raiders to join him in their mountain stronghold. Those others would be tattooed and wear labrets so huge that they tripped upon them when they walked! They would try to make the boy point out the way that Supnah's band had gone; then they would follow and kill them all.

The thought was so anguishing, it drove back the boy's fear and replaced it with anger. "Karana will tell the Ghost Man nothing! Karana is not afraid! This boy's father is the mountain, and his mother is the mist! Karana is alone! He has no band!"

Beside the fire, the girl looked up, as startled by the sharp outcry of the child as the dog, whose ears went up.

Torka measured the boy shrewdly through half-closed eyes. He reached out and pressed gently upon the child's bandaged thigh. When the boy gasped with pain, Torka nodded. "Karana is not made of mist or stone. In time, he will tell Torka where his band has gone."

Karana hissed and bared his teeth like a cornered lynx, hating himself for having blurted out any words at all. Now they knew that he could understand them. Now they knew that he could speak. Now they would never stop asking their questions. But he would tell them nothing. One day his leg would be healed, and he would run away, find his father and his band, and lead them here to kill these strangers. If only they were ugly, they would be easier to hate. If only they were not so kind, it would not be quite so hard to keep up his guard against them. If only the girl were not such a good cook, the smells of roasting meat emanating from her fire would not make his stomach lurch and gurgle in betrayal of his resolve not to be hungry. Where was Supnah? Why had he not returned as he had promised? Karana would not allow himself even to think that his father might not have survived the winter. Supnah *would* return, and soon. Karana was finding it very hard to be brave.

The eyes of the old one swept over him. It was as though the wings of an invisible bird had brushed against his skin.

"Hmmph," exhaled the old man in a voice that revealed nothing of himself. "Do not try to be so bold, Little Hunter. We are not ghosts. We are all that is left of the People. You are of our band now."

6

While Torka and Umak hunted with Aar upon the tundra far below the cave, the boy slept in the sun on one side of the ledge, and an unhappy Lonit cracked marrowbones with a stone on the other.

The full, yellow light of the cloudless morning washed over her. Lost in thought, she took no notice. She was remembering another light: the invisible light that had burned within the cave when she and Torka had "caught fire." It had been brighter than a thousand Arctic mornings, warmer than the sun at noon upon an endless summer day. In that light, she had been Torka's woman. Fully his at last, she had trembled with gladness, knowing that in all the world there was not a female left alive to take him from her side, nor was there a man who would say that she was not worthy of him.

Her happiness had been such that she was actually thankful to the great mammoth who had destroyed the lives of many so that joy might come into her life. Lying warm and exhausted from lovemaking within Torka's arms, she had drifted into sleep, too blissfully content to feel guilty about her gladness. Those who had been harsh and cruel to her were dead. The only two who had ever shown kindness to her were here beside her. Together they would make a new life, a new People. A sweet, euphoric contentment had absorbed her consciousness as she had willingly slipped into the sweetest dreams that she had ever known.

The sense of bliss and gladness had remained with her until the animal had cried out and she had known that it was not an animal. When Umak had returned with the boy in his arms, she had taken one look at the child's face and had nearly swooned with dread. It was Torka's little son, returned from the dead to remind her of what a selfish creature she was. Had she actually been glad for his death? No. Her heart bled for the children who had died beneath the rushing, ripping onslaught of the killer mammoth. She had been foolish to think that Torka had made love to her; he had used her to sate his need because she was the only woman available. How he must long for Egatsop!

She sighed with pained resignation. Torka would have another woman soon, she was certain of it. She paused in her work. Her eyes moved to rest upon the boy. His existence was proof of the existence of others. No longer could Lonit cling to the belief that she was the only woman in the world. When Torka had thrown the boy's foul, tattered rags off the cliff, Lonit's practiced eyes had noted that they must have been beautiful once, for they had been sewn of many strips of furs that had been joined with infinite precision. The hands of his human mother had sewn his garments with pride and love. Karana had screamed in rage as he had made a pathetic, lurching grab for those garments. Lonit knew that the intensity of his attachment to his clothes had little to do with the clothes themselves; it was a manifestation of his love for the woman who had made them.

Lonit wondered what she was like. No doubt she was beautiful, like her child. It must have torn her heart when she had been forced to abandon such a fine son. But why had Karana's parents left him? He was well beyond the years during which it had been acceptable among Lonit's band to expose a child. The fact that he had been able to survive on his own proved that he had been strong and able to hunt. Perhaps he had *not* been abandoned? Perhaps he had been lost in a storm and even now his people were backtracking along the game trails in their search for him. Lonit did not want to think of that. She preferred to think that they had died of starvation during the long, bitter time of the winter dark.

The sun was so warm upon the ledge that the marrow in the bone that Lonit had been cracking softened and grew oily and rich with scent. A fly buzzed in, fighting the wind with transparent wings as it began a greedy exploration. Another joined it. Still lost in thought, Lonit absently waved them away as she was confronted by a sobering truth: She wanted the boy's people to be dead. She wanted to be alone in the world with Torka as her man and Umak as the patient, caring father whom she had never known. But it was not likely that an entire band would starve to death, and the boy's behavior drove that point home to her. Fighting against pain and fever, he dragged himself to the lip of the cornice and sat staring across the tundra. Lonit watched him and knew that he was certain that it was only a matter of time before his people returned.

But they had not returned. It had been many days since Umak had carried Karana down from the heights. The hours of light were growing longer. Soon night would become a thing of the past, and still there was no sign of Karana's people. Lonit's eyes focused upon the boy. His leg was healing very slowly. It was still hot and so full of pain that he could barely move it. Had Torka not insisted that he spend his nights out of the wind, he would have remained on his mat of piled skins, there on the other edge of the cornice, and never stirred at all, except to relieve himself. Still, Umak said that his wound *was* healing. Fragments of bone from the splintered end of the spear were beginning to work their way out of the inflamed thigh. Umak said that this was good, for it was the splinters that caused the festering. The wound still bled a little and sweated clear fluid, but it no longer oozed the thick, greenish secretions that had caused the old man so much concern in the first few days after he had speared the boy.

Karana's appetite had returned, although he still refused to eat in front of any of them. He snarled at Lonit each time she came close to place an offering of meat before him. When Aar ventured near to steal the neglected portions, the boy clouted him across the nose. Insulted and intractable, the dog stayed near the child, waiting patiently. When no one was looking—except the dog, and Lonit from her place at the far side of the fire pit—Karana wolfed down every morsel of food that she had brought to him. Covertly, she had observed the boy's growing interest in the dog. His initial fear of the beast gradually became curiosity. Intrigued by having a wild animal in such close proximity, he had begun to toss it the joints that he had not quite scraped free of marrow. Each day his toss grew shorter, drawing the animal closer and closer, until one day he held out a generous scrap of meat and Aar was eating out of his hand.

From that day, when not hunting with Umak, the dog stayed beside the boy. In the cave or on the ledge, Aar could be found at Karana's side, sleeping next to him in the night, absorbing sunlight with him by day as the boy sat with his back against the mountain wall and kept his vigil over the empty tundra far below, patiently awaiting the return of his people.

Lonit sighed again. Soon now, they would come.

Torka was also convinced of it. He seemed reborn, no longer sullen and reflective but eager to greet each day. He had no time for Lonit. When he was not hunting, he was busy with his weapons, working and reworking his spears, knapping and reknapping his projectile points. Lonit was convinced that he occupied himself to keep his man-need quelled, and when Karana's band came, he would choose someone worthy from its women to warm him in the night. Meanwhile, when darkness fell, he built a signal fire on the ledge, sheltering it from the wind within an open-ended baffle of skins laid around a brace work of bones.

"If Karana's band is out there, they will see Torka's fire. Soon they will come."

The boy had listened with wide-eyed apprehension, as though he feared that the flames would attract ghosts instead of men; but as time passed, he began to relax a little. Both Umak and Torka ignored his hostility. They spoke to him and shared their thoughts, and Torka showed him the People's way of making weapons out of stone and bone, and Umak told him tales of magic and myth, and although he would not speak in acknowledgment of their open concern for him, the fear and hatred that had gleamed from wide, dark eyes when they had first brought him to the cave was less apparent now.

Still, he kept his unrelenting daylight vigils and snarled at Lonit whenever she brought food to him. She had given up trying to communicate with him. In time, he would speak again. In time, he would lose his fear. In time, his people would come, and who knew what would happen to her among strangers, when her own band had barely tolerated her.

She had said as much to Umak. He had listened pensively and understood her fears, for he himself suffered similar apprehensions. Here, alone with Torka and Lonit, he was a hunter again, needed again, strong again. Within a band, he would be only one more old man living out his days until his time came to walk away upon the wind.

They had sat together the night before, close to the fire, while Torka and the boy slept. The sounds of meltwater

cascading down from the ice pack had filled the darkness.
Now and again, from somewhere deep within the mountain
itself, there was the low groan and grinding sound that had
become familiar to them.

Umak had seemed suddenly to come to grips with an
unspoken argument that he had been waging with himself.

"The People were not the *only* people," he said. "There
are other bands. We are not alone. Umak says that it may be
the people of the tundra are like the great herds of caribou.
Once they were one bull, one cow, then one herd with many
calves. Calves grow. They become many bulls, many cows.
The bulls lock horns in combat. Blood is shed. The younger
bulls break away from the main body of the herd. Cows
follow to form a new herd. Like this it happens, many times.
Soon there are many herds, each moving its own way, each
following its own route of migration in endless search for
food, forgetting that there are other herds until not one cow
or one bull remembers the beginning."

"This woman is happy here upon the mountain. She is
content with Umak and Torka as the only members of her
'herd.' "

"It is so with Umak. But no man or woman may hold the
wind. It will blow what it will to us. And whatever comes, we
must be strong."

Now flies were landing on the back of her hand and
crawled between her fingers, buzzing and circling as they
feasted on the oils that had risen from the marrowbone. She
flicked them away with disgust and rose to her feet, wiping
her hands on the hide apron that she had made of unwanted
scraps left over from the garments she was sewing for her
men.

She could see them now: two solitary figures striding
toward her, with Aar trotting along to one side, tail up and
bouncing. They had taken a fair-sized ground sloth; its bulky
shape was unmistakable as they took turns dragging it. Its
thick pelage would make a wonderfully thick sleeping mat,
and its extraordinary claws would make excellent tools with
which to dig the late-summer harvest of edible tubers. The
happiness of anticipated pleasure filled her, then disappeared.
The warm, sweet springtime wind moved around her. It
brought no warmth or sweetness. Remembering Umak's words
about the wind, Lonit considered it a hostile thing.

Her eyes scanned the tundra. Were people of another

band there, just beyond the mountainous, snow-mantled horizon, walking toward her even as she gazed? No! It was not possible! She could not bear to think of it. Yet she could not help herself. Torka would welcome them. He had said so. He had spoken enthusiastically of safety to be found in numbers and of workloads eased. Umak had accused him of planning to go off to hunt the Destroyer. He had not denied it, but Lonit was certain that the last thing on his mind was hunting mammoths. He was thinking of a new life, of a new woman, perhaps many women, and Lonit knew that he would have it all. What woman would not eagerly open herself to pleasure him? What hunting band would not welcome a man of Torka's skill and daring among its ranks?

And what of Lonit?

She drew in a breath. It was bitter.

Her mother's words rose from the past. ". . . there is no place in the band for an ugly girl . . . you must be useful . . . you must be brave . . . you must be strong. . . ."

The bitterness within her grew. *Lonit has been all of these things. And still Torka will choose another. But Lonit is strong. Let the wind blow to her what it will. Lonit will not be afraid.*

She would still have Umak. She would stay with him, to serve him as a daughter—or as a woman if he wished it. She would be all things to him, and when the time came for him to walk away upon the wind, she would walk with him to gentle the journey for him. Together, they would set their spirits free upon the wind. It would not be a bad thing. Without Torka as her man, Lonit had no wish to go on living.

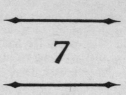

7

The long, lengthening days, which yielded to star-filled nights, continued to pass. Below the mountain, grasses greened and grew tall. Across the tundra, flowers of every shape and shade imaginable burst into bloom. In the high, precipitous alpine canyons, groves of miniature dogwood became spangled with white, four-petaled stars, while willow catkins turned gold with tiny blossoms, and dwarf bunchberry and cranberry flowered and began to set fruit.

Flies, gnats, and great hordes of whining mosquitoes formed black, veillike transparencies over pristine lakes and ponds. Birds were everywhere. Fishing hawks and eagles rode the thermals, soaring and banking above rivers in which salmon had begun to run. Geese of myriad sizes and varieties vied with ducks, swans, turnstones, and sandpipers for prime nesting sites within the wetlands. Cranes and herons stood serpent-necked and stilt-legged in the sedge marshes, while loons called and lobe-toed phalaropes splashed and spun within the shallows of uncountable streams as they ducked their heads beneath the water to scoop up larvae and freshwater crustaceans with their beaks.

Foxes and hares, ptarmigan and owls lost the last of their winter-white coloring. They were brown now, or red or gray, or mottled combinations of all three. Along the wide, stony outwash plain that lay at the base of the mountain, a herd of blocky, short-maned horses paused to drink, caught the scent of man, nickered nervously, and moved on. Not far away, in the now-luxuriant scrub growth of a meadow on the fringes of the tundra, a winter-weakened yak fell to the predations of a ravenous short-faced bear and its cubs. A rusty-gold pride of shaggy-coated lions dozed in the long grass downwind of a small herd of musk ox that grazed the mountain's southern flank.

And in the deep, spruce-shaded canyon below the aerie of Torka, Umak, Lonit, and Karana, Umak followed cloven foot-prints along the hard-packed spine of a still-existing snowbank. Within a grove of stunted birch trees, he sighted his prey and brought down the bud-antlered bull moose with one throw of his spear. Struck through its heart, the animal dropped to its knees, woofed once, then keeled over, dead.

The old man's cry of triumph echoed up the mountain walls to set vibrations running deep into the silt underpin-nings of the summit ice pack. Somewhere deep within the glacier, an enormous lateral fracture cracked lengthwise and stressed the masses of ice on either side of it. Imperceptibly, the lower mass slipped just a little; but the entire glacier groaned, cracked open into fissures along its surface, and stretched subtly downward to accommodate the changes within itself.

The movements and sounds had been no more and no less than the usual erratic shiftings that the old man had grown used to over the past weeks, so he paid no heed to them now. High above him, where the sun struck the south face of the ice mass, a lobe of white a quarter of a mile thick oozed forward to overlay its stony, vertical foundations. A family of large white sheep, which had been feeding on the green tufts of a sky-high meadow, leaped into thin air and skittered down the mountain wall. A teratorn, circling in the blue, clear vault of the sky, cast its shadow on the gaping, mile-long mouth of a thousand-foot-deep crevasse that had not been there a moment before.

At the back of the canyon, a thin avalanche of small stones and bits and pieces of glacial ice clattered and rolled for thousands of feet before landing not far from where Umak stood. But the old man had seen many such rockfalls since he and the others had come to the mountain.

Torka was coming toward him, his own spears in hand. Umak uttered a little whoop of pride. He had beaten Torka to the kill! Aar was already sniffing at the carcass and lapping blood from the wound. Umak raised his arms and shook them to show his victory, knowing that the bull moose he had slain was in its prime. Coupled with the many antelope that they had taken, plus the sloth and the woman meat that Lonit had snared with her traps and bola, the ton and a half of meat that the moose would yield would be more than enough to feed them all for the rest of the summer, through the fall, and on into the time of the long dark and beyond. If they wished, they need not hunt again but could spend their time at leisure while Lonit worked at the endless tasks that times of plenty presented to those of her gender.

When Torka came near to appraise the kill, Umak spoke his thoughts to him, adding: "Lonit is one woman. There is much meat. In this new place, it may be that the spirits who give power to the hunter will not mind if these two help Only Woman In The World."

"Lonit is not the only woman in the world."

"When Umak sees others, then he will believe that there are others. In the meantime, there is much meat to butcher, many hides to work—too much for Only Woman In The World."

Torka sighed, doing his best to restrain annoyance with his grandfather. Umak had not referred to Lonit as Almost A Woman since he had awakened to see Torka and the girl sharing the same sleeping skins on the morning that they had discovered Karana. Torka did not like to be reminded of that morning or of the night that had preceded it. He avoided Lonit when he could. She stirred memories of their coupling and the feelings toward her that he had never felt for anyone but Kipu and his grandfather. It disturbed him to have to admit that, in retrospect, he remembered feeling no such tenderness for Egatsop. Passion? Yes. Possessiveness? Yes. Pride in knowing that the most beautiful woman in the band had accepted him? Yes. But lately, when he looked at Lonit's tall, slender figure bent over her drying frames, or sewing, or cooking, he found loveliness in her every move and gesture.

By the standards of the People, he knew that she should not seem beautiful to him, but she did. When watching her patience with the wounded child or her devotion to Umak, Torka always found himself thinking that Egatsop would never have been so patient with another woman's child or as devoted to an old man who had need of his pride. Although Umak did his best to pretend otherwise, there was no mistaking the fact that he was strong in the morning and tired and stiff-jointed each afternoon. Egatsop would not have understood why Torka would stand back and allow Umak to stalk and make a kill that *he* could easily have made in half the time, but somehow he knew that Lonit would understand.

He had seen her listen to the old man's tales, pretending that he had not dozed off midway through a story only to awake with a start and repeat it all over again from the beginning, unaware that he had been asleep at all. He had seen her surreptitiously pound Umak's meat before roasting it, and he had known that she did this to spare the old man's teeth, which must be growing brittle. So many little things, all done when she thought herself unobserved. It was impossible to despise such a girl.

He knew now that he had completely misjudged her. He had come to care for her deeply, but he did not want to care. The caring could cripple his resolve to find and slay the beast that had destroyed his band. Each time he looked at Karana, he saw his lost, beloved little boy and knew that before he could allow himself to care for anyone or anything again, he must drive his spear into the eye and brain of World Shaker and see the monster fall and breathe its last.

"Umak says that he will help Lonit. Only Woman In The World will be glad to have another pair of hands to work the hides and cure the sinew and prepare the meat."

The old man's statement drew Torka from his reverie. He looked at his grandfather and knew that he had been right to mislead him into thinking that he had beaten him to the kill. He looked vibrant, arrogant, almost young again. The placement of his spear in the moose told Torka that, despite the encroaching infirmities of old age, he was still a hunter to be reckoned with. Coupled with his powers as a spirit master, Umak would be an asset to any band. The thought was steadying.

Torka repeated the compliment aloud, then went on: "When Karana's people come, it will be a good thing to share our meat with them. They will welcome us. And Lonit will have the hands of many women to help her with her work."

"*If* Karana's people come!"

"They will come. They would not abandon such a son as Karana. Torka says that the boy was lost in the storms of the time of the long dark. Even now, hunters are coming in search of him."

"The time of the long dark was longer and darker than any that this old man can ever remember. Never has Umak seen such storms or felt such cold. If the boy was lost, his people will think him dead. They will send no one to search for him."

"If Karana were Torka's son, Torka would not stop searching until he found the bones of his little one and placed them
with his own hands to look at the sky. *Only* then would Torka
believe that his son had given his spirit to walk upon the
wind."

"Hrmmph! Torka would not have lost his son in the first
place, no matter how fierce the storm, no matter how white
the wind. It took a crooked spirit to tear the life from Kipu's
heart. But Umak says that Karana has been abandoned. His
people will *not* come!"

Torka rose, impatient with the conversation. He knew
that Umak must have his doubts about joining with a new
band; he must be worrying about his age. "You will do well
with a new people, Father of my father. You are Umak! You
are spirit master! You will be strong. You will follow the game
again. Life will be good. You will have women again. You will
be proud again. You must not be afraid."

The old man's face frowned in righteous indignation. "Umak
does not fear for Umak!" His arms went wide, then up and
out as though to encompass the entire hunting range that lay
at the base of the great mountain. "Torka has brought Umak
and Lonit to a good place. We have made a safe encampment. We have much meat. We do not need others to help
us survive. In this place, we could stay forever!"

The impassioned outpouring of the old man was contagious. Torka responded with equal intensity. "Forever is how
long Torka will take, if that is what he must take to find and
kill the Destroyer!"

"Hah! So it *is* as Umak has said! Torka waits for Karana's
band so that he can walk away from this old man and from
Lonit and from Karana and say to the great mammoth: 'Torka
comes to you now, across a far land, seeking one who has
destroyed the People, seeking to kill one who cannot be
killed! And if Torka dies now, it does not matter, because
Umak and Lonit and Karana are safe in the care of another
band!' "

Torka stared at his grandfather. It never failed to amaze
him that, just when he began to accept the fact that Umak
was a man of failing faculties, the old man's mind snapped
and sparked and cut through to the very quick of his own
thoughts. The image of a brittle-toothed, sinewy elder sitting
stiffbacked by the fire vanished. Before him was Umak, fiery

tempered, wily tracker of beasts, slayer of bears, teacher of infinite wisdom.

"Come with me, then!" he urged. "When Karana's people come and Lonit and the boy are safe, we can go together. Together we will kill the Destroyer and return to tell the tale!"

"Hmmph! Even if Karana's band come, Thunder Speaker is far away, and this old man says that this is good. The memories of the Destroyer are bitter! Let them go, Torka. Forget what has been. Look at what is. Life is good now. And if this spirit master's eyes have seen clearly, then Umak says this: When the time of the long dark has come and gone, when the first blue light rises with the setting of the starving moon, Lonit will bring forth new life, and the People will be reborn. Will Torka say then that his life does not matter? Will he then say to Umak: 'Come, let us leave our woman and child to the care of those who lose or abandon their own?' Hmmph! Torka will do as he must. But Umak will stay with Lonit. To this old man, her life is worth more than the death of a mammoth."

8

The sun stood still in the sky. The world turned upside down. The northern lights shone by day, and the wind rose to transform their colors into rainbows that ran like rivers over the land.

Only Torka saw these wonders. He was not certain why he saw them. He did not want to be happy over Umak's revelation, but the more he thought about it, the more the sense of wonder grew within him. Perhaps it was because they had all been so close to death—the old man, the girl, the hunter, the boy, even the dog. In a sense, they had all walked upon the wind only to be rejected by the spirits, to be cast out of the world they had known, not to die but to be reborn in a new world; and now their rebirth was being confirmed in the promise of the new life that was growing within Lonit as surely as summer was ripening upon the land.

Perhaps Umak was right. The Destroyer was far away, in a part of the world that they had left behind. Life was good on the mountain. For the first time, Torka realized that as long as his remnant little band held together, the People could not be destroyed. The People lived on in Umak and Torka. Through Lonit, they would be reborn to survive in generations yet to come. Perhaps it *was* time for Torka to release himself from the past and to send his memories of the great mammoth walking away upon the wind . . . at least until Karana's people came. Now he would think of other things. He would care for Lonit and their coming child. He would think about the future. And savor the renewed joy that he now found in the wonder of living.

* * *

They acted so strangely toward her. Lonit could not understand why. She had made a clean, orderly encampment for them upon the ledge and had set much meat to dry and many hides to cure on the long, broad lip of the cornice. She was content with her woman's work, but they insisted that they help her with it. She felt demeaned by the sight of her men scraping away at hides, cleaning and twisting sinew. Were they dissatisfied with the quality of her labor? Humiliated, she had applied herself with extra care and vigor, only to be scolded, told to rest, and ordered to stop working so hard.

It was very confusing. What else was a woman to do? Men hunted; women *worked*. And how much rest could one female need? Ever since Umak had brought down the moose, and he and Torka had piled its meat into its own skin and devised a pulley to haul it up onto the ledge, they had treated her as though she, and not Karana, were injured and in need of special care. She would catch them watching her in the most curious ways, as though they waited for her to say something special, or as if they expected her to be sick.

It was perplexing. Her appetite had never been better. She felt well and strong, although her breasts were tender, and she waited apprehensively to experience her time of blood. What would her men say when it came? Would they be content to banish her to the far reaches of the cave? Or would they send her away to sit out her time at the base of the mountain wall? The thought made her shiver with dread. She was glad when her time of blood did not come, although she wondered why it stayed away.

Lonit knew only what she had been able to observe, that the time of blood came with some sort of mystic regularity that had something to do with the phases of the moon. But twice more the moon went through its cycle and her time of blood did not come. She was relieved. In the meantime, half of her wished that her men would stop treating her so strangely, while the other half rejoiced in incredulous disbelief. Torka was being kind to her. For reasons she did not understand and would not even think to question, he did not seem to hate her anymore.

The sun stayed longer and longer in the sky. Then, one day, it did not set at all. Sunset came, but the sun did not disappear. Instead it hovered low upon the western horizon, like a lambent coal glowing softly in the blue fire pit of the sky, then slowly slid northward in the lingering twilight. At midnight, the sun began its slow descent toward the east. Hours later, a new day was born. Not once had the sun left the sky.

And still Karana's people did not come.

Lonit saw that the boy was brooding. He barely touched his food. "Lonit will gather eggs for Karana," she told him.

The boy glowered. Lonit smiled. Karana still kept his silence and maintained a mask of hostility, but Lonit had seen subtle changes in his behavior over the past weeks. She had observed that fresh eggs, raw or cooked in the ashes of the fire pit, were his favorite food. His leg was healing nicely, although it would probably be many moons before the torn muscles would be as good as new. His fear of the spirit master had gradually become awe as Umak spent hours with the boy, telling him tales of the People, teaching him to play bone toss, and sharing with him much of the same knowledge that he had shared with Torka when Torka had been a boy. Not to be outdone, Torka also doted on the boy and took time out from the working of his own weapons to fashion a spear for Karana out of a long bone taken from the moose.

"Soon Karana will hunt with Umak and Torka. This will be a good thing."

The boy had not replied, but he had taken the spear and hefted it, shaking it at an imaginary quarry. And then, for the first time, he had smiled.

Lonit had watched the relationship of her men and the boy grow. Karana was gradually filling the void that Kipu had left in their lives. She was glad for this, but sorry for the child. No matter how kind and caring Umak and Torka were to him, it was obvious that he still longed for his own people. For all of his fierce bravado, he was still a lonely little boy. Sometimes, when the men slept or were off hunting, Lonit heard him whispering softly to the dog. In Aar, Karana had found a companion in whom he could confide his secret hopes and fears. Aar found an affinity and empathy with the child perhaps because the dog was, for all of its strength and voracity, little more than a lost pup itself. Boy and dog were always together now. They slept back to back, actually touching, and when Karana sometimes whimpered in his sleep, the dog licked his face and whimpered soft encouragement back to him. Karana would throw a skinny little arm around Aar's neck and cuddle close. The dog made no attempt to move away.

The day was hot and windy. Torka volunteered to accompany her on her search for eggs. They went down the mountain together, with Lonit marveling at his open concern for her safety. He carried her gathering nets over his shoulder and went down first, reaching back to steady her descent as she followed.

She had already gathered most of the eggs that were available near the mountain's flank. One of the few lessons that her mother had taught her was to never take *all* of anything. This was the way of the band, Torka confirmed. A few eggs here, a few plants there, a few head of game or geese, and always there would be more to greet the hunters and gatherers in the following time of light.

They went out onto the tundra, deep into the sedge marsh where the geese were now molting the last of their flight feathers. They would be bound to the earth while they raised their young. New feathers grew meanwhile to replace the old so the geese would be strong when they flew away into the face of the rising sun in the last lingering days of summer before the time of the long dark.

Torka paused. It was very windy. The grasses hissed all around. The waters rippled and splashed as waterfowl, suddenly alerted to their presence, took to their wings in a cackling, honking, squawking hysteria. Since many were devoid of the long, strong feathers that allowed them to fly, many gained no altitude at all, instead crashing through green walls of grass to disappear without grace or dignity into another portion of the marsh.

Torka laughed.

It was such a rare sound, Lonit looked at him, startled and pleased. He was no longer the same man who had walked the wind and led her and Umak to the mountain. He had lost the gauntness of winter. The sun had bronzed his face. Her love for him was so intense that it nearly choked her. Despite the wind, the day was hot; she could barely breathe.

"Look," said Torka, raising his arms. "The wind has blown the flies and biting ones away across the plain. Let us take advantage of this. Such a day may not come again until the time of the long dark has come and gone and a new summer is born!"

He gave her no opportunity to reply as he put down his spears, dropped the egg-gathering nets, stripped off his clothes, and plunged into the cold shallows, hooting with delight as he splashed and wallowed like a child.

"Come!" he called.

It was a command. She could not refuse. It was good to peel off her summer tunic; it had grown much too tight across her breasts, no doubt the result of all of the food that her men so generously shared with her. Yet she had found it strange that only her breasts should grow fat while the rest of her remained lean and her belly tighter than it had ever been.

Removing her boots, she walked into the shallows, gasping against the unexpected chill of the water, hoping that Torka would not find the sight of her too repulsive.

As she came toward him, he grew suddenly quiet. The expansive, boyish expression of absolute carelessness vanished from his features. She paused, knowing that the sight of her had ruined his happiness—but when he got to his feet and came to her, she knew that the sight of her had only banished the boy and roused the man.

His eyes moved over her slowly. His hands followed. When he touched her breasts, she gasped and shivered as though the wind had suddenly turned cold. But she was not cold. She was aflame. His palm pressed gently against her lower belly to lie flat against its tautness, and slowly a smile moved upon his mouth as he nodded.

"Lonit is beautiful," he said, and drew her to him in an embrace of exquisite tenderness, holding her, enfolding her in his arms. "Lonit is Torka's woman. This baby . . . it will be a good thing."

"Baby?"

He did not speak. He breathed the breath of his life into her nostrils, then lifted her and carried her out of the water. Gently, he lowered her onto the tundra, and more gently than that he made love to her. Beneath the golden eye of the midnight sun, Lonit knew that it *was* love, and when at last they lay joined, exhausted and fulfilled, she understood why she had not shed a woman's blood and needed no one of her own gender to explain to her how she had come to be carrying Torka's child.

9

Now they were lovers. They shared the same sleeping skins. The days ran on, one into the other, like golden fish leaping through the mesh of a skeining net that would not hold them.

And still Karana's people did not come.

The boy was walking again, with the aid of a crutch that Umak had made for him out of a caribou antler. His wound was still painful and he limped badly, but he continued to keep his vigils on the ledge, patiently waiting for his people as he watched Umak and Torka hunting on the tundra far below the mountain.

Berries began to ripen in the canyons. The hunters accompanied Lonit on gathering forays and stood guard over her as she dug for edible tubers. To humor her insistence that they store as much as possible against the threat of starving times, they went with her into the wetlands and stood by admiringly as she refined her skill with her bola by hunting geese and other waterfowl. Even with the first roundness of pregnancy beginning to show, she was still as swift and lean and agile as a young doe.

"Hmmph. The longer Umak looks at Only Woman In The World, the less ugly she becomes."

"Lonit is not ugly," said Torka defensively, and did not correct his grandfather for referring to her as the only woman in the world. For Torka, she *was* the only woman. He rarely thought of Egatsop these days, and when he did, it was a sad and tender remembrance. The possessiveness and the rage against the way she had died were gone. She was dead; he had placed her to look at the sky with his own hands. Lonit was his woman now. He knew that he would never desire or love anyone the way he loved Lonit.

Hatchlings were flying. Young foxes, wolves, and lions were learning to hunt. Burrowers and rodents were watching the unwary among their young learn how to die. Bison and musk ox, horse and camel, antelope and yak, the great browsing herds grazed their way ever eastward across the steppe beneath the great mountain. Soon the first of the season's migratory birds would rise from the tundral wetlands to wend their way into the face of the rising sun. Karana looked out across a world that had been tinted rust by the first frost of autumn.

Where were his people? Why did they not come?

Lonit sat in the sun on the far side of the cornice. The boy heard the soft sound of her voice as she hummed to herself while she sewed. She was stitching new boots for them all. Her voice was soothing. The boy did not want to be soothed.

His brow furrowed as he stared out across the world. Aar had followed Umak and Torka down from the heights. The old man had discovered bear sign in the canyon. He and Torka had decided that they would dig a pit trap for it at the head of the canyon. Such a large and potentially dangerous animal was not welcome in their hunting range, and bear meat was among the best if eaten fresh. Rich and sweet, it would be a feast for them all. The fat of the animal would burn long and steadily in Lonit's oil lamp. Its thick hide would provide warm winter leggings and overvests for them all.

But Karana was not thinking about the bear that would soon die at Umak's and Torka's hands. He was thinking of his people. A deep, aching hurt formed at the back of his throat. Was his father dead? Could it be that Karana was the only member of his band to survive that last terrible winter? Or was the old spirit master right? Could it be that his people had abandoned him?

The supposition was one he had not allowed himself to consider. Supnah would never have abandoned him. *Never.* Yet now he remembered the anguished look that had contorted his father's face when the magic man, Navahk, had spoken to him. And he remembered the way that the magic man had smiled at him. It had been a smile full of secrets, dark secrets, like insect larvae hidden deep within the belly of a wounded longspur that he had once found upon the spring tundra. The little bird had looked all right; he had thought that it was only stunned and shivering against the cold. But when he had lifted it from the snow, the worms that were eating of its damaged breast squirmed and wriggled against his palms as, with one last shudder, the tiny bird had died.

The memory was so unpleasant that Karana closed his eyes and shook his head, trying to blot it from his mind. He hoped that Navahk was dead, his own belly eaten out by worms. He could not understand how his father could have taken the advice of such a magic man. Perhaps it was because they were brothers? Perhaps it was because, long ago, Karana's mother had adored Supnah but avoided Navahk, and Supnah felt obliged to compensate him for that?

Perhaps Karana would never know the answers to these questions. Supnah, Navahk, and his band were far away. Karana was alone with strangers, and as time continued to pass, he was finding it harder and harder to remain hostile toward them. It was clear to him now that the old spirit master had not meant to hurt him. Still, he resented the old man for his refusal to believe that Karana's people would return.

He opened his eyes. He looked around the well-stocked, meticulously maintained encampment and had to admit to himself that life here with Umak, Torka, Lonit, and the wild dog was good—so good that sometimes he actually hoped that his people would not come for him.

But they would. He *know* that they would. To wish otherwise was to be a disloyal son. He clenched his teeth and set his mouth into a scowl. Karana would wait for his people. Soon now they *would* come.

The dog alerted them to danger. They had been busy digging the pit trap, cutting down spruce trees and hacking them into stakes onto which the bear would, they hoped, fall and impale itself. To be certain of their quarry's death, they had baited the canyon with freshly killed marmots into which they had inserted deadly slivers of bone that had been ingeniously softened and bent double. Pointed on both ends, when swallowed by the bear, the bone splinters would be straightened by its digestive juices, expanding into lethal rods that would pierce the animal's intestines. Weakened by pain and internal bleeding, such a bear could be tracked and killed

by two men. It would be dangerous, but if the bear avoided
the pit trap, they would have no other way of successfully
bringing it down with minimal risk to themselves. It was not
a way of hunting that either Torka or Umak liked, but both
men knew that even with a full complement of hunters there
was no prey more dangerous or unpredictable than a bear
unless it was an enraged mammoth.

Their main problem had been keeping Aar from making
off with their marmots. They kept throwing stones at the dog
to keep it from snatching the deadly bait, and the dog,
insulted and confused by their behavior toward it, had turned
and started back toward the ledge. So it was that Aar came
upon the bear and alerted the hunters to the fact that they
were about to become the hunted.

For one moment, the great bear froze in the brush at the
neck of the canyon. Standing on all fours, it was over six feet
tall at the shoulder. When it stood erect to sight its prey, it
was more than twice that. It had a push-faced snout and a
wide, overslung lower jaw. Its huge, shaggy body rippled
with an underlayering of fat, and its small yellow eyes fixed
the hunters as it shook its enormous head and slobbered out
of a gaping maw of a pink-lipped mouth that showed teeth
more suited to ripping flesh than grinding berries.

The great head dropped. The eyes did not blink. The bear
made no sound. It charged without warning, but Aar's sudden, lightning-swift counterattack distracted it. Confused by
the dog's frenzied barking and bold, circling, snapping lunges,
the bear paused. It turned first one way, then the other as it
attempted to swat the audacious dog. Its movement allowed
Torka time to level and hurl a spear. It went deep into the
bear's shoulder, quivering harmlessly but not painlessly in a
layer of fat. The bear growled now, rearing up and shaking
itself. With the spear still projecting from its shoulder, it
came down onto all fours again and ran straight toward Umak.

The old man never flinched. With his spear in one hand
and his dagger in the other, he crouched, waiting. The bear
was a blur of brown as it filled his vision. Behind Umak,
Torka raged at his grandfather to run, but he did not. A
lifetime's worth of hunting wisdom and experience galvanized
his senses. Sight, sound, smell, taste, and the sensory nerves
at the tips of his fingers all functioned at their maximum
levels as Umak, spirit master, bent them to one purpose. He
was master of his own spirit now, in complete control of his

body and emotions. The light that burned at the back of a man's eyes when death was near was white-hot within his own eyes now. He stood his ground until he could smell the breath of the bear and one huge, clawed paw flew outward toward him in an attempt to swipe off his head.

In that instant, his mind and body were consumed in the bright inner fire of pure intent and absolute fearlessness. The eyes of man and beast met as Umak lunged forward to drive his dagger deep and his spear through the bear's left eye socket straight into its brain. The animal swept over the man like a breaking wave of brown fur. When it fell, it fell with Umak in an embrace of death.

Torka's heart was in his throat and his knife-edged whalebone bludgeon was in his hand. Time seemed to throb in cadence with his pulse—and it was fast, much too fast. He was breathless, unable to react to what he had just witnessed. And then, in an explosion of energy, he cried his grandfather's name. As Aar leaped upon the fallen bear with slashing, ripping teeth, Torka joined him, hacking and slicing with his weapon. He knew that he was sobbing. He did not care. The great bear was dead, with Umak's spear in its skull and Umak's dagger deep in its thorax, and all that Torka could see of his grandfather were his legs sticking out from beneath the monstrous mound of ruined fur and bleeding carcass.

Then one leg moved, and the other. From out of the bottom of the mound came a weak and angry voice. "Torka can skin this great bear later! Umak may be a spirit master, but what he has killed is not going to get up and walk away! Get this old man out of here!"

Night had returned to the tundra. And in its star-filled darkness, the little band feasted on the meat of the great short-faced bear. Umak had not come away from the encounter unscathed. The bear had half-scalped him, but as wounds went, it was not so bad. He sat proudly while Lonit sutured it. He remembered his failure with the wolves and smiled as he thought: *This wound is a good thing. It has given back to this old man his pride.*

They shared their food with Aar. Karana sat close to Umak as Lonit built their fire high. For the second time since he had come to live with them upon the ledge, the boy spoke.

"Karana is glad old man alive."

"*Hmmph!* This old man is not so easy to kill!" replied Umak. "And Umak is glad boy has decided to use his mouth for more than eating and scowling!" He gave the child a cuff to the side of the head. It was gently done. The boy smiled as he watched Umak don the bear-claw necklace that Lonit had made for him. The old man had salved his wound with a paste of willow pulp and urine. The curative oils of the willow soothed the rawness of his sutured scalp. Ammonia in the urine would discourage infection. Although he was tired and hurting, Umak had never felt stronger or younger or more deeply at peace with himself. In his old age, he had faced down and killed a bear that was even larger than the great white bear that he had slain in his youth.

"This is not the first bear that Umak has taken," he informed the boy. "No. Long ago, when this old man was a boy no bigger than Karana, the bear spirits said to their little ones: 'Grow strong. Grow wise. Grow wary. Umak is growing to manhood, and he is all of these things!'"

He told his story then. In the high, ruddy glow of the dancing fire, they sat close together in the darkness of the cave, enchanted by the spell that he worked with his words. Umak of old was born out of the dark to live again in the light of Lonit's fire, to hunt, to walk the savage tundra, to live as a youth again in the magic of the night until, in the dying glow of the flickering shadows, the old man, weakened by blood loss and exhausted by the events of the day, fell asleep.

Karana looked at him adoringly, sighed, put his head on the old man's knee, and contentedly lost himself in his own dreams of adventures that had been nurtured by Umak's tales. Aar slept beside the boy, and Lonit lay asleep on her side upon her new mattress of ground-sloth fur.

A weary Torka looked at her with love. His eyes drifted to the old man and the boy. He was reminded of the many nights during his own childhood when he had slept close to his grandfather, with his head on Umak's knee, nourished by his wisdom and his strength. It seemed so long ago, yet with no effort at all, he could call it all back—all of it . . . too much of it.

Sadness touched him. It erased the soft, warm mellowness of his mood. In the darkness, pale from loss of blood, Umak looked frail and worn. The youth who had leaped to life through the magic imagery of the spirit master's tales was irretrievably lost to the past.

Suddenly uneasy, Torka rose and went to stand at the edge of their aerie. He could not put from his mind the realization that, had it not been for the warning given by the dog, he and Umak would probably not have survived their encounter with the bear.

The wind touched him. It had the chill, dry bite of autumn to it. Beyond the mountain, the world was a vast, textureless sprawl of darkness. Stars, like cold white embers throbbing on the sleek black skin of the night, defined where earth ended and sky began.

Where were Karana's people? Were they out there now, far across the tundra, staring toward the mountain and wondering at the fire's glow high on its eastern wall?

Or was it as Torka had feared from the beginning? Were they alone in the world? He was happy now, with Umak and Lonit and the boy in this strange high camp that they had made above the game-rich land. But without another band to give strength to their numbers, they would be doomed to live out their days alone, always at risk of imminent death. Umak was an extraordinary hunter, but he was an old man who would not be able to hunt forever. If Torka were injured or killed, how long could Lonit and their coming child hope to survive with only a wild dog and an injured boy to protect them against the dangers that would face them every day of their lives?

Not long, he thought.

And while Umak, Karana, and the dog dreamed the deep, restful dreams of those who were content, Torka sat bundled in his sleeping skins against the mountain wall at the edge of the cornice. He watched for distant fires, for signs of other bands, then slept the fitful sleep of one deeply troubled. His dreams were of wolves and roaring walls of water, of frozen wastes of endless tundra, and of a mammoth with eyes as red as blood and shoulders as high as the mountain. He saw himself as a condor, his feathered arms spread wide upon the wind. And then, as in a dream dreamt long before, he became a lightning bolt, a spear of silver, streaking down toward the mammoth, down toward death as thunder rent the sky and he entered the flesh of the Destroyer, piercing it to its very heart.

He awoke with a start.

The thunder had been real. He could hear it now and see the evanescent flash of lightning upon the far horizon. He stared, wondering for a moment if he had heard another sound within the thunder, a higher, sharper sound—the screaming trumpet of a mammoth.

He listened. There was only the sound of the distant storm. Somewhere, high above the cave, something shifted within the summit ice pack. Torka paid no attention to it. He closed his eyes. It was nearly dawn. He slept again, and this time he did not dream at all.

When the sun rose above the eastern mountains, its light spraying across the tangled, icy sprawl of distant summits and spreading across the miles to pierce his lids, Torka came up out of darkness, shielding his eyes with the back of his hand, certain that he had to be dreaming. There was no wind. The silence was so absolute that it hurt his ears, and the color of the dawn was so intense that it seared his vision. It filled the great sweep of plain with shimmering golden light. And in that light, something was moving, schooling in a long stream like fish swimming beneath the surface of a light-dappled lake. And in the silence, slowly, sound was growing.

Within the cave, Umak, Karana, and Lonit slept heavily in the last, lingering shadows of the night. The dog rose and came to stand beside Torka. Tail tucked, ears back, head out, Aar stood at the lip of the cornice and surveyed the tundra. Now Torka was certain that he was dreaming. The dog never came close to him intentionally. They hunted together for Umak's sake and they shared the same cave, also for Umak's sake, and now for Karana's as well; but Torka and Aar shared a mutual distrust. Aar had not forgotten that Torka had once tethered him, and Torka would not allow himself to forget that Aar was still a wild beast.

Now the beast was growling, so intent upon the vision that was rising in the lake of morning light that it paid no heed to Torka as he rose and stood.

Man and dog surveyed the world together. Slowly the light began to fade. Slowly the sound allowed definition. Torka stared in disbelief. He closed his eyes and stared again. The vision was still there, real. He was not dreaming. Slowly, from out of the northern sweep of the vast, undulating tundral steppe, people were coming toward the mountain.

PART IV

WORLD
SHAKER

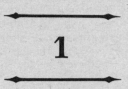

1

They were not Karana's people. The boy leaned on his crutch and stared down at them with a sinking heart that was buoyed only by the fact that they did not look like the Ghost Band either. They were a small, bedraggled band of fewer than thirty weary travelers. Their clothing was roughly made. They wore no labrets, nor were their faces painted, although they were so encrusted with soot and grime that at first they appeared black.

They paused at the base of the great peak, murmuring among themselves at the unprecedented sight of a wild dog keeping company with men.

Torka and Umak stood together on the ledge. Aar stood in front of them, barking and snarling as though he had appointed himself spokesman for his man-pack. Lonit and Karana stood to one side. When she leaned close to ask the boy if they were his people, he growled at her and shook his head in a vehement display of disgust.

"Karana's band not look like *that!*"

His negative reaction affirmed Lonit's growing feeling of foreboding. She did not like the look of the newcomers, but until Karana spoke, she was certain that her apprehension was caused by her resentment of them. After her lifetime of dreaming, Torka was her man at last. Alone in the world with him, she would be his woman forever. Together they would create a new band, and the People would be reborn. Now her dream was shattered. Among the people who stood looking up toward their aerie, there were bound to be women more worthy of Torka than she. He would not want Lonit anymore. She would be an embarrassment to him. When their child was born, he would not consent to hunt for it. He would turn his back upon them both.

Staring down at the newcomers, Lonit hated them and herself. If only she were not such an ugly, unworthy girl, she could rejoice at their coming. Yet, slowly, hope began to lessen her fear of them. Even from the distance, she could see that their clothes were ragged, not from wear but due to shoddy construction; it was as though the women who had sewn them had not bothered to take the time to fit them properly or stitch them with any care. The women stood apart from their men, bent nearly double under the weight of enormous, lumpy-looking packs. Lonit could see that their skirts were worn and uneven, neither fringed nor trimmed with any sort of contrasting fur. The men were also clad in ragged-edged garments. Other than their weaponry, they carried no loads at all. A few short, squat young boys were walking out of the main body of the group on either side of a bison-skin clad hunter who wore his stiff black hair pulled into a single tuft at the top of his head. Lonit stared. The tuft seemed to be spraying out of the man's skull, but even though he walked into the wind, his hair was so stiff that it barely moved. He carried spears in both hands. With arms raised, he was shaking them as he cried out in a high voice that bespoke friendship.

"Wha tha ah mateh? Galeena khum! Khum ah frend!"

In his necklaces of wolf paws and freshly taken bear claws, Umak ignored the weakness that his scalp wound had brought on him. He stood as tall as he could. He held a spear arrogantly in one hand. He was determined to show only strength and disdain to the newcomers. He shared Lonit's apprehension. He did not like the look of this band, and could not understand a word of the language that its headman had spoken. Karana was looking at him, waiting for him to respond with the infinite wisdom of a spirit master. Lacking such wisdom, Umak chose to remain silent for long moments during which he scowled with a great display of authority. His chin went up. His mouth turned down. His eyes half closed as though he were looking beyond this world into another plain of existence that only a spirit master's eyes could see.

"Dhag Meh, Galeena khum ah frend! Dhag Meh bahd beh mah oh spaweh?"

The words of the tuft-headed man hung in the air. Torka

frowned, straining to understand while Karana came close to Umak, impressed by his scowl and the wonderfully insolent way that he stood glowering down at the strangers. Wanting to win praise from the old man, Karana spoke. "Karana knows man talk. Man asks who on mountain. Man says his name Galeena. Galeena says he would come to us. He asks us not kill him. He says he friend. He calls this band Dog Men. He asks if Dog Men be men or spirit."

Umak was impressed, as were Torka and Lonit. Torka nodded to show his approval.

"It is good that Karana knows the words of other bands," he said.

"Hmmph," Umak snorted, noting that Torka and Lonit knew what Karana had not yet discovered—that their spirit master's knowledge was not limitless.

The boy was delighted by Torka's compliment. He stood a little straighter and imitated Umak's haughty demeanor. "Karana be like spirit master someday! Know all things. But Galeena speaks same words as Torka. Many bands, all speak same words. Just say different."

Umak cocked his head. His scowl became a smile. He had been right when he had told Lonit that the People were like the great herds of caribou! They *had* been one at the beginning. Now they were many, and the words that they spoke were slowly changing as they ranged farther and farther from the center of Creation.

The light of comprehension was born within Umak. "Dhag Meh . . . Dog Men. Galeena khum ah frend . . . Galeena comes as friend. Hmmph! It is good that this spirit master can speak to Galeena and his people."

And this he did. He raised his spear arm and shook it. "Galeena khum ah frend! Umak is spirit master! He says to Galeena: Come! Be welcome! Dog Men have much meat to share!"

It was a mistake. The old man knew it a moment after Galeena came up onto the ledge with a half dozen of his hunters following right behind him. The stink of the strangers preceded them up the wall; and it was a more offensive stench than that in which Karana had wrapped himself for protection against predators. This was the stench of filth—of unwashed bodies and clothes and of something else, something threatening. Tension walked with these men. Karana had to kneel and put his arms about Aar to keep the dog from attacking. The animal lowered its head, and every hair upon its back stood on end as a low, steady growl came out of its snarling muzzle.

Umak did not have to look at Brother Dog to share its instinctive sense of danger. He was sorry that he had invited the newcomers without first conferring with Torka. If anything went wrong, Umak knew that he would be fully to blame. But what could go wrong? he asked himself. They were men. Hunters. Once they had washed themselves and aired their clothes, they would be no different from the men of the People who now lay looking at the sky. But why did they hold their weapons so defensively? Why had they brought none of their women and children up onto the mountain with them? Umak snorted quietly, assuring himself that the newcomers were afraid of those whose spirit master had bent the will of a wild dog so that even the smallest among them could touch the beast as though it were his brother. He stood a little taller. He scowled a little more disdainfully. It was good to know that men feared his powers once again.

Torka eyed the newcomers warily. His hand tightened around the sinew-wrapped haft of his whalebone bludgeon. He could not have said why he had taken it up, but the moment the strangers had begun the ascent of the wall, he had felt the need to show them a sign of strength. Why? Men hefted weapons against game and predators, not against their fellow hunters. Men did not hunt men. Yet, the moment he had looked into Galeena's small black eyes he had seen a bold rapaciousness in them that had made him glad that he held his weapon.

Galeena spoke. Politely.

Torka replied. Politely.

Galeena grinned, and all six of his spear-carrying fellow hunters grinned with him.

Torka felt fury race through his veins. Galeena was eyeing Lonit in a way that made Torka want to brain him. His fingers flexed around his weapon. "This woman is Torka's woman," he told him in a tone that left no room for debate.

Lonit flushed. She bowed her head, dropping her lids, and moved to stand behind Torka, wanting to be shielded from the strangers' sight. She did not like them. There was something in their eyes and smiles and the way that they carried their weapons that frightened her. She wished that they had never come. Yet, their coming had caused Torka to speak words that she had never thought to hear him speak to others. A new band had walked into their world, and Torka had not denied her. The realization was heady.

Galeena took a step forward. Aar nearly leaped out of Karana's arms. Threatened by the dog, the man froze. His hunters aimed their spears at Aar. Karana felt suddenly light-headed with fear, but he kept his place and tightened his grip around Aar's neck. He knew that his little arms could not hold the dog if it chose to spring to the attack, but his softly spoken words kept the dog at his side. "Hold, Brother. Until Spirit Master speaks, these smelly ones are welcome among us."

Galeena eyed the boy and the dog, measuring the moment and finding a powerful magic in it. He looked at Torka, saw his strength and unmistakable resolve to stand against any threat to his band. But it was such a small band: one hunter, an old man, a young woman, a boy, and a wild dog. A strange company, one to be wary of until Galeena was absolutely certain that it was not more than it appeared to be. "Yuh Dahg Meh, spaweh payeh?" he asked directly.

Torka strained to understand the words. Umak grasped their meaning and replied with pride. "Umak is spirit master!" When Galeena's features clumped into a mass of humps and seams that showed his lack of comprehension, the old man repeated in the newcomer's dialect. "Umak spaweh masteh! Umak's people . . . payeh . . . you call Dog Men. We are strong with spaweh, spirit!" It would do no harm to embellish their status. The spirits of the mountain *had* been with them, allowing them a safe encampment, protecting them during the hunt. Umak was gratified to see the look of uncertainty and restrained awe upon the faces of the newcomers when they looked at Brother Dog. It made him feel almost omnipotent as he spoke to the strangers with his chin jabbing up and his eyes looking down his nose at them as though they were ignorant children coming to him for their first lesson in the wisdom of the People.

Galeena's eyes narrowed shrewdly. He had not failed to note Umak's tone of condescending superiority. He appraised the fresh scalp wound on the old man's head and thought: *He may command the spirits of this place and of that wild dog, but* some *animal did that to him. His magic is not so great. He is mortal, this spirit master. And those who stand with him, they are mortal, too.* He nodded. He grinned, displaying brown, furred, wide-gapped teeth as though he considered them to be objects of beauty that all should admire and envy. He gestured outward, indicating the spacious ledge and the fine encampment that Lonit had made.

"Ghu khamp this," he said, openly coveting the many skins and racks of drying meat, fish, and fowl, as well as the sacks of dried berries and roots. Like Umak, Galeena had quickly grasped the subtle differences in the dialects of the two bands. He altered his own with pleasure, wanted Umak to know that, although he claimed to be a spirit master, he had misjudged Galeena's potential for understanding. "Galeena's band, we see fiah this khamp from long fah way. We khum. Now we khamp this khamp. Be safe from Big Spirit in this high place we shah with Dhag Meh."

The world shook beneath Torka's feet; yet the movement was within him as his heart leaped within his chest and nearly staggered him. "Big Spirit?"

"You not know Big Spirit? Big Spirit shake world! Big Spirit kill many Galeena's people. In fah place, many die. Galeena's band meets many bands at place wheh tundra and forest meet. Much spruce theh. Many mammoth browse wheh Corridor of Storms begins. Bad place. Mountains all ice theh. High to sky. Walk like meh. Make sound like wumeh wailing. Wind neveh stop. Blow all time."

"And Big Spirit?"

Galeena grunted, not wishing to be hurried by Torka's impatient query. It required concentration to form the words in a way as to be understood by the Dog Men. "We make khamp theh. Where Corridor of Storm begins. We hunt mammoth. We kill. Many bands togetheh. We take much meat. We feast. Then Big Spirit khums, hiding in skin of animal it khums . . . looking like mammoth it khums . . . but too big for mammoth. It kills. Many run. Its red eyes see all. Big Spirit follows. Its tusks kill men, like this! Its feet kill wumeh and children, like this! It cries out. Then it goes. And meh come out of hiding. Meh try to track Big Spirit, to kill Big Spirit. Rain khums. Much storm leaves no tracks to follow. But Galeena and his people, we say this good. We khum fah place. We seek high khamp. Away from Big Spirit. Galeena says Big Spirit walks fah tundra, looking foh meh to kill. And meh cannot kill Big Spirit. It is like mountain. It lives foreveh!" He paused, observing the affect his words had on his listeners. "You, Torka, you know Big Spirit?"

"Torka knows Big Spirit."

"Torka meet in fah place? Maybe Big Spirit kill many Torka's band, too?"

"It is so."

"That why Torka's band small! *Very* small. Torka bring to high place be safe! This good! This khamp *very* good khamp! Room for many. Galeena's people, we khum! We stay! We make one band with Dog People! Old man Spirit Masteh, he talk spirit talk for all! Galeena's band, no spirit man us. Mammoth kill. Now good times for all togetheh. Many make hunt safe! Many live easy! It be good thing!"

2

It was not a good thing. Galeena did not ask, he took. He put his weapons aside, but still he took. Peacefully, his people came up onto the ledge. They did not ask anything of its occupants. Their greater number allowed them the privilege of simply dropping their belongings wherever they wished. When Lonit attempted to direct the women to the part of the cave best suited to their needs, they swept her aside and ignored her protests. Suddenly, her orderly encampment was one of confusion and disarray as the women rifled through her stores and stuffed their mouths with berries and wedges of fat. Lonit stood back, waiting for Torka or Umak to come to her aid with them, but they had similar troubles of their own.

Galeena had clearly taken over. He barked commands to his surly hunters and kicked at the few young boys who were the only children in the band. One of them threw a short, poorly balanced spear in Aar's direction. It missed the dog, but Karana did not miss the boy as he leaped at him and knocked him to the ground. Umak pulled them apart. Karana was so angry that he was oblivious to the pain in his leg; he knew only that Aar had disappeared.

"Brother Dog will come back," assured Umak.

"To this? This no longer Torka's cave! This Galeena's wallow!" protested the child.

The boy was right. Galeena's men were hunkering in the shadows, devouring Lonit's carefully preserved meats. They tossed the scraps randomly about and relieved themselves at will, wherever and whenever the need presented itself.

"Over there . . . on the sedges with that! And over the side with the rest of it! You keep that up and the whole ledge is going to smell like a bison wallow!" Torka raised his voice, then thought better of it. Galeena and his band already looked and smelled as though they had come up out of days of rolling in a muddy dung heap. And their numbers totally overwhelmed any authority that Torka attempted to maintain.

Torka watched them with thoughtful contemplation. They were a filthy, disgraceful people. He had no doubt that, had he tried to stand against their occupancy of the ledge, they would have forced their way past him, even if they had to throw him off the mountain to do so. Still, given time, rest, and food, their manner was bound to improve. They too had suffered beneath the deadly shadow of the Destroyer. As much as Torka disliked them and was angered by their forced intrusion, he could frame no logical argument against Galeena's intent to join forces and share the occupation of the ledge for the betterment of all. Adjustments would have to be made on both sides. And with other women to assist her, Lonit's workload would be eased, and she would have those of her own gender to assist her at the birth of their child. Karana would have friends his own age. Umak would be able to be a spirit master again, with a real band to pay him homage. And he, Torka, would have men to hunt with; the dangers of the kill would be lessened considerably.

And Galeena was probably right about Big Spirit. His sentiments echoed Umak's certainties. The mammoth *was* a spirit. No man could hope to kill it—not without risking becoming a spirit himself. His eyes strayed to Lonit. She was coming toward him, clutching her personal belongings. Compared to the women of Galeena's band, she was the most beautiful woman in the world. He was proud to know that he had put life into her belly. He recalled their many lovemakings and thought of the child that would be born to them toward the end of the time of the long dark. He imagined its cries and the smile that would dimple Lonit's face and bring warmth to her antelope eyes when the infant at last took suck upon the firm, round breasts that he so cherished.

He smiled as she came to him. All thoughts of the great mammoth left his mind as he drew her close. Life was good. The future promised much to him. With Lonit as his woman, Torka was no longer ready to throw his life away.

3

Galeena's people ate as though they feared that they would never eat again. They stuffed themselves until it seemed that they could eat no more, but they did eat more. And more. Until Lonit protested to Torka that soon all of their winter provisions would be gone.

Galeena overheard her. "Wuhman no worry! Tomorrow men hunt. Both bands together, we take much meat. Have plenty eat for all khum dark time winteh."

The sun stood high in the sky. Exhausted by what Galeena said was a very long trek to the mountain, his people lounged upon their own filthy sleeping skins and upon the hides and furs that they had freely seized from Lonit's stores. Scratching at their vermin-infested bodies, some of them slept; others gnawed bones, wolfed meat, gulped fat, cut wind, belched, and coupled freely. Now and again, some of them rose to defecate or vomit; then, thus purged, they ambled back to their sleeping skins to doze or eat or copulate within full view of the unruly boys who scoured the cave for leftovers.

Never in their lives had Torka's people seen others behave in such a despicable manner, nor had they ever seen such rowdy, offensive youths. Torka would have asked Galeena why the boys had no one to feed them; it did not seem logical to him that they could all have been orphaned. And there were simply too many women in Galeena's band. No young girls. No toddlers. No infants. And no elderly, either, for that matter—just men and women in their prime and a pack of nearly a dozen animalistic boys who ran wild amid the adults, foraging for food and harassing everyone, especially two greasy matrons who sat by themselves beside a sloppily made fire where no man joined them. They were evidently widows;

Torka had seen them fight for their share of food as savagely as the boys. Now, as he watched, one of them whacked at the boys with the thighbone of an antelope as the other one stared wistfully across the cave at Umak. The old man ignored her, and Galeena showed no concern over the screechings of her embattled hearthmate or for the brawling boys. The headman was too busy beneath his sleeping skins with his appropriated food and the two giggling, guffawing women who were his wives. Torka knew that he would get no answers from Galeena until the man was rested and sated.

Torka was sickened by the stench and crowding, and at his insistence, his little band had relocated their fire stones, sleeping skins, and what Galeena had left them of their personal belongings. They moved well out of the center of the cave, almost onto the exposed lip of the cornice. The new site was not without drawbacks. When the weather changed, or when the wind grew strong, they would have to build a weather baffle to keep themselves and their little fire sheltered and dry. It did not matter. The air was breathable here, and the stench of Galeena's people was not totally overpowering. No one objected to their moving; no one even took notice. Galeena's people were too occupied with their own sleepy, gluttonous pastimes.

As Lonit rearranged her fire stones and Torka and Umak settled themselves, Karana glowered unhappily. "Karana does not like these smelly ones. Torka should take his spear and make them go away."

"Torka is one. They are many. Karana must remember that they have come far. They have suffered much. They are tired and hungry. In time, when they have rested, they will change their ways. They cannot live like this *all* the time! Karana will see that this is so. And in the meantime, Torka says that it was not so long ago when Karana was a smelly one himself."

The boy flushed angrily. "Only to keep the big-toothed animals from eating me!"

"Perhaps it is the same with Galeena's band?" suggested Torka.

Ignoring the stares of Umak and Lonit, Karana knew that he was speaking out of turn, but he did not care. If he did not speak his fears about Galeena's band, he would have no hope of convincing Torka to change his mind about them. He lowered his voice, speaking in the tone of a conspirator.

"Galeena's people *bad* people. Maybe they *are* Ghost Band! Maybe they eat *us* when all meat is gone! If Torka cannot drive them away, then Spirit Master must make them disappear! It would be a good thing. Then Brother Dog will come back. Then this will be a good camp again!"

Torka's brows came together thoughtfully. "Galeena's people are not ghosts, Karana. If Umak made them disappear, we would be alone . . . at great risk again . . . and Karana would have no other boys to talk boy-things to. He would have only a dog who cannot understand or speak to answer."

Umak harrumphed at this, but before he could speak in defense of the dog, Karana bristled and replied hotly.

"Karana does not talk to those who have tried to kill his brother! Aar *does* understand! And Karana says that one of Brother Dog's droppings is worth more than *all* the boys of Galeena's band!" With this he limped off to stand at the very edge of the cornice, leaning on his crutch of antler, missing his brother dog more than words could ever say.

Slowly the sun slipped behind the mountain to leave the eastern world in shadow. Darkness began to fill the cave. Galeena's people slept. A chill wind drove Karana back to Lonit's fire. Neither Umak, Torka, nor Lonit said a word about his earlier display of temper. He sat in sullen silence, trying to think of a way to apologize without altering his position. Galeena's people were all that he had said, and more. He knew it and would not change his mind. He must make Torka change his.

In the light of the rising moon, a wild dog howled, and from across the unknown country to the east, another dog answered, then another and another.

Karana tensed.

Umak listened. He nodded reflectively, trying not to be distracted by the eyes of the matron. Alone among her people, she was still awake. How long had she been staring at him? And how many winters had come and gone since a woman had looked at him like that? Hmmph. She was not young, but she was not old, either. Beneath her slovenly garments and layers of filth, she might even prove to be human. The possibility was intriguing—so much so that, when he spoke in reference to the dog, he knew that he was not speaking of Aar at all. "Perhaps Brother Dog will not long be alone, without a mate to share the meat that he brings to his camp?"

* * *

Lonit looked at Torka and sighed as she heard the lonely sounds of the wild, distant animals. Moonlight was silvering the night. "Perhaps Aar will find one of his own kind. It would be a good thing." In the glow of the moon, Torka had never looked more handsome as she thought: *Lonit has found her place beside Torka at last. Even in this camp, with these smelly people all around, it is a good thing.*

Karana glared at them. The old spirit master had the oddest look on his face. And Torka and Lonit seemed to see nothing but the reflection of the moon shining in their eyes as they looked at one another. He suddenly felt alone, as though, despite the crowding of the cave and the presence of those who had taken him into their band, there was no one in the world for him, not even a wild dog. For the first time in longer than he wanted to acknowledge, he thought of his people. So much time had passed since they had walked away into the snow-driven mists, promising to return for him and the children. Now, when he tried to recall his father's face, he did not see Supnah at all; he saw a composite of Torka and Umak. Supnah was far away, lost in the misted past, but someday he *would* return . . . if he could. But Karana was sure that if something had happened to his father, Karana would have known it. And yet, despite his certainty, he saw not his father but the leering, contemptuous smile of Navahk, Magic Man.

Karana shivered. His certainty shriveled. He willed his memory of Navahk away, but it would not go. The magic man's smile lingered at the back of his mind. His white serrated teeth, with canines as fanged and sharp as any wolf's, bit at Karana's conscience.

Karana is an ungrateful son who has forgotten his own people.

Was the accusation his own, or was it Navahk's? He could not tell. He only knew that it was true.

Clouds drifted intermittently across the face of the moon. Within the cave, darkness thinned and thickened. Karana pulled his sleeping skins around his narrow little shoulders. Beside him, Umak drew the skin of the great short-faced bear around himself. It was not fully cured, but the boy knew that if the old man did not keep it close, Galeena or some member of his band would probably try to steal it. As the boy watched, Umak drifted into sleep, as he often did, sitting upright, nodding trancelike, as though he were not asleep at all but in communion with the mystical powers of the mountain. Karana envied him. He wished that he had the power of a spirit master so that he could will the sneering image of Navahk from his mind and make Galeena's people disappear.

The wind was rising, and Karana could hear it hissing against the mountain. From somewhere high above the cave, small stones tumbled, their sound muffled as they plummeted through the veils of one of the innumerable waterfalls that would continue to bleed out of the summit ice pack until the first frost of autumn turned them solid. Karana listened. The dogs still howled. It was a lonely, desolate sound. He wondered if Aar was out there. He wondered if the dog would ever come back.

"Sleep now," Torka said. "Tomorrow we will hunt. Torka will bring back prime meat, and Karana will wet his skinning dagger in blood."

Karana lay down and tried to sleep. Torka and Lonit bundled together. It was very quiet in the cave. Only the howls of the distant dogs disturbed the familiar sounds of wind and mountain. Galeena's people snored, but the sound was muffled beneath their piled sleeping skins. Karana felt the night growing all around him. He longed for the warmth and strength of the dog beside him. *If the smelly ones should go away, Aar would come back to his man-pack. Then Karana would not be alone.*

He sighed. He flung a small, slender forearm across his eyes. He tried to sleep. The moon hung low in the western sky by the time he succeeded. The dogs were silent. Far away across the tundra, a blue-eyed, black-masked animal sat alone at the crest of a hillock. It stared up at the mountain. Toward dawn, it slept, whimpering in its dreams.

In the darkness at the back of the cave, a woman of Galeena's band stirred and wept softly in the arms of a scar-faced young hunter; neither had participated in the debauched feasting of their people. They had no appetite for anything; the grief upon which they feasted had deprived them of all but a deep and unremitting sadness.

"Have you been awake all night, Iana?"

"To sleep is to dream, Manaak, of Big Spirit. . . ."

"Big Spirit is far. It cannot come to such a high camp. Galeena has led us well, as he promised. We will have a new life." His words were a bitter combination of consolation and sarcasm.

"Big Spirit is *here*," she said, sighing, and placed a hand over her heart. "With little Ripa, our daughter . . . with all of those who died. Why does he kill even the little ones, Manaak? Why is he so angry?"

"He is a spirit. A *big* spirit. He may do as he wishes."

She shuddered. Her hand moved from her heart to touch his face, to linger upon the still-fresh scars. "But what will stop him? No man can kill him, Manaak! No man! Galeena has sworn it."

"I will kill Big Spirit," Manaak vowed.

"You must not speak so! If you challenge Galeena again, he will do more this time than have the others cut your face!"

Manaak did not reply. He held her close, wrapped his arms around her, and felt their unborn child move against his forearm. Beyond the darkness of the cave, he could see the fading stars prickling the night. He could hear the *shh* sound of the waterfalls that bathed the face of the mountain. It was a soothing sound, but he was not soothed. "Did you see the little one? The boy with the limp? The one they call Karana?"

"I saw. . . ."

He heard the catch in her throat. Deep within him, his sadness became anger. "We could have carried him. *I* could have carried him. Antu was small, and like Karana, not hurt beyond healing. I *could* have carried him. I *wanted* to carry him. I—" His voice broke. He could not go on.

Her fingers caressed his lips. "Galeena is headman. The decision was his. You fought. He cut your face. It was the second time you stood against him, Manaak. And you have said the words yourself. Galeena has led us well, to a new life, to a place where Big Spirit cannot come."

"To a place without children."

"What was done had to be done for the good of the band. Galeena has said so."

"These Dog People have not thrown away their little one. Their old man hunts. And he is so old, Galeena would have put him out of our band many winters before he could live to look as he does. Yet he is strong. He hunts and is of use to his people. The one called Torka says that the old man killed the great bear whose skin he wears."

"The ways of the Dog People are not our ways," Iana soothed. "They too have faced Big Spirit, but look how few of them are left! The one who leads them, this Torka, looks bold and brave, but he has yielded his camp to Galeena, so he must be weak. You see, Galeena's ways are best. He has led us well. He was right to—" She stopped, unable to continue. The sadness within her was so great that her soul swam out into it and nearly drowned.

Manaak felt her go limp within his arms. He rocked her as though she were a child. He thought of Ripa, the little daughter whom he had seen die beneath the feet of the killer mammoth, and of Antu, the son he had been forced to abandon when Galeena had led his band into the storm so that his hunters would not be forced to join the other bands whose headmen had elected to pursue the great mammoth and try to kill it. Later two of the survivors had caught up to them and recounted the way their fellow hunters had died. Even though their spears had tasted the blood of Big Spirit, the beast had gone its way, immortal. That was what Galeena had said, gloating while his hunters nodded in affirmation of his decision to abandon the hunt for a creature that could not be killed. Only Manaak had not agreed, thinking that, even though men had died in the attempt to kill it, at least they had tried. At least they had not turned their backs and run like frightened dogs.

"Sleep," he whispered to the woman in his arms, and he felt her relax and yield to sleep at last.

But Manaak did not sleep. He sat with his back against the mountain wall, and wrapped in the shadows of the ebbing night, he watched the sun rise above the soaring, glacier-ridden peaks that rimmed the horizon of the unknown world to the east.

Deep within the mountain, something moved, sighed, and moaned. It was a terrible sound, like some huge, living thing trapped within the stone and trying to get out. Yet it was a whispering rather than a roaring. Then it was gone, and Manaak wondered if he had imagined it.

At the entrance to the cave, the man who called himself Torka rose and faced the dawn. He peeled off his tunic and trousers, then went out. A few moments passed before he returned. His body shone of moisture, and his hair was dripping wet. Manaak frowned, knowing that Torka must have allowed the icy water of one of the cascades to wash over him. It was a strange thing for a man to do, he thought, then decided that it must be some sort of religious ritual unique to the Dog People.

Torka stood in the light of the rising sun, allowing it and the morning wind to dry him. Manaak saw the power of his body and the new scars that marred him. Had the mammoth done that to him? Had he, like Manaak, come close enough to Big Spirit to look into its red eyes and smell its foul breath and see the blood of his people upon its tusks?

Manaak thought of his dead children and of his sad-eyed woman. Then he thought of Galeena, who had led his band into the storms that had decimated them.

Manaak's mouth flexed downward. Slowly, gently, he eased Iana from his arms. Carefully, wishing to rouse none of Galeena's people, he made his way across the cave and approached Torka. He was impressed by the man's alertness, for Torka turned to face him before he came close, eyed him watchfully, and scowled with pinched nostrils when Manaak stopped beside him.

They stood shoulder to shoulder. Torka was taller, and stronger, if Manaak's judgment of such things was sound—and it usually was. His eyes narrowed, measured, searched, and found what they were seeking. Iana had been wrong; there was no weakness in Torka. "Galeena seeks safety for his people in Torka's cave." He hissed the words provocatively. "Galeena hides from his fears like an old wuhman hiding from those who would put her out of her band to die. What does Torka seek?"

"Torka has found what he has sought. Safety for my people within a new band."

"And what does Torka fear?"

The question took the warmth from the sun. Torka saw the answer shining darkly in the other man's eyes.

Manaak nodded. He smiled, but there was no happiness in the smile, only a twisted, burning affirmation of his own hatred. "Torka has seen Big Spirit . . . he has seen his children die . . . and he has looked into the red eye of the beast that Galeena says cannot die."

"It bleeds. It *can* die."

Manaak's smile deepened. He turned slightly, gesturing out across the tundra. "It is out there somewhere. Be it flesh or spirit, it *is* out there. It looks for men to kill, for children to crush, for bands that have not found safety in high camps like this."

Torka's brow furrowed. "Galeena is wise, then. He seeks safety for his people, as Torka has done. Together our two bands will live and hunt as one . . . in safety."

Manaak's face contorted with disgust. "There is safety for no man, wuhman, or child as long as Big Spirit shares the world with us!"

Now Torka gestured broadly and angrily. He resented the pointed censure that he saw in Manaak's eyes. "Big Spirit is far away. It walks another world."

Manaak shook his head. "Big Spirit will khum someday for your children and mine. Unless we kill him."

"We?"

"Torka! Manaak! Together!"

The old, terrible longing to kill the Destroyer came rushing back to roar inside Torka's head. He took in a breath and tried to quiet the roaring with common sense as he spoke earnestly to the man who called himself Manaak. "Two men cannot kill the Destroyer. Even if they had the power of lightning to speed their spears and set fire to their hearts, we would still not be enough."

Manaak nodded, relaxing a little. He smiled again, and this time it was a smile, not a grimace of frustration. "Two men could set fiah to the hearts of many men. And with many hunting together, it could be done."

"Galeena has said that he has no wish to hunt the great mammoth."

Manaak shrugged. Sunlight was bathing the interior of the cave. The people of his band were stirring, and their headman was rising, rumpled and retching, from his bed skins. Manaak's smile disappeared. "Galeena may not be headman foreveh," he suggested, then turned and left Torka to consider the meaning of his words.

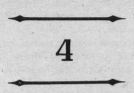

4

Crack!

The sound was an explosion of power as the two bull musk oxen came together with the skull-splitting intensity of the autumn rut.

Torka leaped to his feet. He had his spears in hand before Karana shouted the news that he had sighted the herd grazing in the willow scrub on the outwash plain. Torka was beside him in an instant. They stood together on the lip of the cornice.

"Look!" exclaimed Karana, pointing off. "Many musk ox!"

Torka looked, then beckoned to Galeena's people and gestured them forward. "Come! Now we will hunt! Together!"

Not one of them moved. They stared at their headman, waiting for a signal from him. No signal was given.

Galeena yawned. He lay on his side, his tufted head propped on an elbow, with his two women sitting cross-legged and stark naked on either side of him. "Not hungry. Hunt tomorrow," he announced, and reached up to tweak the nearer nipple of his younger woman as though it were a fruit that he thought of picking.

The woman giggled and shook herself.

Torka was annoyed. Galeena had promised to hunt. A day and a night and a morning had passed, and still he lounged in lazy squalor. "Come!" Torka attempted to persuade him. "See for yourself! A man can spend only so many hours on his back with his women. Come away now, before you find yourself as soft-bellied as a female. Look! There are musk oxen below the mountain, so close that this man can feel their life spirits riding the wind, asking to be hunted!"

Slowly, Galeena sat up. Slowly, his fingers twisted the

nipple of his woman until she cried out. He roughly shoved her back, released her breast, and smiled when he saw frustration in Torka's eyes. It gave him pleasure to irritate this man. He did not like the way Torka tended to assume authority. Galeena yawned again, widely, with profound deliberation. Then, when the yawn was done, he said, "Not hunt today. This day be nearly finished."

Impatience hardened Torka's words. "So is the meat that was to have been food for Torka's people during the time of the long dark."

A low murmuring went through the members of Galeena's band. They looked from Torka to their headman, awaiting his response to Torka's audacity.

It came with an insolent smile. "When the meat gone, we hunt then."

Never in his life had Torka heard such foolish reasoning. Wait until food was gone before seeking more? Lounge on one's buttocks while an entire herd of musk oxen grazed within one's hunting range, and never lift so much as a spear to take meat? It was unthinkable! It was an offense to the spirits of the game. He said as much.

Beside her fire, Lonit shrank within her garments and stopped stitching the new winter gloves that she was sewing for Karana. Across the ring of stones, Umak rose. She knew that he would have gone to stand with Torka, but the weight of the great bearskin slowed his steps. He wore it as a robe, and with the head of the huge beast balanced atop his own, he looked twelve feet tall, yet she barely saw him. She looked aghast at Torka, remembering the laws of her band: One did not set oneself apart. One strove to be like all others, to exist within the whole for the survival of the whole. Torka had chafed against such strictures before, and clearly he was chafing now—so much so that it frightened her as the stunned incredulity of Galeena's people had quickly settled into well-focused anger. Torka had openly impugned the judgment of their headman. By so doing, he had indirectly impugned them all, for they had chosen Galeena to lead them.

Several hunters rose, took up their spears, and shook them warningly at Torka as the boys skulked out of the shadows to stand behind Galeena. The headman's women scowled, while at the back of the cave, sad-eyed Iana looked on listlessly and Manaak stood up and stared expectantly at Torka.

More than the threat of the raised spears of Galeena's hunters, it was Manaak's expression that cooled Torka's temper and reminded him of his place. Whatever grudge the scar-faced Manaak held against Galeena, it was Manaak's grudge, not Torka's. Galeena might not be headman forever, but he *was* headman now. He might appear to be little more than a lazy, flatulent fool, but his people had thought enough of him to follow him, and he *had* brought them to a safe encampment. Whether he liked him or not, Torka had to concede that Galeena had accepted him and his people into his band without question.

He rebuked himself for his impulsiveness. He had been wrong to challenge Galeena. The man had come far. If he was not ready to hunt, Torka must accept his unreadiness with understanding. It was not as though the herd of musk oxen was going to disappear; the habits of the animals were such that, unless threatened, they would remain where the browsing was good. The bulls would be charging and rutting or muzzle-deep in the autumn-yellowed willow scrub. Last spring's calves, fat now and sprouting the stubbly beards that were characteristic of their species, would be looking on while the cows bawled and slobbered and were impregnated by the bulls.

Torka's hand tightened about the hafts of his spears. It was not the way of the People to refrain from hunting when stores were low and game was near, but it was evidently the way of Galeena's people. He recalled Umak's words: *In new times, men must learn new ways.* So must it also be within a new band.

He sighed regretfully. His blood was up for killing, but he could be cooled. "Torka will hunt tomorrow," he deferred amiably to Galeena.

The headman's greasy brow expanded outward toward his even-greasier hairline. His topknot skewed to one side as his loose-skinned scalp twitched and slid over his broad, foreshortened cranium. He leered smugly at Torka as though he had just gulped down a piece of contested meat without sharing so much as a bite. "Torka hunt when Galeena say hunt! Torka not hunt when Galeena say not hunt! Or Torka go! Take people and leave Galeena's khamp!"

"*Galeena's* camp?" Torka nearly choked at the man's brazen insolence.

The malicious glint in the headman's eyes was unmistakable. His people saw it. Once again they murmured among themselves. Pleased, they nodded and smiled.

Torka's eyes narrowed. His willingness to compromise was shattered by the realization that Galeena's refusal to hunt had nothing to do with weariness; it had to do with his desire to put Torka in his place and demean him before his own people, as well as before the members of Galeena's band. So far, he had succeeded. Torka was aware of little Karana looking up at him expectantly, and of Lonit looking away, pretending not to see his shame. Torka knew that within the skin of the great bear, old Umak was watching him. If he backed down to Galeena now, he would never again be able to command respect from anyone, especially from himself. But for the sake of his little band, and for his unborn child, he must walk cautiously in pursuit of his pride.

So it was that he assumed an Umak-like stance, head high, chin up, mouth down, his face as hard and blank as stone. "Hmmph. Galeena has said that his people and Torka's people will be one band. Many will hunt safely and live easily. Torka would not speak against the wisdom of Galeena. Rather would Torka say that in the time of the long dark that will soon send the sun to hide beyond the western edge of the world, the wisdom of Galeena will speak for itself."

Galeena's people looked in confusion to their headman. They waited for him to tell them whether Torka had spoken in deference or sarcasm.

Galeena glowered. He was not sure himself. Beside him, Ai, his younger woman, sat very straight. She was staring at Torka with an interest that no female belonging to one man should ever show to another without the expressed permission of her mate. He backhanded her across her face so hard that he cracked her nose. It spurted blood. Her small, pudgy hands flew to her face. When she cried out, he hit her again.

Disgusted, Torka turned away. He went to sit at his own fire. Karana followed. And at the back of the cave, Manaak observed the harried, resentful expression upon Galeena's face and smiled.

The day ended. A night passed. A new day began.

Umak rose with the dawn and leaned close to Torka, indicating Galeena with a nod of his head. "That one is bad. That one has a heart that is small and rotten with too much pride. But that one is also stupid. This old man can make his heart smaller. But Torka must not challenge Galeena again. Torka must watch. He must stand back and observe how Spirit Master masters the spirit of Galeena."

With these words, he donned his bearskin and his necklaces and balanced the head of the great short-faced bear upon his own. If the weight of the huge skull stressed his scalp wound, he showed no sign of pain. He streaked his cheeks with ashes—bold strokes that gave his features a look of imperious disdain, as though he were at odds with the universe and confident that he was somehow more powerful than the forces of the earth and sky.

He rose and flung his arms wide. Chanting loudly, he strode to the very edge of the cornice. He made invocations to the dawn, not in words but in syllables, at first short and staccato, then long and drawn out, as though the wind were sucking the words from his head.

When he turned at last to face those whom he had awakened, the sun stood at his back. He shone like an eagle soaring in the very heart of a midsummer noon. He looked magnificent, larger than life. When he threw back his head and howled, from across the miles far below the mountain Brother Dog howled back.

His audience stared, transfixed and awed.

When his howling stopped, the wild dog was also silent. With a harsh, whooping cry, Umak flung his arms straight up, nodding his head so that the skull of the great bear appeared to be moving of its own power. One of the matrons swooned with fright, and the ferret-eyed boys were sobered. Even Torka was impressed. Umak swayed, and Umak danced. But it was not Umak—it was the great, short-faced bear that moved and breathed. When the shadow man within it spoke, he spoke with the voice of the great bear, and Galeena's eyes went so wide that they appeared ready to pop from their sockets.

"Today the spirits of the game await the spirits of the hunters!" roared the great bear that was Umak. "Today will be a good day to hunt!"

And it was so.

Even if the sky had poured rain, or clouds had gathered to whiten the tundra with snow, no one who had witnessed Umak's transformation into the bear spirit would have thought to question him. They took up their weapons and went out, men and boys together—all save Umak and Karana, who stood watching with the women on the ledge.

"Soon we will join them," soothed the old man, one hand upon Karana's shoulder, sensing the boy's need to follow the hunters. "When we are healed and strong, we will run ahead of them and show them how it is done, and all will envy this old man and this small boy."

Karana looked up along the wall of fur that was shaded by the out-thrusting head of the great bear. Umak was in there somewhere. The boy could see the jab of his chin, the black hollows of his nostrils, and a few wisps of his hair threading through the claws and paws of his necklaces. "Will Brother Dog run with us, Spirit Master?"

Umak heard the longing in the boy's voice. It touched him. He too missed the company of Brother Dog; but last night and the night before, the baying of wild dogs had joined Aar's howling to puncture the darkness. Umak reflected on this and spoke his thoughts. "We have found a new band. So too has Aar found others of his own kind. Our brother will have no need to hunt with his man-pack now."

"But we are his brothers!" protested the boy. "How can we know that he is happy with his own kind? Karana is not happy with these smelly ones! Karana is—" He stopped. His words had grown loud, and the women of Galeena's band were staring at him, as was Lonit. He saw the reproach in their eyes and glowered resentfully, waiting for Umak to speak.

But Umak made no reply. He had forgotten all about Karana, and the farthest thing from his mind was concern for the whereabouts or welfare of a wild dog.

The two matrons were coming toward him. They were carrying offerings of meat scraps piled onto platters made of the pelvic bones of large grazing animals. They were both looking at Umak in *that* way again. And they were completely naked.

Blood beat behind Torka's eyes. It was all that he could do to keep himself from shouting with the joy of exhilaration. It was, as Umak had promised, a good day to hunt. The sky was clear. The sun was warm. The wind blew to cool them and to keep the biting insects away.

Although Torka hated to admit it, it was obvious from the first that Galeena knew what he was doing. He led his men

well, in the same age-old way of hunting musk oxen that
Torka had learned as a boy from Umak and the hunters of his
own band.

They did not approach the herd head on. They went
around it in stealth, in small groups that did not come together until they were well beyond the grazing grounds of
their prey.

Now they formed into a single line. The wind was their
ally, blowing their scent away from the herd. They stood
squinting, facing into the wind, with the good, rich stink of
the animals exciting their need to hunt.

Galeena's arm went up, signaling the men at either end of
the line to begin to move forward. Slowly, the line became a
loop. Gradually, it enclosed the herd, leaving it only one
route of escape, into the dead-end glacial canyon in which
Umak had slain the moose.

It was a while before the animals realized that they were
being herded. The tundra scrub was high enough to conceal
the crouching, stalking hunters. Then the first bull caught
sight of them. It froze; then its head went up, its nostrils
working as though trying to disavow what its small eyes had
already confirmed to its brain.

But there was no denying the presence of the hunters
now. They stood erect, their spears at the ready. Galeena
screeched a signal that echoed out of the mouth of every man
and boy who burst forward in a howling tide of enthusiasm
for the chase to come.

"Ow-yah! Hai!"

They raced forward like men pursued by hornets. The
oxen panicked and ran before the hunters until, sensing
entrapment within the canyon, they whirled and paused to
form a protective circle on the high flank of the mountain. It
was a defensive formation that served them well against wolves
and lions. With their calves safe inside a bastioning circle of
outward-facing cows and bulls, the musk oxen lowered their
heads and displayed their massive upcurling horns to the
two-legged flesh-eaters who came howling and yipping at
them like wild dogs.

But they were not dogs—they were men, and much more
dangerous. They were not intimidated by the oxen and kept
well away from the ripping horns, not once coming close
enough to place themselves in danger. Their spears gave
them the advantage of distance, and their knowledge of their

prey gave them absolute supremacy. They knew that the musk oxen would not charge them. The animals would not break their defensive circle. They would die where they stood rather than abandon their calves or wounded to the predations of the hunters.

And so the men and boys of Galeena's band killed them, and Torka joined in until at last he stood back, wondering why the hunt continued. They had dropped over three-quarters of the herd. Only two old bulls remained standing, and a few cows and calves. The dead and dying animals would provide so much meat that their women would be hard-pressed to prepare it all. Still the hunt continued, with Galeena's men and boys making dashes in to retrieve their spears so that they might be used again and again.

Torka was appalled. To take *all* of the musk oxen would be to destroy the life spirits of this herd forever. He could not believe that Galeena would allow his hunters to do such a thing; it was against the strictest taboos of the People to kill in such a profligate manner. Always a few animals must be left, for it was said that if the last calf died, so too would the last child die in the time of the long dark when the herd animals refused to come to be hunted by those who cared not for their continuance.

Scar-faced, hard-eyed Manaak came to his side. "Why Torka not hunt? Do you fear a few old oxen as much as you fear Big Spirit?"

He was gone before Torka could reply, but the words had gored him. Still, he would not have killed again had Manaak not provoked the last of the old bulls into a charge.

It was the largest animal in the herd. Over five feet tall at the shoulder, it was massive, with grizzled, shaggy hair cascading to its fetlocks. Every square inch of its fifteen hundred pound body was layered with muscle except for that portion of its skull above its eyes. That was horn.

Galeena had already placed a spear into the old bull's shoulder, so that blood loss and pain caused the animal's head to drop. Its broad horns seemed to flow together above its brow, like a flattened band that spread downward into deadly, upturned points at either side of its eyes.

Manaak hurled the last of his spears, which buried itself beside Galeena's weapon. The bull's knees buckled, then locked. It did not fall but fixed its antagonists with small, pain-filled eyes. Behind it, one of the few surviving calves bawled, and at the bull's cloven feet, another bull lay on its side, eyes glazing, tongue lolling as its rib cage heaved in the last paroxysms of death.

"I will make the final kill!" proclaimed Manaak.

"Only if you can get to your spear before I get to mine!" Galeena answered Manaak's challenge.

As Torka stared and as the others goaded them on, Manaak and Galeena approached the bull. They feinted this way and that while the boys came up from behind the animal. Clambering over the bodies of dead and dying oxen, they poked at the bull's already bloodied hindquarters with their spears until an enraged cow forced them to retreat.

Blood was showing in the thick, dark pelage of the bull's shoulder. It was salivating heavily—thick, pink foam that betrayed internal injuries. It wheeled just as the boy who had driven Aar from the ledge tripped and went sprawling flat on his belly.

Incredibly, the bull charged. It was nearly dead on its feet, but rage fueled its effort. Several men loosed spears at it, all falling short. It was Torka's spear, longer and lighter than the projectiles used by the hunters of Galeena's band, that buried itself in the soft flesh at the base of the bull's cranium. It sliced deep. Torka's position had allowed him the perfect angle for the killing throw, and his strength, skill, and the quality of his weapon made it possible. His projectile point severed the balance center at the back of the bull's brain, and cerebral hemorrhage did the rest. The animal dropped dead inches short of crushing the fallen boy.

On the ledge where he had been observing the hunt with Karana and the women, Umak roared with pride, and the women, including Lonit, shouted with amazement and delight. The hunters and boys came to Torka to speak their approval and tell him that never had they seen so fine a throw.

Only Galeena said nothing. The exhalation that hissed through his gap-toothed mouth was deep, reeking of resentment. And although the boy who had fallen was Ninip, his only son, he felt no gratitude to Torka for having saved the boy's life. The boy had been careless. He had tripped and shamed his father. By saving his life, Torka had shamed Galeena further. And every man, boy, and woman in his band had witnessed the humiliation. He would never forgive Torka. Someday he would make him pay.

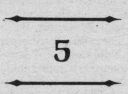

5

The women came down from the ledge, and the butchering began. Umak joined them in his bearskin robe. He walked through the slaughter scene with the same imperious disdain as a great heron striding through a marsh.

"Hmmph. Just as Spirit Master said, a good day to hunt." He would not let them forget that he had foretold their good fortune. As the hunters skinned their many kills, he stood stoically by. His face betrayed none of his inner turmoil over the wanton slaughter of the entire herd. What was done was done. If the life spirits of the game were offended, nothing could change that. Tonight he would make spirit smokes and send songs of veneration to the life spirits of the musk oxen. Perhaps that would satisfy them. If not, they would know soon enough. In the meantime, his songs and smokes and ritual dances would impress the people of Galeena's band, especially the matrons. That, at least for Umak, would be a good thing.

To Lonit's surprise, the hunters of Galeena's band took part in more than just the skinning of their kills. She was amazed to see them force their women to stand back while they slit the throats of each animal, cut out its tongue, and hunkered down to eat on the spot.

As she watched, Torka cut the tongue from the bull that he had killed and brought it to Umak.

"For Spirit Master, whose magic brought much meat."

The old man grunted, obviously pleased by Torka's deference. As Galeena's people stared, apparently unaccustomed to youth serving to age anything other than orders to walk away upon the wind, Umak accepted Torka's offering as though he had not the slightest doubt that it was his due. He held the tongue high in a gesture of thanksgiving to the spirits. He made a loud and lengthy chant of praise to the animal whose flesh he was about to consume. Then, after cutting off and setting aside a small portion that Lonit was certain he would bring back to the ledge for Karana, he slit the tongue in half with his fleshing dagger and offered a share to Torka.

She saw them both pause and look for her among the women before settling down to eat together in silence. She was relieved that they had not seen her or called her forward to join them. She had deliberately chosen to stand at the back of the group of watching women, stooping, trying to make herself small so that she would not stand out from the crowd. From the way that the women hung back, she knew that they expected to receive none of this part of the kill. As among her own band, the choice portions were reserved for the hunters.

If Torka or Umak had invited Lonit to share in their feast, they would win only enmity from Galeena and his men. And Torka had already won more than his share of that from Galeena.

Lonit could see it in the headman's small, rapacious eyes as he looked at Torka as though he were an animal whom he would like to hunt. Lonit was disturbed by the sight of him. He sat on the haunch of the dead bull that Torka had slain, as though the animal had been *his* kill and not Torka's. She liked him less now than when she had first seen him. He had frightened her then; he frightened her more now.

The wind had dropped. It was warm and sluggish and did nothing to cut the smell of blood that rose from the dead and dying musk oxen. Satiated with tongue meat, the hunters began to fling their leavings to the boys. The youths leaped forward to fight viciously among themselves over every scrap while the hunters turned their attention to other delicacies. As Lonit watched, they gouged the eyeballs from the musk oxen with their thumbs and greedily began to suck the rich, black juices.

Lonit salivated, recalling the days when she had wandered the tundra with Torka and Umak and they had generously insisted that she share these delicacies with them. Those days were gone forever. She sighed with longing for them and was glad when she was called to work with the other women as the butchering began in earnest. Activity would drive back the bittersweet memories.

Now there were skulls to smash and bodies to dismember. Brains must be scooped and cherished for the tanning of hides. Sinew must be separated from meat and saved. Fires must be made. Flesh must be smoked and roasted. Bones must be cracked, and marrow must be melted. The hunters were already urinating on the freshly taken skins. Once saturated, the skins would be wadded into tight bundles and kept warm by the fires. In a day or two, the skins would be soft enough to work, and the long hair of the musk oxen could be easily combed free. Then the women would spread them, scrape off the last of the flesh, and bind them to the drying frames to begin the long, tedious process of transforming rough skins into supple garments.

As Lonit took up her stone fleshing knife and began to work with three other women to cut the fat-rich hump of a large bull into long, bloody steaks, she ate freely of the meat. It was warm and sweet. Yet, strangely, it was also bitter, for as she ate, her mind wandered to the hunt in which the great bull had been slain. She was unsettled by her recollections of the wanton, wasteful slaughter of the musk oxen. She could not forget the pitiable sight of the little calves bleating for their mothers and the way the brave bulls had deliberately taken spears into their sides rather than abandon their old and weak and their stumbling babies.

The taste of the meat was suddenly repulsive. Lonit swallowed and tried to think of other things. To one side of her, the sad-eyed woman whom the others called Iana worked in silence. Across from her, the other two women, who had introduced themselves as Oklahnoo and Naknaktup, ate and worked, laughed and chattered. They mocked the musk oxen for their stupidity. Lonit found herself resenting their words, reflecting on the ways of her own species. She wondered why humans—so much wiser and more adaptable than any animal—were rarely as self-sacrificing and caring of their own as the brave, dumb oxen that had died this day. She spoke her thoughts and was immediately sorry.

"Bah!" Naknaktup, the younger of the two matrons, snapped a rebuke. "Musk oxen not brave! Musk oxen stupid! If they run, they not all be dead now!"

Oklahnoo snorted in agreement. She was twice as plump as Naknaktup and several years older. From the set of their features and the sound of their voices, it was obvious that the two were sisters. She appraised Lonit as though she had doubts about her sanity. "Is good thing musk oxen not think like people! If oxen run away, if leave behind young and sick, we take only *some* meat. But because oxen stupid, because they stay with old and weak, we kill *all*! Does Torka's wuhman say this not good?"

The woman had asked a question. Lonit was bound to answer. "It is *not* good! There are no cows or bulls left to make new calves. The herd is gone *forever*. Never again will hunters feast upon its meat and offer thanksgiving to its life spirits."

Oklahnoo shrugged. "What matteh that? We feast *now*! This is not only herd musk oxen in all world! We find more. We kill many. *Foreveh!*"

"Eh yah!" added Naknaktup.

The sad-eyed woman looked up from her work and suggested that they get on with theirs. "Much meat to butcher. Sun will not slow its walk across sky while wuhmen talk."

Oklahnoo flashed a smile in which her well-worn teeth were like mottled, mossy pebbles that have lain too long at the bottom of a stagnant pond. Her fleshing dagger was a large, rounded, crudely knapped stone that fit within her palm like a nut within its shell; where it protruded along the heel of her hand, it was razor sharp. It was with this edge that she sliced into the meat of the oxen's shoulder, speaking with relish of how she had managed to suck hot blood from the neck of a still-living calf. The hunters had slit its throat and cut out its tongue, but they had not severed its jugular vein. It had still been alive when Oklahnoo had fallen upon it. She chortled as she imitated the sounds it had made when she had buried her face in its torn throat. She used her arms to show the way it had kicked.

Lonit suddenly felt nauseated. The sisters were the same twosome who had come naked to Umak to offer meat and whatever else he would have of them. He had taken the meat and nothing else; but he *had* appraised them with interest. Lonit could not understand why. She found them revolting. Like all of the women of Galeena's band, they were filthy. Their hair looked as though it had never known the soothing pull of a comb. A lifetime's worth of grease thickened the snarled strands. As they hunched over their work, they chided her again for her concern over the fate of the musk oxen.

Lonit made no reply. She knew that they would not understand her feelings any more than she understood theirs.

Could they not know that someday their own lives might be in jeopardy, forfeit but for the intervention of someone willing to put himself at risk for their sake? Did they consider themselves somehow beyond injury or illness or the onset of old age? Would they be so filled with laughter when the members of their band sent them away to walk the wind because they could no longer forage and fight for the leavings of those who were stronger and younger?

Lonit's eyes strayed across the killing scene. Three or four women worked to butcher each musk oxen. The men and boys lounged about, restoring the energy that they had spent in the taking of so much meat. Not for the first time, Lonit noted that this was a band without children or babies or old people. She did not have to ask why. The young, the old, and the infirm were always expendable during times of trouble. And these *were* times of trouble—or had been until Galeena had brought his people through the storms of adversity to a safe encampment upon Torka's mountain.

Her eyes rested upon her man. How proud of him she was! And of Umak, who hunkered beside Torka, scraping marrow from a broken leg bone with the marrow scoop that she had made for him. He did not look like a man at all but like a great bear; it was almost amusing to watch him, to see the delicate marrow scoop disappear into the human face that was hidden beneath the head of the animal. It was difficult to remember that the strong, clever spirit master was an old man who, not many moons ago, had volunteered to walk away upon the wind so that the People would not suffer for his sake.

The realization was distracting. Umak had survived. The People had died. And Lonit and Torka were alive only because of the wisdom and concern and inestimable strength of one old man who had not been considered fit to live. Through storm and cold and against the predations of wild beasts, they had stayed together and fought for one another until, at last, they had found safety within a new band. Soon Lonit would bear Torka's child. And all because of one old man, the People would be reborn.

One life *did* matter. To risk one's life to save another was *not* the act of a fool.

Within her womb, Lonit's baby moved to affirm her thoughts. Her free hand went to her belly. The child within it was still very small, but it was strong with life and rippled within her like a tiny fish shivering within the confines of a protected pool. Usually the movement of the unborn child filled her with joy, but now it filled her with shadows. This baby would be born in the time of the long dark. Umak had told her this would be so. But could he assure her that a child born under the starving moon would be allowed by the people of Galeena's band to live? Would the matrons, Oklahnoo and Naknaktup, laugh at her as they now laughed at the musk oxen if she were forced to expose her baby to the spirits of the storms? And would Torka allow it?

Lonit suddenly felt ill. Distraught, she rose and, without bothering to explain her hurried departure, went to stand alone, away from the killing site. She faced into the wind. It was too warm to soothe her. She was pale with nausea, and there were tears in her eyes when the sad-eyed woman followed and came to stand beside her.

The woman looked at her out of a gaunt face that would have been pretty were it not layered with soot and grime. She wore a stained, ragged dress that was stretched like a drum skin across the huge distension of a well-advanced pregnancy. When she spoke, her voice was soft and deep and sweet with empathy. "Torka's wuhman have baby in belly?"

Lonit nodded.

The sad-eyed woman smiled and nodded. "Iana think this so. First time baby, this?"

"First time baby."

Again she nodded. "Is good thing. First time baby best. Hard to bring, but best. Iana will help. Lonit not be afraid. Iana have babies before. Two babies. And help bring many more."

Lonit frowned. Many babies? And not one of them alive to ride firmly bound to its mother's back? Had the deaths of her children saddened Iana's eyes? Many had died when the Destroyer had rampaged through Galeena's encampment, but perhaps Iana's infants had been victims of the long, cold nights of the starving moon, which all too often had driven the women of her own band to expose or abandon their newly born. She shuddered. She did not want to think about it.

"Lonit not be sad," said Iana, indicating with a bloodied hand the slaughtered herd of musk oxen. "Not for them. Betteh all die. Betteh die than be sad for lost calves . . . for lost mothers . . . for lost fathers. Iana say, betteh all die than some remembeh."

Lonit frowned and shook her head, understanding that Iana was not speaking of musk oxen at all. "No. It is *not* better to die. It is *never* better to die. And this woman will *never* abandon her children!"

Even though her face was darkened by soot and grime, Iana's face paled visibly. Her eyes went very wide, and for a moment she stared at Lonit as though she was not quite certain that she had heard her correctly. Then, lowering her head, she sighed and whispered: "Not speak so. Galeena say, Lonit do. Is way of band."

"Lonit is *Torka's* woman. Galeena camps in Torka's cave. Galeena eats of Torka's meat. Torka speaks, Lonit answers. To *Torka.* Not to Galeena."

Iana shook her head slowly, almost wistfully. "Much man Torka. But Galeena headman this band. Lonit listen what Iana say now. Lonit *remembeh*: Torka must do as Galeena say . . . or huntehs of Galeena, they kill Torka. Then Lonit be sad. Then Lonit say: Betteh die than remembeh!"

6

They worked until the sun went down, and still the butchering was not finished. So much meat. So many hides. So much blood. Wolves came. And dogs and foxes—concealed by the shadows of encroaching night, but they were there, waiting.

Umak waited for Aar to come into the light of the fires that had been made. If the dog was there, he kept to the shadows, and the old man knew that Brother Dog would not come to him that night or any other—until he broke company with the people of Galeena's band. And this he could not do . . . nor did he wish to.

At sunset he made a dance to the dying and stripped naked to bathe in the nearest of several deep, icy pools that lay at the base of the silt shoulders rising from the outwash plain. He made a ritual of the bathing. Torka guessed correctly that it was a ruse. Umak saw his grandson trying hard not to smile as, at Umak's request, Galeena and his people solemnly stripped themselves of their garments and waded out into the water to be "purified" by the old man's magic.

And it was magic to coerce such filthy folk into doing that which they had never done, supposedly to gain the power of the day that had brought them luck during the hunt and to keep the spirits of the game strong and sanctified within themselves. These were what he had assured them they would gain through their sacrifice of bathing. And he made certain that they were thoroughly doused, especially the matrons.

From the ledge, Karana watched the night gather and the fires of the hunters burn like suns upon the outwash plain.

He sat alone and from his aerie saw the predators gather around the butchering site. He looked for Aar among the shadowy forms. If the dog was there, Karana could not see him. The lonely boy sighed, wishing that he could have participated in the hunt. Tomorrow, when the butchering was done, Umak and Torka would bring him tongue meat—he was certain of that—and Lonit would have saved hump steaks for him and would roast them to his liking.

But now he was alone with his memories and his dissatisfaction. He sat in the darkness, holding the spear that Torka had made for him across his knees, with his small fists curled around the smooth, white length of its haft, and thought of all the chants that he had heard old Umak make. He tried them out himself, hoping to find the right sequence of syllables and chanting rhythms. Now and again he lifted the spear high into the night, an offering to the spirits. If he held it high enough and shouted loudly enough, perhaps they would hear and heed his wish to make the magic that would cause Galeena and his wretched band to disappear. But nothing happened.

The hours passed. He knew that upon the plain the armed hunters took turns forming a circle to guard the meat from the many predators that lay in wait to steal a portion. Karana knew that they would have a long wait. Galeena was too gluttonous to share a meal with anyone without a fight.

The night thickened around him. The stars disappeared. Clouds had covered them.

Karana sighed, wondering if his chants had brought the clouds. Perhaps he had worked weather magic instead of make-people-vanish magic? Something would be better than nothing. He rubbed his injured leg. It ached. The weather *was* in for a change. He hoped it poured rain onto Galeena's butchering site; that would show his people what a luckless headman they had chosen to lead them.

But the clouds held no rain. They were only the cold congealed breath of the mountain. They smelled more like winter than early autumn. Karana bundled his sleeping skins around him and lay down to sleep.

When he awoke, Aar was beside him, curled close. He was certain that he was dreaming, but the dog was real enough. The dried blood on its shoulder and the fresh scabs on its nose told him that, as did the warm, rough licking of the animal's tongue.

"Brother Dog!" Karana joyously wrapped his skinny arms around Aar's shoulders and held the animal as though it were indeed the brother of his heart.

The dog whimpered and licked his face with increased enthusiasm.

The boy touched the dog's wounds and frowned. "So you have not been accepted by your own kind. Nor have I been by mine. Have you found a Galeena ruling the dog pack? Well, Karana has found a dog ruling the man-pack. You were right to run from Galeena. He is bad, as bad as the dog that did this to you, my brother."

They lay close, not sleeping, merely resting and finding comfort in their closeness. Deep within the mountain, the familiar restless surge of sound sighed and groaned and then was silent. Karana listened. It was quiet . . . unnaturally quiet. With a start, he realized that the waterfalls that cascaded downward from the summit ice pack had frozen.

"It will be winter soon," he whispered to the dog.

Aar's head was up. He listened to the silence and was as discomfited as the boy by it.

"Karana does not think that he can spend an entire winter in this place with Galeena and his people. Karana is working hard to make the magic that will make them disappear."

The dog whined and licked his face; it was almost as though it had understood the child's words and wished to tell him that, even though he was doomed to failure, Brother Dog would not judge him for it.

Karana sighed, his enthusiasm for his ability as a magic maker quashed by common sense. "If Torka will not drive Galeena away, Karana will leave this place. Together we could be a band. Karana and Aar. It would not be a bad thing."

The dog sighed softly, and Karana lay still, thinking about what he had just said. *It would not be a bad thing. It would be an impossible thing.*

Unless his leg healed.

He closed his eyes. He would try to make the magic that would do that; it could not be as difficult as summoning the clouds. And he *had* done that, hadn't he?

He slept and dreamed of dark, savage miles of storm-swept winter tundra, of children dying beneath the cold fire of the aurora borealis, and of a small boy following the flight of an eagle to a Mountain of Power where he had lived alone, as an animal, for far too long.

He awoke with a start. The sun was rising above the snow-streaked mountain to the east. Brother Dog was gone. And for the first time since he had been trapped in Torka's snare, his leg did not hurt at all.

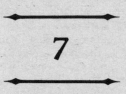

7

He watched the sun rise. He watched the sky spirits build a huge rainbow ring for the sun. It was extraordinary, filling the sky. Karana smiled. Clouds were gathering again. Slowly the circular rainbow faded, and the air began to grow warm. Karana knew that it was going to rain. He wished that Brother Dog had stayed to share the morning with him, for when the first raindrops began to fall, they made the morning more wonderful than any morning that had ever dawned before. These raindrops were special, for Karana knew that he had made them.

His leg was aching again, but not so badly that he doubted his magic. It felt so much better, in fact, that he rose, took up his crutch of caribou antler, and tossed it off the ledge.

He watched it fall. From now on, the only staff that he would carry would be the spear that Torka had made for him. Soon he would hunt again. Soon his people would return. Soon, if Umak refused to make the magic that would drive Galeena's people away, Karana would do it instead. He would watch Umak's every dance and gesture, memorize every nuance of every chant, and absorb the old man's knowledge until he too was a spirit master. He would turn Galeena's people into lemmings and order them to follow their filthy headman over the ledge to their deaths. Aar would come back then—he was certain of that. And when his people returned, he would greet them with Brother Dog at his side. Umak would step forward in his bearskin, with his necklace of wolf paws and bear claws, the head of the great bear balanced atop his own. He would put a hand upon Karana's shoulder. Together they would stand before Navahk, magic man, and Umak would say: "Behold Karana, Boy Who Brings

Rain. Behold Karana, whose magic is strong in the shadow of this spirit master." And Navahk would not smile, for in the presence of Umak and Karana, his own power would be small indeed.

The premise was exhilarating, but only for a moment. Great black squall lines were massing along the horizon to the northeast, and lightning flashed nearby. Thunder shook the world, as well as the boy's confidence. Far below the ledge, the hunters, boys, and women were scurrying about. Karana squinted against the distance and saw Umak waving his arms at the sky. Galeena was directing the hurried packing of meat into hides. The butchering camp was being abandoned. The people were preparing to return to the shelter of the cave. If the full fury of the storm broke upon them, the way would be difficult and dangerous.

A knot formed in Karana's belly as he watched Torka walking beside Lonit, carrying most of her share of their load along with his own. What if she were to stumble and hurt herself and her baby as she ascended the wall to the ledge? With each raindrop, the chances of such a mishap increased, for the way would be slippery and treacherous.

Karana was suddenly cold with dread. He had caused this rain. It was not falling hard yet, but it would be. He had willed it to be so. He had wanted the people of Galeena's band to blame their headman's wasteful way of hunting for having angered the sky spirits. But now that he thought about it, they had shown no reticence when it came to slaying the entire herd of musk oxen. They would probably not blame Galeena at all. They would blame their new spirit master. They would say that, by failing to deter the storm, Umak had proved that his magic was that of a weak old man.

Karana felt sick. He would have to make the storm go away. But how? He had not the slightest idea of what he had said to call down the spirits of the rain. He had merely copied what little he remembered of Umak's atonal chants. There were no words. There were only snatches of sound that made no sense to anyone who was not a spirit master.

It was raining harder now—big, cold drops. He extended his arms and allowed them to form a clear, cool lake within his cupped palms. For the first time, Karana realized just how foolish he had been to assume the responsibility for the use of such powers. If Umak were blamed for the storm, he would have to step forward and admit his blame before everyone, regardless of the consequences. The prospect was terrifying. With a purely reflexive action, he flung his arms upward and released the rain that he had held captive within his hands.

"Go back to the sky! Tell the spirits of the air that Karana has called you by mistake! Tell them that Karana is sorry!"

In that instant, a bolt of lightning struck downward along the mountain wall. It came so close to the ledge that Karana could smell it and feel its power tingling in the air all around him. When thunder followed almost instantaneously, he jumped straight up. His head was so filled with the sound, he did not hear the sharp, grinding, almost human cry that came out of the summit ice pack. He was absolutely positive that the sky spirits had come to punish the audacious boy who had dared to steal the magic chants of Umak so that he might become a master of spirits.

He was master of nothing. He was only Karana, a little boy, who would never take the powers of the spirits for granted again. Yet, as he stood on the ledge, the wind veered sharply. The great squall lines reversed direction. The rain stopped.

And Karana knew that he had made it so.

They came up onto the ledge, rejoicing that Umak had turned the storm away. They spoke of the grandiose invocations that he had made to the sky and of the wonderful dance that he had done on behalf of the hunters. Karana stood by and said nothing as they dumped their meat, hides, and horns without ceremony. No one except the storm had witnessed his encounter with the sky spirits. That was best. He had never seen Umak look happier. The old man behaved like one half his age as he preened under the doting attentions of the matrons. The two sisters aggressively vied for his favor. Karana had to concede that, since their dousing, they were not so bad to look upon. He was glad for Umak, and had no intention of telling anyone that he was responsible for the comings and goings of clouds and rain.

He was very tired. He felt as though the lightning bolt had drained away a portion of his spirit. He dozed beside Lonit's fire while the men and boys made several additional trips back to the butchering site. He heard the youth whom the others called Ninip make a caustic remark about his uselessness. Torka countered it while Karana pretended not to hear. Soon his leg would be strong and flexible again. He would show Ninip who was useless: Boy Who Brings Rain, or Boy Who Falls On Face Before Bull!

Through deepening sleepiness, Karana heard the women speak of how clever Galeena had been to discover this high, dry encampment. He heard them say that had it not been for their headman's resourcefulness, they would have been forced to camp as they had always done, on the open tundra, at the mercy of every storm. Here, thanks to Galeena, they could sit out the weather and work their hides and prepare their meat with little concern for the elements. Karana muttered to himself but was too weary to remind them that *he* had found this cave, and had it not been for Torka's fire, Galeena would never have thought to bring his people to the mountain. Galeena was a man of minimal imagination, brave only when he had armed hunters at his back.

Karana rolled over and closed his eyes. He was almost dreaming now: Aar was at his side. He hunted with Torka, in the shadow of a great bear that was Umak, while Lonit followed close behind with an infant upon her back and her bola in her hand. It was a fine dream. Karana savored it and knew that the best thing about it was that Galeena and his people had no part in it at all.

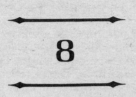

8

It was nearly dark by the time Galeena announced that all that was going to be brought up from the butchering camp had been brought. Although everyone knew that there were still carcasses that had not been fully stripped; no one protested. They had taken the best portions. The rest would have to remain behind. Everyone was exhausted, and the storm that had been sent into retreat that morning was advancing now.

They slept through the worst of the deluge. By morning the rain had turned to sleet. Torka rose to secure the weather baffle that he had raised the night before to keep his little family warm and dry. As he looked at the sleeping forms of Karana and Lonit, he was troubled by a concern that had nagged him since yesterday.

Darkness had forced them to abandon further trips to the butchering site, and the weather would make any descent of the wall dangerous. But they had left so much meat behind! They had killed so many musk oxen that, even if the weather allowed, they could not possibly have butchered them all. Unguarded carcasses at the killing site, which was close to the mountain, would invite predators. If the predators lingered, they would pose a threat to anyone who left the ledge to hunt, fish, or gather tubers and berries.

He had said this to Galeena, but the headman had shrugged and said they would be cautious and kill the predators if they proved a problem. Nevertheless, Torka remained troubled. He wanted to speak his mind to Umak, but the old man had passed the night with the matrons at their fire. Torka saw that he now sat cross-legged before the ring of stones, frowning as he stitched at the sleeves of the tunic Lonit had made for him. He had a lap full of what looked like the flight feathers salvaged from the teratorn that they had killed so long ago. Torka had no idea what Umak was doing with them. The matrons buzzed around him like flies. He swatted them away, so intent upon his work that he did not hear his grandson when Torka called out his name.

It was Galeena who came to him. "Is good thing we khum this dry khamp, uh?" He indicated the foulness of the morning with a snap of his head. "Torka still worry about leaving meat? Galeena say stop. If beasts khum to eat of Galeena's kill, it will be good thing for them. And for us. Fat beasts slow. Not danger to men. Torka worry too much."

Torka eyed Galeena and spoke his thoughts. "Galeena has eaten well of Torka's kills. Galeena grows fat. But on the hunt, Galeena is not slow. He is a danger to the beasts who would feed off the meat that he has wasted."

The headman considered Torka's words. There was good in them, and bad. Compliment and insult mixed together like summer-ripe berries mashed into rancid fat to mask its stink. No man had ever spoken to him as Torka spoke . . . except Manaak—and Manaak had paid. He thought of the way Torka had shamed him by saving the life of Ninip, his son. Again he vowed: Torka will pay. Grinning, Galeena slapped him familiarly upon his back. "Torka always think his way betteh?" he said, pressing with an oily amiability that reeked of insincerity. Beneath the oils were sharp barbs, set to snag.

Torka raised a brow. "It is sometimes difficult to accept new ways. Does not Galeena also find this true?"

Galeena was aware that several of his hunters, his women, and his son were watching him. He was also aware that Torka had subtly turned the barbs of his question back in his own direction. He was not about to be caught. With a definitive snort, he said that he found no trouble adapting to new ways, provided they were worthy of his consideration.

This said, he sauntered to the rim of the cornice. He stood just far enough back to keep out of the rain. He hefted his tunic, loosened the sinew tie that bound his baggy trousers around his waist, and freed an enormous, blue-veined penis. He proceeded to relieve himself. "All see! Galeena piss new way! Torka's way! Not in cave. Over rim of ledge!" As he had expected, the wind blew his urine back at him amid clouds of steam. He laughed and turned to face into the cave. "All see what happen when Galeena piss Torka's way!

Torka make killing throw on hunt! Torka save life of worthless boy! But Torka best learn not to piss on himself before he tells Galeena to accept new ways!"

The hunters howled. The women guffawed. Umak stared, taken aback. And young Ninip flushed deeply with shame.

Torka knew that he would be wise to let the insult pass, but it was too much for him. "Indeed. But Galeena should know that among Torka's people there is a saying: A man who pisses into the wind holds his brains in his hand."

Galeena was speechless for only a moment. "Torka's people are *dead*," he reminded venomously, putting the cutting edge of a thinly veiled warning to his tone.

"Not all of us," replied Torka, measuring his adversary, wondering if he would ever be anything else.

That night they danced. After a day of laying out hides, setting meat on racks of bone to dry, and preparing yards of precious sinew, they felt the need to celebrate such a rich bounty. They danced, and their fires danced with them—high, wasteful fires built of the last of Lonit's carefully dried sod and bones and lichens. When she protested, saying that if the weather did not improve they would be hard pressed to find fire makings to last them through the time of the long dark, Naknaktup silenced her. Oklahnoo reminded her that it was still autumn. Iana said that winter was far away. And Ai, the younger woman of Galeena, assured her that they would have plenty of time to gather and store the kindling and makings of future fires. Tomorrow. Or the next day. Or perhaps the day after that.

In the meantime, they kept their fires high. Smoke filled the cave and blackened its rocky ceiling. Eyes smarted and nostrils burned, but Galeena's people seemed not to notice. They clapped their hands. They stamped their feet. They praised the spirits for having brought them to this safe, high encampment. They praised the musk oxen for having been stupid enough to allow Galeena's hunters to kill them all. They praised each other for everything, anything, and absolutely nothing. They formed a line, then a circle. The circle opened and closed. The dancers sang. They formed a line again and moved like an oxbowed river, snaking back and forth around their fires.

"Khum! Torka's people! Galeena say you dance tuh!" It was Ai. Small and plump, her wide, round face shone in the firelight. It was greasy and blotched with soot from the fire. Her nose was swollen from Galeena's earlier clouting, but amidst the fall of her shoulder-length black hair, her face was still pretty. Very pretty.

Torka could not keep himself from smiling back at her as she took his hand.

"Khum! she urged, and led him off to take his place beside her among the circling dancers.

He hesitated only a moment, making certain that Lonit was following. She reached for his free hand, but the circle closed. The line broke. Wondering why she looked so distraught, he was surrounded by a press of dancers, each moving to his or her own rhythm, each chanting his or her own song.

Someone took her hand, pulled her half off her feet. Lonit gasped, startled to find herself in Galeena's embrace. He was dancing as he held her so close that she could barely breathe. She had not realized how strong he was. His right hand curled about her waist, held it high against her back, hurting her, forcing her to move with him as his free hand touched her in ways that no man except her father had ever touched her—invading the lacings of her tunic, grasping, deliberately hurting her. She tried to pull away, but he jerked her wrist upward. Again she gasped. He leered at her, wolf-eyed in the firelight darkness. All around, dancers moved, lost totally in the moment. The tip of Galeena's tongue penetrated the gap between his front teeth. It was a lewd and obvious symbol. She was glad for the firelight, for he could not see the blush that flamed upon her cheeks. He leaned close, whispered an obscene suggestion, told her that when Torka's baby fought its way free of her body, she had best remember who was headman of this band if she expected the child to be allowed to live.

He released her then, so forcefully that she spun away from him and nearly fell. When she caught her balance, he was nowhere to be seen. She looked for Torka, but dancers were all around her, sweeping her along.

It was so warm within the cave that she could barely breathe. The firelight made everything seem unreal. She thought she saw Umak dancing with the matrons . . . or was it the great, short-faced bear? She saw the boys leaping and swaying in grotesque parodies of the adults. Disoriented, she wondered if she had imagined the last few moments. Had Galeena actually threatened her? Why would he wish to do so?

The movement of the dancers shoved her along. To her infinite relief, she saw her own fire circle. Karana sat solemnly before it. She forced herself out of the dance, half stumbling as she seated herself gratefully upon her sloth skin. Breathless, dizzy, she shook her head to clear it. When Karana asked if she was all right, she told him that she was fine.

But when she saw the way that Ai was looking at Torka, she was not sure.

The night passed slowly, like a bad dream. For Lonit, the only good thing about it was that Torka did not linger with Ai. After a few moments he left the headman's woman and the dance to join Lonit at their fire. Ai glared after him, as did Galeena. When Lonit asked Torka what he had done to offend them, he exhaled a sigh of annoyance, wrapped his sleeping skins around them both, and held her close. "Nothing and everything," he replied obliquely, then would say no more on the subject.

They slept together until the night was nearly over. Lonit awoke and lay still within Torka's arms, remembering the previous night and wondering if her fear of Galeena had caused her to misunderstand his words. She could see no reason why the man should wish to threaten her and even less reason for him to desire her. She could hear him now, sating himself upon one of his women. Probably the pretty one, she thought, and recalled the way the woman had looked at Torka. Not wanting to remember or to hear more of the breathy, savage coupling, she buried her head in Torka's arm. She snuggled closer to him beneath their sleeping skins and wished that Galeena and his band had never come.

Far beyond the mountain, the howling of a wild dog rose with the dawn. Lonit wondered if it was Aar and hoped that the animal had found a better band than that which had driven it away. She took her memories of Brother Dog with her into her dreams and was sound asleep when Karana rose, took up his spear, and walked out of the cave to stand in the light of the rising sun.

*   *   *

He stood alone. He listened to Aar, and to the summit ice pack shifting and settling on the heights far above the cave. He had heard that sound a thousand times before, yet now, on this cold, clear morning, it was as though he were hearing it for the first time. It spoke to him so clearly that he cocked his head and closed his eyes, allowing its voice to whisper to him not out of the deep, uncharted canyons of the mountain but of his own soul.

Go. Go now. Boy Who Brings Rain is no longer welcome on the Mountain of Power.

The inner voice startled him almost as much as the pressure of Umak's hand.

"Karana rises early to greet the sun," commented the old man.

The boy stared at him, sensing that his words, although gently spoken, had nevertheless been a rebuke. It was for the spirit master to greet the sun.

Yet, as they stood together facing into the rising sun, it was the boy who was touched by its power. Karana's eyes and heart and very being were seared.

Umak was unsettled by the strange, wide-eyed expression that appeared upon the child's face as Karana's voice tumbled out of his mouth, a breath ahead of the fear that colored his revelation.

"The mountain says that we must go from this place. We must go eastward into the face of the rising sun. Listen! Brother Dog calls on the wind and echoes the voice of the mountain. He warns us. We must go from this place, or we will stay here forever!"

"Karana must stop such talk! Because Umak has refused to use his magic to make Galeena's people disappear, now Karana would have us pack up and leave and abandon to them the best encampment we have ever known!"

"It is a *bad* encampment."

"Hrmmph! It has saved the life of one small boy! It has allowed Umak, Lonit, and Torka to live in safety! Karana will anger the spirits of this place with his ungrateful talk!"

"It is the spirits of this place that speak through Karana's mouth!"

Umak was taken aback. "*Umak* is spirit master! Karana is a little boy!"

Karana gulped. Umak was very angry. The boy nodded,

not wanting to upset him. He decided that he would say no more. Umak must be right. He was being presumptuous to assume that the spirits would wish to tell him anything. If they had warnings, they would give them to Umak.

9

Days and nights flew before the sun and moon like clouds driven by the gales of time. Karana listened in vain for the spirits of the mountain to repeat their warnings. After a while, he was glad they remained silent. His leg was not quite strong enough for a trek into far and unknown lands, and even if it were, he would not want to go without Torka, Lonit, and Umak. And they would not believe that the spirits of the great mountain would choose to speak through such a little mouth as his.

In many ways, life was improving upon the ledge. The autumn nights were growing longer. The days were sweet and burnished by the light of the Arctic sun, but there was an ever-increasing quality of fragility to that light. Man and beast became restless in anticipation of the time of the long dark, so even Galeena's people were moved to rise with the sun, to hunt, to gather, to prepare for the lean, dark days to come.

The skies turned white with tens of thousands of migrating snow geese heading south and east. They competed with Lonit and the women of Galeena's band for the last of the season's berries and roots. While the geese fattened on the autumn bounty of the tundra, Galeena's women came down from the mountain to set snares for them, and Lonit took great pleasure in stalking them with her bola, a weapon totally unknown to the people of Galeena's band. Torka was proud to see how the hunters openly admired Lonit's skill with the strange device. They and the boys murmured with amazement at the whirring sound it made as it flew low over the ponds and marshes, and even surly Ninip cried out with astonishment as its perfect weighted thongs hissed around the legs and necks of its prey. Wishing to make a gesture of friendship, Lonit offered to teach the women of the band how to use it, but they were not of a mind to try new things; Ai turned up her flat, now-crooked little nose and said it was easier to set snares than to waste her time attempting to master such a complicated thing as a bola.

The enmity that had strained Torka's relationship with Galeena was gradually softening into a begrudging toleration. Neither man liked the other, but Torka had proved that he was a good man to have along on a hunt, and for the sake of his people, he had not challenged the headman since their last exchange of hostile words. Now that Galeena was finally showing concern for the future welfare of the band, Torka saw no reason to provoke him; his younger woman was already going out of her way to do just that. It was obvious to everyone that, since Galeena had cracked her nose, she was nursing a grudge against him, deliberately focusing her attentions upon Torka in order to antagonize her own man. Torka avoided her when he could. Now she was angry with him, too, which pleased Galeena and made Lonit very happy.

The inner recesses of the cave were once again packed high with provisions for the coming winter. Drying frames were everywhere, and each was weighted with meat and fish and fowl. The women worked skins and fashioned horns and bones into tools of many uses. Umak, happily situated with Naknaktup and Oklahnoo at their decidedly cleaner fire circle, portended good things for those who spent the last days of the time of light in preparation for the inevitable rising of the starving moon. With the two doting matrons to see to his every need and whim, he had no time for Karana. When the boy came to him, Umak waved him away, telling him to seek those of his own age for companionship. Karana shrank back from him, hurt and bewildered by his rejection, but the old man did not notice. He had his women and his portendings, and those were enough to keep any man busy. Arrogant, confident, and fully virile again, he had assumed great status as spirit master of Galeena's band. He might be beyond his years of running down steppe antelope and killing them with his bare hands, but everyone knew that he had recently stood against the great short-faced bear, and he would not let anyone forget that he drew the essence of its power from its skin each time he wore it. He greeted each dawn with a chant in which he referred to himself as Man Who Kills Great Bear Alone. He invoked each sunset with a plea for the return of the sun, in the name of Man Who Walks In Skin Of Great Bear Spirit.

And behold! The sun rose! The sun set! Everyone was impressed. Especially Umak. Because of their confidence in his magic, Galeena's hunters were bolder and better at their kills. Because they feared his power, Galeena's women bathed and maintained a cleaner encampment when, from out of a feigned trance, he insisted that they do so or be eaten by the wind spirits. Torka was openly proud of him, and a beaming Lonit brought him prime portions of meat from her own fire. All the women of the band did so, for as the man who called the spirits of the game to die upon the hunters' spears, Umak was not required to hunt for himself or for his women.

For the first time since their youth had left him, Umak was content with his life . . . except when he was distracted by Karana's watchful eyes. The boy's face was impossible to read, even for a spirit master, so Umak did not try. It was enough for him to see that the boy was walking without the aid of his crutch. Soon Torka would take him down from the ledge to hunt small geese. And all because Umak had used his skills as a healer to drive the bad spirits from the boy's injured leg. The old man was proud of his accomplishment.

And Torka, seeing the change in him, was glad.

"Umak is happy in this new way of life?"

"Hrmmph! To live in one place is not the way of the People! But Man Who Kills Great Bear Alone says that this mountain *is* the Mountain of Power. To this spirit master it gives great strength and wisdom! To those who camp within its walls, it is good!"

Torka could find no cause to disagree with him. Galeena and his people left much to be desired when he compared them to the members of his own band, but life was easier since they had come; and, although Torka often found himself longing to be alone again with only Lonit, Umak, Karana, and the wild dog for company, he had to admit that the future seemed far less threatening. Umak was right. Life *was* good upon the mountain. For the first time in longer than Torka could remember, days and nights were passing with very few shadows.

Until, one night, he dreamed again of the roaring wall of water. It rose up from beyond the horizon to sweep eastward toward the mountain. Black and raging, it drowned all that moved before it, except one indomitable creature that walked through and above it.

It was huge. It was silent. It was terrible in its unwelcome familiarity. Neither flesh nor spirit, its shoulders held up the sky. Its massive, stanchion limbs parted the waters. Its bloodied tusks ripped the fabric of the clouds. Bodies rained out of them. Headless, faceless, crushed, and mangled, they grasped at its shaggy hair and rode its monstrous back, leering at the dreamer across the tormented miles of his memories.

Alinak. Nap. Egatsop. Kipu. The bodies of the People—they were all there, beckoning and speaking to him on the rising wall of the wind, telling him that he could not walk away from them, that they had followed, that they would always follow . . . until he was one of them, a member of their band again, forever.

He twitched in his sleep. He tried to shake the dream away, but it intensified. The beast of his nightmares reached the mountain wall. It was larger than life, but only half the size of his terror as the beast raised its trunk, so the bodies of the dead could clamber upward and leap onto the ledge.

They were mists, smokes, swirling over the sleeping forms of Umak, Lonit, and Karana. He knew them all, and yet did not know them. Those flattened, mangled, hideously smashed, and bloodied corpses could not be his beloved woman, his more-beloved son. Neither had faces, yet somehow they smiled and stared at him before putting their mutilated cloud mouths over the faces of Umak, Lonit, and Karana to suck their life spirits from them.

The beast rammed its tusks into the mountain wall. The world shook as Thunder Speaker trumpeted its triumph over the man who had dared to stand alone against it and live to tell the tale.

Torka!

It spoke his name as its impossibly long trunk encircled his chest, crushed his ribs, and lifted him, carried him out of the cave, and hurled him upward into the night. He flew into the clouds and was blinded by their mist. Lightning flashed nearby. Thunder deafened him as he grasped the bolt and turned it to his purpose.

It was a part of him. *He* was the lightning bolt. It was an extension of his spear arm. It burned and set his spirit afire. It sapped him of his humanity as it transformed him into a living weapon. His arm was not an arm, it was a five-jointed sling of power; its muscles and tendons and flesh were all fused by the lightning into a wondrous device that coiled back and then sprang forward like the limb of a leaping lion. The power of that beast, and more, was his as the lightning bolt was propelled from his hand downward with the speed of a plummeting eagle.

He struck the Destroyer through its red, hate-filled eye. He went down into that hatred, into a lake of blood that choked him and cooled the power of the lightning bolt until it and he lay cold and lifeless within the heart of the great, dead spirit that would never again roam the world to feed off the lives of men.

"Torka!"

Manaak's imperative whisper brought him out of the dream. He stared up at the scar-faced hunter, dazed, dry mouthed, his heart pounding. Dawn was thinning the darkness. Lonit lay warm against his back beneath their sleeping skins, but he was cold, badly shaken, glad that Manaak had awakened him.

"Khum! Listen! Torka must hear!"

Rising carefully so as not to awaken Lonit, Torka drew on his tunic and followed Manaak to the edge of the cornice. The world was blue with cold, and the waterfalls were frozen solid. The wind spoke softly, promising that soon the sun would rise.

From across the endless miles, from out of distant canyons and glacier-choked mountain ranges far to the east, there came a sound that gave substance to Torka's dream.

"Mammoth . . ." Manaak exhaled the word as though it were the answer to a long-chanted prayer.

Torka listened, his heart and spirit as cold and frozen as the waterfalls, until the sound redefined itself and he smiled with relief. "*Many* mammoth. A herd. Very far. Days from this place. A herd means females and young." The dream was fading now. He felt better. He saw the look of disappointment cross Manaak's face and did not care. "Big Spirit . . . World Shaker . . . the Destroyer . . . the one that Manaak would kill, that one is solitary. That one walks alone."

Manaak's eyes narrowed. "Big Spirit was not alone when it came upon the encampment of mammoth huntehs at the entrance to the Corridor of Storms. The mammoths screamed as they died in the bog pits into which the huntehs drove them. Then Big Spirit came. Like the shadow of an early winteh he came and fell upon us like a storm. When he left, he went alone; but it is said that Big Spirit follows the herds. He watches the old, the weak, the little lost ones who wandeh off to die. He kills those who would eat of their flesh. He grinds into the tundra those who would disturb their bones. It is for this he lives: to crush the life spirits of those who hunt mammoth."

"Then he will not seek us here, for we are men who prey upon other kinds of meat."

Manaak shook his head. "It is said that Big Spirit knows and remembehs all. And like Manaak, he does not forgive. Big Spirit is out there somewhere; even as we speak, othehs may be dying in their encampments. Someday it will come to us, and we will have to face it. Galeena may be content to hide in the belly of this mountain, but until Big Spirit is dead, Manaak will listen for the sound of mammoths moving in the night, and Torka will twitch in his dreams."

Torka was troubled by Manaak's words, but as game continued to pass below the mountain in a slowly dwindling parade, no mammoths were seen, and the animals that he and Manaak had heard trumpeting in the distant mountains were not heard again.

Fowl continued to fill the skies by day and to chortle, honk, and quack within the frosty marshes during the ever-lengthening nights. The animals of the tundra were exchanging their summer coats for winter white. Pikas and other rodents feverishly stockpiled the last of the season's available greenery—sticks and stalks and tender shoots that dared to sprout in defiance of the increasing cold. Cached in lichen-lined burrows, these would dry and serve as fodder when snow and ice lay deep and impenetrable upon the surface of the tundral world.

The men of the band hunted with less urgency now. The boys were encouraged to go out on occasional forays as long as they remained within hailing distance of an elder. Karana's leg was much improved, but when he took up his spear and prepared to follow the others, Ninip mocked him for his lingering limp, and Torka was adamant in his refusal to allow him to descend the wall.

"When your leg is stronger, you may go. Not yet."

Karana accepted Torka's words in sullen silence, but he glowered when the others left without him, and would not be cheered, even by Lonit's offering of his favorite pudding, a mixture of finely beaten fat sweetened with congealed blood and pebbled with dried bunchberries and cranberries picked fresh in the canyon at the base of the mountain wall.

The days passed, and the nights, and Torka nodded with encouragement when he saw how Karana exercised his leg until its muscles burned; but the boy continued to limp badly, and Torka refused him permission to leave the cave.

"You will be slow. You will be unsteady. You will be a danger to yourself and to any man or boy who hunts beside you."

"Then let me hunt alone! Let me prove what I can do!"

The boy looked so much like his lost son that Torka had to look away. "Soon," he said, and tried to put his memories behind him. He failed. When he looked again at Karana's earnest little face, he spoke his heart to one who had become like a son to him. "Time passes quickly, Little Hunter. It seems that only a moon ago I was a boy walking in the shadow of my father, eager to prove myself to him and to my people. Sometime between then and now, I became a man, shadowing my own son. And now, my father and my son and most of my people walk the spirit world, and Torka walks with Karana, and both of us are shadowed by the wisdom of Umak, our spirit master. I will ask him to make the chants that will cause the spirits to hurry the healing of Karana's leg. But Karana must remember how much Umak has already asked of the spirits in behalf of one small boy."

"Spirit Master has his women and a new band. He does not care about one small boy."

Torka shook his head. "Karana lives because of Umak's magic. Karana grows stronger because one old man would not let him die. Life is good for us, Little Hunter, so be patient. Be content with the days as they are given. Be glad that between now and the rising of the starving moon, Torka will hunt for you and Lonit will cook for you while Umak shares a common fire with those who have made him feel young again in this high, safe place."

"Spirit Master has forgotten us," pouted the boy.

Torka smiled. "No, Little Hunter. He has remembered himself and has found it good to be a man among men again."

10

It was still autumn, but small, hard flakes of snow driven by a whistling wind stripped the leaves from the willows and whipped the world into a stinging froth of white.

The people of Galeena's band stayed within the cave. They ate and slept and ate again, and when Lonit once again found herself concerned over their squandering of food, the women mocked her for her worrying. Theirs was a well-established pecking order, and they made it quite clear that she was at the bottom of it. But in the main they offered friendship and companionable gossip as readily as they offered criticism and advice. To her surprise, although they made occasional remarks about her appearance, they did not find her repugnant. When Ai made a slur against Lonit's unusually lidded eyes, matronly Naknaktup came to her defense.

"If Galeena lets Ai live long enough, maybe she will watch her own wandering eyes and not worry about Lonit's! This woman live long time, see many people have eyes like Torka's woman. In some bands far from this place people *prefer* eyes like that. So this woman say: If man as fine as Torka take Lonit to be his woman, maybe her looks betteh than ours. And *much* betteh than Ai's since Galeena smash her nose for looking at Lonit's man!"

All of the women laughed at that, except Ai and sad-eyed Iana, who never laughed at anything. Lonit was too astonished to respond. Others with eyes like hers? Whole bands of them? Was it possible? Or was Naknaktup only saying it to be kind? No. Among these women, with the possible exception of Iana, kindness was a word that had no meaning. She knelt with them in a circle around a large oxhide that was in the last phase of scraping. They had all paused in their work—Ai to glare at Lonit with open hostility, the others, except Iana, to snort and guffaw at Ai.

Lonit wished they would stop. Ai's mouth puckered into a knot of resentment that only intensified the mirth of the other women. Lonit could not help but stare at their broad, uniformly round, flat faces. Since Umak had coerced them into washing themselves occasionally, their features were visible—small, even, so similar that they might all have been sisters. Even the plainest of them had the taut, upswept fold of skin that covered their lids and made their eyes appear to slant upward toward their temples. How she envied them their eyes and their round, pretty faces. But nothing else! She was Torka's woman, and she knew that they all envied *her* for that.

Ai was on her feet, wiping her small, pudgy hands on her apronless skirt. "Laugh! Go ahead! But soon Ai will laugh loudeh! Lonit and her man, they think they betteh than us! Keep apart, turn noses up at ou' food, ou' ways! Now Lonit's belly grows as big and round as a summeh moon. Soon Ai *will* lie with Lonit's man! And when Lonit's baby comes, Galeena will neveh let it live. *Neveh!* This woman will make certain that this is so!"

"Sleep now. Do not worry, little Antelope Eyes. Believe me, Galeena's woman cannot say what he, or any other man, might do."

Lonit had waited until very late to speak her fears to him. She had awakened him with a gentle touch, and now he returned it and kissed her brow.

"Sleep," he urged. "Torka holds no fear of the threats of a jealous female."

"Jealous? Why would Ai be jealous? She is Galeena's woman . . . and she is beautiful."

"Lonit is beautiful."

She smiled wanly, wanting to believe him but failing. "Lonit will soon be as Ai says . . . as big and round as a summer moon."

He drew her into an embrace, his broad, strong hand pressing gently upon her belly. "The summer moon is the most beautiful moon of all."

She wrapped her arms around his neck and pressed herself and the child against him, loving him so much that, for a moment, she could not speak. But she *had* to speak. "Lonit has overheard Karana say to Umak that this is a bad camp, that we must leave this place, that the Mountain of Power has spoken through his mouth to warn us away."

"Karana is a little boy. Would the spirits of the mountain speak through him instead of Umak?"

"Umak is old. Perhaps—"

"Umak is spirit master. If the spirits were to speak to anyone, they would speak to him. And he is happy in this camp. Here he has found the power of his manhood again. So do not listen to the babblings of a foolish woman and a more foolish child. Soon Torka's woman will be delivered of our summer moon. Soon the time of the long dark will be upon us. We will stay here, in this high, safe place. It was ours before it was Galeena's. Thanks to Umak's magic, his people are changing . . . a little. In time things will be better between our people." He stifled a yawn and shifted his weight against her. "Lonit will see. Soon this will be a good camp again."

She wanted to disagree, to speak to him of her troubled memories of the night when the fires had burned high and the people of Galeena's band had danced and she had imagined that the headman had threatened her; but Torka had drifted into sleep, and she was yawning and growing heavy-eyed. Perhaps it was just as well. Galeena had made no further advances to her, nor had he threatened her in any way. The night of the dancing fires seemed long ago, part of a half-forgotten bad dream. She sighed, glad to allow her recollections of it to fade. In Torka's arms, with their unborn child sleeping high beneath her breasts, life itself seemed a dream. She closed her eyes and slept, smiling because she knew that no dream could be sweeter, or more unbelievable to her, than what she was now sharing with Torka.

It was a time of the telling of tales. Umak spoke first. When his voice began to crack and it became apparent that the weather was going to keep everyone confined to the ledge for the remainder of the day and night, Galeena took over. Whereas Umak's tales were intricate, allegorical stories that spoke of man and beast and their eternal conflict and union with the forces of Creation, Galeena's stories were straightforward, rather unimaginative tales of bold adventures in far places. In Umak's stories, man and beast were always subservient to the powers of the earth and sky. In Galeena's tales, he and his band were the central figures around which all else moved. Sun, moon, stars—all revolved around Galeena. He spoke of strange-sounding hunting grounds in which he and his hunters killed until all of the game was gone. He spoke of feasts that lasted for days on end, until all the food was gone and he and his band were forced to move into the hunting territory of other bands. He spoke once more of the Corridor of Storms, a game-rich but terrifyingly narrow, wind-scoured passage of open grazing land between mile-high mountains of solid ice . . . mountains that shifted and moaned like women in labor and sometimes came crashing down in huge avalanches to bury men or beasts traveling beneath them.

Now for the first time, the tone and emphasis of his tales changed. Here, in the cold, wind-wrapped shadow of his memories of the Corridor of Storms, Galeena the storyteller reluctantly conceded that even the mighty Galeena, hero of his tales, was only a mortal man after all.

"How many die neeah Corridor of Storms, wheyeh mountains walk like people?" His question was part of his story chant.

"Many die neeah the Corridor of Storms, wheyah mountains walk like people!" his hunters responded in unison. His women keened as though they were one. The boys of his band listened with wide-eyed wonder even though they had heard the tale so many times that some of them were able to mouth the words in silence as Galeena spoke them aloud.

"Do they die of the mountain falling?" Again Galeena's question was a part of the story.

"They do not die of mountain falling!"

"Tell us then what kills the people!"

"The wrath of Big Spirit kills the people!"

"Ai-yah! And who is wisest headman of all bands? Who keeps people safe from falling mountain? Who leads people from Big Spirit when he khums to us like storm?"

"Galeena!"

"And who tells his people to hunt Big Spirit neveh moh? What man saves life of this band while othehs follow Big Spirit and die?"

"Galeena! Ai-yah-hay! Ga-lee-na!"

He beamed at their open adulation, then scowled when he saw that, alone among his hunters, the scar-faced Manaak remained silent and visibly unimpressed. Even Torka seemed taken with his storytelling. He sat cross-legged at his own fire circle with Lonit and Karana. All three of them faced into the cave, watching Galeena as he postured and puffed out his chest.

"Where lies this Corridor of Storms?" asked Torka.

"Eastward. In the face of the rising sun," replied Manaak.

Galeena snorted with incredulity. "What kind hunteh not know Corridor of Storms?"

"This kind," admitted Torka evenly, not in a mood to be riled. "Torka is a man of the west. Torka cannot know what he has not seen."

Again Galeena snorted. "What kind know-nothing people live in west not know moh mammoth browse in east?"

"People who follow the caribou have little concern for the ways of mammoth," Torka said. "To us, the meat of a mammoth is fit to be eaten only during the worst times of the starving moon. It is too tough. It tastes too much like the bitter sap of the trees that it eats. Even the smell of its flesh offends us."

"Ha!" blurted Galeena with explosive enthusiasm. "Bands khum from all places to join at great encampment. Kill many mammoth. Tough meat makes tough people!"

And smelly meat makes smelly people, thought Karana with disgust. Suddenly an idea burst into his consciousness, and he wondered why he had not thought of it before. "At this great camp where many bands come . . . has Galeena seen the band of Supnah? He leads many men, many women. He is not much for mammoth meat, but in starving times . . ."

Galeena did not appreciate the child's interruption. "What care yuh this Supnah?"

Karana told him, and Galeena grunted, telling the boy that he *had* seen and shared a fire with a man named Supnah.

"Big band. No little ones. No babies. Some wuhmen. And magic man. Navahk, is that name?"

Karana's eyes grew round. "Navahk. It is so."

Galeena grunted again. He told Karana that he and his band had met with Supnah and his people while they were still en route to the great encampment. They had both taken a few caribou. They had shared a cooking fire, and Galeena had invited Supnah to continue on with him to the great gathering of mammoth hunters close to the entrance of the Corridor of Storms. Supnah was unfamiliar with the area and had expressed his dislike of mammoth meat.

"Last time Galeena see that man, he was still at fiah. Long time back now. Supnah say he stay that place, hunt moh caribou, then go on, following herds whereveh they lead."

"But he promised to come back for me, for all the children. He—"

"Said nothing of son. Said nothing of childs. So Galeena says now to Karana, that after Big Spirit killed many in camp of mammoth huntehs, Galeena led his band back west, away from Big Spirit, looking for this Supnah, thinking maybe two bands be betteh than one. But Supnah gone. Supnah follows caribou. And Big Spirit follows Supnah. Galeena sees tracks. So Karana forget Supnah, forget all huntehs who walk the tundra with no high, safe mountain to keep them safe from Big Spirit!"

Karana's head was swimming. He knew that everyone was staring at him. He did not care as he blurted: "You saw the tracks of Big Spirit and did not follow Supnah to warn him?"

Galeena's people murmured. The boy's question had sounded like an accusation.

"Follow Big Spirit?" Galeena shook his head. "What foh this man do that? Galeena is not ready to send his spirit walking on the wind! Huntehs hunt *game*, not crooked spirits! And why does Karana care what happens to one who walked away and left him to die?"

"Because I have *not* died! Because he is my father! Because his band is my band! Because I know that if he *could* have returned for me, he *would*! And because, unlike Galeena, Karana is not afraid of Big Spirit!"

He knew at once that he had grievously overstepped his place. Lonit gasped, and he heard Umak exhale a muted harrumph even before he saw the black, sobering look on Torka's face.

Torka reprimanded him strongly and angrily. "Not until Karana has faced Big Spirit, as this man and Galeena and his hunters have done, will he know the meaning of fear. Be it spirit or flesh, many brave men have died trying to kill the great mammoth that has many names. This is a little boy with a mouth twice his size! Until he is a man, with the weight of a man's responsibilities upon his back, let Torka not hear him challenge or criticize the ways of his elders, for while their wisdom is great, Karana possesses no wisdom at all!"

Karana was shamed by the rebuke, but not so cowed by it

that he failed to see how it soothed Galeena and mollified his hunters. They all murmured favorably at Torka's speech. The women nodded, and the boys followed Ninip in a chorus of jeers. Karana hung his head. He heard Umak say that Karana was a boy who learned quickly and would not repeat his mistake. He felt sick, betrayed.

To ease the tension of the moment, Umak began to tell a tale. His two women rose and urged the others to pass the meat. Once again, the people of Galeena resumed their endless feasting.

Lonit offered an aged ptarmigan egg to Karana. It was one of his favorite foods, but he waved it away. He had no appetite. Far off across the tundra, muffled by the falling snow, a wild dog howled. Or was it a wolf? Karana could not tell.

Suddenly restless, he went to stand at the edge of the cornice. Umak's chant filled the cave. The words drifted like smoke into the boy's head. There *was* magic in the Mountain of Power, he thought. A dark and subversive magic that turned even such brave and honorable hunters as Torka and Umak into compromisers who could find wisdom in the excesses and cowardice of a man like Galeena.

This boy will not stay in this place. It is a bad camp. As Brother Dog has left it, so too will Karana go. He will follow his own people eastward, into the face of the rising sun. And no matter what Torka says, Karana will not be afraid!

But as he looked down along the icy, precipitous route that he would have to take in order to leave the cave, he *was* afraid. He had climbed this face of the mountain many times before his injury. In sun, in rain, in sleet, in snow, he knew every foot- and handhold. At best it was a time-consuming climb and not without danger. At worst it was deadly, and only a fool would try it.

Karana was not a fool. He had survived alone upon this mountain too long for any man to accuse him of that. Yet Torka had done just that in front of the entire band.

There was a hot, hard lump at the back of Karana's throat. When he tried to swallow it, it would not move. He had not realized just how much he had wanted Torka's approval or how much the denial of that approval could hurt.

The snow had stopped. The air was very cold. The wind seemed to be holding its breath. Soon the snow would begin to fall again, but now Karana could see the sun. It was a small, dull yellow eye that stared at him through miles of shifting clouds. Something about it made him think of Navahk, the magic man, watching him, smiling his hate-filled smile, daring one small boy to follow where brave hunters dared not go.

The change in the weather was causing Karana's leg to stiffen and ache. He knew that Torka would be proved right about him if he tried to make the climb down from the cave alone. And when he fell to his death from the icy wall, somehow Navahk would know and the eye of the sun would grow wide with pleasure as, miles away across the tundra, the magic man smiled. Unless . . .

Speculation pricked him. He remembered the pulley and sling that Torka and Umak had devised to heft the heavier portions of dismembered moose up the mountain wall. The device had seen much use since that day. It was flimsy, and if not carefully balanced, as much meat fell from it as was successfully brought up the wall.

Karana will be careful, vowed the boy. *In the deep, dark shank of this night, while everyone sleeps, Karana will go. No one will miss him. This is no longer his cave or his mountain. Torka's people are no longer Karana's people. They are of Galeena's band now.*

The day seemed to go on forever. As snow continued to fall, the people of Galeena's band grew tired of eating and listening to story chants. They drank a foul liquid that their women had prepared and stored in bladder flasks. Soon half the flasks were drained, and while Torka knapped projectile points and Lonit busied herself with her sewing, Galeena's people showed little inclination to engage in productive work. They dozed, and when they woke, their speech was slurred, and for a little while they were much given to laughter. Then their mood changed. The hunters coupled with their women as though they were angry, so quickly that afterward the partners were irritable and argumentative. The boys were forbidden even to sip from the flasks and soon grew bored and fell to squabbling so viciously that Ninip hit another boy with a rock and Umak had to be summoned to suture the scalp of the screeching boy.

Karana sat by himself, bundled in his sleeping furs close to the edge of the cornice. It was better to watch the snow fall, cool and clean and silent, than to observe the activities within the cave. In his mind, he had already left it. When Lonit came to him and tried to persuade him to come in from the cold, he ignored her. Had Torka come with even the slightest word of apology, he might have weakened and lost his resolve to leave. But Torka had not come, and although Karana was disappointed, he told himself that he was glad. Torka had become a stranger. Anyway, he told himself, he would have to grow used to the cold, which would be his one constant companion until he found Brother Dog and the two of them set off across the tundra in search of Supnah's band.

Beside the headman's fire circle, Ai whispered incendiary words to Galeena. Well-pleased by her behavior of the last few days, he accepted her advances. Smashing a woman in the face was a good way to deal with troublesome females, although Ai had taken longer than most to stop sulking. Now, as she handled him, he sighed with pleasure and nodded at every word of flattery that she was whispering into his ear. As she opened herself wide to his impatient rutting, he did not doubt her for a moment when she told him that he was the best of all men at all things.

But then Weelup, his second woman, whispered the words that Ai had told her to say under threat of being tripped the next time she descended the mountain wall: "Some say Torka is bettch." Weelup cringed as she spoke and rolled away in anticipation of a blow.

It came.

Galeena hit her hard across the back as he shriveled, his mating with Ai ruined. "What wuhman say that?" he demanded with murder in his eyes.

"No wuhman," soothed Ai. "*Torka* thinks he is best man at all things. Always Torka challenges Galeena. Torka does not eat from our fiahs. Torka does not drink from our flasks. Torka insults our men by lying only with his own wuhman."

Briefly, at the back of his anger, Galeena knew that no man had offered to share a woman with Torka. It was up to the headman of a band to make such a gesture first. And Galeena had deliberately chosen not to do so. If any man was guilty of insulting another, it was he for not extending such a common courtesy to another. Torka did not seem to mind. The young man was obviously more than content with his own strange-eyed female, and Galeena was glad, because he had no desire to share either of his women with a man of whom he was clearly jealous.

Ai ran her small, warm palms over his chest and lifted her head to lick and nip at his skin. "Galeena not worry what Torka say or what other wuhmen and men of his band may think. Ai hears the old ones say that long ago, Galeena was best man of all at great gathering where many bands come to hunt and dance the *plaku* at the entrance to the Corridor of Storms."

"Old ones? Long ago? . . . Galeena is best man *now*! If wuhman dance *plaku* in this khamp, Torka could not come close to matching this man's prowess!"

Ai smiled and buried her face in his chest lest her smile become laughter at his expense. "Galeena not have to say this to Ai! Ai is Galeena's wuhman, she wants no man but headman! Ai knows that Galeena is best of all!"

"Ai will *see*!" He shoved her away and was on his feet, declaring that his people must prepare for a *plaku* immediately.

Silence fell.

Galeena's people stared at him with stunned and gaping incredulity.

"*Plaku! Plaku!* Make ready! Make ready!" he ordered, watching as the men's blank faces wrinkled into lecherous grins and the women's hands flew to their mouths in a vain attempt to suppress their titters.

Ninip hooted and led the boys into a snickering little clot of whisperings as Iana came to take Lonit by the hand and draw her away from Torka to sit with her at her fire circle.

"*Plaku* not for woman with baby in belly," she explained, and had time to say no more before Naknaktup joined them.

The older woman gloated as she informed them that Umak was indeed a great and powerful spirit master, for he had put a baby into the belly of one who had thought herself long past bearing.

Lonit was so delighted, not for Naknaktup but for Umak, that she forgot to ask why she had been drawn away from Torka's fire. Now the old man *would* be young again, for the child that Naknaktup would bear him in his last years, the child that would strengthen him and renew his purpose in living—not just to posture and preen and make his wonderful magic but to pass on the gift of his life to one whose spirit had been formed with his own loins.

"Yuh see! All wuhman will want Umak! They will dance the *plaku* for my man! This wuhman will be proud!" Naknaktup beamed.

"*Plaku?* What is the *plaku?*" pressed Lonit.

"It is a dance that is done at the great encampment of mammoth huntehs near the entrance to the Corridor of Storms. *Plaku* . . . the *dance of wuhman's choosing*. It is a sharing of pleasure, from one band to anotheh, from one man's wuhman to anotheh wuhman's man," explained Iana.

Lonit blinked, not liking the sound of this at all. "Who shares? Who chooses?"

"All share, but it is the one time when the wuhman may choose. One man. Many men. Any man they would desire to lie with. Any man except their own man. For this one time."

"Not *my* man!" protested Lonit.

Naknaktup laughed at Lonit's exclamation. "*Any* man, my little one. Torka . . . Umak . . . Galeena . . . any and all! More wuhmen want one man, more proud his wuhman be!" She clapped her large, work-roughened hands together with delight as she savored her memories. "This wuhman live long, see many things, dance at many *plakus*. Long time back, before Galeena become headman this band, Naknaktup see him take on *all* wuhman at great gathering!"

"That is not possible!"

"Galeena youngeh then," conceded the matron, adding a conspiratorial wink. "Very small gathering that time. Not so many wuhmen, and *plaku* last long time. But Naknaktup tell Lonit that Galeena has one big, hungry, rising bone! That one reason huntehs make him headman this band. Any man with bone that big—"

"My own Manaak once took three wuhmen same time," Iana interrupted, obviously not wanting to hear Galeena praised. "When Manaak finish, all three wuhmen filled and happy. Not dry and bruised like Galeena leaves wuhmen afteh his pounding! But that no matteh. All wuhmen want Galeena. He headman. No wuhman but Iana want Manaak now that he has scars on his face."

Lonit was in despair, yet she saw the sadness on Iana's face and wished to soothe it. "Among this woman's people, a man with scars is a man who is envied by others. Manaak is strong and has a fine face. His scars say that Iana is lucky not to have to share her man with others! Lonit does not want to share Torka!"

She looked so distraught that Naknaktup reached out and swept her into a motherly embrace. "Listen to this wuhman, little one. Manaak has scars because Galeena cut him. Manaak's scars mark him as man apart . . . as man who will die if he challenges Galeena again."

Iana put a gentle, empathetic hand upon Lonit's arm. "You *will* share your man, Lonit." Her voice was as soft and sad as her eyes. "The *plaku* is a dance of our people. You and Torka are of this band now. If Torka is chosen and refuses one of our wuhmen, he will not be a man to envy. Our huntehs will be angry. They will hold Torka while Galeena cuts his face or maybe even drives him from this place. Then Lonit will become Galeena's wuhman. Then Galeena will kick Lonit until Torka's baby dies. Then Lonit will live by his fiah and share his sleeping skins with Ai and Weelup until Galeena grows tired of her. Then Galeena will send Lonit to follow Torka, to walk alone into the wind, to be food for beasts."

The men of the band built a single fire in the center of the cave. It was a smoky, careless pyre heaped high with the bones and refuse of recent meals. They dragged their sleeping skins close and seated themselves around it, leaving a broad circle of open ground between themselves and the flames. Here the women would dance. The hunters made lewd jokes about the dancers, and wagers as to whose prowess would be tested and by whom. When Torka made no move to join them, they called out to him, patted the ground where they wanted him to sit, and reminded him that he was a man of their band now. No man of the band could stand aside during a *plaku*, nor would any male who had a breath of spirit left in him wish to do so.

They all laughed at that. One of them suggested that perhaps Torka was a different kind of man. Another replied that since he had yet to join with one of their women, there was no way to tell if he even *was* a man; although he was a fine hunter and his own female seemed to be evidence enough of the workings of his rising bone.

Torka felt his face flush with resentful embarrassment. He was aware of a pitifully distraught Lonit sitting far off across the cave with Iana and Naknaktup. He could not bring himself to look at her. He wanted to speak out, tell Galeena's hunters that, among Torka's people, it was not expected of a man to copulate with other men's women in order to prove his virility; but he knew that they had spoken the truth when they had said that he was of their band now. The People were dead and gone. And Umak's sage words of advice were proving their validity more and more every day: *In new times, men must learn new ways.*

Even if they neither like nor approve of them, he added to himself, reluctantly joining the circle. He sat down beside Manaak and, for a moment, was distracted by Karana staring judgmentally from the shadows just beyond the circle of hunters; then the boy was gone, off to mope at their own fire circle no doubt, and Galeena was summoning Umak to join the others.

"Hrmmph!" was all the old man said as he came forward in his bearskin robe and his softly clicking necklaces of claws and paws. Over the last few days, he had completed stitching the flight feathers of the condor to the seams of the sleeves of his tunic. When he raised his arms, he appeared to have wings, as though he were not a man at all but some strange, otherworldly combination of bear and bird. He held his arms high for a moment, waiting for the exhalations of awe from those who observed his display; they came, mainly from the women. Satisfied, he folded his legs beneath him, laced his arms across his chest, and stared stoically into the flames.

But only a rock could have sat stoically through the *plaku.* As a prelude to the dance, the women circulated among the men with flasks of the oily, thick, foul-smelling drink that Torka had managed to avoid over the last few weeks. It was a revolting mixture of blood and fermented berries and juices, of mosses and fungi, and of willow bark pounded into pulp and then chewed by the women until it became totally liquified and mixed with their saliva.

Now he had no choice but to drink, and to drink deeply. To do otherwise would be to offend the people of Galeena's band, who set much store by the potion. He gagged twice, but managed to swallow down a mouthful. The men nodded. The watching women tittered and moved on.

He soon understood why they drank it. It had nothing to do with flavor, for the taste was even worse than he had thought it would be. And he knew in less than a minute why Galeena and his people were so often indolent and lethargic. One swallow of their women's potion, and he was warm and blinking. His shoulders tingled. The soles of his feet seemed irritably sensitive. He worked his toes. The sensation was exquisite. His eyes were suddenly taking in light and substance differently than they had ever done before. The cave, the fire, the men seated around it, the women moving slowly with their flasks of fluid, all seemed as beautiful as the first dawn at the ending of the time of the long dark. He felt somehow larger, stronger, yet as light as a small boy riding snugly bound to his mother's back as she walked out across the tundra in the long-gone days of his earliest childhood.

But he was not a child. He was a man seated among other men, watching as the women slowly stripped themselves of their garments; watching as they slowly oiled their bodies with fat and rubbed their breasts, bellies, and the soft, dusky inner curves of their thighs with leaves of aromatic wormwood; watching as they slowly joined hands and, facing away from the men, began to circle the fire, stepping to the side, not lifting their feet from the ground, but sliding them slowly along the earth; watching as they raised their arms and slowly began to chant; watching as their steps grew wider, allowing firelight to show between their thighs before they scissored closed again.

Slowly.

Everything moved, swam, and pulsed a beat slower than that of his heart; and then his heartbeat was hammering, and the movements of the dancers quickened as they turned. The fire was behind them now, and within the men who watched them. Their bodies glistened. They displayed their breasts and bellies and the soft, oiled triangles of fur that hid softer, moister areas that were not so easily displayed. They tilted their hips, rolled them slowly, allowing glimpses of vistas rarely seen.

Dry-mouthed, Torka watched, hard with need, entranced, unaware that he, along with the other men, had begun to clap an increasingly strident, quickening rhythm. He had forgotten Lonit. He had forgotten Karana. He had forgotten everyone and everything but the dancers.

Their movements determined the cadence of the clapping rhythm. They smiled as they danced—not wide, tooth-showing smiles, but tight, grim little contractions of pleasure. The brief autumn day that had seemed so long was finally ending. The long shadows of night were filling the cave. The women of Galeena's band danced the *plaku,* and for one brief night they were in control of their men, and they knew it.

The dance continued, each woman moving more slowly as

she passed a man she favored, her knees bent, limbs splayed, hips moving, arms extended upward, shoulders jerking so that her breasts quivered and her round, soft nipples went hard and dark.

It was growing dark. The fire had consumed most of the bones and refuse and was settling now. The circling stopped. Ai danced before Torka and fed another fire. Her back was to him. Her arms were raised, small pudgy hands entwined. With her strong little limbs splayed wide and her knees bent, she rocked her hips back and forth, shifting her weight from heel to toe, flexing her surprisingly slender ankles and supple waist as she stretched upward, arching her rib cage like a well-fed lioness clawing at a tree, and began to answer the fire's sounds with low, hungry mewings.

All around the circle, the hunters had gotten to their feet. They were casting off their clothes and freeing themselves. Torka was no exception.

The dance went on. There was an excruciating moment as one of the younger hunters dropped to his knees, moaning in shame and frustration. Already spent, he would be of no good to any of the women who might have thought to choose him. Torka felt a momentary pang of pity for him. It would be a long time before his woman or hunting partners allowed him to forget this moment.

The women turned as one. Torka looked into Ai's face and saw features as savage and impassioned as an Arctic storm— and, despite the heat of the moment, every bit as cold and uncaring of all but its own release. In that instant, Torka knew that Ai had provoked Galeena into calling for the *plaku* so that, while the headman was distracted by other women, she could demand from Torka what he and Galeena had both denied her. She was a bold, selfish, manipulative creature who was responsible for the shaming of the young hunter and for the hours of worry that her threats had brought to Lonit. He was filled with loathing for her; but the loathing did nothing to cool his lust. If anything, it inflamed it.

All around the circle, the women of Galeena's band were choosing partners. Torka saw or heard none of their ferocious joinings.

Ai was smirking at him, displaying herself, handling herself as only a man should handle a woman. Her eyes fastened on the erected height and width of that portion of his body that she had so long desired and now so thoroughly aroused.

Little pearls of saliva appeared at the corners of her mouth. She licked them away as she came forward to fulfill the threat that she had made to Lonit.

He hated her, yet wanted her and would have taken her even if he had not known that to refuse her would be to insult Galeena and risk being cast out of the band. It was not his welfare that concerned him. It was Lonit's, and Umak's, and that of his unborn child. With the time of the long dark soon approaching, they needed the protection of the band . . . as much as he needed to have Ai now—but on his terms, not hers.

He fought back an urge to snap her in half and sate himself upon her lifeless body so that she could find no satisfaction in his release or in Lonit's humiliation.

Lonit.

Her name was in his heart as he lifted Ai from her feet, gripping her firmly beneath each armpit, deliberately hurting her. He felt her tense and try to twist free of his grip as she realized that she had lost control of the moment.

He lowered her slowly, browsing, biting, thinking of the wild stallions of the steppe as he took her down and impaled her so violently that he knew he had hurt her. He was larger and harder than he had ever been. Too big for her, but not for Lonit. The realization gave him immense pleasure. He thrust deep, heard her cry out in pain, and knew that Galeena's legendary organ was overrated. Release came, and it was as violent as the penetration. Like a rutting wolf, he remained within her and held her close even though she tried to twist away.

"Ai, Galeena's woman, is this what you have wanted?" He whispered the words into her throat, just below her ear, and took her again with deliberate carelessness.

He lay, still joined, with the bulk of his weight atop her, deliberately ignoring the pressure of her small hands as she pushed upward at his shoulders. She gasped his name and begged him to move.

He did, not to release her, but only to press her harder. He pretended to sleep then, holding her down with the weight of his body as he listened to the other hunters ambling back to their own fire circles or breathing in deep satisfaction where they lay. He feigned snores and breathed them into her ear as he felt her squirm and pant as she fought to free herself from his grip. He held her where she was until sleepiness took the edge from his intent. She was crying softly when at last she managed to slip from his near stranglehold and tiptoe back to Galeena's fire circle.

Torka folded his arm beneath his head and allowed himself to yield to sleep, smiling because he was certain that Ai would never want to lie with him again.

He slept fitfully. His dreams were fragmented images of the past: of Egatsop, beautiful and alive; of little Kipu shrieking with childish delight as he tossed him high into the air, caught him, and tossed him up again; of Big Spirit, shadowing the world, shaking it, destroying it; of Ai dancing naked in the ruins of his life, boldly offering herself to him while Galeena glared at him with killing on his mind and Lonit held an infant to her breast and wept softly.

Lonit.

He reached for her in his sleep. She was not there. His dreams shifted, becoming troubled recollections of his coupling with Galeena's woman and of the way that he had been forced to put Karana in his place. He had found pleasure in his demeaning of the woman but not in his humiliation of the child. That brave, loyal, stubborn little scrap of a boy had come to mean more to him than he would ever have thought possible.

The dream dissolved. He opened his eyes. He stared into darkness. Karana had been wrong to speak so rudely to the headman. Galeena would have been well within his rights to banish the child from the cave as punishment for such behavior. If it had come to that, Torka knew that there would have been a confrontation between himself and the headman. He would no more allow Karana to be put at risk than he would stand aside and allow Lonit or Umak to come to harm. It was for *their* sake that he bore Galeena's filthy ways. It was for *their* sake that he had not turned his back upon the conniving Ai. And it was for Karana's own good that he had given him such a severe tongue-lashing. He would have done no less if the boy had been his own son.

The thought brought a revelation. In Kipu he had lost a son. In Karana he had gained another. If Lonit bore a male child, it could mean no more to him than Karana. They would be as brothers, and Torka would name them both as his sons. Surely the boy must know this!

But how could he know if Torka had not told him? He had

only to recall the hurt, angry expression upon Karana's little
face and to remember the look of despair in Lonit's eyes
before the *plaku* had begun to know that neither of them
understood what drove him or the depth of his feelings for
them. It was not the way of the People to speak such thoughts
to others.

In new times men must learn new ways.

Umak was right. Torka would go to them now. He would
hold Lonit close and assure her that Ai was nothing to him.
Nothing. He would look Karana in the face, his eyes focusing
directly into those of the boy so that Karana would have no
doubt that he spoke with a true spirit, and he would name
him *son.*

In the thinning darkness, Torka rose and stepped quietly
over the sleeping bodies of yesterday's *plaku* dancers. Pre-
dictably, Galeena had the most women around him. Any of
the females of the band would gain status by coupling with its
headman. He had not gone back to his own fire circle. Ai
slept there alone while her man lay on his back with sleeping
women entangled around him, their arms and legs entwined
like a clutch of worms.

He was disgusted by the sight of them. *When the time of
the long dark has passed, when Lonit is strong again after the
birth of our child, if Galeena has not changed, then Torka
will leave this place. There are other bands out there. They
are bound to be better than this one.*

He walked around a hairy mound that he knew was Umak.
Two naked women lay snuggled close beneath his "wings."
The head of the great bear seemed to smile up at him as he
passed. Torka smiled back, thinking that the old man truly
was a spirit master; he had mastered his own spirit and willed
it to function as a young man's again in his old age.

His smile vanished when he reached his own fire circle.
The weather baffle sheltered Lonit's sleeping form, but Karana
was not there. Nor were his sleeping furs, his clothes, or the
spear that Torka had made for him.

11

Karana had been gone for hours, and all that time snow had been falling steadily, covering his trail. The wind was bitter, and the mountain sheathed in ice.

Galeena declared that a search was impossible, and his hunters agreed. Although Umak was visibly distraught, one look at the mountain wall forced him to agree with the headman. Yet Torka decided to follow Karana.

He dressed, then lowered himself on the sling controlled by ropes of twisted rawhide, as Karana had done. Even though it was more difficult and more dangerous for a grown man, Torka was so concerned about Karana, he did not think about his own safety.

He searched for hours, plodding eastward, certain that Karana would be seeking his people where Galeena claimed to have seen them. He would be heading toward the distant mountains, making his way across the savage, unknown land toward the place that was called the Corridor of Storms . . . where Big Spirit walked the world, destroying the lives of men and crushing small, vulnerable boys who dared to walk alone because they believed themselves to have been abandoned by their friends.

Across the endless miles, he shouted Karana's name. The wind blew his voice back into his face along with stinging particles of hard, pelletlike snow, which reduced visibility so much that, for a short while, he lost his sense of direction.

As darkness gathered beyond the swirling, howling, wind-driven white, he suddenly thought of Lonit and his unborn child. If he were to die, they would be at Galeena's mercy with only a frail old man to protect them. Torka's sense of frustration was absolute. For their sake, he must return to the mountain, but to turn his back on Karana now meant abandoning the boy to certain death.

His grief was unassuageable when, at last, he committed himself to the homeward trek. When he reached the base of the mountain, Manaak was waiting for him.

"Tomorrow," said the scar-faced hunter. "This man will go out with you tomorrow. Perhaps two will find what one could not."

Faint but real hope stirred. "Tomorrow," agreed Torka, and knew that in Manaak he had found a friend.

They climbed the wall together in darkness, each man clutching the sling's rawhide ropes and supporting the other. Manaak had poured ashes over the wall to lessen the slipperiness of the ascent. It did some good, although both climbers nearly fell several times. Only the ropes of the sling, steadied from above by Umak, kept them from losing their balance completely and allowed them to keep a reasonably firm grip on the wall. When they finally clambered onto the ledge, the hunters of Galeena's band commented on the impressiveness of their climb—and on the foolishness of it.

"It is not a good thing for a hunteh to risk death for the sake of a child," scoffed Galeena. "That Little Lame One has gone to feed his spirit to the storm. He is scrawny, but he will make meat for wolves and lions. He was not good for much else than that from the beginning, this man thinks. Torka must forget him now."

Torka pulled his ruff back and shook snow from his shoulders, then looked at Galeena out of tired eyes. The headman was obviously feeling cockier than ever since he had awakened after the *plaku* with several women in his arms and a passive Ai at his fire circle. He was a hard, arrogant man who had no understanding of compassion; but with the exception of Manaak, his hunters were loyal to him, not in spite of these qualities but because of them. With Galeena as their headman, they could live as soft and as indolent a life as their habitat allowed; and upon the mountain to which he had led them, life was soft indeed.

Torka eyed them with contempt, knowing all too well that there was not a man among them who would hesitate to drive a spear through his heart if Galeena asked it. So, although he would have liked to strike the headman down for the words he had spoken so callously against Karana, he said quietly: "Among Torka's people, it is not considered a good thing to abandon the dead before they *are* dead. The Little Lame One survived alone for many moons upon the tundra. His courage led him to this mountain and to this cave. He is still alive. In the warm new garments that Lonit has made for him, he will curl up like a fox against the wind, with his back to the storm. He *will* survive. Torka *will* find him. Torka will ask none of Galeena's men to risk themselves."

Tomorrow came. The storm intensified into a driving blizzard that shook the very foundations of the world. Although Manaak said that he was ready to accompany Torka on another search for Karana despite the weather, Torka had only to look at the bereft expressions upon Lonit's and Iana's faces to know that he dared not venture out this day. In frustration, feeling that he had to do *something*, he kindled a signal fire and hunkered down beside it.

Ninip sauntered near. "Little Lame One is dead! Not even the beasts that gnaw his bones could see Torka's fire through this storm!"

Torka slapped out at him, missing but driving him off. The boy laughed belligerently. Torka ignored him and continued to nurture his fire, sheltering it from the wind, hoping against hope that somehow Karana *was* alive, that he *could* see the beacon and know that there were those upon the mountain who longed for his return.

Hours passed. The storm raged on. Umak phrased an endless litany of chants, imploring the spirits of the wind and weather to turn away from this part of the world so that one small boy might be able to find his way home again; but the spirits that had obeyed his command on the night of the musk-ox hunt did not heed him now.

The storm grew worse. Torka continued to feed his little fire as day became dark and Umak's chants droned on. Exhausted, drained by the energy that it took to keep his hope alive, he stared out across the storm-riven world and thought of the tales that Galeena had told of other bands, of strange lands, of the Corridor of Storms, and of vast, rivering herds of game moving back and forth across the world, vanishing at summer's end, then returning out of the eternal night at the ending of the time of the long dark.

Where did they go in that time when the darkness swallowed them? *Why* did they go? What force impelled them to begin to leave the tundra even before the first gauzing of frost turned the grasses brittle and caused the willow to turn gold? Did the spirits gift them with some secret that was withheld from Man? Did they journey to some far and shimmering plain beyond that place of horrors that Galeena called the Corridor of Storms? Did the sun hide there, warming that far and unknown land and bathing the herds in its precious, life-sustaining light while Torka's world lay cold and dark beneath the storms of the time of the long dark?

And where was Karana now? Was he following the herds, trekking ever eastward in search of his people? Would he find the father whose love meant so much to him that he would not admit that the man had abandoned him? Was he, even now, looking back toward the mountain, hating Torka for having shamed him before Galeena's band? Or was he dead, in the belly of a beast, as Galeena claimed? Was he lying frozen and alone, perhaps, a tiny, forsaken figure looking at the sky forever?

The thought was unbearable. Torka's face was drawn with fatigue when he looked up, startled by Galeena. The headman had come to stand beside him. He was looking down, shaking his head.

"Torka must forget the scrawny one. This fiah, it is waste of fuel. Little Lame One has chosen his path. The way was clear to him. Galeena says that he made the brave choice, asking no man's pity, wanting no wuhman's tears. Now that he is dead, Torka must admit that it is good thing."

Torka's eyes were as cold as the storm. "When Torka with his own two hands has placed the bones of Karana to look at the sky, then and only then will Torka admit that Karana is dead. And even then, Torka will not forget one who was as a son to him. And *never* will Torka say that the death of a child is a good thing!"

All that night the storm raged, and while her man slept, Lonit kept the beacon fire burning. When he awoke, she spoke no words that might cause him pain. She brought food to him and dragged her sleeping skins close to his side so that she might keep the vigil with him. Sometime before dawn, she fell into a deep, troubled sleep. She dreamed of wild dogs running out across a world of white. Land, mountain, and sky, all were as white as bones. She awoke with a start.

Torka was gone. Like Karana who had vanished before him, he had gone in stealth. His heaviest, multilayered winter clothing was gone, and he had taken enough food from their provisions to sustain him on a long journey.

"He has been gone for much time," Iana told her, coming close to offer comfort.

"Why didn't you wake me? Why hasn't someone gone after him!"

"Too much snow. Too much wind," explained Manaak, obviously upset. "If he had told this man that he was going, Manaak would have gone with him. Togetheh we might have—"

"Joined the lame one in the world of spirits!" interrupted Galeena. He came close to Lonit as she stood before her fire circle. He put a heavy hand upon her shoulder and smiled down at her; the smile was a leer. "Forget Torka. No man of this band will follow that one into this storm. Torka not come back. Lonit not worry. Galeena always care for wuhmen." His hand curled around her shoulder.

She twisted away and shrank back from him. "Torka *will* come back!"

"Snow has buried his tracks," informed Ninip, slurring his words vindictively as he grinned at Lonit's misery. "No man could find him in this storm! No man would risk himself for a huntch so weak in his head that he throws away his life for a cripple!"

"Karana is *not* a cripple!" Lonit would have slapped him had he been within striking distance. "And Torka is *not* weak! Would your father not search for you if you were lost in a storm?"

The question caused the boy's wide, dirty face to flame and twitch. The members of his band laughed as Galeena replied: "Not for Boy Who Falls On Face Before Oxen would this man put himself at risk in *any* weatheh!"

For another day and night the storm blew and howled and spat snow at the world. As in Lonit's dream, the land, mountain, and sky all turned white, part of a freezing, tattered cloudscape into which no man who wished to live to see another day would have set himself.

And then, seemingly in a moment, the storm was over, and the sky cleared. The tundra lay white and still, buried beneath the frozen rubble of the storm. A cold sun shone, all warmth bled out of it, as all youth seemed to have been bled out of Umak.

The once-proud spirit master stood on the ledge, in his bearskin robe, with the head of the beast balanced atop his own . . . but the skin was only a skin, and the head was only a skull, and within his own body, he felt like an old man again. For nearly a week the storm had raged, and for all that time, Umak had raged back at it.

Why had the sky spirits ignored him? He had made such a show of his magic. The people of Galeena's band would not have been surprised if he had flown off into the storm like some sort of a miraculous bear-bird that was fully capable of ripping the power from the heart of the storm, of plucking up both Karana and Torka with taloned feet and returning them both safely to the mountain.

He had been enchanted by his own spells. For a moment, when the boy had first disappeared, when Umak had first taken his place upon the ledge and spread his feathered arms up and out, he had almost believed that he *could* fly!

Not until Torka had descended the wall had he been confronted by the truth. He had wanted to go, to lead his grandson boldly down from the heights in search of Karana. He had frozen where he stood, an old man in a bearskin robe, with a stiff leg and an absolute terror of the ice-sheathed wall that he had known he could not hope to conquer.

So he had folded his legs, not like a bear but like a camel, and wrapped his body in the skin of the great short-faced bear. He had hidden within it for days, pretending to be what he knew he was not. He was glad for the bearskin; it made him seem large while, in truth, he felt very small.

Gradually, the members of the band began to doubt him. Oklahnoo watched him with a jaundiced eye. Her sister, a kinder soul—or perhaps simply protective of her man and the child that she carried—continued to bring him food.

"Umak *is* spirit masteh," she assured him. "Umak's magic *is* strong. It is slow this time, that is all. This wuhman say, chant hard."

He was grateful for her encouragement. It helped to cut the sting of the slurs that he overheard the other women make. They were careful not to speak too loudly, just in case they were mistaken; but it was there, all the same. Deep within that part of himself where self-confidence was born, there was an expanding emptiness, where guilt had begun to take root.

Why had Karana left the cave? Because an old man had

been so taken with himself that he had ceased to care about one small boy?

Umak shuddered in almost overwhelming remorse. Where was Torka? He had risked his life to go in search of Karana because a spirit master's powers had failed to bring him home. Now the storm into which he had gone was over. Why had he not returned?

"Please, Spirit Master, you must not stop your chanting!" He looked down, his attention drawn by Lonit.

"The spirits of the mountain, of the wind and storm, they will listen to your words! They have always listened to Umak!"

The girl's expression of faith touched him but did little to restore his own faith in himself. He felt old and stiff-bodied.

"This spirit master, he is tired," he admitted to Lonit.

Lonit sat beside him. "Torka must be tired. Karana, too." She sighed and laid her head against his arm as though she were a child. They sat together in silence, looking across the miles, their faces illuminated but not warmed by the cold, late-autumn sun. Softly, Lonit spoke of the past: about the long, bitter way that they had traveled together since the Destroyer had come and gone from their lives; how an old man who had walked the wind had brought Torka and a frightened girl to a new life; how he had willed the desire to live into her; how he had stood against foxes and wolves and storms; and how always the spirits had listened when he spoke.

"They will listen now," she whispered, her eyes brimming as she looked up at him. "For Torka, for Karana, and for Lonit, they *must* listen. If Torka does not return, Galeena will take this woman to his fire circle. He will kick her until Torka's baby dies. Then Torka will be truly dead. Forever. And Galeena will be glad."

He was so appalled by her statement that, for a moment, he could not speak. Then he stammered: "Why would Galeena kill Torka's baby? These are not starving times."

"Ai has said that it is his way."

"Hrmmph! Not as long as Umak is spirit master!" He rose and readjusted the weight of the bearskin upon his bony frame and began to chant again. His voice was a rasping vibrato that did not quite rise above the occasional deep, barely audible reverberations that emanated from the heart of the mountain, but it was stronger than it had been for hours.

Lonit brought food to him. He did not eat. She brought

him water. This he sipped, to moisten his throat so that it would not fail him.

At dusk, a rockfall clattered down from the heights. From his place upon the ledge, Umak observed it out of fatigue-reddened eyes as it fell along the precipice to the left of the cornice. There was ice in it, and large discolored wedges of snow pebbled with detritus that must have broken loose from beneath the underlayering of the summit ice pack. It was one of countless such slides that he had witnessed since first coming to dwell upon the mountain; yet there seemed to be something different about it. So *much* snow. So *much* detritus. Perhaps it was only the failing light. He could not be sure, nor did he care. He had more important things to occupy his thoughts at the moment.

It seemed that the spirits were not deaf to his invocations after all. His heart soared, for Torka was coming toward the mountain, and Karana walked beside him.

Exhausted by their ordeal, Torka and Karana slept for a day and a night. The boy curled within the fold of Torka's arm, close to Lonit's fire circle. In the predawn darkness of the second day, Karana awoke and looked at Lonit as she began the preparations for the first meal of the day.

"He came for me. . . ." he whispered wonderingly. "He told me that he followed the tracks of wild dogs deep into the heart of the storm. He risked his life . . . for one small boy."

She shook her head, and when she spoke, her words held a gentle and loving admonition. "Of course! What did you expect? He is Torka! Torka would never abandon one of his own!"

12

The last of the migratory waterfowl that had survived the storm were gone from the tundra. The great herds had vanished into the setting sun. In the last days of light, game was growing scarce, but Galeena's people were not concerned. The men of the band hunted with abandon. Although they had already seriously depleted the provisions that they had piled at the back of the cave, they gorged themselves on their fresh kills and left little to be put aside for the long, lean days of darkness that were soon to come.

The women had lost their earlier minimal enthusiasm for work. Most of them were pregnant now, and Lonit found herself observing them with increasing concern. They were growing as fat as bears preparing for hibernation. Lazy, sloppy bears. She wrinkled her nose in disgust at the foul smells that had begun to emanate from their carelessly prepared winter stores. In the relatively warm, wind-protected confines of the cave, improperly dried berries were mildewing, and green moss was furring their supplies of meat. When she spoke of her concern, even Iana was surprised. The sad-eyed woman informed her that mildew added a special tang to berries, and nothing was tastier or more tender than meat rimed with green mold.

"Yes," she agreed. "This is so. But it is too early in the season for the mold to be so advanced. It will eat the meat before we do! And the mildew is so thick on the berries that soon they will not be berries at all but gray little clumps of fuzz not fit for eating."

"Everything is fit for eating," said Oklahnoo, overhearing. The others agreed.

Lonit shook her head. "It will be so in this camp! If

Galeena's women are not more careful, we will all be reduced
to chewing hides long before the sun returns at the end of the
time of the long dark!"

They did not take kindly to her criticism. Naknaktup told
her that her pregnancy was making her as fussy as an old
woman, and Weelup added that fussy women, old or otherwise, were not welcome in Galeena's band.

"Torka's wuhman is just like her man," Ai sneered imperiously. "Always she thinks her ways are best! But where are
the people who taught her? They walk the wind while Galeena's
band grows strong and fat in this khamp."

Again the others agreed and added that although Torka
was a man who was good to look at, he was always too
busy—hunting, working his weapons, teaching the little lame
one new ways to hunt, even though this was clearly a waste of
time. Weelup said that Galeena had told her that the other
men had complained that sometimes just watching Torka
made them tired, and the headman still resented the way he
had ignored his wishes and gone off in pursuit of a child who
was better off dead.

"Karana is no longer lame," Lonit corrected her emphatically. "He walks with a slight limp, but he can climb the wall
as well as any man, and better than most of the boys. Sometimes this woman thinks that he looks like a little sheep,
scampering up and down, as surefooted as a half-grown ram."

"Maybe we will eat him in the dark time winter," suggested Ai.

The others laughed. All except Iana. She was looking pale
and wan these days; the other women were certain that her
baby could come at any time.

It was rare for Lonit to speak out in anger, but she did so
now, directly to Ai. "In starving times, this woman will see
you on a spit before she will stand by and allow harm to come
to Karana!"

The other women murmured in startled amazement.

Ai smirked loftily. "There will be no starving times. Galeena
says that neveh again will his band wandeh the winteh dark
in search of food. Food will come to *us* in the dark times.
Galeena has watched. Galeena has seen how the mountain
breaks the back of the tundra wind. On one side afteh a
storm, *much* snow. On otheh side, *little* snow. While the
great herds follow the setting sun oveh the edge of the world,
otheh animals stay. They browse and keep themselves fat for

the spears of Galeena's huntehs. All through dark times, they will eat. All through dark times, Galeena's people will eat *them*. So this wuhman says: Only stupid Lonit worries about meat spoiling. Galeena says, when it is gone, there will be moh. Galeena says, in this khamp, his people will neveh go hungry! And Ai says to Torka's wuhman, threaten me again, and *all* of yuh Dog People will be sorry!"

Lonit stared, aghast, not at the threat, but at Ai's careless and utterly disrespectful attitude toward the unpredictable and all powerful forces of Creation. Ai's words had flown in the face of the spirits of the game and defied the powers of the starving moon.

"Beware, woman of Galeena. The spirits grow angry with those who assume too much," warned Lonit, and from that moment on her world was filled with shadows that had nothing to do with the ever-shortening days. No matter what Galeena might say, or how Ai might unquestioningly echo him, the starving moon *would* rise. And once it stood high in the great, black sky, it might not set again until all of the people who dwelled upon the mountain were dead, as punishment for the arrogance of their headman and his woman Ai.

On the far southwestern horizon, a plume of volcanic smoke rose from one of the tangled, snow-mantled peaks that, in daylight, appeared to be holding up the sky. But since it rose during the night, the plume went unseen.

Beneath Torka's sleeping skins, the mountain dropped and rose so subtly that its movement merely caused him to sigh and draw Lonit a little closer. When the roaring of the distant eruption reached his ears, it was so muted by distance, it seemed to be no more than a slight rising of the wind. But high above, on the glacier that smothered the summit of their mountain, the mile-long crevasse that had opened on the day that Umak had killed the moose now gaped wide.

Upon the tundra, small animals felt tremors deep within the permafrost and scampered out of burrows and hiding places. Birds took flight, winging across the full face of the moon. Wolves and dogs made low, confused howls and yaps. Game animals huffed and circled restlessly as, miles away, a herd of mammoths trumpeted its uncertainty to the night. And from a distant, sprawling passageway that cut a swath of open grazing land between two continental ice sheets, an answering trumpet came, high and shrill—unmistakable to any man or beast that had heard it before.

It was that sound that woke the people on the mountain and had them on their feet, listening in terror.

Chunks of ice fell from above; then all was quiet. The people looked out across the blue, moonlit world, and Naknaktup pressed close to Umak, asking the spirit master what had disturbed the night.

Wind spirits, thought Lonit, for the quiet was absolute except for the soft whispering of the wind against the mountain.

Umak felt the wind against his face. It was cold, a winter wind that made his bones ache. His breath congealed into clouds before his eyes, veiling the banking flight of the birds that were returning to the earth like falling leaves.

The silence thickened and expanded, then entered the cave and pulsed within it. There was not a man or woman or boy who was not steeped in the terror of his or her own private fears—including the spirit master.

Umak remembered Karana's words of warning: *We must go from this place. It is a bad encampment. We must go, or we will stay here forever.*

Yet he knew that to go from the high, sheltering safety of the mountain into the savage, unknown distances of tundra that were now under the first shadows of the time of the long dark would mean certain death . . . not for the entire band, but certainly for an old man with aching bones and an aging matron swollen with child. Umak had walked the wind once. He was not ready to do so again. He wanted to live long enough to see himself reborn through Naknaktup and also through Lonit; for the life that would come into the world through her also would be Torka's. A third generation of spirit masters, an unbroken line into the future born from the loins of one old man.

The thought was so heady that it actually warmed him until the dark cloud of Manaak's words drew the old man back to the moment.

"It is Big Spirit that walks the night. It is that great ghost that makes the mountain tremble and the beasts cry out in feah. It has followed us, as Manaak has always said it would. Now we must hunt it! Now we must kill it before it kills us all!"

The women broke into an anguished keening. The hunters grumbled and looked anxiously at one another. Galeena was clearly angry.

"This man heahs no beasts!" the headman said, gesturing outward into the night. "This man heahs no ghosts! What disturbed the night is gone now. Galeena is sick of Manaak always talking about Big Spirit. Galeena says that if Manaak ever sees that great ghost, he is free to hunt it alone. As for Galeena, he has found a safe khamp for his people. What shook the world is silent now. It will not come to this place."

"No man may say what the spirits will do," said Umak.

Galeena faced him furiously. "That spirit walks in the skin of a mammoth. Mammoths do not climb mountains. And Galeena does not hunt mammoths unless they are safely mired in bogs!"

"That could be arranged," suggested Torka. "With enough men working together, we could track it down, discover where it is browsing, and lure it into a trap we devise."

The excitement in his voice did nothing to ignite anything but alarm in the other hunters. Only Manaak was inflamed by it.

"It would be a good thing. Those who walk the tundra would foreveh sing praises to those who killed Big Spirit!"

"Men *cannot* kill spirits," said Umak, waving a warning hand at Manaak to silence him. "Men make praise songs to appease their anger. Men walk lightly in the spirits' shadows and make the songs that will cause the shadows to fall upon other parts of the world."

"So that other men may be killed?" Torka's question was sharply edged; he had heard the uncharacteristic chord of expedience in Umak's voice. It both angered and startled him. Karana was right: Umak *had* changed since he had become spirit master of Galeena's band.

"Galeena does not care about othehs!" said the headman, and when his hunters all sighed with relief and murmured in agreement, he flashed his wide, gap-toothed grin and slapped Umak upon the back with approving familiarity. "Wise men will listen to their spirit masteh! Wise men will make the songs that will keep Big Spirit fah away, walking its own part of the world!"

"Make all the songs you will," said Torka grimly. "This man has dipped his spear into the blood and flesh of Big Spirit. If that one walks into our world, it will take more than songs to drive it away."

Galeena eyed him with dislike. "Torka always knows *everything*! He is not the only man to have faced the great ghost! Torka and Manaak want to fight Big Spirit, you make spears. *Many* spears. *Strong* spears. *Sharp* spears. If Big Spirit comes, Galeena will let you kill him. *If* you can. But now, Galeena says listen to the night: It is silent. Big Spirit walk anotheh part of the world. If you wish to follow, Galeena says *go*! He will not stop you. But as for this man and his huntehs, we hunt meat, *not* spirits. We will stay here. Foreveh!"

On the far horizon, the volcano returned to sleep, as did the people of Galeena's band. The night passed in silence, except for the whispering of the wind and the deep, somnolent murmurings of the summit ice pack. Toward dawn, Manaak came to Torka's fire circle.

"This man goes now to hunt Big Spirit," he whispered, prodding Torka with a gloved hand. "Does he go alone, or does Torka come with him?"

Torka backhanded sleep from his eyes. He looked up to see that Manaak was dressed for traveling and hunting: His spears were thrust through his pack, his snare lines were looped around one shoulder, and over the other hung his game bag with its extra supplies of projectile points and tools for knapping, butchering, and other assorted uses. Torka frowned as he propped himself onto an elbow. He replied softly so that he would not disturb Lonit or Karana, who slept on either side of him. "Unlike Manaak, Torka does not feel alone in the world. Unlike Manaak, Torka could not leave this camp without looking back. Unlike Manaak, although Torka *would* risk himself if he thought that he had a chance of killing Big Spirit, Torka will *not* abandon his woman because Galeena has goaded him into pursuing his own death."

Manaak hissed in anger. Torka's sarcasm had cut clean through to the bone of truth. The scar-faced hunter thought of his woman as he exhaled his frustration. "Big Spirit is out theh. Someday it will come. Someday, for the sake of our wuhmen, we are going to have to face it."

"Someday. Not now. Who will hunt for our women in the dark time of the starving moon if we do not return? They are both big with child. It is for them that we must stay. Torka has been thinking much about it. We *will* do as Galeena suggests: We *will* prepare our weapons and make many strong, sharp spears—enough for every man in the band. If Big Spirit comes to browse below our camp, we will have the advantage. This man does not think much of Galeena's ways, but he is right when he says that mammoths cannot climb mountains. Do not be so eager to die, my friend. We cannot be certain that it was the voice of Big Spirit that we heard. Be glad that the great ghost walks far away, in another part of the world, and know that if it *does* come to us, we will be ready for it."

Manaak was not a man easily swerved from his course once he had committed himself to it; nevertheless, Torka's words made sense. Disgruntled and not fully mollified, he went back to his own fire circle.

Torka lay awake, envisioning how it would be if the great mammoth did come. The men of Galeena's band would stand together in a line along the lip of the cornice. They would hurl spear after spear down at the beast. They would create a rain of death, and the beast whom Galeena's people called Big Spirit would flee or die.

It seemed so easy . . . too easy. He was aware of the wind and of the sound of something moving, shifting deep within the core of the mountain. It was a familiar sound, but had it always been so constant? So like a heart beating arrhythmically?

"Listen. The mountain is alive. Once it was a friend. Now it warns us away."

Karana's voice had been no louder than a sigh, yet Torka was startled by it. The moon had set hours ago, but starlight illuminated the boy's face. Torka saw the worry in his eyes. "Away?" he asked the boy. "Into the time of the long dark? One hunter, a boy, a woman with child, and an old man? How long would we survive?"

"Umak is spirit master! His magic would make us strong!"

"Umak is happy in this camp. He would not leave it."

"Then we must go without him."

"Never. Torka would not abandon you, Little Hunter. Would you ask him to abandon the father of his father, to walk away from one who saved his life, and Lonit's, *and* Karana's?"

The boy chewed his lower lip for a moment before he replied. "Spirit master no longer cares for anyone but himself. But Manaak and his woman would come with us. We would be a band. Karana may be little, but he *is* a hunter! And Torka is the best hunter of all! Torka found Karana in the great storm. Only the cleverest of trackers could have done that!"

"Cleverer trackers were after you—a pack of dogs—and from the way they were running, it was obvious that they were on the scent of prey. This man made a guess that *you* were that prey. It was fortunate for Karana that something drew them off so that Torka found you before they did."

"If Brother Dog was with them, Karana would have come to no harm."

"Do you still think of that one? Forget him. Aar has found a pack of his own by now, and if that was the pack that trailed you, do not doubt for a moment that Brother Dog would have joined the others in their kill. Men and beasts cannot be brothers, Karana."

"Hmmph!" exhaled the child in an excellent imitation of Umak. "Torka's people live with Galeena's band!"

Torka laughed at the comparison and shook his head sagely. "For now, yes, because it must be so. But with the exception of Manaak, there is not one among them whom Torka would call brother."

13

The mountain was silent. Dawn yielded to a cold, bright day of absolute perfection. The animals of the tundra grazed and hunted. No mammoths were heard, and the strange restlessness of the previous night seemed like a half-remembered dream. The people were reluctant to leave the cave but could not quite understand why. Umak made special chants of propitiation to the spirits of the sky and mountain. As though summoned by his song, a huge teratorn with vulturine wings swept the sky, and a small family of delicately boned steppe antelope ventured from the willow scrub to graze close to the base of the mountain. The fears of the previous night forgotten, Galeena and his hunters went down from the mountain, and as Torka stood back in revulsion, they killed the entire little herd.

It was nearly dark by the time they returned to the cave. As was their way, they settled in to spend the night feasting as though there were no tomorrow. Sated by their gluttony, they slept for all of the next day and night and lounged in contented indolence for two days more.

Motivated by boredom and the desire to indulge themselves in the savory flesh of fresh-killed lamb, they left the ledge to track an elusive flock of Dall sheep into the shadowy heights of the narrow canyon where Umak had killed the moose and the great short-faced bear. The sheep were fleet and agile. They leaped and bounded upward along the walls of the chasm as easily as cloud shadows. Excited by the chase, the hunters pursued them even though the confines of the canyon were intimidating to those who were used to hunting upon the broad, open miles of the tundra. Galeena led them into the heights, and the boys scattered through the frost-brittled scrub and dark groves of stunted spruce, sending ptarmigan and hares racing for better cover.

Torka watched them and wondered if they were very brave or very stupid. Perhaps in people as unimaginative as Galeena's band, the latter induced the former. He told Karana to stay close and to keep his spears at the ready. The same thick, high ground cover that had hidden the great short-faced bear could be hiding equal dangers.

Despite a slight limp, the boy kept up with him. His leg was strong again, and although the other boys taunted him for his stiff gait, Torka noted that Karana refused to rise to their baiting. He demonstrated his mettle by going anywhere that they dared to go, by never complaining or asking that any exception be made for him. The leg *had* to pain him at times, but if it did, he never spoke of it; only an occasional tension at the corners of his lips betrayed the extent of his effort.

They continued on until a projecting, down-thrusting lobe of the summit glacier blocked their passage. Further penetration into the canyon was impossible unless they ascended the ice. The sheep skittered up ahead, their small, sharp hooves cutting into the snow, sending fragments of it exploding outward as they raced for their lives. Galeena's well-thrown spear took an adolescent ewe through the neck. Manaak's weapon flew to embed itself in the haunch of a ram. Several animals stumbled and rose to run on, half of them with spears protruding from various portions of their bodies. Others fell, their white coats red with spattered blood, their bleats drowned by the howling of Galeena's hunters.

Torka told Karana to go forward and make a kill if he wished. The boy was off in an instant. Torka did not move. He stood transfixed, momentarily disoriented.

The glacier . . . it had not been there before—he was certain of it. He eyed the soaring, dirty-faced mass of ice that blocked the way before him. Several spruce trees lay broken and half-buried in a rubble heap of rock-hard boulders of snow, which the boys and hunters of Galeena's band were scrambling over as they climbed to retrieve their kills. Those trees had been erect when Torka had last seen them; they had composed the little grove in which Umak killed the moose. Now, as he studied the snow and ice in which the trees lay all but totally buried, he realized that he was not looking at a glacier but at the accumulated debris that had been falling away from the underlayer of the summit ice pack ever since he had led the others to the mountain.

Manaak came toward him, carrying his ram slung over his shoulders. He was curious as to why Torka was not participating in the hunt. When Torka shared his thoughts, Manaak shrugged and told him that it was the same everywhere. "Old men in far khamps they say that ice spirits grow strong. Ice spirits fall from sky. They coveh the earth. Stay on mountains. Not melt. This mass of ice, it will grow in the dark time winteh. In shady canyon like this, even in summeh, not all of it will melt. Next dark time, it will grow again. It will fill the canyon, grow so high it will join with the main summit glacier. In the next time of light, it will begin to walk out of the canyon, grinding all before it. This man has walked fah and hunted many game trails. In the fah mountains, whole passes are disappearing under ice that walks. In many places, game must find new ways to come through the mountains to the land of good grass."

Torka understood at last why his people had waited in vain for the caribou to return along their usual route of migration. "From where do the herds come, Manaak? Have you traveled there, into the face of the rising sun?"

"No man may do that. The herds come from out of the rising sun, through the Corridor of Storms, from oveh the edge of the world where no man may follow."

"I wonder. . . ." Torka's musing was curtailed before it was fully begun.

A terrible high, raking screech reverberated through the canyon. It was followed by the pain-filled screams of a boy and by the shouts and curses of men.

The lion-size jumping cat had been feeding off the carcass of the camel that it had killed several nights before. The cat was old, with a partially joined spinal column, and an arthritic hip. Its limbs were short, giving it hyenalike proportions, as though the bodies of two distinctly different types of animals had been joined by mistake. This cat was no swift-footed predator of the open tundra; this cat was designed to spring. Its brain was small. Its disposition was surly. In its waning years it had become a particularly nasty and unpredictable aggressor. When Ninip and the other boys accidentally flushed it from its cover, it sprang for a quick retreat up the face of the icefall; but its hip hurt enough to make an upward vault too painful to consider. With its short, lynxlike tail twitching, it wheeled and spat, swiping out at the boys and hissing as it displayed the two fangs that would someday win others of its species the name saber-toothed.

This cat, a prowler, a lurker, and leaper, was always ready to hurl itself upon dull-witted prey that happened to browse too close to where it lay waiting to pounce. And pounce it did, leaping at the boys who shouted and stamped and menaced it with the few spears that they had not thrown after the fleeing sheep. With all of its power projected into its spring, the lion-size cat was a blur of long, tawny fur. Its lower jaw appeared to have unhinged itself as it flapped back against its throat. Its mouth gaped impossibly wide, allowing its fangs, which were half as long as the forearm of a man, to project forward.

Ninip was its target, but the boy sidestepped just in time, pulling his nearest companion into the way of the cat. When the animal hit the boy, its canines plunged straight through his thorax. He went down hard, with the cat on top of him. One of the animal's fang tips cracked against a rock that lay beneath the boy's punctured back. The cat yowled against the pain of a shattered nerve, drew out its teeth, and stabbed its victim again and again, all the while scratching and tearing at the boy's midsection until its paws and body were red and fouled with the color and stench of its victim's disembowelment.

The boy was not dead. He could make no sound, but his hands spasmed at his sides and his limbs jerked convulsively. The cat was eating him alive.

Karana threw his spear. All the other boys had fled, and the men of Galeena's band were watching. Why they were making no move to come to the fallen boy's aid, there was no time to guess. In his excitement, Karana had thrown one spear short of his target; but he still had another, his best one, the spear that Torka had made for him. His small hand curled around the haft, balancing it lightly. From the corner of his eye, he saw Ninip glowering at him.

Karana advanced slowly, spear arm bent, the weapon levering for just the perfect balance as he made ready to throw. He was aware of Torka and Manaak running toward him, their spears at the ready. Torka held his whalebone bludgeon in his left hand. Karana drew in a breath of resolve and aimed. He wanted to make the killing throw. Then all men would call him Lion Killer instead of Little Lame One.

Torka would be proud. And Ninip would never have cause to mock him again.

Watching Karana, Ninip knew his intent. He was suddenly furious. How dare the little lame one stand up to the marauding cat as though he were the bravest boy in the world? He would never be able to live down the ridicule of his companions or the disgust of his father if he stood by in fear of the great cat while puny Karana made an attempt to kill it. Galeena still held him in contempt for having stumbled before the charging ox. Ninip would never win his respect if Karana made this kill.

With a burst of energy that eclipsed his fear, Ninip raced to Karana's side and snatched the spear from his hand just as the smaller boy was about to release it. Caught off-balance by a violent elbow jab to his side, Karana fell as Ninip gave out a loud, triumphant whoop. The spear was light and long, much different in balance from the heavier, thick-shafted weapons made by the hunters of his own band. He sought the right position from which to make his killing throw, but his movement had caught the attention of the cat.

It moved so quickly and unexpectedly that Ninip had no opportunity to react. In one great leap it was on him, knocking him down. He fell on his side with the spear still in his hand, uselessly pinned to the ground by the downward pressure of his head against his forearm. Instinct had caused him to curl into a fetal tuck, protecting his vital organs from the ripping claws and stabbing fangs of the cat. With his thick winter clothing his only protection against the predations of the beast, he screamed out to his father to kill the cat before it tore him to pieces.

High above the canyon, the giant condor that was often seen circling in the sky flew across the face of the sun, drawn by the sounds of death and killing. Its shadow distracted the cat, which looked up for an instant, long enough for Ninip to see his father and the other hunters standing immobile. Not one of them was even making an effort to lift a spear. They were going to stand there and watch him die.

He could not have said when Torka's spear struck the cat. Manaak's followed. The cat seemed to lift straight up off the ground, whirling and backing away, making the deep, ugly rasping gargle that felines make when they are cornered and in a rage.

Ninip did not move, uncertain if his limbs and arms were still connected to his body or if he was even alive. Slowly Torka moved into his line of sight to stand between him and the cat. Ninip's vision was blurred by blood—his or the cat's, he could not be sure. Torka was making low, hostile mewings to the animal, baiting it, calling it to him. He held his strange, knife-edged whalebone club. Ninip felt faint, confused. Why was Torka putting himself at risk for one who had never done anything to deserve his concern?

As Ninip watched, Torka crouched. He gripped the narrow, sinew-wrapped end of his weapon in both hands. He continued baiting the cat until, with a shriek of rage, it hurled itself at him. He leaped aside with supreme agility and grace, spinning around as he did so. The long, sharp edge of his weapon severed the outreaching taloned paws of the cat. It landed before it realized that its feet were missing. The stumps would not support its weight. Screaming and stunned, it fell rump over head as Torka closed on it to smash its skull with three brutal downward strokes of his bludgeon.

Like the boy whom it had disemboweled, the saber-toothed cat died slowly.

If Galeena had had his way, Ninip would have been left behind to die beside the mutilated body of the disemboweled boy. The headman was openly angered by Torka's killing of the cat.

"Again Torka risks his life to save a useless one! Did Torka expect othehs to join him in his risk? No. A band needs *men, huntehs,* not clumsy boys!"

The other hunters all spoke in agreement. They resented Torka's display of bravery, which had shown them a standard by which they had no wish to be measured.

Torka looked incredulously at Galeena. "Ninip is your son."

"Bah! What is son? This man has had many sons before. Will have sons again."

It was difficult for Torka to comprehend the extent of his callousness. "The spirits have been generous to Galeena. The cat broke a tooth while attacking the other boy. It must have been in pain, so it did not stab Ninip. He is badly scratched and bruised, but with care, he will be healed soon enough."

"You saved him, you heal him! Galeena will not claim that clumsy one as his own!"

14

The ice that formed on the ponds was bottom deep now and would not melt until spring. Daylight was little more than a brief blue haze. While the cold, dry wind blew hard out of the northwest, Iana went into labor twice, but both episodes stopped short of producing a child. Manaak was restless. Umak made child-come-forth chants to no avail, and Ai smirked behind his back and whispered to Galeena that the spirit master's magic was certainly less than effective. The old man harrumphed and said that Iana's child would not be born until its spirit was ready; Oklahnoo eyed him skeptically while Naknaktup pointed to Ninip and boasted that the boy was alive only because of her man's healing magic.

For Umak's sake, Torka did not argue with her. Ninip *was* recovering, albeit slowly. The incident with the cat had changed him. His combativeness and arrogance had bled out of him. Black and blue, sore and sutured, he sat in passive dejection beside Torka's fire circle. Although Torka had once detested the boy for the way he had treated Karana, now Torka worried about him. Ninip would not eat unless food was forced upon him. He would not speak unless spoken to, and then his replies were limited to grunts and mumbles. His onetime companions wanted no part of him except to taunt and mock him as cruelly as he had once taunted Karana. His bright, ferretlike eyes had gone blank. He seemed to have lost the will to live.

Karana gloated. He was openly resentful of Ninip's newfound place beside Torka's fire circle. He was glad that the other boys had turned on their former leader. He found it infinitely satisfying to know that he was no longer the sole object of their animalistic pranks and derision.

As for Torka, a strangely disturbing malaise had settled upon him since his killing of the cat. Sometimes, as he would work upon his weapons, he would find himself looking at Ninip, wondering if he had done the right thing. The headman had not put his own life in jeopardy, even for his own son, because he had others to consider—his women, his band, and the other boys. And Ninip *was* clumsy; he probably never would make much of a hunter. Among Torka's people it had been considered a grievous affront to the spirits of the game to squander meat upon anyone who might prove a liability to the band. Why should it be different among Galeena's band? In the depth of the time of the long dark, the lives of his people, as well as those of Torka's little family, might depend upon the food that he was now forcing upon Ninip. He sighed, dissatisfied with the course of action to which he had so thoughtlessly committed himself.

With his back propped against the mountain wall and his buttocks cushioned by the grass-stuffed pockets of furs that Lonit had stitched to form a knapping pillow, he paused in his work. He had been reshaping damaged projectile points with his fire-hardened antler hammer. Despite the hide pad that kept the palm of his left hand from being accidentally cut or bruised, his hand ached with fatigue. How many spearheads had he braced against it while shaping them with his right hand? All that he had set aside for redefinition. He was surprised. It did not seem that much time had passed since he had first begun to work, but there they were, arranged in a line beside his hammer stones and flakers.

He found himself wondering once again where the great herds of grazing animals went in the last days of autumn before the world went cold and the long, storm-driven time of the long dark began. From this aerie, he often watched the sun rise and set in a pale, ever-diminishing arc that was barely in the sky long enough to grant any warmth. Soon it would be only the faintest glow on the southern horizon, and then it would be gone completely. *Where?* he wondered. *Where does it go? Could not men follow it, tracking the great herds perpetually eastward to . . . what?*

His thoughts paused in midflow. He had led his people to the mountain. He had lighted the signal fire that had drawn Galeena's band across the miles, and although the man was filthy and flatulent and full of his own overinflated sense of self-worth, there *was* safety in numbers. With the time of the long dark beginning to settle upon them, it eased Torka's mind to know that Lonit and Karana and Umak were safe, sheltered within the mountain like infants secure within their mother's womb. Danger lay out there, on the open tundra, in the growing cold and dark where the Destroyer walked, looking for men to kill.

The days that followed were intensely cold. The wind slid down off the summit ice pack to mingle with the fierce, dry tides of air that blew out of the vast distances of Asia and the far north.

Lonit spent most of her time with Iana. When the sad-eyed woman had experienced the first of her unfruitful contractions, the other women had drawn her away to the very back of the cave lest the spirits of her suffering contaminate them all. There had been talk of sending her from the ledge to wait out her travail in a pit hut at the base of the mountain; but those women who were with child thought twice about this. Although it was customary for women in labor to be kept apart, it was one thing to have one's man erect a little birthing hut at the fringes of an encampment, and another to be alone on the tundra while the rest of the band was high above and far away. Umak said that in new times, men *and* women must learn new ways. Everyone was relieved, and a grateful Iana was allowed to stay while Manaak went down from the mountain to gather dry sedges and grasses and to cut sods from the tundra that would be used to soften the floor of the cave upon which she would give birth. He returned by way of the pulley, reporting that the permafrost was growing thick; soon the land would be frozen rock hard.

Lonit was unable to understand the unwillingness of the other women to sit with Iana. With the exception of Naknaktup, who came occasionally to lay a questing hand upon Iana's belly and brow, they all appeared to be totally unconcerned. When Iana's pains began again, they and their men kept far away from her.

Lonit took Iana's dry, cold hands within her own warm palms and held them tightly. "Lonit will stay. Lonit will help. Lonit will sing woman songs for Iana, but Iana must tell Lonit how they go, because the women of Lonit's band walked the spirit world before they could teach her."

"Songs? Among Iana's people, theh are no songs for

this." She gasped, held her breath, and gritted her teeth until the wave of pain that washed over her had ebbed away.

Lonit released her hands and stroked her brow. "Among Torka's people there were *many* songs. Happy songs. Sad songs. Songs for every happening. Especially for *this*! Listen. Umak makes the child-come-forth chant for you! It has great magic!"

"This woman's baby does not seem to heah it."

"Because the women do not sing their own songs. Always Lonit would hear them when she was a litt!e girl. This woman would listen and try to imagine how it must be for the women within the birth hut. The hut was always so far away that Lonit could not hear the words of the women, but she could hear the rhythm of their song. It went like this."

She sang softly, searching for the right tone, for the perfect cadence. She found both. Her voice was as sweet as clear water running over smooth stones on a summer day. It seemed to cut the chill of the cave, to bring the sun back into the sky.

Within the cave, everyone stopped what they were doing and turned to look and listen. Torka's heart swelled with love and pride. The song was no more beautiful than the woman who sang it.

Iana sighed. She was soothed until the next contraction. Then she cried out, gripping Lonit's hand so tightly that the younger woman winced but made no move to pull away. Iana was weak, exhausted, and beyond comfort. "Go from this woman, Lonit. There is no help for this slow-to-be-born child. Birth is like death. It must be endured alone."

Lonit would not leave her. For what seemed endless hours, she stayed with her friend and sang her sweet songs of life until she had no more voice. Was it day or night, morning or afternoon? In the nearly perpetual twilight of the beginning of the time of the long dark, it was impossible to tell. The wind drove thick, storm-heavy clouds between the earth and the sky. Darkness consumed the world. Iana's moans and cries went on and on. Umak did his best to continue chanting, but like Lonit's, his voice was gone.

"Your magic is no good, old man," Ai openly derided him.

Hours passed. Iana's ordeal continued. The people of the band began to murmur about bad spirits. Weelup and Ai complained that they could not sleep. A disconsolate Manaak defied the others of his gender by going to his woman and cradling her in his arms. An equally disconsolate Lonit wept when she saw the grief on his face and crept from Iana's side to seek solace in Torka's embrace.

It was Ai's incessant wheedling that finally drove Galeena to his feet. Even when he picked up one of his spears his intent was not clear to Torka, Umak, or Lonit; but Karana knew, and the members of Galeena's band made sounds of approval.

He advanced purposefully, telling Manaak to step aside. "That woman's noisemaking has gone on too long. It is not a good thing."

Manaak saw the spear poised in the headman's hand. He did not move. For love of Iana, he had forgone his need to track and kill the great mammoth that had crushed the life from their tiny daughter. For love of Iana, so that she would be assured the protection of a band when the birth of their third child became imminent, he had stayed with Galeena's band. For love of Iana, he had not slain the headman when he had forced him to abandon his injured little son. And now, for love of Iana, he would fight Galeena to the death before he would stand aside and allow a spear to be thrust into her.

Galeena did not misread the challenge or the hatred that he saw in Manaak's eyes. Manaak had always been trouble. It would be good now to put an end to him. He readied to thrust his spear.

But it was Manaak who thrust himself at Galeena. Younger, leaner, and faster, Manaak sprang at the headman, who went down with a *whoof* of surprise and a curse of outrage. But he was strong, and anger made him doubly powerful. He managed to free himself of Manaak's hold, and in a moment both men were on their feet, glaring at one another.

Galeena called back over his shoulder, demanding that one of his hunters silence Manaak's woman forever while he did the same to her man.

Torka did not remember getting to his feet; but he was standing with his whalebone bludgeon in his hand as Lonit broke like a startled doe and raced to Iana's side. He called her back, but it was too late. Instinct born of affection and loyalty to the only female friend she had ever had in her life drove her to throw herself protectively across Iana.

"Galeena is a hunter of game, not of women with babies

in their belly!" she cried, looking up at the headman with fire in her huge, round eyes.

The women cried out in dismay, amazed at her audacity. The men picked up their spears and glared at her menacingly as they closed ranks around their leader.

Galeena, comfortable with his armed hunters behind him, smiled his wide, ugly, gap-toothed smile at Lonit. But it was not truly a smile; it was a malicious leer of intimidation. "Long time back, this man warned Torka's wuhman to remembeh who is headman of this band. Galeena thinks maybe she will learn now. This man thinks, moh than one baby in belly will not live to take its first breath if Lonit does not get out of Galeena's way."

"And Galeena will not live to take another breath if he threatens Torka's woman again!" said Torka, and suddenly Umak was beside him, a spear in both hands, looking enormous in his bearskin; and beside him, looking very small and very bold, was Karana, brandishing the spear that he had retrieved from the body of the slain saber-toothed cat. Manaak joined them, his face congested with fury.

"This was Torka's encampment before it was Galeena's!" snapped Karana. "By right, Torka is headman here!"

The tuft of hair on the top of Galeena's head shook as his brows expanded toward his temples. He laughed. "This man sees two huntehs, a boy, and one spirit masteh who has lost his powers! Galeena says that by *might* this encampment belongs to whoever can hold it!"

His men, over a dozen strong, looked at one another, then grinned malevolently at Torka as they shook their spears in his direction. Their women set up a brief ululation in support of them.

"Strike them down," hissed Ai hungrily. "They have challenged Galeena fah too often. It is a bad thing that they live. It will be good to see them die. They will make meat for us in the dark time winteh."

Galeena appreciated her words. She reminded him of the leaping cat that had disemboweled the boy and nearly eaten Ninip. If that boy's mother had been more like Ai, he would never have turned her out into the winter dark after she had completed suckling the boy. He would have kept her for inspiration. Ai made him feel young and bold, but not quite bold enough to ignore the expressions of resolve on the faces of his adversaries. He and his hunters easily outnumbered them, but their spears were sharp, and he had seen what Torka could do with his bludgeon.

The wind was rising beyond the cave. Its sound distracted Galeena. Wild dogs were howling in the distance, and their voices gave Galeena as much inspiration as the cruel, vindictive advice of his younger woman. He cocked his head. He would like to kill. He would like to see Torka and Manaak and their allies dead and on his women's roasting spits; but Galeena preferred confrontations to be weighted in his favor. If he speared Torka's woman, he would be likely to be speared himself, and there would be no pleasure in that.

So he said with cloying sweetness as he gestured broadly: "Why men fight over wuhmen, uh? Torka, Manaak, and old man whose magic is as weak as his old bones, you take your wuhmen, and your little lame boy. You go. *Now!* It will be good thing!"

The implication of his words was obvious. Nevertheless, it took his hunters and their women a few moments to realize that Galeena was condemning Torka and his people to certain death. He stood with his spear poised to strike Lonit. His men adjusted their weapons so that, if it came to a contest, there was no way that Torka and the others could hope to come out of it alive. He laughed again. They laughed with him.

"Torka not happy? Manaak not happy?" he slashed them with the questions. "Galeena is reasonable headman! He not keep people in band when they are not content! So go! Take your wuhmen with babies in belly! Take your old man who makes no magic! Take your lame little one! Go into the storms of the time of the long dark. Galeena, he does not care what you do, or where you go! Galeena will stay in this safe, high khamp foreveh!"

They could stand up to Galeena and die in the cave or take their chances on the open tundra. The latter was their only option. Reluctantly, they took it.

Manaak descended the wall first, to steady the guide ropes as first Iana and then Lonit were lowered in the sling. Umak followed after making the appropriate curses upon Galeena. The headman and the people of the band laughed at him. Ai squawked at him like a riled goose and told him to save his magic and his curses; he would no doubt have need of both before his spirit left his body to walk upon the wind of time of the long dark.

He growled back at her and pulled his bearskin close. He would descend the wall like a man, not like a pregnant female; but before he did, a wailing Naknaktup begged to accompany him and would not be dissuaded, although she keened as she was lowered from the ledge.

Torka stood alone, facing Galeena, asking to be allowed to take what was his by right: the barest makings of a new life. "I ask you only for those things that were mine before you came to this camp—a few skins, the rib bones to make a sledge, the—"

"The dead have no rights in this khamp or any otheh. You go with what you have on. This man gives you your life. Everything else, Galeena takes as his own."

With the spears of every man of Galeena's band leveled at him, Torka began his descent of the wall. Eager to join the others, he took hold of the pulley ropes, inserted one foot into the sling, and began to lower himself.

On the ledge, Galeena leered, and a laughing Ai took up a butchering blade and began to saw away at the rope.

"Stop!" Ninip rose from where he had been sitting immobile beside Torka's fire circle. He had been watching in silence as the man who had saved his life had been degraded by his father. As he looked at his father now, Ninip wondered dully why the affection and respect of such a man had ever seemed so important. Beside Torka, Galeena cast a filthy, twisted shadow. Although Ninip was stiff and sore, he stood tall and straight as he shouted at Ai to leave the rope alone.

Everyone else yelled at her to keep on cutting. She looked toward Galeena, awaiting his command. He told her to keep on with her work. She made a little exhalation of pleasure and did as she was told.

This time, to the shock of everyone who watched, Ninip hurled himself at her and knocked the blade from her hand. She fell in a heap as Galeena cried out in outrage.

"Torka will die if she does not stop!" shouted the boy.

"*That* is the idea!" Galeena shouted back.

Halfway down the wall, Torka heard their words, jerked inward on the rope to force it to swing back toward the wall. It was rimed with ice, but he grabbed for a hold, found one, and kicked loose of the sling. He clung off-balance for a moment before the hold ceased to be a hold. Facing into the wall, he slid a good twenty feet before he managed to stop his fall and cling tightly, breathing hard.

Above him on the ledge, Ninip looked down and sighed with relief. "Torka has saved this boy's life at the risk of his own. Ninip will follow Torka now! Neveh again will this boy claim Galeena as his own!"

The statement of intent and defiance was Ninip's last. Galeena threw his spear with all of his power behind it. It drove straight through the boy's back, into his heart, and stopped only when its bone head pierced his chest. At Galeena's signal, his hunters followed suit. The force of the many direct hits drove Ninip straight off the ledge.

Night had fallen. It wrapped the outcasts in a protective blanket of darkness as they drew the spears from Ninip's broken body. In silence, Manaak took the weapons, as Umak said that they would mean the difference between life and death in the new life that they must now face together. Above them, Galeena and his people were howling as they threw stones and refuse down from the ledge. One of the hunters took up Torka's bludgeon, menaced them with it, and began to descend the wall by way of the pulley. It was a mistake. Ai's dagger had done its work. The rope broke the moment he trusted his weight to it. He fell like a rock and landed like one.

Torka retrieved his bludgeon, then left the man moaning and twitching where he lay. Torka lifted Ninip and held him in his arms as he led his band of outcasts away from the mountain. As long as it was dark, Galeena and his hunters would not follow. They would not put themselves at risk. They would stay in their high, safe encampment, not even venturing from the cave to bring the fallen hunter back up the wall so that he could die in the arms of his woman, safe from night-stalking predators.

They came soon enough. Dire wolves. The man named them as he screamed for Galeena to help him. He screamed for a long time. Neither Galeena nor the wolves heeded him. Torka and his people heard him, and although they walked on into the hostile night without looking back, they knew that as long as the wolves fed upon him, their small band would be safe from predators.

*   *   *

They buried Ninip on the outwash plain, in a little burrow that they dug and lined with evergreen branches of spruce. It was a pungent, fragrant grave. They laid him down in it, and because it was small, they curled him up like a fetus. Umak made songs of thanks to the boy whose brave spirit had overcome its inherent nastiness and had, through his gift of weapons, through the sacrifice of his death, given them all a chance to live.

It was a solemn moment. Naknaktup wept in memory of the boy's mother who had not been allowed to live past the days of his weaning, and Lonit was filled with a terrible empathy for one who had known the pain of a childhood devoid of love. Karana was troubled, sorry that he and Ninip had not exchanged so much as a friendly look in all of the time that they had lived together. They might have been friends . . . in time. But now there was no time. Ninip's life was over.

They piled many stones over the little grave so predators would not eat his flesh or scatter his bones. Not one of them had ever buried another human being. Always the bones were put out to look upon the sky forever; but somehow, that did not seem right. On the tundra, the skin of the land was too thin to allow for the digging of a grave, and the permafrost was rock hard. In the black, shadowing presence of the mountain, the ground seemed to welcome Ninip's body. For reasons that none of them could name, it seemed right that he should be placed here, safe from predators, within the flank of the mountain upon which he had given up his spirit for them.

Torka took one of the spears. With the stabbing dagger that he carried at his belt, he notched out its maker's identification mark and inscribed his own. Across it, he incised the double lateral lines that had been Ninip's mark of ownership. Then he broke the spear across his thigh and placed the pieces upright upon the grave.

"So that the spirits of the mountain will know that Torka claimed this boy as his own. So that Galeena will know. It is as Ninip claimed. Not even in the spirit world would Ninip claim Galeena as his own. Ninip is of Torka's band. Forever!"

They went on. Manaak carried Iana. The shock of the past few hours had stilled her pains, but in the blue haze that was all that would be of the next day's light, her labor began

again. One great contraction broke the water in which the
unborn child was cushioned from the jolts of life; and the
infant came forth in a gush, so quickly that Umak had no time
to frame a single child-come-forth chant. He made a praise
song instead while Manaak nearly fainted with relief, and
Karana said that the newborn boy would grow to be a very
wise man because he had the good sense to refuse to be born
into Galeena's band.

They rested only long enough for Iana to be tended by
the women.

"We must go far from this place," said Manaak. "It is not
Galeena's way to be forgiving. He will come for us if he can.
Like a pack of wolves, his huntehs will fall upon us while we
sleep. We *must* go on."

For a day and all of a nearly endless night, they walked
and rested, rested and walked. Manaak carried Iana until she
insisted that she was strong enough to walk on her own; and
this she did, although it cost her dear. Nevertheless, when
Umak offered to make a litter of his bearskin robe, she
refused.

"Your magic lives in that, Spirit Masteh," she told him,
holding her infant close. "It may not work quickly, but it *is* a
strong and wonderful magic that has given this son to me."

Two days later, they came upon the carcass of a large
bison. It had been old and sick, and whether it had died of
natural causes or been killed by wolves was impossible to say.
Only a small portion of it had been eaten: belly, throat, eyes,
tongue, and the upper flank. The rest was intact, and it was
an easy task to drive away the smaller carrion eaters that had
evidently just arrived to feast upon it. From its ribs they
erected a framework for a small pit hut and draped its hide
and Umak's bearskin over it.

Iana made no objection; in fact she smiled as she gratefully lay down within it, out of the wind.

"We will all dwell within the life-sustaining warmth of
Umak's magic," she said.

And so they did.

It began to snow. And the snow kept falling, a soft,
windless snow that covered the land and filled the world with
silence . . . until a terrible roaring shattered that silence. The
earth shook, and their little shelter shivered as though against
a wind, but there was no wind.

In terror, they clambered from their shelter and squinted

against miles of white stretching away forever all around them. In all those miles, nothing moved. In all those miles, there was no color at all except the black, soaring bulk of the Mountain of Power, Galeena's mountain. They stared, perplexed and then awed. The entire upper quadrant of the mountain was moving. The vast, mile-thick skin of the summit ice pack was fracturing, slipping, sliding downward as the supersaturated underlayers of scree and till, overstressed by the weight of the new accumulation of snow, suddenly refused to support their burden. In great, dark sheets of debris, the underpinnings of the glacier were giving out, causing the glacier itself to override them.

As Torka and his little band of outcasts watched in stunned silence, the entire east-facing flank of the mountain, including the cavelike ledge and all of its occupants, was buried forever beneath the geological debris of centuries.

Karana tugged gently at Umak's hand, and then at Torka's. "The mountain *was* warning us."

The old man harrumphed as Torka nodded, drew Lonit close, and said quietly: "Galeena was right. He *will* stay in his high, 'safe' encampment forever."

PART V

THE CORRIDOR OF STORMS

1

Alone on the winter tundra, Torka set his little band to the tasks necessary for its survival. The weather cleared briefly. They worked together in stunned silence, still only half-believing the enormity of the catastrophe that had destroyed Galeena's band and had nearly befallen them. They used every scrap of the bison carcass, eating as they worked to scrape precious, life-sustaining marrow from its joints, then setting aside the long bones of its legs, which would later be fashioned into spears. They extracted sinew from its meat and plucked the long, tough strands of hair from its tail and mane so that these wiry filaments could be braided into snare nets for birding and rodent catching and into lines for ice fishing.

By the time the weather closed in again, they had used the bison's horns to break up the frozen tundra and hack out a larger, deeper circle over which they reerected their pit hut. With sods banked high all around, it was a warm refuge from the cold wind and hard-driving snow as, far off across the tundra, a wild dog howled as though in protest to the storm.

Karana cocked his head in the darkness. "Listen. Brother Dog has seen the mountain fall. He mourns for us."

Umak listened to the distant, mournful cries of the dog. He held Naknaktup close as she silently grieved over the deaths of her people; however, he was not thinking of her or of the members of Galeena's band. He was remembering another night, another storm, and an old man who walked away upon the wind while a wild dog followed and kept him from dying. He closed his eyes. Where was Brother Dog now? And by what selfish enchantment had Umak gone so long without wondering about the fate of the brother who had saved his life?

The wind rose. It took the sound of the dog and whipped it away across the world so that, within the pit hut, the voice of the wind was the only voice that could be heard. Manaak and Iana slept in each other's arms as their infant suckled contentedly.

Lonit drifted off to sleep. She lay nestled close to Torka. His right hand rested lightly across her belly. The baby moved. The *future* moved.

Torka listened to the wailing of the wind and reflected on the events that had made him headman of this tiny, vulnerable band. He had never wanted to be headman. Yet now that he thought about all that had brought him to this desolate, storm-ridden place, it seemed that, ever since Thunder Speaker had rampaged into his life, some invisible force had been directing his steps. Testing him. Leading him. But why? Where?

The questions followed him into sleep. He dreamed of distant lands stretching eastward beyond the Corridor of Storms, of lands warmed by the rising sun, where flocks of birds filled the skies and herds of game roamed the valleys. The dream was so intense and of such a fine and glorious land, that he awoke half-hoping to find that he had been transported there. But around him, the world was cold and black. Beyond the pit hut, the storm raged, and winter ruled.

There was no time. No days, no nights, no dawn, no dusk.

There was only darkness, and in that darkness the wind lived and breathed its dry, cold, savage breath in a ceaseless exhalation that flayed the world and raked the skies clean of clouds.

And in that endless dark, beneath those cold skies, Torka and his little band survived. Food was scarce, but such a small group of people needed little to sustain them. As game dwindled in the vicinity of one camp, they moved to another. They warmed themselves with meager fires fueled with small bones and dried dung, and as they left one encampment to seek out another, Lonit encouraged them to gather stones and pebbles. They were rare on the open tundra, but life upon the mountain had taught her how valuable they were for taking in heat and radiating its precious gift of life-giving warmth for many hours after even the most carefully tended sods, bones, and fragments of dung had burned away to nothing.

They walked across the rolling land, their direction determined by the game that they followed and by the bite of the subzero wind. Without the heavy winter garments that they had been forced to leave behind, they were at a profound and deadly disadvantage until they were able to contrive suitable cold-weather clothing out of the most unlikely skins and furs imaginable. Whatever they hunted and killed, they ate and wore. In the skins of fish and birds and squirrels they went forth. Badger and fox, lynx and hare and lemming—their skins were cursorily treated and stitched into patchwork gloves and boots, hoods and surplices. The intestines of their prey were opened, their contents shared among all members of the little band; then the opaque casings were dried over their fire, oiled with melted fat, and transformed into parchmentlike sheets that were fashioned into outer tunics that effectively broke the wind.

From hunting camp to hunting camp, they moved and prospered. Although heavy with child, Lonit had never felt better. Naknaktup had recovered from the initial queasiness of her pregnancy, but she still brooded over the loss of her people, especially Oklahnoo, her sister. Along with a fully recuperated Iana, Naknaktup worked with Lonit to set snares and sew, to butcher and scrape skins, and to pound fat into oil as she shared Iana's joy in her tiny son and outspokenly anticipated the birth of her own child.

"This wuhman so old, she think she neveh again have baby," she said, beaming as brightly as though she had swallowed a piece of the summer sun. "Umak *is* great spirit masteh! This wuhman proud to be his wuhman!" Then the sunlight slowly faded from her eyes, and her smile sagged as memories clouded her happiness. "So many little ones this wuhman have. All dead now. Killed. Sent into storms. Or eaten in dark time winteh."

Lonit's eyes went wide. "Eaten?"

"Galeena not like little ones. Keep only some few strong childs. If times bad, in dark times winteh, when game is scarce and men not like to hunt in cold, Galeena kills little ones. Babies make good meat."

Now Lonit at last understood why there were no children in Galeena's band and why Iana had shown so little enthusiasm over the impending birth of her baby. The Destroyer had not killed all of the little ones of her band; Galeena had.

Naknaktup was perplexed by Lonit's surprise and obvious revulsion. "Torka and his people not eat babies?"

"We do *not!*" she cried, then recalled the rumors that had circulated in the winter camp of her own band before the great ghost mammoth had come, rumors that Teenak, the headman's woman, had killed and portioned her newborn infant to be used as food. Her hands crossed protectively over her own unborn child. "Never in this new land, in this new band, will the people of Torka eat their children. *Never!*"

Naknaktup and Iana looked at one another, then both of them smiled hopefully at Lonit. "May this be so," they said in unison.

"It *will* be so!" she replied emphatically.

The two women nodded.

The sun was back in Naknaktup's eyes as she said: "Then life with Torka's band *will* be a good thing."

And it was so. Each camp seemed to be a little better than the last. The men hunted successfully, taking Karana along with them so that he might learn from their skills and experience. The women shared the work of life, preparing not only food and clothing but all of those little things that raised the quality of their existence from mere subsistence to a level that allowed them a modicum of pleasure.

They laughed. They sang the songs of life. Umak filled the hours with wondrous tales. Manaak and Iana's infant wailed and whooped with lustful, aggressive exuberance for life. He had survived those first few tentative weeks of life in which it was not certain if a child truly possessed a life spirit; now there was no doubt of that. Manaak's new son was old enough and strong enough to be named and thus acknowledged as a member of the band. They called him Ninipik—Little Ninip. And there was no doubt in anyone's mind that the brazen spirit of the brave, dead boy had come to live again within the body of Manaak and Iana's little son.

Torka would always remember the exact moment in which the idea came to him. He was on the way back to camp with Manaak and Karana after several hours of successful hunting. The three of them had taken two steppe antelopes, a winter-white hare, and four fat ptarmigan; nevertheless, the sight of a large herd of horses stopped them dead in their tracks.

"Look at that. . . ." drawled Manaak, salivating. "All of that red, sweet meat on the hoof, standing just out of range of our weapons, as if they knew the exact distance that our spears can fly."

"We should make longer spears," suggested Karana.

"Longer spears would be too light to take such heavy-bodied quarry from this far away," replied Manaak.

"Then we should make longer, *heavier* spears!" retorted Karana.

Manaak laughed. "Our speahs are fine for taking horse, Little Hunter. What we need are longeh *arms*!"

It was the last sentence that snagged in Torka's brain and hooked itself into his thoughts so that he could not be free of it. He mulled it over and over, all the way back to camp, all the way through the meal that Lonit had ready for him, and when he slept, he dreamed about it.

The dream was in part a memory. He saw a young girl holding up one of the long wing bones of a condor. She marveled at its lightweight structure and asked how such a fragile bone could support the weight of such a great wing. He saw himself, kneeling, working the wing, fascinated by its anatomical structure, intrigued by the strength and elasticity of the powerful tendons that gave a springlike movement to the muscles and bones.

And then, in a recollection of a dream within the dream, Torka saw himself as a man with the wings of a condor; wings that carried him high above the world, that made him weightless and allowed him to experience the awesome thrust and power of flight. He was a spear hurtling across the sky, a spear that controlled its own passage.

He awoke with a start, his right arm bent, fist against shoulder. Slowly, the idea uncurled within his mind as his arm curled outward. He lay flat on his back. Again and again, he bent his arm inward, then straightened it, feeling the workings of muscle, bone, and tendon. The idea grabbed him, forced him to his feet, and hurled him out of the pit hut. He stood erect beneath the savage Arctic sky, a man in darkness with the light of inspiration igniting his soul. He took one of his spears from where it rested with the others against the conical exterior walls of the pit hut. He tested its weight and balance. The idea was growing in him; shapeless but not without direction. He hefted himself squarely on both feet. He pivoted to the right, leaning back, back, until all of his weight was on his right limb and he was twisted, helixlike, until he could twist no more. His power was now concentrated within the right side of his body. He could feel it deep within his calf and thigh as, through the controlled tension and angle of his foot, he willed himself to whirl around. He felt his power uncoiling, releasing itself upward along his body as he hurled himself forward, caught his balance on his left foot, steadied it with his right, and threw the spear.

It flew up and out in an arc against the stars. It sliced through the frigid air as cleanly as Torka's creative imagery sliced through his brain. He caught his breath, stunned as the idea flared to life and took shape until, in the darkness, he saw it clearly and cried out to the stars.

"*This* is how it flies!"

Umak peered out from the pit hut, frowning as he saw Torka throwing one spear after another toward the stars. He asked his grandson if he thought that the lights in the sky were prey that men might hunt and eat, then informed him that bad spirits had gotten into his head if he did.

Torka ignored Umak. The idea had taken direction now. It led him, and he followed eagerly, throwing his spears toward the stars. With each release, he felt the source and the redistribution and the flow of his power radiate through him into the shaft. He understood that, as in his dreams, the spear *was* an extension of the man.

Again and again, he retrieved his spears and threw them, *feeling* the throw, understanding the mechanics of it, remembering the great, long bones of the condor's wing and realizing that the beginnings of the idea lay in that moment when Lonit had wondered how such lightweight bones could support the flight of such a great bird.

It was not the size of the bones; it was their length, the elasticity of their tendons, and the multiplicity of their jointing. The power of a man's spear lay not in the weight of the shaft but in the tension that the man released through every bone in his body. The snap-and-fling action of his wrist was as crucial to the throw as the long, sustained push of the powerful muscles of shoulder and back.

"Torka?" Manaak came out into the night to stand beside

him, obviously worried about the strange and apparently irrational behavior. "What *are* you doing?"

"You were right!" Torka said, slapping him on the shoulder. "We need longer arms! Another joint! Perhaps two! And more tendons to bind them tight and allow for greater thrust!"

Manaak stared, his mouth agape. "Come back into the pit hut, friend. Umak is already making chants to drive the bad spirit from your head."

Torka smiled. "The spirit that has come into this man's head is a good spirit—so good that it may change the way we hunt forever!"

Torka was right. It took him several weeks of experimentation and frustration, of failure and mediocre success and failure again; but soon he had devised a harmless-looking device with a handgrip at one end and a barbed tip at the other. Carved out of the pelvis of the bison, it was the length of his forearm. With the grip held in his right hand and the butt of his spear braced against the barb—the narrowing, pointed end of the shaft facing back over his shoulder and gripped midway along its length between his thumb and index finger—Torka had designed a crude missile launcher.

With practice it became a second forearm and wrist, allowing him to increase the power and snap of his throwing arm, more than doubling the speed and distance of his spear's thrust.

Manaak, Umak, and Karana each insisted upon making his own spear thrower, and soon they were hunting with Torka in amazed delight as their women stood by and were glad.

"With the new tool, the hunters can stand well back from the game and make their kills in safety," observed Lonit proudly.

"It is a good thing," agreed Naknaktup.

And Iana, no longer sad-eyed, smiled and nodded; but her smile would have fallen had she heard the words of her man as he knelt beside Torka over the body of the horse that they had taken.

"Look how deep the spearhead has gone into the flesh . . . straight into the lung . . . and from such a distance!" Manaak fingered the wound that his weapon had made. "With the right projectile points, a man could dare to hunt mammoth with this spear throweh."

Torka looked at the other man and shook his head. "Torka has no taste for mammoth."

"The one that Manaak would hunt, he would hunt to kill, not to eat."

"Then Manaak will hunt alone," said Torka.

"If Big Spirit comes, we will stand togetheh."

Without warning, Torka struck out at him. Manaak fell sideways, more surprised than angry; his thick winter garments had cut the sting of the blow, but nothing could have lessened the anger that he heard in Torka's voice.

"You speak with a tongue that will bring ruin to us all!" accused Torka. Manaak had named the unnameable. Here, in this wide, rolling land where their women had no recourse to a high, safe ledge upon which they could seek shelter in time of danger, Manaak had spoken the name of the beast that Torka feared more than death. He reached out and jabbed Manaak's shoulder warningly. "Life is good! Your woman smiles in a camp where there is meat. Your infant suckles, and mine readies itself to be born out of my woman's womb. We have responsibilities in this life! Are you so eager to die, Manaak? Are you hungry to have me die with you? Without us, who will hunt for our women in the time of the long dark? How long will they live with only an old man and a little boy to protect them?"

2

They ate the horse's flesh for many days. Slowly winter began to wane. It had been cold and dry, with little snow; but now, as the time of the long dark approached its end, the weather changed. The wind turned, drawing moisture-laden clouds inland from distant polar seas. Snow fell and fell. Above a thick and storm-swept cloud cover, the starving moon rose over the tundra.

As Torka and his little band moved from camp to camp, game became harder to find. Low on the eastern horizon, when cloud cover allowed, they could see the first promising glow of sunlight above the tangled summits and glaciers of distant ranges, but hibernating animals still slept beneath the ground, safely hidden from the prods of the women by deep, hard-packed drifts of snow, and when browsing animals died from lack of accessible forage, they, too, were buried as soon as they fell. Wolves and wild dogs sang the song of hunger as they prowled the lonely, wind-driven landscape. And the people of Torka's band grew lean and began to starve.

They made an encampment in the smothering, howling whiteness. They lived on wedges of fat that had been meant for use as tallow for their oil lamps. Lonit was approaching the end of her pregnancy. She wondered if she would have milk for her baby. Although Iana had not spoken of it, Lonit knew from the fretful sounds her infant made while nursing that her milk was not flowing as it should. Naknaktup knew it, too. Occasionally Lonit would catch them both looking covertly at their men, and at Torka in particular. Since they had been forced from Galeena's mountain, they had all looked to him as headman. Umak made the magic; Torka made the decisions; and Manaak was second in command. They had assumed their roles as easily as they donned their garments. Only now the decisions were growing more and more difficult, and it was natural for them to be questioned.

"Why do the women watch me like that?" Torka asked Lonit.

"They wait for you to command Iana and Manaak to give up their baby to be food for us all."

"This man will never ask such a thing!"

"It is what Galeena would have done."

"Torka is *not* Galeena! Torka does not eat the children of his band! The children are the future of the People! It is for them that we fight to survive the winter dark!"

He had spoken loudly, and in anger. The pit hut was small. His words were heard by all. Lonit looked at Iana and Naknaktup with an I-told-you-so expression written across her face. Manaak made a grunt of approval. Karana looked at Torka wonderingly, recalling the way Torka had risked his life to find him in the storm; now, more than ever, he knew that Torka was unlike any man he had ever known. Umak harrumphed with pride that Egatsop had been wrong about his grandson. Torka's innate compassion was not born out of softness; it was the foundation upon which his wisdom was building.

"We *will* survive. To make new life! To hear the laughter of our children! For this, we hunt! For this, we live! For this, we will now make the songs of life in the winter dark, loud songs so that the sun may hear us in its faraway part of the world and hasten to return to its children!"

They sang, and from out of the winter dark, wild dogs sang back to them.

"They are close," said Torka.

The people fell silent, listening.

"Do you think Brother Dog is out there?" asked Karana.

"Somewhere. Yes. If he lives," replied Torka.

Umak closed his eyes, turned his face upward, and breathed deeply, drawing in the sound of the dogs, sieving it for an answer to his unspoken question. His mind remained blank. Dogs sounded alike. He harrumphed, disgusted with himself. *Umak is spirit master. If Aar is near, this old man should know it in his bones!* But his bones knew only the cold and a deep, aching stiffness. *Umak is old*, he thought, then opened his eyes and glared into the darkness defiantly. "This man is not so hungry that he would hunt and eat his brother!"

"Nor is Karana!"

Torka eyed the old man and the boy sternly. Manaak had already slipped on his hunting coat. Iana was readying her snares. Torka nodded at their intent. He told Umak and Karana that wild dogs were fair game for starving men who must think of the welfare of their pregnant women and children. "If Umak and Karana have made a spirit bond with the dog they call Aar, so be it. They will stay here and guard the women. Manaak and Torka will hunt and set snares. And if Brother Dog has found a place among the pack that howls, he had best be wise and run far, for Torka will have no second thoughts about killing him."

They traveled eastward under lowering clouds, following the song of the wild dogs. They picked up spoor and were heartened. They trotted on, the wind rising at their backs.

The tundra rolled on ahead of them. Surface snow blew in the wind like transparent veils of mist. They stopped to rest and eat one wedge of fat apiece, scanning the world, making certain that they kept their bearings so they would have no difficulty returning to camp.

Manaak thumped his chest to indicate his satisfaction with their prospects. He rose, shook his spear thrower, and said boldly: "With this we *will* bring home meat!"

Torka would have cursed him for his outspoken arrogance, but he had already trotted away. Torka followed.

Hours passed. The dogs seemed to be leading them. No sooner did they reach a place from which the dogs' song had come, than their spoor led them on again.

"It is as though they stop and wait, calling us on, leaving sign by which we may follow," commented Manaak thoughtfully.

"They are dogs, not men!"

"Yet Umak calls one of them brotheh."

Torka did not appreciate Manaak's reminder. He ignored it and went on until bison sign brought him up short. He realized with a start that he and Manaak were not the only hunters afoot. The dogs were on the trail of their own game, and it *did* seem as though they were going out of their way to cause the men to follow.

"The spirits are with us!" exclaimed Manaak.

"It may be so," said Torka, wishing that Manaak would not speak so freely of things that had not yet come to pass.

Manaak caught the undertone of censure in Torka's tone. His impatient nature was irked by Torka's innate caution. "Look, at your feet, bison sign everywhere! See how they have gouged through the snow with horns and hooves, have rooted with their noses to get at the grass stubble that lies beneath! A big herd! Not more than two days ahead of us! Khum! We will go back now and tell the othehs. The promise of much meat will give us the energy we need to move our encampment near to the grazing grounds of the bison. Soon we will hunt! The bison will be amazed at the poweh of our spear throwehs! We will drink their warm blood and feast upon their flesh while we laugh at our hungeh beneath the cold face of the starving moon!"

Torka was so appalled by Manaak's brazen, thoughtless boasting that he could not speak. Deep within his gut, fear churned like schooling fish. He felt nauseated as he realized that Manaak had just broken the same taboo that Nap had broken on the day that Thunder Speaker had walked into their lives to destroy their world. He had dared to name his prey before actually sighting it. And worse than that, he had vocalized his intent to laugh at the spirit of the starving moon.

Torka was suddenly painfully aware of the wailing wind. It slapped at his back. He shivered, not against the subfreezing wind but against a greater cold as a terrible wave of premonitory dread swept through him.

"Come," he said. "I smell storm in this wind. We have been out from the encampment long enough."

For a thousand miles, the wind swept across open, treeless land, blowing ground snow before it until earth and sky were indistinguishable. Umak stood facing into the wind, relief flooding him.

"They come! At last the hunters return to us!"

Manaak emerged from the whiteness, so elated by his news that he embraced the old man. "Bison, Spirit Masteh! The dogs led us to them! A great herd! We will pass this storm and dream sweet dreams of meat in the winteh dark! We will move our khamp, and then we will hunt! Oh, *how* we will hunt!"

He swept the old man ahead of him into the pit hut.

Shaking off snow, he shared his joy with them all and tossed to Iana the single hare that his snares had taken.

"It is not much meat for now!" he declared. "But we will all eat of its flesh and cook its bones in a boiling bag over what little fat we have left for our cooking stones. Soon we will eat hump steaks, and our hands will glisten with blood and oil! Tell them, Torka! Tell them of the bison sign, and of the size of the herd that . . ." His words trailed off. He squinted into the dark interior, looking from face to face. "Where is Torka? He was ahead of me when I stopped to pick up this hare. He should have been back by now."

Outside, the wind struck so hard at the pit hut that the entire structure shook. Lonit let out a cry of dismay and, with Umak and Karana following, went out into the storm. Frantically, she called out to Torka, but the wind took her voice and fragmented it, blowing it away across the tundra in the opposite direction. Torka would never hear it. And if he did not, he would never be able to find his way back to the encampment in the shrieking, driving whiteness of the blizzard. *Never.*

"In such a storm . . . how long can a man live alone without food or shelteh?"

Manaak's question cut Lonit to the bone as Umak drew her back into the protection of the little hut and out of the lung-searing bite of the subzero wind.

Voices.

From out of the roaring emptiness, from out of the boiling whiteness of the storm, Torka heard men speak. Their sharp, guttural commands drew him back into consciousness. He looked up from the bottom of the ravine into which he had fallen and saw figures trotting along the rim.

One. Two. He counted a dozen men, furred and cowled in the dark, shaggy skins of bison, with spears in their hands and backs bent as they moved against the wind. Then they were gone, enveloped in the blowing snow. And in all the world, there was only the sound of the wind, and in the boiling whiteness nothing moved.

Nothing.

Except the man at the bottom of the ravine.

Alone and disoriented, Torka shook his head to clear it, telling himself that the figures had not been real, *could* not have been real. They had been ghosts walking the blurred edges of his consciousness. Dreams. Nothing more than dreams.

His head ached with questions. How had he come to be lying inert at the bottom of this deep, irregular crack in the surface of the earth? Where was Manaak?

The questions brought immediate answers. He remembered that Manaak had paused to kill and string a hare that had tangled itself in one of his snare lines. It had been snowing very hard. They had been walking along the slope of a steep incline, one of many conical little hills that pocked the otherwise flat terrain like blisters. They had used them as marking points to guide them back to their encampment, but in the wind-driven snow, although the hills ranged from thirty to over a hundred feet in elevation, they had been difficult to spot. Manaak had said something about hoping that they would be able to find their way home, and Torka had replied that they would do so, provided they did not linger until the storm grew worse. So, when he had gone ahead, Manaak must have assumed that he had continued on without him. With the wind shrieking all around, neither man heard the sound of the inner core of the little hill collapsing; Torka had only known that one moment there was solid, snow-covered ground beneath his feet, and the next he was falling as that ground opened without warning. He could not have known that the hill was not a hill, or that the broad, flat, circular expanse of land over which they had been traveling was an ancient silt-filled lake. Over millennia, water that had once glistened beneath the Arctic sky had been thickened into a stew of soaked sediment that was the outfall of erosion in the distant mountains. Surrounded by permafrost, excess water froze to form hard cores of ice that slowly bulged above the surface of the ground. Except for their presence in otherwise flat terrain, they looked like any other hills, but warm summers transformed the texture of their frozen centers, and cold winters redefined them until pressure and expansion rent them with fissures and filled them with air pockets. Torka's weight had been enough to cause one of these rifts to open; the resultant crack in the side of the hill had opened beneath him and caused his fall into the now-open air pocket beneath.

It had happened so quickly, so unexpectedly, that he had had no time to react before his head hit the side of the ravine. He had no idea how long he had lain unconscious, but the storm had blown itself into monstrous proportions. The ravine provided a natural refuge. He knew that he dared not try to get back to the encampment until the wind dropped and the snowfall lessened. As he stripped off his outer coat and stretched it across the top of the narrow fissure to serve as a roof that would keep the weather out and his body heat in, he could only hope that Manaak had found his way back to the encampment or had found shelter against the elements. Meanwhile, in his many-layered garments, he locked his gloved hands beneath his armpits and wished that his snares had entrapped a hare, as Manaak's had done. Salivating, he tried not to think of food. He thought instead of oil lamps and glowing fires of sods, and tried to will himself warm.

His head began to ache dully again. He closed his eyes and slept until, out of the howling whiteness of the storm, the Destroyer walked within his dreams. He saw it clearly, a moving mountain half-invisible within the blowing snow as it moved inexorably toward the encampment of his people.

He awoke with a start. As on that terrible dawn of long ago, all of his senses screamed: *Danger!* He listened. Had he heard the trumpeting of the great mammoth? No. There was only the sound of the wind wailing, screaming, and moaning—a sound to put demons into the mind of any man. But *that* demon was far away. Best to forget it, to sleep, to preserve all energy for the maintenance of precious body heat. Above the narrow cleft of the ravine, the air became colder as the wind continued to rise. The storm would rage for hours. Nothing would be moving within it.

Nothing.

Fleetingly, he thought about the conjured images of ghostly men that had first awakened him. Briefly, he half remembered something that Karana had said, had feared so long ago.

The Ghost Band.

What had the boy said of it? They come in the time of light, to steal women and boys, then to vanish as though they had never come at all, leaving burning encampments and the bodies of the dead and dying as the only proof that they existed at all.

He told himself that he was being as fearful and overly imaginative as Karana. This was not the time of light. It was the worst winter storm he had seen in many moons. Nothing would be afoot in such a storm. Nothing.

Except ghosts. Except spirits.

"No!" he spoke the admonition aloud, and although the wind drowned his voice, the mere exhalation of a human sound was comforting.

He forced his thoughts to drift. At length he slept lightly, one hand curled around the haft of his bludgeon, the other on the one spear that had not broken in his fall.

Within the encampment, Naknaktup awoke. The storm had lessened. Her people slept—deep, troubled sleep—but Naknaktup was not troubled. The storm would end. Torka would return. If Umak believed this, Naknaktup was certain that it would be so. Her confidence in her spirit master was complete. He who was old had put the spirit of new life into one who was old enough to have begun to suspect herself barren. Truly, Umak *was* a maker of miracles. And the weight of the miracle that he had implanted within her womb was now pressing against her innards. She sighed against her need to relieve herself as she rose, drew one of her sleeping skins around her shoulders, and went out.

The wind had dropped considerably, but it was still snowing and bitterly cold. Naknaktup was glad that her baby would not be born until the full return of the time of light. She smiled as she waded through the snow, daydreaming about warmer days and the sweet smell of her infant, how it would be to cuddle it and suckle it, and—

She stopped. Shadows were moving in the snow. Dark, hairy shadows, as though bison stood erect on their hind limbs and stalked prey in the guise of men. She counted the shadows. One . . . two . . . *many*. And all carried their weapons in such a way that Naknaktup immediately sensed danger.

They came out of the wind, leering at the startled woman who stood with her graying hair whipping in the wind. Visions of light and warmth and of suckling babes vanished as Naknaktup managed to cry out an undefined warning just as a spear struck her breast and pierced her heart.

Inside the pit hut, the others were instantly alerted by her dying scream. Assuming that a predator had attacked her, Umak and Manaak grabbed their spears, glad that the weather had caused them to store them inside instead of outside, as they usually did. They shouted at Karana and told him to stay out of the way. Iana clutched her baby close, and Lonit wished that she still had her bola so that she might be of help.

Younger and faster, Manaak pushed Umak aside so that he would be the first one to leave the pit hut.

"Umak is spirit masteh! Manaak is hunteh! Let him walk before you!"

"Hmmph! Naknaktup is Umak's woman!"

Manaak would not yield. He wanted to be the first man out, the first to face wolf or bear, lion or mammoth. Mammoth! How he hoped it *was* the great ghost. His lust to kill outweighed his common sense, eclipsed the small voice that shouted at the back of his brain: *If it is Big Spirit, we will all die.*

He came out of the pit hut breathing hard, prepared to face Big Spirit but totally unprepared to face hostile, predatory strangers of his own species. For one fatal moment he stared at them, his spear poised in his hand. It was his last moment. Two spears found him. One drove straight through his neck. The other entered through his belly and drove its barbed nephrite head through his lower back, severing his spine. Disbelieving, he suffocated on his own blood as his knees buckled and he dropped to the snow. The last thing he heard was Umak shouting his name as the old man came bursting out of the pit hut from behind him.

Umak never saw the blow that felled him. He came up out of the shelter, leaping at his attacker. He had seen Manaak fall, and he had seen what had dropped him. Old he was, and no longer as strong as he had been in his youth, but in this moment, he knew that his woman was dead, *and* his unborn child. His rage made him young. His rage made him powerful.

But youth and power were nothing to the shadowed form who stood behind him, to one side of the entrance to the pit hut. The man swung downward with the heft of his spear, to send Umak sprawling.

It was silence, not sound, that woke Torka. The wind had stopped. Eager to return to the encampment, he shook snow from his outer coat, donned it, took up his one good spear, and with his bludgeon at his belt, climbed out of the ravine.

In the thin, transient light of day, the world was white—

the land, the sky, were snow white, cloud white. He squinted against the glare. Soon it would fade. If he was going to find his way back to the encampment before dark, he would have to hurry.

When the depth of the snow allowed, he moved at a lope, his muscles gradually relaxing as movement warmed them. Experience enabled him to find his bearings with little trouble. Now and then he paused, noting landmarks that would have been unrecognizable to all but the most seasoned tracker; softened by the overlayering of snow, everything looked different. But he was Torka. The blood of many generations of spirit masters flowed within him, and Umak had taught him well.

He went on and did not look back. Soon a dark, uneven stain of smoke became visible on the horizon, pinpointing the exact location of the encampment. So they had built a signal fire to guide him home. He was glad. It would make the way easier, although he wondered what they had found to burn that would yield so much smoke. He quickened his step, thinking of the warmth of the pit hut, hoping that Manaak would be there to greet him, and longing for the soft arms of his woman.

Lonit! He almost cried her name aloud as he imagined her dimpled smile.

As he crested the top of a low, rolling slope, his thoughts veered sharply, and the brightness went out of the day. He did not slow his pace as he looked back over his shoulder.

From the way their tongues lolled from their mouths, the pack of dogs must have been following him for some time.

Instinct told him to keep on running. Wisdom forced him to stop and face them. On the top of the slope, high ground granted him an advantage. He could never outrun them. But he could kill a few and, after he had put the rest to flight, take his kills back to the encampment. The dogs would not make good meat; they were far too lean. His little band, however, was in a state of near starvation and would rejoice no matter what he brought them. And if he skinned it first and ate its blue eyes before returning to the pit hut, they would never know that they fed upon the flesh of Brother Dog.

Aar's black-masked head was unmistakable amid his tawny-eyed, gray-haired cousins. He was very thin, with ribs showing and scars across his nose and high at his shoulders; but he was clearly an animal in his prime now, the second largest dog in the pack, with broad, slavering jaws and a wild, half-mad look in his eyes.

"'Brother' Dog . . . we meet again. This man sees that you have reverted to kind, as he always knew you would."

Aar's head went down, neck outstretched, ears back. Beside and slightly ahead of him, the largest male growled, and, as though by command, every animal in the pack followed suit.

Slowly, Torka loosed his bludgeon and raised it with his left hand while holding his spear at the ready in his right. The dogs understood his threat. Several took a few halting steps back, but their leader, the largest male, snarled. He took two steps forward and froze, his hair bristling along his shoulders and spine.

Torka stood immobile, allowing the dog to perceive no fear in his stance. "Come," he invited. "You are the biggest. You will make the most meat."

The dog's head twisted a little, as though it tried to understand the words of the man. Aar moved up beside it, shoulder to shoulder, tension rippling in his muscles as he strained to hold himself back.

"Ah, Brother Dog, Umak would not be happy to see you now or to know the fate that you have chosen. Come, try to feed upon Torka, and Torka will make certain that you are never hungry again!"

Starvation had made the dogs bold. They closed ranks behind their leader. The big male led them to attack, and yipping and yowling they came at Torka without hesitation. They poured up the slope toward him, and he swiped down and across with his bludgeon. But even as his weapon came in contact with the side of the big dog's jaw, he saw to his amazement that the leader had another enemy.

Aar was at his throat. If the weapon had not killed him, the slashing teeth of Brother Dog would. The big gray dog fell sideways. Others swarmed over him to meet the swiping death dealt to them by Torka's club. Not once did he have to use his spear. With Aar fighting by his side, turning on his own kind in defense of Brother Man, Torka was able to brain the most aggressive members of the pack. The rest ran in whimpering retreat. All but one—a shaggy, heavy-bellied female, who had stood back from the melee, stared up the slope at Torka and the dog, as bewildered by Aar's behavior

as Torka was overwhelmed by it. For the first time since
Umak had insisted that Aar was his spirit brother, Torka
knew that the old man had been right all along. Stunned, he
dropped to one knee. The dog stood close, but not too near,
staring at him out of a bloodied face. Tentatively, Torka
extended a conciliatory hand.

"*Brother* Dog . . ." he acknowledged, and although he
did not understand how it could be, he knew that somehow
the dog was more than an animal. In a strange and bewilder-
ing symbiosis, the dog had chosen to place its loyalty with
Man. "We have not been friends, you and I," said Torka,
"but from this day on, truly we *will* be brothers."

Torka would have prepared the slain dogs for transport to
camp, but as he began to do so, he saw the tracks. Frozen in
the bottom layer of hard snow, the wind had blown away
their covering of soft powder. Torka stared, touching them,
noting their differences.

Many men.

Aar sniffed at the footprints with interest, and the female
dog did the same. Torka was struck cold with dread: The
furred, armed men that had walked along the rim of the
ravine at the height of the storm had not been figments of his
imagination. They had been real. Karana's words came raging
back into his head as his eyes fastened on the distant signal
fire that he knew was not a signal fire at all.

*The Ghost Band . . . it comes in the time of light to steal
women and boys, then to vanish . . . leaving burning encampments and the bodies of the dead and dying as the only
proof that they existed at all.*

With Aar at his side and the female dog trailing at a wary
distance, Torka raced for home. The pit hut was a pile of
charred, stinking rubble by the time he reached it. He stood
in shock, cold and immobile, as memories of another encampment raked his soul. Death . . . death . . . everywhere.
A voice screamed within him. *No! Not again! No!*

He moved forward quickly, hoping that the bodies that he
saw would rise to mock him, parties to some obscene jest.
They did not rise. Manaak was dead of massive spear wounds,
but the weapons had been drawn from his corpse, and he lay
in a frozen pool of his own blood. Naknaktup sprawled where
she had fallen, on her back, hideously mutilated, with her

unborn child ripped from her belly and placed in a position to suckle wounds where breasts had once been.

Had there been food in his belly, Torka would have vomited. He used his spear to steady himself, searching for Umak and Lonit and Karana, half hoping that he would not find them, then going mad with blind, directionless rage when he could not. He cried out their names, and Iana's. The wind blew them back at him out of miles of empty, desolate darkness.

Aar's soft whimpering drew him to Umak's body. The old man lay half-buried in the rubble of the pit hut, so blackened by burns that he was unrecognizable until, from out of the ashes and charred skins and bones, softly slurred but unmistakable sound reached Torka's ears.

"Hrrum . . . mphh . . ."

Frantically Torka cleared the rubble of the hut away, and when he looked down at his dying grandfather, he bowed his head and wept like a child until a blackened, bony finger poked at his tears.

"Tears are the blood of a man's spirit. Do not let it bleed. Strength is born in the spirit. Torka will need his strength . . . to track Lonit and Karana and Manaak's woman. . . ."

"They live?"

"No thanks . . . to this old man. They took them east . . . in the last waning hours of the storm. . . ." A deep, low garble rose to choke him. His hand fell to grip Torka's forearm as he willed himself to endure his pain. "Torka . . . must go . . . now. . . ."

Gently, as though he held an injured child, Torka gathered his grandfather into his arms and held him close, as if, through the power of his love, he could keep death away. "We will go together, as Umak once brought Torka out of the way of the wind, to a new life, so Torka will carry Umak until he is well and strong again."

"Hrrmmph! That would not . . . be . . . a good thing." His lungs had been seared in the fire; blistered tissue made every word an agony. But he was Umak. He mastered the spirits of his pain, and although he fought for every phrase, he smiled as he spoke, knowing that even now, at the very end of his life, he *was* a spirit master. In a rasping whisper, he spoke to Torka of the past, and of the future that now rested with him. "The People . . . they live in you . . . forever."

"Forever . . ."

Aar lay down and nuzzled his snout beneath the old man's hand while the female dog, still untrusting of Man, lay down at the edges of the ruined encampment.

"My brother, once more it is time for this old man to walk away upon the wind. But this time, Brother Dog will not stop me. . . ."

The wind rose. The darkness thickened. Far off within the distant eastern ranges, there was a roaring *within* the wind, a trumpeting. Torka listened to the easily recognizable voice of a mammoth. Thunder Speaker? World Shaker? The Destroyer? *Or Death itself*, he thought, filled with hatred for the beast whose predations had ultimately brought him here, to this terrible moment of absolute despair.

"Listen. It walks before us . . . into the face of the rising sun!" Euphoria lightened Umak's voice. Within Torka's arms, his body rose, then fell back.

"Father of my father?" Torka dared not ask the question.

Aar answered it. With his head pointed skyward, Brother Dog cried a high song of mourning for the spirit of an old man who walked the wind at last.

3

Within the freezing dark, a light glowed like a cold white eye that stared unblinking across the miles. The furred, cowled men pointed and grunted with obvious appreciation as they prodded their captives with their spears.

"Klamah! Klamah!"

"Hurry! Hurry!" echoed Karana in his own tongue, belligerently leaning into the wind and walking as slowly as he could.

Ahead of him, Iana tripped, and when Lonit bent and tried to assist her to her feet, her reward was a brutal spear poke to the back that sent her sprawling. Infuriated, Karana sprang to her defense, but his hobbles brought him up short, and now all three captives were on the ground.

Those who had taken them were not amused. Long, barbed spears gave clear commands that words did not have to speak. The two women helped each other to their feet. Karana rose, made a grab for one of the offending spears, and was kicked so hard that he ended on the ground again.

Was it the blow? Or was it something else? The boy sat clutching his gut, gasping for breath as something moved deep within his chest and belly. Like clouds scudding across a full moon, he saw shadows, *felt* them within himself, and knew with a bleak, expanding emptiness within his heart that Umak was dead. The spirit of the old man who had touched him now moved within him and around him. He reached out to grasp it, to hold the invisible substance of what had once been the soul of Umak, but such things could not be held. And yet, as he was booted to his feet and pushed along by his captors, somehow it was still with him. He cocked his head

and realized that it would be with him always, a part of him
forever.

"Hmmph!" he exclaimed, and did not wince when the
blunt end of a spear was rammed hard into the small of his
back to silence him.

They walked for hours. The cold white light was a beacon
toward which the fur-clad men directed their steps until,
toward dawn, the light disappeared and they paused to rest,
hunkering down in the snow to eat their traveling rations
before curling up to sleep. When they awoke, one of the
heavily garbed men took the infant from a passive Iana and
handed the baby to Lonit. He said something to the others,
low and grating words that made them laugh with dark intent. Several of them came to his side to join him in taking
turns sating themselves upon Iana. Manaak's woman neither
yielded nor resisted. She lay with them like a limp, vacant-
eyed doll.

Lonit closed her eyes and held the baby close. She knew
that it lived only as long as Iana complied with her captors'
wishes. Memories of death—terrible, bloody, purposeless
death—ran red behind her lids. She opened her eyes and sat
shivering, close to Karana.

"Why have they not killed us? And why did they not gut
me along with poor Naknaktup?"

The boy, cross-legged beside her, stared out across the
darkening miles. "Karana knows only what he has heard
others say of the Ghost Band. They steal women and boys.
Naknaktup was older than you, and no beauty. When we
reach their encampment, the Ghost Men will take us down
into the earth and we will die to this world forever."

Lonit's mouth worked with bitterness as she listened to
the animalistic grunts and moans of pleasure that her captors
made as they found release within Iana. "They are men, not
ghosts," she said. "So we must continue to walk slowly, to
drag our feet so that our tracks are clear. Our captors think
that they have killed or captured us all. They do not know of
Torka. They must never know what gives strength and hope
to Lonit and Karana."

The boy nodded. Unconsciously, he mimicked his beloved spirit master as he crossed his arms over his chest,
jabbed his chin skyward, and turned his mouth down.
"Hmmph, it *is* so," he said in a whisper of what he wished
was absolute certainty. "Torka *will* find us!"

*   *   *

But the weather changed and the wind turned. Once again it blew with a demonic intensity that whipped fallen snow into smothering rivers of air. Travel was impossible. Footprints were erased from the world, and after two interminably long days and nights of storm, a bereft Torka emerged from the lee of a tundral hillock, where he and the dogs had curled against the cold, to look upon a tundra that was wiped clean of any trace of those who walked ahead of him.

For a long while he stood staring, listening, his heart as empty as the land that stretched before him. Then resolutely he went forward into the face of the rising sun. The dogs snuffled as they trotted beside him, as though querying his reasons for traveling into unknown land.

"Lonit is there, and Karana," he informed them, unaware that he was doing the very thing for which he had so often criticized Umak; he was talking to the dogs as though they were capable of understanding his words.

The days that followed were brief intervals of pale, wind-tattered light through which Torka loped with Aar at his side and the female dog following at a wary distance. The nights were long spans of wind-chilled darkness through which he tried to sleep so that he could travel with little or no need of rest in the hours of light. But on the third night, he awoke in the deep darkness that precedes the dawn and, for the first time, fully focused on the bright star that burned cold and white on the mountainous horizon. The star did not move! It was *not* a star. It was a beacon! He cursed himself. The marauders were traveling by night, gaining the extra hours, following a signal fire that could not be seen by daylight.

He was immediately on his feet, scooping up his weapons, then moving toward the light. The dogs whined, but he ignored them. The mountains were near—long, hulking ranges smothered by glaciers. There was the strong smell of ice in the wind, but he caught neither sight nor scent of travelers or encampments. If those who had taken Lonit, Karana, Iana, and little Ninipik were members of the Ghost Band, they were well named. Trailing them was like trying to follow a cloud after it has vanished from the sky. But now, at least, he had a light to guide him.

He traveled all that day, keeping his course straight for that part of the mountains where he had seen the light. He stopped only long enough to appease his exhaustion, sleeping little, eating less. Although the land was rising, the mountains seemed no nearer. He went on, into the night and the next day until fatigue dropped him and he lay upon the tundra, watching the dogs hunting for themselves. They worked as a team, sharing their food and their sleeping place. He thought of Lonit, and his pain over her loss was unbearable. He buried his head in his forearm and slept without bothering to eat. When he awoke, it was to Aar's nuzzling of his hand. The dog stood over him. The animal had placed the midsection of a hare, with head and extremities chewed off, before his face. Aar stared at him, apparently waiting for him to eat the offering. Torka was hungry enough to comply. As he gnawed the unexpected gift, he recalled the many times that, at Umak's insistence, the food of the band had been shared with the dog.

The light was close now. The marauders strode forward with confidence. Exhausted, Lonit again felt the deep pull of pain creep from her lower back around her pelvis. She had listened to enough woman talk within Galeena's encampment to know that such pains were the onset of labor. Her infant, *Torka's* infant, was ready to be born. *Torka!* She bit her lip to keep from crying out his name.

The mountains were dead ahead of them, and the land beneath their feet was slowly rising to meet them. Karana had been walking apart from the women. Now he came to walk beside Lonit.

"From the crest of the hills, I saw him!" His voice was a whisper that somehow managed to roar with triumph. "A man with two dogs running at his side! It was dark, but in the starlight, I saw him! It *has* to be Torka!" For the first time since the raiders had come to the encampment, he saw Lonit's face dimple into a tremulous smile. For the last two days, she had looked so pale and wan, he had begun to fear for her; so he did not tell her that what he had seen had been so far away that the image had appeared to be no more than three tiny shadows moving upon the snow-whitened land. Not one of the Ghost Men had noted the movement. But Karana had seen it. He had *known* that it was Torka because, as on the ledge when the spirit of the mountain had warned him of danger, something within him had spoken the truth of Torka's presence to his soul; but he did not think that Lonit would believe him. "We have only to slow our captors down

for another night—perhaps two—and leave whatever signs of
our passing we can, to help him follow us."

Her smile faded. Her eyes strayed to the hulking, shaggy
forms who stalked out ahead of her, using their spears as
prods to assure the firmness and depth of the snow that lay
beneath their feet. Behind and to each side of her, other men
walked—ugly, tattooed men with hideous bone labrets piercing their lower lips and protruding downward over their
chins like carved, saliva-slickened fangs. *Killers,* she thought.
*Men who carry spears and daggers not only to hunt and
protect themselves from predators, but to enable them to be
predators of their own kind.* "If Torka comes for us . . ." She
stopped herself before she spoke her fear aloud and thus
assured that it would come to pass, but the words were in her
eyes as she looked at the boy. *If Torka comes for us, they will
kill him.*

Ahead of her, the man in the lead suddenly stopped,
raised an arm, and called out what sounded like a greeting.
Lonit and Karana looked ahead, puzzled, but glad for the
opportunity to rest . . . until they saw figures coming toward
them out of the foothills. They carried torches of what appeared to be tallow-soaked grasses and skins bound onto the
rib bones of large game animals. Soon they were there,
breathless, smiling, ugly men who embraced the marauders
as though they were long-awaited brothers returning from a
hunt.

And so they were. Only their quarry had not been game,
it had been slaves. Dizzied by a concept too alien to comprehend fully, Lonit found herself the object of their scrutiny as
they pulled back her hood and passed her from man to man.
Each of them handled her, touched her belly, and seemed
pleased as they exchanged animated words of congratulations
to her captors. They put their hands on Iana then and examined her strong, bawling little son, nodding, grunting all the
while. Then they turned their attention to Karana, poking at
him, leering as though he were a nubile young girl, handling
him as provocatively as they had handled the women, until
the boy screamed in outrage and made one of them regret
that he had removed his gloves before beginning his trespass
into Karana's garments.

Lonit cringed, certain that they were going to strike Karana
dead for his action. They laughed instead and pushed the boy
as though he had pleased them. The man he had bitten

sucked blood from his wound, loosed a snare line from his belt with his free hand, and while two others held Karana, he looped the sinew cord and slipped it around the boy's neck.

"Shliank!" he exclaimed, and jerked the tether hard, pulling Karana close.

Lonit did not have to speak his language to know that he had just announced to all that Karana was now his. For the first time, she noted that this man's labrets were more elaborately carved and twice as long as those of his kinsmen. In his dark, shaggy bison skins, he was a grotesque but undeniably powerful man. Fanged like a beast, his face was so darkened by the swirling black patterns of his tattoos that, even in the light of the torches, she could see nothing but the pure, dangerous savagery of his features. When he commanded the others to move on, not a man among them hesitated, and when Karana strained against his lead, the man only jerked it harder. Strangling, the boy was forced to follow.

Toward the light.

It was an eye glaring at them from the side of a narrow, elongated mound that rose at the base of the foothills. And then, slowly, the eye opened. Men emerged from it.

Fear crawled within Lonit's belly as she balked and was prodded onward across broad stretches of snowfree talus that would never hold the tracks of men. Karana walked ahead of her, choking as he fought against the pull of the tether. On and on they walked, up the side of the embankment, into the eye.

Lonit cried out in terror. Behind her, for the first time since Iana had been forced to endure rape for the sake of her child, Manaak's woman made a sound. It was a soft, squirming, mewling exhalation that begged for mercy. For herself. For her baby. For Lonit and Karana.

But there was to be no mercy for any of them. This was the destination toward which they had been driven. There would be no turning away from it now. Hard, unyielding hands gripped Lonit from behind, shoved her forward onto the mound, then upward toward the eye. She saw at last that it was only a gaping hole within the shoulder of the embankment. From deep within the earth, light shone, and a hideous, animalistic, fanged face grinned up at her as, against her will, she was lifted up by the back of her armpits and handed down, down, into the eye, to waiting hands.

She nearly fainted as heat and stench and light enveloped

her. Placed onto her feet upon moist and slippery ground, she was surrounded by leering, naked men with oiled bodies that were tattooed from their foreheads to their toes, including their genitals.

Again she was handled, her garments invaded, her belly touched. She tried to break away but was mocked for her efforts, turned around and around, pressed against, then pushed forward, deeper into the eye, down along a stinking, slippery-floored corridor that ran deep and then laterally beneath the surface of the mound.

It opened into another passage, with a short, nearly vertical stairway with a framework of bones, which led into a small, skin-lined room in which many spears were stacked, and out of which several torchlit tunnels branched.

Disoriented, Lonit, for the first time, succumbed to despair. Behind her, Iana was weeping. Karana was nowhere to be seen. As Manaak's woman was forced into one tunnel and Lonit was pushed ahead into another, her thoughts were like frightened birds flying into a storm. *Karana was right. These men are of flesh, but also are ghosts. Not even a tracker as skilled as Torka will ever find us here.*

It was Aar who first picked up the scent of Man and ran in circles, snuffling, nose to ground, tail wagging madly while the female dog cocked her head with curiosity and watched him. When Torka found the first of the tracks nearby and recognized the bootprints of Lonit and Karana, he whooped with joy. The female dog cocked her head in the other direction and whimpered softly, thoroughly confused by the behavior of the males of her pack.

"Torka will find his woman," he vowed grimly. "And in stealth, with bludgeon and blade and spear hurler, this one man will make many men pay for what they have done."

They went ever eastward, toward the mountains until they reached the talus slopes and lost the trail where the snowpack ended. Aar picked up the scent and ran in several directions, returning at last, as darkness claimed the world, to where Torka sat alone, hoping to sight the night fire by which he might be guided. But there was no light except that of the cold, distant stars. From the east, he heard the not-too-distant sounds of mammoth. A calf calling, a cow's reply, and then the voice of another calf, older than the first, but high with adolescence and quivering with distress. The dogs heard the mammoths' cries, and their heads went up as they whimpered softly, as though in sympathy.

Torka was suddenly struck by the realization that, like the dogs, he understood the communications of the mammoths as clearly as though they had spoken to one another in his own language:

"*Mother! Where are you? I am afraid!*"

"*Child. Be still. I will come for you.*"

"*Mother. My sibling is in trouble. Come quickly!*"

"*Children. Be calm. Do not be afraid. By light or dark, I will stand with you.*"

Torka listened. The mammoths' sounds continued, then stopped. The cow had comforted her little ones. His thoughts astounded him. How could this be? Mammoths were prey. They possessed the spirits of beasts, not men. Mammoths could not love or grieve or worry. Or seek vengeance against those who had brought their loved ones to grief or destruction. Or could they?

Suddenly bitterly cold, Torka looked at the dogs lying curled one against the other. The female had abandoned her pack to be with Aar. Why, if she did not love him? His own love for Lonit was like a stone within his throat, choking him with his need to find her and Karana and to avenge the deaths of Manaak and Naknaktup and his beloved grandfather.

Memories of a huge, hate-maddened red eye crowded in on him. The Destroyer's attack had come as he and Nap and Alinak were trying to butcher the fallen cow. Had the Destroyer been her mate? Could the great mammoth have loved her? Could an animal think like a man? *Love* like a man? *Hate* like a man?

No! Torka was certain that it could not be so. In time, he would kill the Destroyer and drink its blood in the name of his lost band, Egatsop, Kipu, and his infant daughter, who had not lived long enough to know any of life's joys.

His mouth was set. His eyes stared out across the dark and savage land. Now he had other prey to hunt—murderous, woman-stealing, slave-taking men. And for one man alone, they would be every bit as dangerous and as difficult to kill as any mammoth.

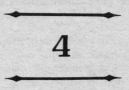

4

Lonit screamed, but her voice was absorbed by the suffocating, airless confines of the tiny room in which she lay. It
was one of several cubicles that were located at the end of the
Ghost House's innumerable warrenlike underground passage-
ways. Like the tunnels, its walls and conical roof were braced
with rib bones and mammoth tusks, then chinked with the
same thick mud of human feces mixed with grass and refuse
that covered the floors. The entire room oozed and stank and
emanated heat like a festering wound.

Lonit screamed again and gasped for air.

Several tattooed women sat around her as she labored to
give birth. They had placed her upon a bed composed of
several thicknesses of mildewed furs lain across a mattress of
moldy grass and lichen. Beneath the bed, a frame of mammoth ribs kept the mattress from spilling over onto the warm,
fetid slime of the floor. In the dull, flickering glow given off
by two oil lamps that burned on stands of caribou skulls
propped onto bone posts, the women's faces were a blur of
oily, darkened sameness until one of them folded into a smile
of empathy and understanding. She rose to see to Lonit's
plea.

Naked except for a loincloth of feathers, the woman was
nearly as tall as Lonit. She reached the apex of the room's
ceiling with no difficulty and removed a large sod from its
center. The warm, stinking air rushed up and out, forming
vapors as cold air entered.

Lonit drank it in. It was sweet, it was clean; it was from
the world above, where Torka lived and looked for her and,
by now, must have given up all hope of ever finding her. It
took all of her effort to keep herself from calling his name.

One of the women snapped a rebuke at the woman who had opened the air vent. The tall woman closed it, and the other women mumbled in appreciation. Lonit nearly retched as the stench of the room closed in on her again. The tall woman, seeing her discomfort, reopened the vent. The other women spoke to her sharply, in what sounded like several different dialects, but the tall woman merely glared at them, her tattooed hands resting on wide, tattooed hips. The others rose, one of them yelling a sentence that ended sharply with the word *gulap*. The tall woman responded with an even sharper sentence that ended with the same word. The others rose as one in a communal huff and left the cubicle by way of a low, hide-covered exit that was little more than a hole in the wall. The tall woman sighed, shook her head, and came to sit with Lonit.

"Gulap will come anyway," she said.

Lonit was startled to hear her own language spoken.

The tall woman smiled at her obvious recognition of their shared tongue. "You and Aliga, we talk same talk. Must come from same part of the world. Far away. To the west, yes?"

"Yes!"

Aliga's smile thinned into wistfulness. "Times were good there. A long time back. It is best we forget. This place stinks like a corpse in summer, but it is good to know that in spite of all this stink, we *are* alive."

At that moment another contraction took control of Lonit's senses—a pain so intense, so absolute, that for a moment nothing existed except the pain. A tide of excruciating pressure bore her down, down until . . . slowly . . . it began to ease.

Aliga lay a questing palm across her abdomen. "Your baby will come soon now."

"Where is Iana? I would have her with me now."

"Your friend, she is with the men. She is new, so they will use her for a long time. Be glad you are here. After the baby comes, I will give you a drink if you want, to make bleeding last long time. No man will touch you while you bleed."

"What have they done with Iana's baby?"

"Strong boy, that baby! Many women here will be proud to suckle him. When he is bigger, Ghost Men will take him to the great gathering of mammoth hunters not far from here.

Ghost Men will trade him for many good things, and for more women."

Lonit stared, afraid to ask the next question. "And Karana . . . will they trade him, too?"

"Little one with limp? No, he is pretty like a girl. Ghost Men will use him like a woman. In some bands, such boys are valuable to hunters on long treks without their women." She saw the expression of incomprehension upon Lonit's face. "On long treks, boys do not bleed, boys do not get babies in belly. More valuable than women to some." She sighed, with infinite sadness. "Your friend is lucky to have a boy baby. This woman hopes you have the same. Then Ghost Men will let your baby live . . . if Gulap says the omens are good."

"Gulap?"

"She is oldest sister of headman, the mother of his favorite sons. She is very old now, and very smart. Very clever to live so long in a band such as this." Aliga grew suddenly quiet. Women's voices could be heard approaching the blood room. Aliga put a warning hand on Lonit's wrist. "Be brave, be strong, Woman Of The West, and say nothing to anger Gulap. The headman has said that you will belong to him when your bearing blood has ceased to flow. He has said that he will tattoo you himself. This is a great honor but has made Gulap very angry at you. Never again will her brother look at her as he has looked at you."

"But this woman is ugly! Why should he want me?"

Aliga looked at Lonit as though she could not believe what she was hearing. "You have the eyes of the running doe. It is considered a mark of great beauty among many bands. It is as rare as the white lion, or the call of the loon whose back bears no stripes. The rare thing, the unusual thing, it is valued above all else. You are beautiful, Lonit, Woman Of The West. Can it be that no one has ever told you that?"

"Only one. But it has been enough. . . . It has been *everything.* . . ."

All night long the mammoths cried sad sounds of mourning. Torka slept fitfully until dawn softly colored the tundra and an incredibly foul stench came to him on the back of the east wind. The dogs had smelled it, too. They had risen as one, turning toward the stink, and then away from it. They exhaled through their nostrils as though trying to cleanse them; then, suddenly restless, Aar began to circle and sniff again, whimpering to himself.

Torka rose, recognizing the smell of Man in the wind. It was twice as foul with rotting refuse and offal as that of the ledge after Galeena had taken it over. It was undeniably the stench of an encampment. But although he scanned the horizon until his eyes teared and burned, he could see no signs of life at all . . . until Aar turned, faced due north, and froze.

Torka followed the eyes of the dog, and for a moment he too was unable to respond.

A long column of people was advancing toward him—too many people to constitute the marauding band for which he had been searching. He could see females bent beneath heavy loads, and men carrying spears and snow prods. If there were small children, he could not see them. A small group of hunters was trotting toward him, calling out, their spear arms raised. He stood his ground, with his own spear at the ready and Aar growling at his side.

The men were dressed in finely worked skins, and as they approached, they bore the scent of those who did not live in squalor. The leader of the group paused just out of spear range, his arm raised. Another, younger, man came forward to stand beside him. He wore garments stitched entirely of the white belly skin of winter-killed caribou. He also raised an arm, and as he did, the hawk talons that were strung from the bottom seam of his medicine bag jangled in the wind.

Torka did not move until the first man threw down his spear as a sign of peaceful intent. The man in white did the same, although Torka sensed a certain reluctance in his gesture.

"We seek the great gathering of mammoth hunters at the entrance to the Corridor of Storms." The voice of the first man was as clear and devoid of threat as a cloudless sky.

"We have heard the call of mammoths in the night. We would hunt!" The second man's voice was as lean and sharp as a well-knapped projectile. "Where is your band, Man Who Walks With Dogs?"

It was not the tone of the men's words that struck Torka. It was their dialect. He knew it as well as he knew his own—it was Karana's tongue. As he took note of the number of the strangers and the lack of children among them, he knew instinctively that these were Karana's people.

With no further concern for his own safety, he threw down his spear. "I am Torka! I seek the Ghost Band that has stolen my woman and Karana, son of Supnah! If you are that man, then join with me. This day we will hunt men, not mammoth!"

Within the Ghost House, Karana feigned sleep. Stripped of his clothes, he lay very still, afraid that movement would draw his tormentors back to resume their unnatural mauling of him. He could hear them now, sloshing urine over themselves in the adjoining sweat room. He had pretended not to understand them, even though his natural gift for unraveling the various threads that composed the markedly different tongue had served him well. Now that they had sated themselves upon him—and upon one another—they spoke of pursuing other prey.

The sound of the mammoths had excited them almost as much as their manhandling of Karana. It was evident from the way the beasts were calling that one or more of them was mired. The others were staying close, trying to help or to offer comfort.

The marauders spoke of how the headman had already led a large party of scouts from the Ghost House to determine the whereabouts of the mammoths and of the pleasure they would all soon take when the killing of the beasts began.

Karana listened, hating them, hating the way they had bruised him deep inside his body where no man had the right to bruise another, let alone a half-grown boy. Their voices rose and fell. Karana's hatred rose and congealed into an unswervable resolve.

Go. And while you hunt, I will take up my clothes and escape, upward like smoke through the vent of this room before anyone can catch me. I will find Torka and lead him here. Together we will see if Ghost Men bleed as easily as the men and women whom they kill for pleasure.

The premise was invigorating, but it suddenly occurred to him that he had no idea what they had done with his clothes. His eyes strayed along the contours of the bone ladder that led upward to the vent of the room. A cold and hostile world lay there, through the sod hatch. If he moved quickly, he could make his break for freedom now. Not one of the robust, well-fed Ghost Men could follow through the vent, but Karana was small and agile enough to wriggle through it if he tried. He trembled at the challenge, then at the realization that he had no hope of survival without his clothes—unless he found

Torka immediately. And what were the chances of that? What if he had been mistaken about his sighting? What if the shadows that he had seen moving upon the tundra had only been tricks of the wind and the starlight?

From off along one of the stinking, labyrinthine tunnels of the Ghost House, Karana heard Lonit cry out. He felt her pain and knew her fear. He closed his eyes tightly, commanding the spirit of courage to grow within him. Lonit was Torka's woman. To Torka, he owed his life. Within the Ghost House, Karana, Lonit, Iana, and little Ninipik were already dead to the world above.

Perhaps a naked boy might survive, he thought as, slowly, he rose from the foul mattress of furs and lichens.

Torka is alive. Torka is near. As on that cold, clear morning when the mountain had spoken to him from out of his own spirit, the voice that told him that Torka was alive was a spirit voice. Karana could no more have disregarded it than he could have ignored the cries of Lonit. He had heard women in labor before. Lonit's time was very near. And Karana's time to escape was now.

Naked or clothed, he might never get the chance again. In absolute stealth, he peeled back the bed furs from the mattress, and with the speed of an eagle launched from its perch, Karana flew up the ladder, shoved the sod to one side, and forced his body through the vent, back into the world of the living.

With Aar on the scent and leading them as though he were master of the pack, Torka and the men of Supnah's band advanced across the tundra in search of the Ghost House, following the stench of Man that had briefly risen from the earth to foul the wind. For a moment it returned, strong and sweet with the stink of hot urine and decomposing refuse and fecal matter. Then it was gone, as completely as though they had imagined it.

They paused, scenting like animals. Supnah's even, weather-lined features were taut with concentration as, beside him, the man in the skins of winter-killed caribou knelt, balancing his weight upon the balls of his feet. "Is my brother, Supnah, certain that he wishes to follow these Ghost Men when we have spent half a lifetime successfully avoiding contact with them?"

"If Karana is with them, Supnah will follow," replied the older man.

"Karana *is* with them," said Torka emphatically. "And this man says that ghosts do not leave tracks by which they may be followed."

Navahk, magic man, eyed Torka out of cold, heavily lidded eyes that seemed to see right through him. Torka could not remember ever having seen a handsomer man, or one whom he instinctively distrusted more. Not even Galeena had elicited such a negative reaction from him at their first meeting. Perhaps his experience with that headman had adversely colored his attitude toward all strangers? He could not be certain. He felt no repugnance toward Supnah, even though he found it difficult to overlook the fact that he had abandoned Karana. Nevertheless, Torka saw the resemblance to the boy in the father's weatherworn face, and responded to the clear-eyed intelligence that honed his features and defined his open, albeit cautious nature. Supnah was totally unlike his younger brother.

The magic man's every word and gesture were guarded. His long, full mouth was set into a perpetual smirk, as though he held a great and wonderful secret that no man save him would ever know until it was too late and even then it would not matter, because no one but Navahk was capable of understanding it. Torka had not been with Supnah's band for more time than it took to tell them of how Karana had followed an eagle to a safe refuge upon the Mountain of Power before he had felt the eyes of the magic man boring right through him. He had turned to look at the man, and Navahk had smiled in the most friendly manner, showing wide, perfect teeth that were oddly pointed, as though he possessed an entire mouthful of canines; but it was not the man's unusual teeth that caught Torka's attention and put him on guard. It was his eyes. There were depths within them that warned of treacherous undercurrents. For reasons of his own, although he smiled and pretended otherwise, Navahk was not glad to hear that Karana, his brother's son, was alive, nor was he eager to take the opportunity to rescue him from the Ghost Band.

But Supnah was elated. He seemed half a lifetime younger. "Karana was abandoned by this man once. It will not be so again!" He put a strong, beautifully gloved hand upon

Torka's forearm. "It is good that the spirits have guided us to this meeting."

"It *is* good," agreed Torka.

Navahk, magic man, said nothing.

The hunters shook their spears, and all agreed that if Supnah willed it, then it was time to hunt the Ghost Band; too long had that band preyed upon others as though their fellow men were beasts who might be hunted like animals.

Navahk's smile deepened. "Can men hunt spirits? It is said that, because the Ghost Men possess no true flesh, they must steal the women of human bands. Otherwise they would have no sons. Can we feel anger toward them for that?"

"Were it your woman they had stolen, you would have no need to justify your anger," said Torka coldly. "And this man says to you that they took more than women from Torka's camp. They took furs and what little food we had. Ghosts do not need to eat or to clothe themselves. They sound less like ghosts than like men who would rather prey upon the women of other bands than take the time to raise girl-children of their own."

A murmuring went through the hunters. The corners of Navahk's lips pulled inward, creating hollows beneath his high, rounded cheekbones. "It is said that they are great, shaggy spirits, with the bodies of bison and the stabbing fangs of leaping cats. It is said that their faces are black, and that the only time that men may look upon them without being killed is when they come to the great gathering to gain women for trade goods. They come in the mist and disappear into the mist. No men have ever dared to hunt them as we do now."

Again the hunters murmured. This time they looked to Supnah, waited for him to refute his brother. He was momentarily at a loss for words.

Torka knew that Navahk was playing upon the fears of the others. Was the magic man afraid? Torka measured his smile, his eyes, and the straight, lean lines of his body within the white casing of his clothes. No. Torka was certain that fear was an emotion that did not come easily to Navahk. There were subtler motivations beneath his reluctance to pursue the Ghost Band. His tongue was as cold and quick and dangerous as a river in spring flood. From the way the others behaved toward him, it was apparent to Torka that Supnah was not the only decision maker in this band. Navahk's judgment was sought in all things. Together Supnah and Navahk shaped and steadied the lives of their people; but although Navahk openly shared in the leadership of the band, Supnah bore the ultimate responsibility for its successes or failures. No wonder the magic man smiled, thought Torka, remembering that Karana had told him that it was because of omens seen by Navahk that Supnah had left his son to care for the other children of the band while the adults went off in search of food. The memory disturbed him. Why would Navahk have advised such a thing? And how could Supnah have listened to him?

Ahead, in the distant turnings of one of the mountain canyons, the mammoths began to call to one another again. Distracted and suddenly impatient, Torka gestured toward the sound. "Go, then. Hunt mammoth. This man will search for the Ghost Band. For his woman, for the woman and child of one who was a friend to him, and for a boy who has been as a son to him, Torka will go on alone. He is not afraid."

He had meant to goad them, to sting their pride, and by so doing force them to commit themselves to the course that he so desperately needed them to take. Alone, he had virtually no chance at success. With nearly twenty armed men beside him, success might just be assured.

But they stood and stared. Their magic man's statements had robbed them of their zeal. Even Supnah seemed uncertain now.

"How can we know that Karana is still alive and not a spirit?" the headman asked.

Torka felt disgust for Supnah. He was weak, and Navahk manipulated him like a strip of soggy sinew. He was not fit to be headman. "We cannot know. We can only try to find out." With that, he turned and walked away before he lost control of his tongue and made a statement that so impugned the manhood of Supnah that his own life would be forfeit. If Karana, Lonit, Iana, and little Ninipik were to be found, he would have to find them alone.

He lengthened his stride, so frustrated and angry that he was half-blind with suppressed rage. Aar and his female ran ahead of him, noses to the earth, tails up, cutting wide circles until, suddenly, Aar stopped dead in his tracks.

From out of the east, a small, naked boy was stumbling toward them.

*   *   *

The old woman's face was black. There was not an inch of her skin, including her eyelids and ears, that was not tattooed with swirling dots that whirled over her features in patterns resembling the ribboning spirals of the aurora borealis.

Lonit stared at her through a haze of exhaustion and ebbing pain. Never had she seen such a hideous apparition. Green mold colored the woman's brows and lashes. Repeated rinsings in urine had brittled her hair and bleached it yellow. It fuzzed around her face like an aura of matted spider webs upon which some animal had relieved itself. Her features were hidden in folds of oiled, weathered skin that was full of peaks and valleys. And out of those peaks and valleys, a chasm opened—it was the woman's mouth. From out of the mouth poured words that Lonit could not understand, but they were spoken in the voice of youth, not age. It was like hearing a newborn infant cry out with a voice of an adult. Lonit was so startled that, for an instant, she forgot the fear that had come to her when Gulap had entered the Blood Room.

Now Gulap smiled, displaying small, tattooed teeth that had been filed down to points—a mark of beauty among the women of the Ghost Band. She shook a rattle over Lonit. It was a hollowed sloth's claw into which the bones of rodents had been placed. They made small, dry clickings, punctuating Gulap's words. As she spoke, the other women began to keen. Gulap's smile widened.

Lonit closed her eyes. The pain was returning; it was a terrible, strapping pain that encircled her back and belly like an invisible belt that was being tightened and tightened until she was certain that it was going to cut her in half. The sound of the women's low mourning seemed to intensify the pain. They held her upright in the birth position. She was glad for that. She was too weak to kneel alone. But she wished they would stop their ululations. She wished—.

Pain suddenly ripped upward into her body as, with a brutal thrust, Gulap turned her rattle into a dagger that entered Lonit, pierced the water-filled caul that surrounded her baby, and pulled out. Lonit's eyes were wide as she screamed against the violation. Only the tension of her muscles, locked in the vise grip of a contraction, had kept the now-bloodied claw from penetrating the flesh and bone of her baby.

Gulap spoke. Gulap shook her head. She watched Lonit

protectively recoil, violently tearing herself from the arms of the women who held her. Aliga was closest. She looked sorrowful and repentant as she translated Gulap's words to Lonit.

"Gulap says she will end your woman pains. Gulap says it is better that your baby die. Gulap has seen bad omens for you: Your milk will be poison, and your infant will be unfit to suckle from any woman's breast."

"And so she will guarantee that by putting a hole in my baby's skull before it can take its first breath!" Lonit glared at Gulap, wanting the woman to know that she was not duped by her pretense to magic.

"Do not look so at the wise woman," cautioned Aliga.

"She is not wise, she is wicked! Tell her that this woman wants no part of her help with the bearing of this baby! Tell her that Lonit has no desire to be her brother's woman! Tell her that if she will stand aside, Lonit will have her baby and then leave this place. With Iana and the boy Karana, Lonit will go far and never look back!"

Aliga's head swung from side to side. "We would all go far and never look back if we could. If Gulap were to let you go, the men of this band would kill her."

"Tell her my words!"

Aliga shrugged and did as Lonit asked, showing no surprise when Gulap grinned with malevolence as she spoke directly to Lonit.

Aliga translated. "Gulap says that the boy Karana has run naked into the cold. He has been gone for a long time now and must be dead. When those who have left the Ghost House to hunt mammoth return, they will be very angry and will punish the hunters who were careless enough to allow such a pretty boy to escape. Even now Liquah and Tlah look for his body. When they find it, they will skin it. Gulap will make a dress of it for you to wear when your bearing blood has ceased to flow. It will make the headman smile to take you and what is left of the boy at the same time. And in the meantime, Gulap says that Woman Of The West should not worry about her baby. It is cursed. Male or female, it matters not. The minute it is born, Gulap herself will take it out and feed its spirit to the wind."

Brother Dog welcomed Karana with such enthusiasm that the boy was knocked flat. The hunters of Supnah's band would have speared the beast that seemed to be devouring their leader's long-lost son; but Torka shouted "hold," and in a few moments Karana was running toward them again, with Aar trotting happily at his side, licking at his hand while the female dog followed, whimpering in confusion.

Never had the hunters of Supnah's band seen a boy walk with a beast as though it were his brother. They whispered among themselves, wondering by what magic the small, naked boy stumbled past them, with an animal loping at his side as though its spirit were enchanted into believing that it was a human being instead of a wild dog.

Navahk watched and listened resentfully as Karana paused before his father and accepted the obligatory welcome from the headman of his band. For a long time, Supnah looked at the boy with eyes that spoke of a love that was deeper than his words could express. He put his hands upon the child's shoulders. He called him Boy Who Follows Eagle. He wrapped him in clothing brought quickly by other members of the band.

Karana was proud to accept the name. He was glad to be reunited with his father. Yet there was a strange, bittersweet emptiness within his heart where filial love should have been. Supnah had turned his back upon him and abandoned him to the storms of the time of the long dark. On the other hand, Torka had risked his life to face into those storms in order to save him. It was Torka to whom he owed his loyalty now. It was Torka to whom he turned, embracing him shamelessly, as a son embraces a beloved father. When Torka returned his embrace and called him Little Hunter, that childhood endearment was more welcome than the bolder name that Supnah had given him. Boy Who Follows Eagle. He *was* that. But he was also Little Hunter, and he knew that he would always be Torka's son. And Lonit's brother.

"She lives," he said. "She cries out in childbirth, and her life is in great danger in the most terrible place that this boy has ever seen. This boy will take you there. Together we will bring Lonit out of the spirit world and back into the world of the living!"

"So they *are* ghosts. . . ." Navahk's words were half statement, half question, spoken in a tone as soft as the finest sinew.

Somehow, as Karana paled, Torka felt a sinew noose fall around his neck and tighten.

"Look!" Karana pointed eastward, glad to look away from his uncle.

Barely visible upon the distant talus slopes, two figures were trotting toward them. They moved in the stop-and-start way of trackers, and only the angle of the sun kept them from sighting Supnah's hunters in the shadows of the rolling tundra.

"Ghost Men," whispered Karana.

"You cannot be sure of that," said Navahk.

The boy nodded. "Their house is there, under that long mound that looks like a hill. They will be trailing me, I think. They would not want any of their captives to escape to bring others back to their hiding place or to tell others how easy it would be to kill them there. It would be like smoking badgers. The Ghost House is a great burrow with many tunnels and breathing vents; but the vents are very small, and there is only one entrance. Block that, close the vents, and they would all die."

"Or stand with spears at ready at the entrance, send fire into the vents, and then close them. They would come pouring out like the vermin they are rather than suffocate." Torka smiled at the concept; with a few refinements, it might work.

"Spirits are immortal. Those who would hunt them are risking their anger," said Navahk obliquely.

"The Ghost Men have risked *my* anger!" Torka shot back. "And now I will prove to you that they *are* men!"

He asked no man to follow but commanded Karana to remain behind. With his bludgeon and spear thrower at ready, he stalked those who sought Karana. It did not take him long. The first man never saw the spear that killed him. The second whirled, looking for adversaries who were not there. When Torka showed himself, he was so far out of normal spear range that the man threw all three of his spears, plus those of his fallen comrade, and not one of them came close. Torka smiled when he saw panic take the man. Now the Ghost Man was seeing a ghost.

He took his time picking up the man's spears. Slowly he gathered them, tested their balance, and found them crude but serviceable. The Ghost Man watched him, backing up, almost tripping over himself as he finally turned and began to run.

Propelled by his spear hurler, Torka's spears flew like missiles, one after the other. The first two landed ahead of the man, stopping him in midstep as the third pierced his back, to emerge through his belly, and two more embedded themselves in the backs of his thighs. Torka's mouth twisted with satisfaction as, from behind him, Supnah and his men approached, amazed by his prowess and the "magic" of his spear thrower.

"No magic," he told them, and offered to fashion a spear hurler for any man who wished to have one . . . but after they helped him to rescue his woman. They mumbled among themselves. He barely heard them as he leaned over the dying Ghost Man and rolled him onto his side, ignoring his cries as pain ripped through legs, in which spears were still imbedded. "You are no ghost," he snarled, remembering Manaak and Naknaktup and Umak as his hand curled in the leather at the man's throat. "Tell them what you are."

The Ghost Man's eyes bulged in his black face. Beneath the tattoos, the skin was paling as the luster of life began to fade from his eyes.

"Tell them!" Torka insisted, shaking him, savoring the knowledge that he roused pain.

"Man . . . I am . . . a man . . . I am. . . ."

"Soon a dead man," Karana said, jerking the spear from the man's gut, knowing that in doing so, he disemboweled him. He would die slowly. As Karana had suffered slowly, under this man's maulings, under his weight, and under the terrible knowledge that this was the man who had hit Umak from behind and thrown him into the blazing pit hut to be burned alive.

5

They went forward under a lowering sky. Karana led the way, glad that Navahk had chosen to remain behind with several other men, who would guard their women against any large flesh-eaters that might come against them.

They were halfway to their destination in a world the color of slate when they dropped to the ground and lay flat. Their eyes slitted against the rising wind, they watched from the lee of a tundral slope as armed men emerged from the Ghost House and disappeared into one of the canyons that cleft the base of the eastern ranges. The wind blew toward them out of those high, glacier-choked vastnesses. The smell of ice was very strong. Now and then, the cry of a shrieking mammoth pierced the silence.

"They have gone to hunt the great tusked ones," said Karana. "The Ghost House will be nearly deserted, except for a few guards and the captives. We will steal back our women and be gone before those who hunt mammoth can return."

Supnah eyed the horizon speculatively. "The guards . . . we will have to kill them. This man has never killed another man."

Karana looked at his father, wondering if abandoning children to the winter dark was not the same as killing them.

"The Ghost Men are predators of their own kind," said Torka. "By their actions, they have made themselves prey to be hunted by other men. When they are dead, the people of the tundra will live without fear of their predations. To kill them . . . it will be a good thing." He trembled against a terrible resolve as he watched the last of the Ghost Men enter the distant canyon. *When they return, they will find their encampment as I found mine*, he thought. *When they return, they will die . . . but not until they see the corpses of their brothers and loved ones left for carrion, as I have seen them leave mine.*

Through low, narrow, stinking tunnels, the old woman walked and chortled, gloating over the obscene victory that she was about to claim.

The baby in her arms was beautiful, as beautiful as its mother and as strong. Gulap sucked at the remnants of her teeth. Her grin became a grimace. Woman Of The West had fought for this infant like a cornered lynx. She had scratched and bitten, and when the others had obeyed Gulap and tried to hold her down, she had resorted to a hard, outward kick that had caught the old woman squarely across the chin. Gulap's tongue explored the swollen, tender area beneath her lower lip. She could taste blood in the spongy depression where two teeth had been. Her grimace twisted downward into an expression of hatred that made her appear even uglier than usual.

Seated along the steamy, bone-lined tunnel that led toward the entrance to the Ghost House, one of the guards shuddered as he watched her pass. Would all females become as hideous as the headman's elder sister if allowed to live past the years of their prime? He closed his eyes and went back to dozing, sorry that he had looked up at her in the first place.

She stalked on, her booted feet slipping a little in the ooze of the floor. A little farther along, another man stood dozing on his feet. She gave him an elbow jab to his ample paunch as she walked by him and turned back, chuckling at his expense as he grabbed at his gut.

"Come! Put on your clothes! Gulap needs a man to walk ahead of her to keep her safe from flesh eaters as she goes to offer them this useless meat."

"A girl-child?"

"Not for long!" she exclaimed, squawking like a malevolent old bird until the guard opened the way before her into the world above. It had taken him only moments to slip on his surplice and loose-fitting boots. For what she had in mind for him, he would not need to be out in the cold for very long. He was up the ladder with all of the graceless ease of a bear bellying up a spruce tree.

Now the cold wind struck down at her, shriveling her

happiness as it reminded her of her lost youth—for despite the heavy garments that she had donned for her venture, she was chilled to the bone. Her filed teeth ached deep within her gums. She clamped her small tattooed lips in a grimace.

How many years had passed since she had been a resilient young girl impervious to the weather? Too many! How long ago had she been a bold and seasoned traveler mocking the slave women of the Ghost Band when they balked at crossing an icy autumn river? Too long! When the captives had wailed, she had flailed at them with small, hard fists, and when they cowered naked against the cold and the ice-thickened water, begging for their clothes, she had kicked them. Her bones would crack from such treatment today.

Now, as the freezing, heavy wind embraced her old bones, it invaded the loosely fitting upper portion of her tunic. Her free hand reached to pull up her hood, then stopped. It would do no good. The cold would find her flesh no matter how many layers of skins and furs she wore. Even within her sleeping nest of grass and lichens in the Ghost House, with all of her sleeping furs piled over her, she would shiver and her bones would ache—and she would lie awake, remembering her youth and the warmth of men who had once slept beside her. The men slept with young captive women now. Beautiful women. And she would grind what was left of her teeth and know that she would sleep alone until the end of her days.

"Mother . . . hand up the meat so that you may more easily climb the ladder!"

The guard's voice cut her as deeply as the chill of the wind. *Mother?* She was not that man's mother! Her reaction to his unintentional insult warmed her, for warmth always came from anger . . . and from the pleasure she found when inflicting pain on those who possessed the youth and beauty she could never have again.

She was suddenly no longer interested in performing the ritual murder of the baby in her arms. It was too young to fear her, to cower, and to show terror of her. It could but die, bleating like a goat. But its mother? That one could warm her old bones and take the ache from her teeth. Not through death, for Gulap would need the permission of the headman for that. It would probably come in time; but Gulap needed to be warm *now*.

Impatiently, she handed the infant up to the guard, telling him to take it far enough from the entrance of the Ghost House so that it would not draw predators.

"Pack its mouth with snow, and its nostrils. Let it suffocate. It is a bad death. But slap it first, so that it cries. I want its mother to hear it scream."

He shrugged and took the child. Its life or death was of no concern to him, but infant killing was woman's work. He silently cursed the old hag for sending him out into the bitter wind to attend to such a demeaning task while she returned to the warmth of the Ghost House.

As he climbed out of the mound, he could hear her chortling happily, shaking her bloodied sloth's-claw rattle. He hoped that she would trip and fall and impale herself on it.

Then he looked at the infant within his arms. The "meat" looked like its mother. He smiled, visualizing the blood-stained tip of the sloth's-claw rattle. He had seen Gulap use it. The mother of this child would live to lie beneath many men, but never again would she bear meat that would be offered to the storms.

They lay in wait. Hidden behind the mound, they let the man climb out of the earth. He stood with his back to them, breathing in the cold, clean air of the tundra as the wind combed through the stinking, matted strands of his bison-skin coat. He did not turn around.

It was the last mistake in judgment that the man would ever make. Supnah grabbed him from behind as Torka, his blood so stirred that he made no use of the ladder, leaped down into the interior, with his spear in one hand and his bludgeon in the other.

All along the labyrinthine corridors, the torches were flickering and dying. The strong smell of smoke and the stink of burning hides began to permeate the interior of the Ghost House, but try as she might, Aliga could not open the vent to the Blood Room; it seemed to have frozen shut.

Lonit did not care. They had taken her baby. They had exposed Torka's child. She was a captive in an underground world where she had no hope of ever seeing her man again. Her labor had been long and hard, but the birth itself had been quick and without complications. Nevertheless, as she lay upon her back, thinking of Iana's horrible fate, which she would soon share, she watched the wicks sputtering in the oil lamps and thought: *The room grows dim, but it does not matter. This woman can feel the light of her own life going out.* She closed her eyes. *It will be a good thing.*

Aliga shook her. "Lonit! Listen! Do you hear voices? Far off toward the entrance to the Ghost House. *Male* voices cursing in our own tongue."

The weariness of childbirth had made Lonit groggy. Compounded by the lack of air, she was sleepy, drifting in her own thoughts, only half hearing Aliga. "Iana. Where is Iana? I have not heard her baby cry. It must be a good baby."

Aliga bit her lip. This was no time to tell Lonit that Iana's baby had *not* been good, that it had grown colicky and irritable when held to a strange woman's breast. Annoyed by its fretfulness, Gulap had brained it.

And now, suddenly, Gulap was in the room, one hand holding the hide flap in the doorway aside, the other gripping her rattle. Slowly, she advanced. Slowly, she jabbed upward with the bloodstained tip of the claw, shaking it until it hissed as she spoke. No doubt assuming that some of the hunters had returned, she ignored the sounds that poured into the Blood Room from the various interconnected tunnels. Her eyes were ferret bright.

"Stand aside, Aliga. Woman Of The West and Gulap will spend some time together. With *this.*"

Aliga stared not at the old woman who stood, stripped naked again, as stringy and desiccated as a wind-dried haunch of old meat, but at the upraised tip of the hideous claw. Deep within her loins, mutilated muscles contracted involuntarily as she recalled her own impalement and the grunting sexual satisfaction of the tattooed hag who now stood eyeing Lonit. Aliga's heart went out to the young woman. She was so weak. She would be unable to fight against Gulap, and if Aliga tried to intervene, the men would punish or even kill her. No one challenged Gulap. *Ever.* She was the elder sister of the headman. She had born him many sons. None of them would stand against her.

The old woman grinned, shaking the rattle to punctuate each step she took toward Lonit.

"Spread her legs!" she commanded, and Aliga, sickened, moved forward and did her bidding.

Lonit's eyes fluttered open, and she attempted to raise her head as the hag bent before her, motioning Aliga aside.

But now the old woman looked up, startled by the sudden intrusion of one of the other female captives.

"We will suffocate!" she gasped. "We will be smoked like fish over a smoldering fire capped by a skin basket!"

Gulap was confused. "What are you saying?"

"Strangers have come! They have sealed the vents! Even now they run through the tunnels, killing the guards who try to escape in search of air. Next they will come here! They will kill us all!"

Aliga's face showed a mixture of dread and delight. "In this place we are already dead!" she snapped, then recoiled as the hide doorflap was flung wide.

The man who forced his way through the low entryway was tall and mad-eyed from killing. He pushed the wailing woman aside, and as she fled, he stood staring past Gulap and Aliga to the bed of furs upon which Lonit lay. His hair, his clothes, his strongly handsome face—all were red with the blood of the Ghost Men. The killing end of his spear and the long, strangely curved blade of bone that he held in one hand were slimed with gore.

The old woman blinked, appalled and aroused by the sight of him. He was Power. He was Death. He was the most perfect and beautiful man she had ever seen. And she knew that he was going to kill her.

The sound that came from her throat was a half growl, half purr. As the perfect man looked at her, she could tell by his expression that never in his life had he seen a more hideous woman.

His revulsion struck deep into her pride. Her heart was beating hard, fast. *Old. Gulap is old. Old. Old.* Her heart hammered the word again and again until it shrieked out of her mouth, and in a leap of loathing, she flew at the man, slashing out at him with the rattle, wanting to ruin the beauty of his face, to destroy his youth and his life with the deadly claw.

He feinted to one side and sent her stumbling past him. She wheeled and came at him again, still shrieking. The pointed tip of her sloth's-claw rattle raked his shoulder, drawing blood as it pierced the layers of his sleeve and the flesh beneath. He tripped her, and she fell in a twitching heap, her heart bleeding as it beat its last faltering rhythm around the claw that had become imbedded within it.

*   *   *

Aliga was so lightheaded with terror that she was certain she was going to faint. Gulap was dying. In a moment, her own life would end. The stranger was moving toward her. To her amazement, she did not want to die. Noting that his dark, wide eyes were upon Lonit now, she swallowed hard and launched herself to stand between him and the weakened girl.

"No!" she cried, surprised at her own courage, which caused her to remain, feet planted firmly, between the exhausted young woman and the death-dealing stranger. "You will not touch Aliga's sister!" she told him, wishing that she were not trembling so, hoping that her almost complete nudity would not provoke him to rape as well as murder.

His eyes took measure of her. He saw her fear, but he also saw her bravery. Slowly the killing madness bled out of his expression. His hands relaxed upon his weapons. "Do not shiver so, Aliga. Your 'sister' is my woman. No harm will come to her, or to you, from Torka." He moved past her to kneel beside Lonit's bed of jumbled skins and furs. He put aside his weapons and tentatively touched her face, whispering her name as though he feared to speak it lest she vanish.

Her hands moved to fold over his as life welled up within her and flickered within her eyes. "Torka?"

He drew her carefully into an embrace and held her as though the substance of his own life was dependent upon her.

"It *is* so," he said, kissing her, breathing the warmth of his life through his nostrils into hers, and joined with her, mouth to mouth, life to life. "We are one," he whispered when the kiss was done. "Torka and Lonit . . . one life. *Forever . . .*"

The men of Supnah's band emerged from the Ghost House in silence, sobered by what they had done—neither rejoicing nor lamenting the fact that they had slain others of their own kind. They left the bodies of the marauders where they lay and led the once-captive women to freedom.

Torka carried Lonit in his arms as Karana came to them. "Look!" cried the boy, ecstatic, holding up a tiny bundle. "Karana has taken good care of her for Torka and Lonit! But now she is hungry, and this boy cannot feed her!"

Lonit sobbed with relief as Karana eagerly placed her tiny

daughter into her arms. Torka looked at the infant and saw that she had her mother's antelope eyes. He wanted to smile and be glad, but for the moment he could feel nothing. There was a dark, cold emptiness expanding within him. It stank of the blood of the men whom he had killed.

The baby fussed at Lonit's breast. Fatigue and stress had combined to keep her milk from flowing. Aliga came near, bundled in furs now to protect her from the bite of the wind. She reached up, offering to take the infant to Iana to be nursed.

"In time, Lonit's milk will flow. For now, let Iana suckle it. Perhaps, by feeding your child, Iana will also be fed."

Neither Lonit nor Torka understood Aliga's words until their infant was placed into Iana's embrace. Her sad, now-vacant eyes brightened. Her haggard face eased into a radiant smile. She cooed. She crooned. She put the child to her breast, kissing its tender brow, calling it Ninipik and "little son."

"Where is Manaak's child?" asked Torka.

While Lonit closed her eyes and buried her head in Torka's shoulder, Aliga came to answer his question. "So many spirits walk the wind. . . ."

"*Too* many," replied Torka, his voice as bleak and hostile as the land around him. "And more will follow before this day is done."

They took the women back to where Navahk and the others awaited their return, and when the captives told them of what they had endured, there was not a man in Supnah's band who did not agree with Torka that their hunt was not over. As long as any Ghost Men remained alive, all their own lives were in jeopardy.

Only Navahk stood back from the others, observing Torka as he sat with Karana and the dogs, refitting the end of his spear with a new point. "For whom do you hunt, Man Who Walks With Dogs? For the good of all, or for yourself?"

Torka did not hesitate. "I hunt the Ghost Men for Manaak, and for a dead child with whom he walks the wind. I hunt the Ghost Men for Naknaktup, a brave old woman who dared to turn her back upon her people for love of an even braver old man. I hunt the Ghost Men for Umak, who was father of my father and master of my spirit. I hunt the Ghost Men for Iana, for Aliga, for Lonit, and for my daughter who has yet to be given a name, so that never again need they fear that 'ghosts' will come in the night to murder their people and steal them away into slavery. I hunt the Ghost Men for Karana, so that no boy may ever again suffer at their hands. And I hunt for Torka. Yes. Because I *need* to hunt them. For *myself.*"

They devised a plan for their man hunt. They would go out in several groups, each scouting the exact whereabouts of the Ghost Men. Once found, they would gather into a single force, surround their prey, and kill them all. The Ghost Men would be absorbed in their mammoth hunt, killing or butchering, totally unaware that others of their own kind pursued them.

Supnah named the men who would stay behind to protect the encampment of women. Karana was told to remain with them and to make certain that the dogs made no trouble; the animals made most of the women nervous. The boy pouted and openly showed his disappointment, insisting that both he and the dogs would be of help to the hunters. Neither Torka nor Supnah would hear another word from him. They told him that they planned to walk into danger and would not put his life at risk.

"We leave some of our bravest hunters here," said Supnah, attempting to soothe the boy's feelings. "Our women must have strong men to guard them. Karana will be one of these. And Navahk, too. It will be a good thing for Karana to be with his father's brother again. Learn from Navahk. He has much to teach us all."

Karana seethed with frustration while Aar nuzzled his hand to offer comfort. Navahk was a tall, smiling figure in white, staring after the departing hunters with unblinking eyes as they walked away and gradually disappeared into the distance.

"Navahk will make the magic to make us strong upon the hunt," said Supnah to Torka as they strode out together.

"Our numbers and the many fine spears that Supnah's men carry will make us strong," replied Torka. He could not have said why he wanted no part of Navahk's magic.

At the edges of the encampment of women, Karana looked up at Navahk and experienced the old, instinctive fear and distrust of the man and his ever-present, insidious smile.

If Navahk saw the boy, he gave no sign of it. He did not move. He kept on staring. He kept on smiling. The wind was hard out of the east now, cold and acrid with the smell of ice, of rotting stone, and of distant groves of spruce. Navahk did not flinch as it blew against him. It whipped the long, white fringe of his sleeves. It lifted the single winter-white flight feather of an Arctic owl that he always wore braided into the forelock of his waist-length black hair. It rippled in the thick, silken white caribou skins of his surplice and leggins.

Karana shivered against the deep, threatening ugliness that he had always sensed lurking beneath the exterior beauty of the magic man. "Navahk . . . *why* do you smile?" he pressed, half-afraid to speak the question, yet knowing that he *must*.

Navahk's smile deepened as he looked down at Karana. "Why does Karana *think* that I smile?"

Karana's eyes were caught in those of the magic man. In deep, black, bottomless sinks, Karana's mind waded as though through pitch. He sank, choking, fighting for breath as, suddenly, within the strangling darkness, light exploded. Vision swam, like sunlight reflecting off huge, towering walls of ice. It was a miles-high world of ice, and in that world, a sound reverberated, such as the boy had never heard: a screaming, a roaring, a trumpeting. And suddenly the ice was falling, breaking apart as the vision itself shattered.

"Karana knows. Karana sees. The son of my brother's woman, of the woman who would have been mine had I been headman . . . knows that he *is* of my flesh . . . he sees the world through my eyes . . . and what he sees betrays the truth of his birth to all but Supnah, who is a fool who sees nothing!"

Karana stared, still trapped in Navahk's eyes. In his *father's* eyes. He felt sick, confused, betrayed. "You left me to walk the wind!"

"Thereby breaking my brother's spirit! I command the band through his mouth. Only for your sake has Supnah ever been strong enough to stand against my will—your sake and your mother's. It was good that she died! It will be good when your spirit joins hers. I have seen your death, Karana. *That* is why I smile."

The boy stepped back, aghast, unable to speak.

The smile was back upon Navahk's face. His eyes strayed once more to the eastern ranges. "The canyons entered by the hunters will lead them to the Corridor of Storms. It is a place of death from which no man has ever returned. Supnah and his hunters will turn back, but Torka will die. I have heard his death in the roar of the thunder." Turning, Navahk reached out to close his fingers upon Karana's shoulder, the fingers curling inward, deliberately rousing pain as his eyes focused upon the boy with purely raptorial intent. "You will die with him—you who should never have been born. Navahk will share his magic with no one!"

Karana wrenched himself free. The magic man reached out to grab him again, but Aar's warning growl stayed his hand

"I have seen your death," Navahk continued. "And Torka's. In the face of the rising sun . . . beyond an endless corridor of ice and storm, you will all die."

Karana was suddenly angry. "We will *all* die. *Someday.* But not today if this boy can help it!" He wheeled then and tried not to think of Navahk's smile as he raced eastward across the tundra with Aar at his side and Sister Dog loping close behind.

6

Distance was deceptive upon the tundra, but the carelessly laid trail of the Ghost Men was not. It led them into the neck of the canyon, deep into a cold, wind-scoured cleft of land between two southeasterly aligned mountain ranges. Through groves of spruce and alder, they moved in silence, as far ahead the distressed cries of mammoths called them on.

It was a dark, high-walled territory—intimidating to men born and bred on the open tundra. Above the bare, black bones of the mountain, massive glacial lobes extended downward from the heights. Torka cringed, recalling the terrifying collapse of the glacier that had capped the Mountain of Power, but he could hear the voices of the Ghost Men now, as well as the cries of mammoths. He went on. For Umak, for Manaak—for all of those who had died at the end of the Ghost Men's spears and for all of those who had been degraded by them—he would not allow himself to be afraid.

The canyon widened ahead, then forked suddenly in several directions. They took the most promising one, advancing more quickly now as they were drawn forward by the catcalls and hoots of the Ghost Men. They were *very* near. The adult mammoth screamed, and the sound echoed in and out of the intricate convolutions of the canyon. They took a few more steps, then stopped dead, knowing that they had taken the wrong turn. The mammoth's cries were behind them now. Nevertheless, they did not move. They were too stunned by what lay ahead.

The world spread wide before them. Never in their lives could they have imagined the staggering dimensions of the landscape that lay ahead. Below them, the mountains fell away to merge with a wide swath of undulating tundral plain. It ran eastward into infinity, between the leading edges of two glacial masses that appalled their senses—two continent-spanning ice sheets. The majority of the moisture of all the seas, rivers, and oceans on earth lay frozen two miles thick within their monstrous vastness.

"The Mountains That Walk . . ." whispered Supnah in awe.

His men murmured softly, reverently. The wind blew toward them out of the east, across distances too huge for men to conjure; but somehow Torka conjured them as his eyes roamed out over that miles-wide ribbon of tundral plain that cut due east between the ice sheets. Thick with the first new grass of spring, it rippled in the wind like the fur of a green animal, and upon its skin other animals were grazing. Distance made it impossible for him to identify their species, but clearly that broad, glacier-walled avenue of tundra was rich with game.

Supnah followed Torka's gaze and shook his head with warning. "The Corridor of Storms is a bad place. No man may hunt there."

"Not even Torka!" panted a breathless Karana.

Torka was startled to see him, and annoyed. He admonished him for following when he had been told to stay behind. The boy gulped an apology, then blurted, "This boy *had* to warn you! Navahk has said that bad things will happen if Torka follows the mammoths into the Corridor of Storms."

Karana's words shadowed every man within the hunting party. They eyed him and the dogs dubiously, until they were distracted by the renewed cries of the mammoths and the taunting of the Ghost Men.

"Navahk has not seen with a clear eye," Torka said. "The mammoths call us away from the Corridor of Storms, not into it."

Supnah's men were glad to turn back to their purpose. Karana was told to stay close as they reentered the canyon and followed the voices of the Ghost Men into the correct fork. It led them to a small valley ringed by sharply defined cliffs. A tiny spruce-lined lake lay at the base of these encircling walls, and in the lake, a spear-riddled mammoth calf lay dead, mired up to its shoulders in the icy sludge of the treacherous, claylike loam that layered the lake bottom.

The Ghost Men stood arrayed along one of the ridges that

partially jutted into the lake. They were just out of reach of the exhausted mammoth cow that raged at them as she smashed her body against the rock in a hopeless effort to get at them. They mimicked and mocked her and hacked at her mutilated trunk with daggers as she tried to sweep them off the ridge. Several spears protruded from her bloodied flanks. Nearby, at the opposite side of the lake, a frightened adolescent mammoth swayed and cried pathetically from a grove of spruce trees while its mother continued her attempt to drive off the men who had killed her baby.

There was something indescribably touching about this besieged little family of mammoths. The cow and adolescent could easily have escaped their tormentors, but the cow refused to abandon her calf even though it lay dead; and the adolescent cried and called with fright as though it were a human child.

Mother! Stop! Come away! Before it is too late!

The exhausted cow cried back in a vain attempt at consolation, then called as though petitioning for help from others of her own kind who might be within hearing distance. Stumbling, she nearly fell into the lake herself as she sobbed and gasped in impotent fury, ignoring her own wounds as she continued her attempts to drive the calf killers from the ledge.

Then, suddenly, as Aar growled and Sister Dog whimpered, the cow stopped and turned. The world shook. Thunder rent the sky. But it was not thunder. It was a great and terrible roaring as, from yet another branch of the canyon, a bull mammoth pounded into the valley.

Its shoulders touched the sky, and the top of its head was in the clouds as it stopped, observing the scene that met its small, red eyes. It was breathing hard. How far it had come, how long it had run, no man could have said, for, as was the way of its kind and gender, it had been ranging alone since it had last cast its shadow upon the lives of men.

It was the Destroyer. It was Thunder Speaker. It was World Shaker. It was the beast of Torka's nightmares. In disbelief, the Ghost Men stared as Death charged them full speed. The cow had been unable to reach them, but as they scrambled for their lives, the giant bull plucked them off the ridge and hurled them high against the cliffs. They broke, screaming and spurting blood from ears, mouths, and noses as they crashed to the ground. Some were dead when they landed. Others lay stunned or screaming as Death ground them into the earth, screaming back at them in a trumpeting rage that obliterated the panicked cries of Supnah and his men as they raced for safety through an offshoot canyon too narrow to allow the great bull to follow.

Only Torka stood immobile, transfixed, watching as the Destroyer comforted the cow. Its mate? Yes. Torka was certain of it. After the killing was done, the bull huffed softly, consoling, caressing, snapping off the offending spears with its great trunk; then it soothed the wounds, scooping clay from the lake and packing the wounds with its long snout until the blood ceased to flow. Together, with infinite tenderness and soft huffings of affection the pair touched the adolescent and drew it from its hiding place within the spruce grove. They went to the lake, then stood swaying as they called to the lifeless calf. With its vast tusks extended, the bull reached out and beneath the limp, bloodied infant, levered up, lifted it from the muck, and laid it upon the embankment.

"Torka!" A terrified and almost infinitely brave Karana had come back into the little valley. He tugged hard at Torka's sleeve as he rasped an imploring whisper. "What is the matter with you? Come! Supnah and his hunters have taken the high ground all along the canyon wall to the west. If the beast tries to follow, it will lodge itself in the narrows. Before it can back out, we can kill it! Its meat will last us forever!"

Torka's hands were closed tightly around the hafts of his spear and bludgeon. He tested their weight against the merit of the boy's words. Karana was right. It *could* be done. Yet now, as at last the moment arrived when he knew that he could avenge himself upon the Destroyer, he wanted no part of its death. The giant mammoth was not a mindless marauder but a creature capable of the same deep emotions as he. Indeed, the beast was no more of a beast than Torka—and less so than Galeena or any of the Ghost Band.

But it was too late for reflection upon the virtues of the great mammoth. It had picked up his scent and those of the boy and the dog who had followed. The Destroyer's head went up. Its ears oared forward.

"Run!" Torka commanded Karana.

Together, with Aar beside them, they fled, racing for survival, knowing that if they could reach the narrow canyon where Supnah and the others waited on the heights, they would be safe.

Halfway there, Karana's weak leg gave out. He fell, stunned, his mind filled with Navahk's smiling visions of death until Torka wheeled back, scooped him up, and ran on. The moment of compassion had cost him. The mammoth was nearly on them. In desperation, he made for the nearest rock face and lifted Karana high.

"Climb, Little Hunter! Climb for your life!"

He turned, knowing that he was all that stood between Karana and death. The light that burns behind a man's eyes when death is near was white hot behind his own. There was a strange thrumming within his ears. Beyond it, he heard Aar's savage barking as the dog ran circles around the mammoth, attempting to distract it as he ran between its limbs, leaping up and snarling. The mammoth demonstrated an amazing grace as it flicked the dog away with a backward movement of its enormous foot. The dog cried out and fell in a heap.

"Brother Dog, we will run together upon the wind," called Torka, knowing that in the next moment he would follow the valiant dog into the world of spirits. Truly they *would* be brothers *forever*.

He stood his ground and hefted his weapons. He called back over his shoulder for Karana to climb. *Climb!* One bludgeon and one spear were all that stood between him and the realm that Torka and Aar would soon walk together.

"Come!" he called to the mammoth. "Thunder Speaker! World Shaker! He Who Parts the Clouds and destroys the lives of men, Torka is not afraid to die!"

What happened next seemed to occur within a dream, within a heartbeat. And yet the telling of it would last for generations. The man held his weapons steady, staring into the eyes of the beast. The mammoth paused. Perhaps in that moment the Destroyer remembered the bold hunter whom it had once left to die in the snow. Perhaps it scented no stench of the Ghost Men who had slain its calf. Or perhaps in the great and legendary wisdom of its species, the mammoth saw in the man one who shared its own great heart, one who would risk himself to save the life of even the smallest member of his own kind.

Whatever the great beast saw, whatever it sensed, it stood for a long time before, at last, it turned away.

*   *   *

Something walked within the ebbing night. Something huge. Something silent. Something no longer terrible. It moved within a shadowed valley, and while the people of Supnah's band rejoiced that the Ghost Band was no more, Torka climbed to the heights of the canyon and looked down, sharing the grief of the great mammoth as it mourned its dead calf.

He stayed in that place until the day was done and another day was being born. Karana joined him, with Lonit, to bring him the good news that Aar had not left the world of the living to become a spirit.

"Hrmmph! Brother Dog is too smart to be killed by a mammoth! He was bruised and his pride was hurt, but while we were hunting the Ghost Men, Sister Dog was having a litter of pups. Aar has his own band now! And Karana has many dog brothers and sisters. It is a good thing! Umak would be glad!"

Torka nodded. Yes. The old man *would* be glad . . . especially to see how the boy was emulating him. Not only in gestures and patterns of speech but in subtler, deeper ways. Navahk also saw it—there was a power within the child. He *would* be a spirit master someday, and a greater magic man than Navahk could ever hope to be.

Navahk . . . Torka did not like the man . . . or trust him. He had empty eyes, as though his spirit had already flown from them to walk upon the wind.

Lonit cuddled close to her man. She held their tiny daughter to her breast, suckling her within the garments of fur that Supnah's women had shared with her. She pointed off, down into the valley where, with heartbreaking tenderness, the mammoths were laying spruce boughs across the body of the dead calf. "It is as though they were people," she whispered sadly.

Torka nodded. She was right. The mammoths *were* like people. *Better* than most people he had ever known.

The dawn was clear and cold. Supnah was approaching them. "Come," he beckoned. "The band readies to move on. We will hunt bison to the west."

The words washed through Torka's mind as he rose. The mammoths were leaving the little valley. Slowly they walked into the light of the rising sun, heading eastward out of the canyon and into the Corridor of Storms. Torka could see it clearly from the heights. The sun shed its light straight down the tundral avenue. He could see game grazing in the distance. Overhead, wheeling above the glacial vastnesses, flocks of wild fowl were flying toward the sun.

He was suddenly trembling. "There is a new world out there, in the face of the rising sun. We will follow the game there, to the east. We will not go back."

Supnah looked as though Torka had struck him. "But no man has ever dared venture into the Corridor of Storms! Death awaits those who journey into the unknown."

A sweet sense of calm filled Torka, as though an old friend had suddenly returned from the spirit world to stand beside him and speak through his mouth. "Umak says that a hunter must face into the light. Only by facing death may his spirit overcome it."

The baby made soft sounds of contentment as it drew life from Lonit's breast. She stood close to her man and looked back, westward to a world that had brought only darkness to her spirit and then forward, into the dawn, into a new world that was filled with light. "This woman is not afraid," she said boldly.

"Nor is this boy," vowed Karana as he smiled, suddenly understanding the vision that he had shared with Navahk. It had not been a vision of death. It had been a promise of rebirth, a vision of a new life in a new land . . . in the face of the rising sun . . . beyond the Corridor of Storms.

Far below them, the great mammoth led his family onto the greening tundra that lay between the glaciers. It seemed to Torka that, for the moment, the largest of the threesome lifted and moved its trunk as though beckoning the man to follow. Torka raised his arm. The mammoth trumpeted. It was a sound that shook the world. Torka smiled, saluting the great beast who had allowed him his life and defined his future.

"This man *will* go forward into the dawn," he said to Supnah, knowing at last that his dreams had been more than dreams. Behind him, to the west, the world was a hostile, hungry place, with half the year in light and half the year in darkness. But ahead, to the east, the sun was rising over herds of game and greening tundra. He would lead his people there, into the dawn, following not the Destroyer but Life Giver, into that warm, bright hunting ground out of which the sun was born.

Into the new world.

Author's Note

This work of fiction has been carefully and painstakingly researched and is based on evidence found by archaeologists, paleontologists, and paleoanthropologists.

The author would like to thank particularly the staff at the George C. Page Museum for their assistance and to praise once again the editorial skills and insight of Laurie Rosin, whose patience and suggestions helped guide and shape the project from the beginning. Grateful thanks also go to Kathy Halverson, Book Creations's research librarian, for her sleuthing on my behalf and for the many gems of documentation that she sent my way. To all the team at Book Creations, whose talents were set to smoothing Torka's way into the New World, thank you.

Thanks to Reva Robins, librarian, for her assistance and interest in the project and for the loan of Asen Balikci's extraordinary work, *The Netsilik Eskimo,* published for the American Museum of Natural History, The Natural History Press, 1970.

Grateful thanks also go to Knud Rasmussen for recording his observations of his Thule Expeditions and to the Smithsonian Institution for honoring the pioneering ethnographic fieldwork of Edward William Nelson by reissuing his magnificent monograph, first published in the *Eighteenth Annual Report of the Bureau of American Ethnology, 1896–97,* "The Eskimo About Bering Strait."

The debate over exactly *when* Man first entered the Americas continues to rage, but most archaeologists do agree that *Homo sapiens* came out of Siberia, hunted and gathered their way across a land bridge that now lies beneath the Bering Strait, and eventually migrated southward to people both the

North and South American continents. Recent finds in Brazil have been dated to 32,000 years of age. Farther north, the vast ice sheets of the Pleistocene all but obliterated any telltale signs of humanity that can be proven to be older than 15,000 to 20,000 years; but we must not forget that the Epoch of Ice lasted for over two million years, and at least *four* times within that period the great continental ice sheets grew to smother the world, then melted again, as they are now in our time.

And who can say that the interval of warmth that we now enjoy is not only a breath of time between the coming and going of the Ages of Ice? Perhaps our cities and civilizations may one day be buried and scoured into oblivion. Perhaps, millennia from now, *Homo futuriens* will pick through the debris of glacial scree in search of our bones and pottery fragments even as we now search the ruins of yesterday's epochs in search of even the smallest proof that once, at the dawn of time, a man whose name might well have been Torka led people out of Asia into a new world to become the first Americans.

BEYOND THE SEA OF ICE would never have been written if Lyle Kenyon Engel had not given this author the inspiration and the confidence to write it.

As the producer of the KENT FAMILY CHRONICLES, WAGONS WEST, STAGECOACH, WHITE INDIAN, and SAGA OF THE SOUTHWEST Series, to name but a few, Lyle's love of Americana was absolute. He had long envisioned a series of novels that would chronicle the lives of the *first* Americans, those unknown men and women of antiquity who followed the great herds of the Pleistocene out of Asia, across the Bering land bridge, to people the New World.

Torka's story is my invention, as are the characters and all the meat that goes onto the bones of a plot before it can qualify as a tale worthy of telling, but Lyle's enthusiasm for the subject matter was the driving force behind the construction.

BEYOND THE SEA OF ICE is as much his novel as it is mine. The initial concept was his. As early as 1979, he had the name of his hero. And because his love of animals equaled his love of Americana, he had the name of the first dog to be domesticated by man: Aar.

In an increasingly complex and callous world, Lyle Kenyon Engel was more than an agent and more than a producer of fiction novels. He was, as one of his authors so aptly called him, the Maestro, orchestrating the creation of books that have brought, and continue to bring, joy to millions of readers around the world.

Lylc, I hope that BEYOND THE SEA OF ICE is one of them. I hope that it is one of the best! And if it is, I thank you for giving me the chance to write it.

William Sarabande
Fawnskin, California

★ WAGONS WEST ★

This continuing, magnificent saga recounts the adventures of a brave band of settlers, all of different backgrounds, all sharing one dream— to find a new and better life.

☐	26822	**INDEPENDENCE! #1**	$4.50
☐	26162	**NEBRASKA! #2**	$4.50
☐	26242	**WYOMING! #3**	$4.50
☐	26072	**OREGON! #4**	$4.50
☐	26070	**TEXAS! #5**	$4.50
☐	26377	**CALIFORNIA! #6**	$4.50
☐	26546	**COLORADO! #7**	$4.50
☐	26069	**NEVADA! #8**	$4.50
☐	26163	**WASHINGTON! #9**	$4.50
☐	26073	**MONTANA! #10**	$4.50
☐	26184	**DAKOTA! #11**	$4.50
☐	26521	**UTAH! #12**	$4.50
☐	26071	**IDAHO! #13**	$4.50
☐	26367	**MISSOURI! #14**	$4.50
☐	27141	**MISSISSIPPI! #15**	$4.50
☐	25247	**LOUISIANA! #16**	$4.50
☐	25622	**TENNESSEE! #17**	$4.50
☐	26022	**ILLINOIS! #18**	$4.50
☐	26533	**WISCONSIN! #19**	$4.50
☐	26849	**KENTUCKY! #20**	$4.50
☐	27065	**ARIZONA! #21**	$4.50
☐	27458	**NEW MEXICO! #22**	$4.50
☐	27703	**OKLAHOMA! #23**	$4.50
☐	28180	**CELEBRATION! #24**	$4.50